PRAISE FOR *THE NEARLY GIRL*

In her latest novel, the *The Nearly Girl*, Lisa de Nikolits takes us deep into the complex workings of an extraordinary mind. Amelia Fisher, the protagonist of de Nikolits's latest offering, reminds readers of the importance of passion and adventure in a world that wishes to keep our wilder urges contained. Like a modern-day Joan of Arc, Fisher's attempts to carve out a "normal life," take her to the fringes of social acceptability—showing us how mythic the idea of "normal" really is. Through a story that surprises, page after page, *The Nearly Girl* will take readers on an unexpected adventure — where the lines between the rational and irrational are blurred. From hoarding to the fear of public speaking, this psychiatric thriller excavates the phobias, idiosyncrasies and character oddities that make us human at the core.
—ANDREA THOMPSON, author of *Over Our Heads*

A playful exploration of human oddities, de Nikolits's latest book asks: What are the consequences when we deviate from the norm? Centred around Amelia, a young woman who only nearly gets things right in life — she catches the wrong bus or shows up on the wrong day — *The Nearly Girl* features a cast of misfits who are all engaged in various forms of self-improvement. With her mother trying end-lessly to improve her body and her tortured genius poet father always awaiting the voice of brilliance to speak to him, Amelia and her family are anything but ordinary. But perhaps the most compelling characters are found in Amelia's therapy sessions, where hoarders, recluses, and claustrophobes alike come together in an enchantingly eccentric group seeking the help of an unorthodox psychotherapist. Yet, we learn from de Nikolits, sometimes self-acceptance is better than change. The story builds with cinematic suspense and surprises, but one thing is for sure: The only crazy thing in this world is trying to be normal.
—JILL BUCHNER, *Canadian Living Magazine*

The Nearly Girl by Lisa de Nikolits is a clever, fast-paced, and enjoyable read with a cast of quirky characters. They range from Henry the supremely creative poet to his estranged body-building wife and her reliable and loving mother, from the not-quite-right psychiatrist Dr. Carroll, who applies his unorthodox cognitive behavioural therapy research called D.T.O.T. (Do The Opposite Thing) to the lovable misfits who populate his required class. And then there's Amelia, Henry's daughter in so many ways, who attributes her inability to conform to the norms of society to her fear of being boringly normal. The novel traces Amelia's life, from her eccentric childhood love of birthday parties outside in the freezing rain to her current predicament of having to take Dr. Carroll's advice to retain the funding that finances her thesis on the unconventional Joan of Arc. In the course of escaping Dr. Carroll's clutches — in more ways than one — Amelia discovers her true self and encourages the reader to do the same.

—GINA BUONAGURO, co-author of *The Wolves of St. Peter's*

The Nearly Girl is completely mesmerizing! Lisa de Nikolits' tale of family dysFUNction is chock full of comedy, drama, and page turning suspense. Anyone who has ever felt alienated by the unwritten rules and norms of society will find a kindred spirit in Amelia, the "Nearly Girl," daughter of a female bodybuilder and a tortured poet, who believes that rainy days are just perfect for picnics on the beach and who fears that getting on the right bus will lead her to a dead end. Told with warmth and humour, and populated with vividly original characters, *The Nearly Girl* illustrates the importance of keeping the magic in an increasingly corporate, cookie-cutter world.

—HEATHER BABCOCK, author of *Of Being Underground* and *Moving*

From the first page you are taken on a rollercoaster ride of suspense, heartfelt compassion, humour, and moments of annoyance for what first appears to be inconsiderate and disrespectful behaviour Amelia's part. Then you find out she suffers from a genetic imbalance passed down from her father combined with extremist traits of her mom. Due to unexpected humour throughout this book, you become attached to this woman and her struggles, and even begin to see her

amazingness. After years of accepting her fate as her cross to bear, she begins to enjoy the freedom from life's responsibilities it gives her … until she can do so no longer with the threat of financial assistance being cut off. Necessity pushes her to try to take charge of her life and illness with a unique new therapy called D.T.O.T. (Do The Opposite Thing). Pretty easy to predict the outcome, right? Not at all! The fast-paced comical drama and antics of dysfunction within family and "family of choice" (friends/co-counselling buddies) leads into an unexpected turn of events when she and her current boyfriend stumble upon her trusted doctor's secretive and very dark home life. This puts them both in grave danger and the rest you have to "read to believe." An ending worth waiting for.
—CAROLYN SHANNON, *Women of Worth Magazine.com*

In *The Nearly Girl*, Lisa de Nikolits, author of *Between the Cracks She Fell*, has created another memorable heroine. Amelia Fisher, who can never quite do what she should, is the nearly girl of the title. The daughter of two incredibly dysfunctional parents, Amelia is required to attend a therapy group to help with her problem. The group's leader, Dr. Frances Carroll, is the most dysfunctional character of all. His mantra, "Do The Opposite Thing," has disastrous results. A very funny book.
—LYNNE MURPHY, contributing author to *The Whole SheBang* and *Thirteen O'Clock*

Amelia Fisher is a brilliant, beautiful, charming, young woman who should have the future and world brightly gift-wrapped in her slender hands. However, she has to reconnect with her acid-dropping, addle-headed father, Henry, a man she hasn't seen since childhood. Then there is her cognitive therapy group led by the unconventional Dr. Carroll, a man whose methods are either genius, or deeply damaging. This sprint-paced novel has it all from restraining orders to sex in office bathrooms, and a nail-biting ending! Lisa de Nikolits's skill is proven in this dynamic rapid page-turner which enchants and delights readers with suspense and unforeseen twists and surprises!
—MICHAEL FRASER, author of *The Serenity of Stone* and *To Greet Yourself Arriving.*

Playwright Henrik Ibsen wrote in 1881, "The sins of the fathers are visited upon the children." Lisa de Nikolits updates this cautionary observation in her latest book, as the reckless life choices of a young woman and her narcissistic, drug-addled mate are visited upon their daughter. Beautifully told, *The Nearly Girl* softens its sting with convivial depictions of Toronto bohemians, before revealing the ugly aftermath of people shipwrecked upon the foolish choices of youth. *The Nearly Girl* is as bleak and beautiful as the Rosedale Ravine after a hail storm.

—ELAINE ASH, Editor, *Walking the Dunes With Tennessee Williams*

A fast-paced and illuminating story where endeavouring to conform to society's perception of normal, exposes the masks of illusion. Amelia Fisher's unconventional upbringing with an LSD-addicted poet father and an emotionally distant body-building mother leads her to attending sessions with a crazy doctor, whose unorthodox method called D.T.O.T., or "Do the Opposite Thing," has significant repercussions on his patients, including Amelia. A chance discovery propels Amelia and fellow attendee, Mike with whom she is in love, into a life-threatening situation instigated by the doctor's own dark secret. Hidden twists abound with growing tension culminating in a surprising ending.

—MANDY EVE BARNETT, published author & freelance writer

The Nearly Girl

ADVANCE READING COPY
UNPROOFED

We gratefully acknowledge the support of the Canada Council for the Arts and the Ontario Arts Council for our publishing program. We also acknowledge the financial support of the Government of Canada.

Cover design: Lisa de Nikolits
Cover photography: Bradford Dunlop

The Nearly Girl is a work of fiction. All the characters and situations portrayed in this book are fictitious and any resemblance to persons living or dead is purely coincidental.

Library and Archives Canada Cataloguing in Publication

de Nikolits, Lisa, author
          The nearly girl : a novel / by Lisa de Nikolits.

(Inanna poetry and fiction series)
Issued in print and electronic formats.
ISBN 978-1-77133-313-9 (paperback).

          I. Title. II. Series: Inanna poetry and fiction series

The Nearly Girl

a novel by

Lisa de Nikolits

Inanna poetry & fiction series

INANNA PUBLICATIONS AND EDUCATION INC.
TORONTO, CANADA

To Bradford Dunlop.
And all the unusual people in this world.

TABLE OF CONTENTS

PROLOGUE

I PUSHED MY WAY INTO THE CAFÉ, cursing the November rain, cursing my glasses for steaming up, cursing my umbrella for showering my legs with icy droplets, and cursing the client who had moved our meeting back by two hours.

"Here! We're over here," one of my colleagues called out and she waved. I recognized her more by her voice than her vaselined outline and I stumbled toward their table.

"I hate this month," I grumbled, trying to balance my umbrella against the wall but it stubbornly fell against me, making sure it transferred its residual water onto my kneecaps.

Spencer, my boss, handed me a paper napkin and I dried my glasses.

"I got you your usual," he said, pointing at a teapot.

"That's black tea," I said, sniffing the tea. "I drink green tea. And when have you ever seen me eat a chocolate chip cookie? You know gluten makes me ill. How many years have we worked together? You can't remember green tea and gluten free?"

"You're so grumpy," Spencer noted. "I nearly got it right." He leaned over and took my cookie.

"You just wanted that cookie for yourself," I accused him and he laughed.

I took his latte and put the tea in front of him. "Here you go, Mr. Nearly," I said and then I stopped as something suddenly occurred to me. I could vaguely hear Spencer objecting to our exchange, but I was trying to encourage a memory to move to the forefront of my mind.

"Earth to Jen, earth to Jen," Spencer repeated, and he snapped his fingers in front of my face, a habit he knows I hate.

"I'm trying to remember something," I said. "Wait…. Right, 'the nearly girl,' that's what they called her. The nearly girl. I went to university with her, so this would have been about five years ago. She had this weird disorder and they made all kind of allowances for her because of it. She was doing her thesis on Joan of Arc. I remember that, too. Whoa, I haven't thought about her in years."

I took a satisfying slug of Spencer's latte and sat back. "She would have loved this weather," I said. "She used to go the beach on days like this. In a T-shirt. She didn't feel the cold and she didn't get sick either. I liked her, but it was hard to be friends with her because she was so unreliable. Like, you'd make plans with her and then she would get on the wrong bus, so she wouldn't show up. Or she'd take the right bus, but she'd show up on the wrong day."

"Was she an anarchist?" Ana, the sales rep on our team asked.

I shook my head. "No, it was a real psychological disorder. She had been diagnosed."

"Convenient," Spencer commented. "It must have been nice for her, to be able to do whatever she liked, whenever she liked, and get away with it, while the rest of us suckers have to play by the rules."

"I don't think it made her life easy," I said. "It wasn't like she was this free spirit with her head in the clouds. She had her torments and insecurities like the rest of us. And she was a dedicated student."

"But how did she manage at university, being like that?"

"Like I said, they made allowances for her. Her father's a famous poet. Henry Berlin."

"Henry Berlin!" Spencer was impressed. "Did you ever meet him?"

"I did. I went to visit Amelia and he was there. He was so shy. He couldn't look at me or talk to me, and he sort of vaporized into another room like a ghost if I was there."

I sat back and rubbed my temples. "It's all coming back to me," I said. "There was a huge to-do about the therapist that Amelia had been seeing, and it was on the news for ages. He was infamous and for a while, the media couldn't talk about anything else."

"What are *you* talking about?" Spencer asked. "Ana, do you have any idea what she's prattling on about?"

Ana shook her head.

I checked my watch. "We've got time," I said. "Do you want to hear the story? In a way it's odd that I've never told you, since Amelia and I were close for a while. But then again, I haven't thought about it, or her, in years."

"We've got nothing but time," Spencer yawned, leaning back in his chair. "Tell us a story, why not?"

"It starts with her parents," I began. "Megan and Henry. Megan met Henry at a poetry reading...."

PART I:
MEGAN AND HENRY (1986)

1. MEGAN AND HENRY

MEGAN MET HENRY AT A POETRY READING one late October evening. The rain had been a steady downpour all day. It was the kind of dreary Sunday that soaked ennui deep into one's bones, causing gloom to marinate in boredom and loneliness. So when a work colleague called and implored Megan to come to a poetry reading, she, on a whim, agreed.

"It's also an open mic," the friend said when they met. "There'll be some weirdos. There are always weirdos at open mics. I've got a planet-sized crush on this writer called Zimmerman Bob. He calls himself that as a protest to Bob Dylan having changed his own name. I think it's ironic that that's his way of protesting, since it means he's changing his own name."

"It is contradictory," Megan agreed, not really sure but wanting to say the right thing. "Isn't Bob Dylan old? Why does your poet even care what he did?

"Bob Dylan's only forty-five," the friend said, which Megan thought was ancient. "And Zimmerman Bob is so in love with him! He calls Dylan the poet of the ages. Anyway, regardless of his stupid name, Zimmerman Bob has just released a collection of short stories that are being hailed by the critics as sheer genius. I'd lend you my copy, but he signed it and it's my most precious thing. I mean, he inscribed it to me; he wrote my name, my actual name!"

"He asked you to come tonight? Why's a short story guy reading at a poetry thing?"

Her friend shrugged. "It's kind of a mixed lineup of readers. Zimmerman Bob didn't personally invite me, but I saw a poster for it so I thought I'd go. I went to his book launch and there were hundreds of people. It was amazing."

Megan pulled her scarf tight around her neck. "I'm glad to get out of my apartment," she said. "I'll sit and get quietly drunk while you ogle Bob Dylan."

"You mean Zimmerman Bob," her friend said dreamily. "Zimmerman Bob. Wait. Let's have a quick smoke outside before going in. I bet he'll be fashionably late and I can try to chat him up on his way in. If he even remembers me, which I doubt."

They stood outside the pub smoking and stamping their feet to warm up. Megan's feet were like ice blocks and she felt damp to the core.

"Look at that weirdo over there," her friend said, and she pointed across the street with her cigarette. Megan's eyes rested on what she thought was a long-haired angel: a blond, tall, barefoot, lean and muscular, T-shirt-wearing angel. He seemed otherworldly, even radiant, and he moved with effortless grace.

"He's so beautiful," Megan whispered, and her friend, Alice, laughed.

"He's off his rocker if you ask me. He's walking through the puddles, and he doesn't seem to feel the cold whatsoever."

The object of their fascination crossed the street and walked toward them. When he reached them, he stopped and smiled, his gaze fixed on Megan. She felt as if the falling raindrops had turned to sparkling diamonds and that every kind of magic was possible.

"Coming to the reading?" he asked and his voice was rich and deep and musical.

"For sure," Alice replied since Megan was frozen stiff and mute. "Are you a reader?" Alice asked, polite but clearly disinterested.

"Yeah, open mic," the angel said. "You?"

"Here to support Zimmerman Bob. I'm Alice."

"I'm Henry," he said, but he held out his hand to Megan who took it and did not let go.

"You're so warm," she said. "You should be cold but you're warm."

"I never feel the cold," Henry replied. "But you are freezing. I'll warm you up."

Alice gave a coarse suggestive laugh but neither Henry nor Megan heard or cared.

Zimmerman Bob arrived at that moment and he grinned at Alice who shook like happy jello.

"Henry," Zimmerman Bob greeted him, and he tipped an imaginary hat. "You honouring us tonight with your verbiage?"

"If you call it an honour, then yes, I am. Bob, this is … wait," he said to Megan, "I don't even know your name."

"Megan," she said.

"And I'm Alice," Megan's friend said to Bob. "I love your book. I carry it everywhere with me. You signed it when I came to your launch but you probably don't remember, there were so many people. It was incredible." She stopped talking and blushed.

Zimmerman Bob smiled. "I remember you," he said, and he almost sounded sincere. "Let's go inside, I'm bloody freezing, unlike Henry here. Henry, dude, where are your shoes?"

"I must have forgotten to put them on when I left the house," Henry said. "Do you think they will let me read if I don't have any shoes?"

"For sure. I'll speak to them."

They went inside. Zimmerman Bob led the way and Alice followed closely. Megan was still holding Henry's hand. They settled into a curved red leather booth and looked around.

"Joint's jumping," Zimmerman Bob said as he got up. "I'll get the first round. Who's having what?"

"White wine," the women chorused.

Henry said, "No thanks, Bob. I dropped some acid and I want to stay pure. Just water for me."

Megan turned to Henry. "Do you take a lot of drugs?" she asked, hating herself for sounding prim and silly, but wanting to know.

"Only acid."

"I heard it fries the brain." Megan could hear the worry in her voice.

"It helps balance my brain," Henry said solemnly. "I see too much when I'm not high. Acid helps me sort things out, keeps things organized."

"First time I ever heard that." Alice was scornful and Henry looked downcast, his long eyelashes girly and pretty, his nose a perfect straight line ending in an upturned tip.

Megan rushed to his defense. "I've heard it can be mind-expanding," she offered helpfully and Henry beamed at her.

Zimmerman Bob came back with the drinks. "Henry, bro, I spoke to Charles and you're copasetic to read. You good to go first? He's ready to start whenever you are. Go on, man. Do us proud." He slapped Henry on the back, signaled to a man standing on the stage, and the MC took the microphone and introduced Henry.

Megan watched Henry walk up to the stage and stand in the glare of the relentless spotlight. She felt a keen terror that he would humiliate himself. She wanted to throw herself in front of him, protect him, pull him back down to sit beside her. She stuffed a knuckle into her mouth and watched him wave greetings as he adjusted the mic to his lanky height.

"Popular fellow," Alice commented, and she took a large swallow of her wine.

"He's a genius," Zimmerman Bob said. "But he's a few sandwiches short of a picnic when it comes to real life. He's got publishers lined up, begging him for a collection of his poetry. He could take his pick, but he won't commit anything to paper. He keeps it all inside his head. Doesn't seem to care about being published and most people think he's insane just for that. Ssh, he's starting."

Henry stood under the bright lights, his t-shirt still wet in patches, and his feet pale and splattered with mud. He shoved his hands into the pockets of his jeans, closed his eyes, and recited without pause or hesitation, the longest, most incomprehensible poem that Megan had ever heard. He spoke for what seemed like hours to her, but she knew it couldn't have been more than fifteen minutes. She only knew that he had reached the end because he finally fell silent and the room erupted into near-hysterical applause.

Henry opened his eyes and grinned.

"The incomparable Henry Berlin," the MC said, taking the stage while Henry, still smiling, ambled back to the booth, sat down, and took Megan's hand as if it was the most natural thing to do in the world.

"Give us a pen, Bob," he said.

"You're going to commit words to paper? Ladies, this is historic." Bob whipped out a pen and thrust it at Henry.

"No, I'm going to write down Megan's information before the night calls me away, as it no doubt will. I leave suddenly," he said to Megan and he leaned in so close to her that his lips brushed her ear. Her entire body stood to attention, as if fireworks had exploded in the marrow of her bones.

"I leave when I need to," he explained, "and not a second sooner or later. I never mean to be rude, and I hope you will understand. I don't understand the timing of it myself. I am here one minute and then I am gone."

Megan nodded, mostly to keep him talking and to keep that beautiful sensual mouth close to her, keep those fireworks exploding. His hair was soft and fine and it tickled her cheek.

Megan took the pen and wrote down every manner in which Henry would be able to find her.

"And here's where I live too," she said. "I live alone."

"Subtle," Alice commented.

Henry ignored her and he pocketed the napkin. He leaned back against the booth and closed his eyes. He suddenly looked exhausted. Black shadows painted the hollows of his cheekbones and he looked bruised where tiny veins showed purple under his skin. His complexion was so pale it was nearly blue. Megan wondered whether she should ask him if he was all right, but he had become impenetrable and closed. She tried to signal Zimmerman Bob for help but he was in his own world, enjoying Alice's charms.

The open mic continued with some fellow playing guitar and chanting while Henry remained motionless, still and inaccessible.

Zimmerman Bob finally made his way up to the front to read and by the time he finished, Megan had no deeper insight as to the worth of his words than before he had begun, but the room loved him and shouted for more. Zimmerman Bob smiled modestly and paged through his book, looking for another poem to read.

Then Henry sat bolt upright. He opened his eyes, smiled sweetly at Megan, withdrew his hand, then slipped out into the night. Megan wanted to follow him but she knew it would be the wrong thing to do. Now, she too wanted to be gone. She wanted to be alone, savouring and exploring the magic of what had happened.

"Don't you dare leave," Alice hissed as she grabbed Megan by the arm.

"You're doing fine by yourself," Megan said, but Alice held on tight.

"At least wait until Bob comes back. You can't leave me here looking like an idiot, all by myself."

Megan sighed and lit a cigarette.

When Zimmerman Bob returned to the table, sweat was running down his temples and his armpits were stained dark grey. "Takes it out of you," he said. "Henry's gone I see. He stayed longer than usual, I'll give him that." He smiled at Alice.

"You were incredible," she said. "Utterly visceral. I find your use of agnostic metaphor mesmerizing."

Megan had no idea what she was talking about but she nodded as if in agreement. "How long have you known Henry?" she asked and Zimmerman Bob laughed.

"You like him. Poor you. I'd say don't go there but it's already too late, isn't it? Henry and I went to junior high together. I will tell you this: he's got the biggest dick I've ever seen on a man. He's hung like a proverbial donkey."

"I don't care about that," Megan said and she blushed. "He's so beautiful. I've never seen anyone so beautiful."

"He sold his soul to the devil for eternal youth, endless beauty and a brilliant mind. I'd kill to be able to dream a scrap of the thoughts he's discarded," Zimmerman Bob said.

"Sold his soul?" Alice was pragmatic. "That doesn't happen these days, does it?"

"Oh, but it does, my sweet," Bob said, and he casually swung his arm around Alice's shoulders. She melted into him.

"Sold his soul," Zimmerman Bob continued. "He did, I tell you. I saw him, howling at the moon, barefoot then too, arms outstretched, shouting 'come and get me, here I am, you can have me in exchange for the purest of arts'. He came back to the dorm a changed man. His soul was … gone!" Zimmerman Bob ended with a dramatic flourish and Alice smiled.

"I'm serious though," Zimmerman Bob said, nodding in Megan's direction.

"I must go," she replied, and she got up, unsteady from everything that had happened and having no idea what that even was.

The readings had ended and people were making their way over to Zimmerman Bob. A line was forming and Zimmerman Bob hauled out a bag of books, ready to sell and sign, but not before he threw one last comment in the direction of the exiting Megan. "He'll be the death of you," he shouted and then he turned to meet his fans, with Alice tidying up his books.

2. HENRY

MEGAN FELL IN LOVE WITH HENRY so hard it hurt. It hurt mostly between her shoulder blades, which made it hard to breathe.

She had rushed out into the cold wet night, hoping, foolishly she knew, that Henry would be waiting for her. But there was no Henry, only a chilly wind that whipped around her feet as she walked home with her arms wrapped around her chest. She hoped, then, to see him waiting for her in the entrance of the stairwell to her apartment, but the stairwell was dark and she was alone. She ignored the elevator and climbed the three flights of stairs, taking the stairs two at a time. Again, she hoped that Henry would be there, outside her door, the door to her tiny bachelor apartment that she'd been so proud to rent all by herself. But Henry was palpable only by his absence.

"Henry," she whispered as she lay awake, replaying his every touch and glance. She could not stop thinking about his pale eyebrows that arched so cleanly, and the expression in his grey-green eyes when he looked at her. She was certain he saw into the core of her being. She thought about his high forehead, his perfect nose, his movie star mouth, the boyish sweep of his hair, and his impeccable cheekbones. His long fingers and large hands — how could she know so much about him in so short a time? Even his ears were perfect.

How could she know? *Because why*, that's why, *because why*.

That's what her mother had always said in reply to Megan's endless interrogations of whys: *"because why, my girly. Because why."* And there was always a finality in her tone that closed any door of doubt. And Megan accepted that now. She accepted that she loved Henry because why. She understood now what it had meant all those years.

Nearly a week later, and he had still not come. Nor had he phoned or emailed. Not that she'd thought he would do either. She had been certain that he would simply arrive unannounced, welcomed and expected, as it should be.

She felt disloyal trying to sleep at night. He was out there, out where it was cold, and she had no right to warmth or rest. She needed to be cold, alone, and awake. It was the only way she could think of to bring him to her.

When he finally knocked on her door, she had, as is generally the case, given up. At least, she had given up for that particular evening.

It was a Saturday night. She was lying on the sofa in her comfiest sweatpants and she was eating a bowl of buttered popcorn and watching reruns of *Celebrity Cooks* on her tiny second-hand television set. When she heard the knock at the door, she hadn't even considered that it might be him. She thought it was the creepy landlord coming to check if she had a cat, knowing perfectly well that she didn't. She yanked the door open, ready to be brusque and there stood Henry. He smiled sheepishly and yet, intimately, as if only minutes had passed since they parted, not the six days, two hours, seventeen minutes and forty-three seconds that her heart had painstakingly counted.

"Hi," he said.

She stepped aside and he ambled in.

"It's a mess," she said, automatically. He shrugged and looked at the TV as if it was an alien from Mars.

"I'm sorry," she said.

"For what?"

"Watching TV. You never watch, right? You're too clever, I know."

"Megan," he said. "You are allowed to watch TV. Can I have some popcorn?"

"Of course. I should have offered, sorry—"

He cut her off then. "Stop that," he said. "What? Do you think I am better than you? I'm not. You'll see. I am here because I like you. I meant to come before and I nearly did but then…" he paused.

"But then?"

"I forget. It doesn't matter. Come and sit next to me and eat some popcorn with me. Do you have any water?"

"Water? Yes. You mean to drink?"

"Yes. I would love a glass of water."

She ran to the kitchen and came back with a glass of water that he downed in a single gulp. "Thanks. Come and sit next to me."

He was wearing the kind of scrubs that nurses in triage wear. His were mauve with yellow and pink triangles. His arms were bare and but he was wearing shoes this time. Shoes of a kind: summer flip-flops with a yellow daisy at the wishbone-join.

Megan thought that he looked like a beautiful, escaped mental patient. She desperately wanted to touch him but she studied his feet instead. They were filthy. "Why don't you feel the cold?" she asked.

"No idea. Just never have. I had tests when I was a kid but they couldn't figure it out. But it's nice. I can do things other people can't."

"But you'd have to be careful too. You could get frostbite and not notice. "

He laughed. "I would notice that. I even have shoes on now. How responsible is that?" He smiled at her as she sat down carefully beside him.

"You want a cigarette?" she asked and he nodded.

She grabbed her pack off the table. Her hands were shaking and she knew that he could see. "I…." She was going to apologize again but she stopped. She lit a cigarette and handed him the pack. She watched him smoke and eat popcorn. When he had finished the bowl, he put it on the floor and gave a contented sigh.

"I love popcorn," he said and she felt as if she had won an award.

"Tell me about you," he said and she was washed with panic.

"There's nothing to tell," she said quickly and she chewed on a fingernail.

"Megan." He was stern. "Stop it. Now, tell me."

"Well… um… my mom and dad live in Scarborough. I did too, until I came here. I wanted to try living on my own."

"And?"

"I like it. I like the quiet. Mom's very chatty, always wants to know about my day, who I spoke to, who my friends are, what we did. I don't have friends. I go to work. I eat lunch in the cafeteria. I do my job and then I come home."

"What about that friend you were at the reading with?"

"Alice? I wouldn't call her a friend. She's on the fast-track at work. She's going to be a big shot. She only asked me to come because she was dying to see Zimmerman Bob and she didn't want to go alone. She and Zimmerman Bob are an item now. Did you know?"

He shook his head, disinterested. "Why don't you have friends?"

"Too boring. I mean, they are so boring. I'm sure they think the same about me, but I don't care. Where did you get those clothes?"

He looked surprised. "Goodwill, I think. I shop a lot there. I do not shop much but when I do, I go there."

She waved her hand around the room. "This is from Goodwill. Though Dad got me the sofa from a friend of his. But the rest is all from there, even the pictures."

"Gustav Klimt," he said. "You got lucky."

"Who? "

"That is the name of the artist."

Megan shrugged. "I liked the way they look. I like the way they make me feel."

"You are a girl after my own heart," Henry said. "You found Gustav Klimt at Goodwill."

Meghan nearly fainted when he said that about his heart. She lit another cigarette and noticed that her hands had stopped shaking.

"What's your favourite memory?" he asked.

"What?"

"What's your favourite childhood memory?"

She tried to think. "Can I tell you later? I don't know. What's yours?"

"Training my cat to go for walks with me, on a lead. I figured if dogs could go for walks then why not cats?"

"Did it work?"

"It did not. Now, Megan, here is the thing that you must know about me."

Henry stopped abruptly, jumped off the sofa, and knelt next to Megan. "I have always seen the world in a different way than everybody else. For example, to me, things are perfectly logical. You have two given premises: one, a cat is a domestic animal, and two, all domestic animals can be trained. Therefore, a cat can be trained to walk on a lead. All of life can be seen as a multiple-linked convergent structure. Simply put: if two lines of reasoning lead to one, that is to say, the premises necessarily imply the conclusion, the syllogism is valid."

"But," Megan objected, hanging on to the part she understood, "not all domestic animals are the same. Your logic carries a wrong assumption. One kind of domestic animal doesn't equal another."

"I think my cat was simply being stubborn."

"Yeah, well, there you have it. Cats versus dogs."

His face was inches away from hers and she couldn't help

herself. She leaned in and he stayed where he was. She under-stood this to mean that he was fine with what was about to happen, and it seemed that she was right because soon they were kissing. She slid off the sofa and they lay on the floor, wedged in between the coffee table and the sofa and when they stopped kissing for a time, they lay still, breathing in each other's exhaled air.

He stroked her hair and she could feel his erection through the thin fabric of his trousers. "Megan," he finally said.

"Yes?"

"I have to leave."

"He jumped up and she scrambled to follow."

"But why? Was it us? Are you sorry we kissed?"

"Sorry?" He grinned. "It was the best thing to happen to me since sliced bread and formal logic, or a slice of formal logic on bread, if you will. No, I just have to go. It's what I do. I have my own clock. I have never figured it out but when I have to leave, I have to leave. I can't explain it better than that."

"Will I see you again?"

He looked baffled. "Of course you will, why wouldn't you?"

"But wait—" she paused. "Do you have a girlfriend? I don't know anything about you." Megan's heart was hammering as Henry walked across the room, away from her. He reached for the door and he stopped.

"It's a dubious honour," he said. "If indeed it can be con-sidered an honour at all. But, if you want to, you can be my girlfriend."

"Really? Seriously? The answer is yes," she said to the closed door and the empty room.

Henry returned several hours later, at three a.m. on Sunday morning. Megan leapt up to open the door. She had been lying awake, thinking about him. She pulled him inside and they crawled into bed together. He moved her panties to one side and pushed himself inside her and she clung to him. He smelled of wood smoke and cigarettes and alcohol and sweat. She breathed in his scent as he moved back and forth with hardly any motion but, oh, it felt so wonderful. He stayed inside her even after he came and they fell asleep that way, joined.

When they woke several hours later, Megan was panic-stricken they would have nothing to talk about.

"I'm hungry," Henry announced, still tangled around her. "What is in your larder?"

She laughed and stroked his head. "Not much. Mostly cans of soup. Mom's convinced that I won't starve if I have enough soup, so she keeps me stocked up."

"Soup!" Henry pulled away from her, his eyes bright. "What kind?"

"Cream of mushroom, cream of tomato, things like that. Nothing exotic or exciting. There is consommé too, in case I get sick and need a clear broth. Soup everywhere you look," Megan said from under the covers, hoping he would be amused by her mother's stockpile.

"Fantastic!" Henry cried. He leapt out of bed and rushed to the kitchen, naked. He began to open the cupboards. "I am in soup heaven! Oh, choices, why doth you maketh my life such a misery? Delectable mushroom or tangy tomato, which of you beauties shall I choose? Megan, I need help!"

She pulled on a T-shirt and joined him in the kitchen.

"Here," he said, handing her two cans of soup. "Put them behind your back. I will close my eyes and you switch them back and forth, okay?"

She did as he asked, and he closed his eyes and smiled happily. "I'm ready," she said, her hands unmoving behind her back.

Henry opened his eyes and pointed to her right hand. "That one," he said, and she gave him the can of mushroom soup. "Which leads us to conclude the obvious," Henry said and he held out his hand for the other can. "Tomato. You are the opposite, so you win the day."

But hadn't mushroom won? Megan was confused. She leaned against the counter and realized that her kitchen could do with some cleaning and she hoped that the finer details of her poor housekeeping would escape Henry's eye. "Do opposites always win?" she asked.

"They do," Henry replied, digging in drawers for a can opener. "Simply because they are the opposite. I am trying to disprove syllogistic theories of consequence and you have just seen one such argument in action. We assume that the one I picked was the chosen one, but your unspoken premise was true only for you. Most of the things we assume in life have zero logical or *a priori* validity." He spooned the soup carefully into a pot. "Do you have any milk?"

"I do," Megan said. "I'm going to make a coffee. Would you like one?"

"For breakfast? No way! But thank you."

He added milk to his soup and stirred it evenly at a low flame, his long fingers holding the spoon as if it was a magic wand. "Perfect," he said, minutes later.

"Would you like a bowl?" Megan asked, cradling her coffee mug.

"No need." Henry carried the pot into the living room and sat on the sofa, his legs cross-legged under him like a yogi.

"I'd break in two if I sat like that," Megan said and Henry looked at her without blinking until she squirmed with embarrassment.

"What?" she asked. "I can see you're thinking something, what?"

"It's just that…" he stopped and ate more soup.

"What?" She was frightened. Was he going to tell her what she already knew? That she was boring and stupid and he had no idea what he was doing there, and as soon as he was done with his soup, he was going to leave forever. "Tell me," she said, feeling sick.

"You criticize yourself all the time," he said, "and it makes me sad. You could sit like this and even if you couldn't, who cares? You have got no idea how wonderful you are, how beautiful, and it makes me sad that you don't know because you should know."

He finished the soup and put the pot down on the coffee table.

"Oh, Henry," she said, "that's the nicest thing anybody has ever said to me."

"But why are you so hard on yourself? Did your parents tell you that you were stupid?"

"No, they're wonderful. They've always told me I could do anything in the world that I wanted to. I could be an astronaut or anything." She laughed and twirled a piece of hair tightly around her finger.

Henry stood up. "I must go," he said.

"Will you come back later?"

"I wish I knew," he replied. "But I don't. I guess we will both have to see."

"You are going to get dressed before you leave, aren't you?" she asked and Henry laughed, looking down at his naked, lanky body.

"It wouldn't be the first time I made that mistake," he said. "Jeez, people are so uptight. We are naturally naked, so what is the problem? But yes, I had better get dressed."

He went back into the bedroom and pulled on his nurses' garb and his yellow flip-flops. Megan dug in her closet and handed him a scarf.

"You're giving me a scarf?" He seemed surprised.

"Yes. Mom knitted it for me. The yellow matches the flowers on your flip-flops."

"So it does!" Henry happily wound the scarf around his neck and slung one end over his shoulder with a jaunty motion.

"You look very dashing," Megan said. "Are you going to the poetry reading tonight?"

"It's only every two weeks," Henry told her. He planted a kiss on her forehead and then he wrapped his arms around her and held her tight. "What will you do with the remainder of your day?"

Megan glanced at the clock. It was already afternoon. "No idea. Have a bath, watch TV. Mom and Dad usually call me on a Sunday and we catch up."

"Where do they live again?" Henry enquired absently, sniffing her hair. "You smell so good. Don't ever change the way you smell."

"I'll try," she said. "Scarborough. They live in Scarborough. How come you're always so warm when you've got so few clothes on? I know I asked you before but I can't remember what you said."

"You probably can't remember because there is no good reason for it," he told her. "No scientific reason anyway. I generate heat like a furnace and no one knows why. I know not, my dearest and now, I must away. I will come back when I can. I mean I will come back, I just don't know when that will be. Are you still my girlfriend?"

"I am," she said, her heart stinging with happiness and once again she was left staring at the closed door and the empty room.

"I am," she repeated.

Then the phone rang and she jumped. She grabbed the receiver, knowing it was her mother on the line. "Mom! Guess what? I've got a boyfriend! A wonderful, beautiful, clever, marvellous boyfriend!"

"Wait," her mother said. "Don't say another word until I get Dad on the line." Once her father had picked up the extension, her mother started. "Tell us all about him, dear. What does he do for a living?"

"He's a poet," Megan said. "A genius. People listen to him like he's the Moses of poetry or something."

"A poet?" her father said. "I didn't know any members of that species were still alive, not to mention making a living at it."

"Well, Henry is a poet. And, he's interested in me! He really likes me."

"Why wouldn't he, dear?" her mother said. "Tell us more about him."

"He's so beautiful. And he's got this unusual condition so he never feels the cold. Even on a day like today, he can walk around outside in flip-flops, without a coat or anything. They don't know what causes it."

"Tell us straight up, Megan," her father said. "Does this fellow have some issues we should know about? He sounds a bit flaky to me."

"Oh no, Dad! He's lovely. You and Mom will love him. Everybody loves him."

"When will we meet him, this beatnik wonder?"

"Dad, he's not a beatnik. What's a beatnik anyway? Whatever, I don't care because he's not one of them."

"This poet then," her mother said. "When can we meet Henry the poet?"

"Hard to say, Mom, he lives by his own hours. Even he doesn't know."

"What do you mean, dear?"

Megan sighed. "You're both depressing me. I was excited to tell you about him but now you've picked holes in him and you haven't even met him. It's because you haven't met him. If you had, and you both will, you would see that he is wonderful. He's a real genius and he's studying disproving some kind of mathematical theory. He makes me very happy."

"And of course we're happy for you, too, dear," her mother said. "You know we worry. It's what parents do."

"Not all parents. Only you two."

"No, Meg. All parents worry. How old is Henry?"

"My age," Megan lied, having no idea.

"Does he do drugs?" her father asked. "He sounds like a drug taker to me."

"Dad! Please stop judging him." Megan thought about Henry's dependence on LSD to bring balance to his life and she decided it would be best to not tell the truth, so she side-stepped the question. "We met at a poetry reading. Imagine me at a poetry reading! And the main poet liking me! I'm so glad I moved to Toronto. I would never have met a genius in Scarborough."

"Toronto's not exactly another country," her father said but Megan objected.

"It is, Dad! It feels like it is. Being at that club and listening to Henry was the best night of my life. It was like another world."

"When did this momentous evening take place?" her father asked.

"A week ago today. Why do I feel like you're both being so horrible when I'm so happy? I don't want to talk to you anymore, so I'm hanging up."

"No, wait, Meggie. We're sorry," her mother said. "It's just, well, remember how cut up you were about Joshua? We don't want to see you so sad again."

"That was different. He couldn't be with me because of his family, because I'm not Jewish. He did love me. It was his family's fault we split up. He couldn't help it."

"Does Henry have any family?"

Megan sighed. "I don't know, Mom. We've only see each other a few times. I feel miserable now, thanks a lot. How to bust my bubble. You guys are the best, you know?"

"Ah, Meggie, don't be like that," her father said quickly. "It's a lot for us to take in: a poet, a new relationship."

"All your dad wants, and all I want, too, is for you to be happy. You know that," her mother said. "I'm sure Henry is lovely. He's keen on you, so he's got our vote."

"I'm sure he's a fine fellow, Meggie," her father said quickly.

"Yeah, sure, Dad." Megan sounded dispirited. "Anyway, I'll let you guys go now. I'll talk to you next week?"

"You know you can bring Henry around any time," her mother said. And then, worried that she had upset Megan even further, she added, "Don't worry, dear, your father and I do know how to talk to poets. I even dated one before I agreed to go steady with your father. My poet was a lovely young man too."

Her father gave a snort that echoed down the line. "Those were stolen song lyrics, Ethel. He was a no good con-artist who looked like James Dean, and that's what you liked."

"He was lovely, wasn't he?" Her mother agreed, sounding wistful. "They weren't stolen, Ed. And I know the difference between songs and poetry. You were lucky I picked you over him."

"Funny to think of you two young and in love," Megan giggled.

"Feels like yesterday," her father said. "Come over when you can, Meggie. You may be happy in the far-away land of Toronto but your old dad misses you, okay?"

"I miss you too, Dad," she said. "I'll come soon, I promise. Work's really busy now, though. They laid-off a bunch of people, so I am getting double shifts. Pay's good though and they like what I do."

"We're very proud of you, Meggie," her mother said. "Take care, dear, and tell Henry we'd love to meet him."

They rang off and Megan sat on the floor, wedged in between the coffee table and the sofa, in the same spot where she and Henry had lain entwined and breathing each other's air. She felt alone and sad and she wished Henry would come back.

Henry did come back. He came back three days later and by that time, Megan was sick with worry. Worried that he had died of the cold or that he had left her and found a new girlfriend. She admitted to herself that she favoured death over infidelity, even if that made her a terrible person.

She arrived home from a late shift on Wednesday night and saw Henry leaning against the banister of the stairwell. She didn't feel much of anything except for quick relief followed by annoyance that her happiness was now reliant on such an erratic person. She scowled at Henry whose wide grin fell to the ground.

"Meg? Are you okay?"

"Tired is all. I just worked two full shifts."

She had wanted to brush past him but instead she melted into his arms and burst into tears. He held her and stroked her hair.

"I don't know how old you are," she sobbed. "Or where you go when you're not with me. I don't know anything about your family. I don't know how you make a living. I think about you all the time and you've been gone so long and I'm so cold."

She hadn't intended to say any of that but it poured out in a rush and then she stopped, having soaked Henry's thin t-shirt. She desperately needed to blow her nose. She pulled away and wiped her nose on her sleeve.

"First things first," Henry was brisk. "You need a hot bath and I'll tell you everything. Everything that I can, anyway. There are things about me that I even I do not know."

He took her hand and led her up the stairs. "I am really sorry. I thought you would be okay."

She unlocked the front door and let them both in. She sat down on the sofa. She knew her make-up had streaked down her face and she felt like a sad clown.

"I've let you down," she said. "Haven't I? I was supposed to be all fine with anything, and I thought I was, but I wasn't. It's my parent's fault. They phoned after you left and they were asked me a bunch of questions. They made it sound like me and you were weirdoes with no future. That's not true, is it?"

"It's not true," he said gently, and he took her hand. "You don't have to be all fine with everything with me, Meg. I'd rather you shouted at me or cried — whatever — but never hide what's going on. I am not going to leave you and I am going to do my best to be more dependable. We will try to make more plans. But first we are going to get you into a nice hot bath and get you warmed up. A bubble bath! That is what you need."

"I don't have any bubble bath," Megan said.

"Shampoo works just as well," he said. "Do you have any candles?"

"Only the plain white ones for emergencies. Dad made me get them."

"Perfect. You get those. I'll start your bath."

Megan dug the candles out from under the kitchen sink and wiped the dust off them. "I don't have anything to stick them onto," she called out. "Candlestick holders have never been on my shopping list."

"We can stick them to the edges of the bath. Don't worry. You will see."

Henry waited until Megan had climbed into the water and then he lit a candle. He poured hot wax, and pressed the candle down carefully. He set half a dozen candles in this way, and then he turned off the lights and sat on the toilet seat, resting his chin on his hands.

He looked dismayed. "Something is missing. You should be drinking a martini. And I should be washing your back but I would burn myself bending over the candles."

"I'm fine," Megan said and she was. "I am happier than I have ever been, Henry. Thank you."

He flashed a beautiful smile at her.

"Where do you go during the day?" she asked. "Can I ask you that?"

"You can ask me anything. I go to the university. At least, I start off trying to go there. Sometimes I don't make it and I am not too sure what happens."

"I don't understand. Do you have blackouts?"

"Nope. It is more like I get distracted. I slip into a daydream and I miss the bus I am supposed to take and I take whatever bus comes along next. I know, rationally, that the bus is not going in the same direction as the one I was supposed to take, but I can't help myself. There is a voice in my head that says 'a bus is a bus' and next thing I know, I am on the wrong bus.

Then I drift around getting off here or there, and I might find a bookstore in which case I can lose a day reading. Or I watch people or I think about my poems."

"Don't the people at the university mind?"

"They think my coming and going is part of my so-called genius. And who knows, maybe it is but it is not something I can control. I have been this way since I was very little."

Henry face suddenly lost its cheer. He cracked his knuckles and Megan winced.

"That's why my mother sent me to boarding school when I was five," he added. "Mother said I was too much of a risk to myself, and my nannies could not control me, and so she gave up."

"When you were five?" Megan sat up and sloshed water, horrified. "Who sends their kid away when they're five? Sorry. I shouldn't criticize your mother. I don't even know her."

"It is fine. Once you meet her, you'll understand. It is also this temperature thing. I am out of sync with the natural world and I am out of sync with other people. Normal people are regulated by temperature and seasons and time but that's not the case with me. And even day and night. I get them mixed up. I do night things in the day and day things in the night. Ordinary people don't do that. They work during the day and they sleep at night. I can start reading a book at two in the morning and I will read until the afternoon of the following day and then I'll sleep. My world works differently from the rest of mankind. Apologies. Womankind. Peoplekind."

"It must make having a job pretty tough," Megan commented, wriggling her toes on the faucet. "I can't see my bosses being okay with that."

"I have never had a job. Not even a summer one. Because I can't. You are right, no one can put up with it. That's also why I haven't had a girlfriend up till now either. I never thought anybody would be able to handle my situation, but then I met you."

"And I let you down by having a huge meltdown." Megan flushed red and her eyes filled with tears.

"No, you did not. You told me how you felt. You didn't say that you didn't want to see me again. Thank you for that, by the way. Have you had a boyfriend before?"

"Yes. His name was Joshua and I was so in love with him. But he and his family are Orthodox Jews and he said there wasn't any point in us seeing each other. He waited until we had been dating for three months before he told me. I would have been better off if he hadn't asked me out at all and I wish he hadn't. I only dated him for three months and then I spent two years crying about it."

"How long ago was that?"

"I dated him when I was sixteen and now I am nearly twenty-two."

"No one in between?"

"No one in between."

They grinned at each other.

"I think I am ready to get out of the bath now," she said.

"I'll dismantle the candelabra," he told her and he blew the candles out.

"Make a wish with each candle," Megan said. "But don't tell me what it is."

He held the towel for her when she got out and he wrapped it around her and patted her dry. "You are so beautiful," he said. "You are my dream girl."

She laughed and was about to say something when he put a finger to her lips.

"Sshh," he said. "You are about to say something self-deprecating and it's not necessary. Besides, I think I should finish drying you in the bedroom. We don't want you to catch a cold."

"Henry," she said, "you really are a genius."

The following weekend, Henry took Megan home to meet his family. They caught the subway to Rosedale and as they got closer, Megan could feel the tension building. Henry's shoulders climbed up to his ears and he started drumming his fingers on his knee. She grabbed his hand. "We don't have to do this," she said but he shook his head.

"We do."

They got off the train and crossed the bridge close to the tracks.

"The houses here are mansions," Megan marvelled. "I've never been here, not in all the time I've lived in Toronto, which isn't that long, but still. And the gardens are works of art, not like where I'm from, where a rose bush and a garden gnome count as landscaping." She was trying to lighten the mood but she could see it wasn't working and she fell quiet, holding his hand as they wound down one street and up another.

The porches were piled high with Halloween decorations, and large clay pots bloomed with purple, burnt orange, and white chrysanthemums. Expensive fall wreaths hung from every door, and carved pumpkins lined the steps. Megan didn't voice her unease but she felt distinctly out of place. She tugged her last-season's Sears jacket down with her free hand and hoped that Henry's parents wouldn't be home.

"There it is," Henry said, a note of desperation in his voice. Megan looked where he was pointing, and she wanted to turn and run. The house reminded her of The Keg mansion on Jarvis Street, where her parents had taken her for her twenty-first birthday. She had heard rumours that The Keg was haunted and she was sure that Henry's family home came with its own crowd of unhappy ghosts.

They stood outside the ornamental wrought-irons gates and Henry dug in his pocket for a set of keys. His face was tight and his hands were shaking as he punched in a security code. The gate opened slowly, as if it too was questioning the soundness of their visit. "I always think they'll change the combination and not tell me," he murmured, more to himself than Megan.

They walked up the long curved driveway and the silence felt oppressive. Megan felt as if she was being watched from all sides and she realized she wasn't holding Henry's hand so much for him as for herself. "Not much noise in this neighbourhood," Megan whispered and Henry tried to smile.

"You have got that right," he said.

He fitted a key into the front door and pushed it open. The door was painted a high-gloss red enamel and an elaborate artificial wreath of maple leaves and berries hung in its centre. Megan thought the wreath must have cost a month of her salary.

The polished hallway was spotless and there was a Persian rug in the centre of the gleaming hardwood floor. A carved antique wooden table held a tall crystal vase , spilling an abundance of roses in shades of pink, peach and apricot.

Henry flicked on a light switch and the vase glittered under the light. It seemed to Megan that there wasn't anything in the house that didn't gleam or shine.

Henry was about to head for the curved staircase to the left of the table when he and Megan heard a voice.

"Henry?"

Both Henry and Megan started in fright. Megan pressed close to Henry, and she could feel his body shaking.

"Dad. Yes, it's me."

"Been a while."

"Yeah."

There was silence.

Henry's father had emerged from a shadowed hallway. He was tall — a good six feet — but he was a wraith, a thin scarecrow frame for the undeniably costly clothes that hung loosely. His cheeks were sunken and the hollows underneath his eyes were black. Megan recalled a moment at the pub, the night she had met Henry, when, after he had finished reciting his poems and was wrung out, she had noticed his eyes closed and deeply shadowed. She could see the similarity between father and son.

"I'm Megan," she said and she went up to Henry's father and stuck out her hand.

Henry's father shook it uncertainly, as if he wasn't quite sure what he was supposed to do.

"Henry?" A female voice this time, and not a happy one at that.

Megan turned to the voice, in time to see Henry stiffen.

"Mother," he said, striving for a casual tone and failing. "I've brought my girlfriend home to visit. I thought she should see the happy hearth upon which I was so lovingly raised."

"I see you've lost none of your gratitude for all the things your father and I have done for you."

Henry's mother scrutinized her son. He was once again wearing his girly hospital orderly garb, his yellow flip-flops, and the scarf that Megan had given him.

"Please tell me none of the neighbours saw you like that," she said, and Henry shrugged.

"They know me," he replied.

"Yes," his mother said. "That is correct. They do."

Megan felt trapped in a malevolent current of hatred and pain. She looked back at Henry's father who hadn't moved an inch and then she turned to Henry's mother, who was frowning with obvious displeasure. She was about to say something when Henry grabbed her hand.

"Mother," he said. "This is Megan. And if you say one nasty thing to her, even one, I will wring your neck, so help me god, I will."

"Now he's turning to violence," Henry's mother remarked to his father, as if Henry was not there. "This is a new development. It must be true love."

Megan eyed Henry's mother. She, unlike the father, was short and heavy around the hips and jowls. She did, however, have Henry's large clear grey-green eyes, his perfect nose, his sensual mouth and high cheekbones. Her hair was Marilyn-blonde and curled as if she had just come from the salon, and she was dressed in a cream shirt and tan slacks, draped with pearls at her neck and wrists.

Megan was reminded of a gold-dusted vanilla macaroon she had seen in a high-end bakery on Bloor Street.

"Megan you say." Henry's mother scrutinized her. "I am Mrs. Arbuthnot-Berlin. This is a surprise, Henry. Here I was, thinking you were entirely asexual all these years."

"You've never understood a thing about me," Henry commented pleasantly. "And now that we have had this fantastic catch-up, I'm going to show Megan my room."

"Change your clothes before you leave," his mother called out as they started up the stairs. "Or at least, throw a coat over that nonsense you're wearing. You have never cared what the neighbours think, but I still do."

Henry ignored her and led Megan down the length of a wide, carpeted hallway, not stopping until he reached the very end.

"How many bedrooms did we pass?" Megan whispered and Henry grinned.

"Five. Two with en-suite bathrooms. Here we are, my room. When I was not at boarding school that is, which was most of my life."

He twisted the door handle and waved Megan inside.

Megan gasped. The room was filled, floor to ceiling, with model airplanes. There were dozens and dozens of them, hanging from the ceiling, the bookcases, and the lamps. They lined the windowsill and there were piles of them on the floor. The only space left uncovered was the bed, which had a wine-covered coverlet and chocolate-brown pillows.

Megan sat down on the bed and stared. "No books?" she asked. "I was sure there'd be books."

Henry tapped his head. "All up here. I read a book and never forget it. Trust me, it's not as wonderful a gift as you might think. I would love to empty my head. That is why I take so much acid. When I am stoned, there is less going on inside, which is a relief."

"When did you do these planes, if you were away at school?"

"I had to come home for the holidays and it helped pass the time. When I am putting a model together, the voices in my head shut up for a bit. It doesn't always work, but for the brief period of time it does, it is a blessed relief."

"Henry," Megan said gently, "tell me about the voices." But Henry shook his head.

"No, no," he said. "I can't talk about them. They get louder when I do. They don't like being talked about. They punish me then."

"It's okay." Megan looked around. "Not even one picture on the wall," she marvelled. "I've never seen anything like this. It's a model airplane museum, that's what it is! Wow. My dad builds bird houses. Our basement is full of them. Mom keeps telling him to sell them at craft markets, but he isn't interested. He says she can sell them if she likes. He just enjoys making them."

Henry grinned. "I can understand that."

He came and lay down close to her, turning her to face him, and he cupped her buttocks with his hands.

"I didn't think I would ever show this room to anybody," he said, and he kissed her. "And now you have even met my family. I bet you haven't had this much fun in years."

"As long as I'm with you, my life is perfect."

She hugged his waist and closed her eyes. There was a knock at the door and Megan pulled away and started to sit up, but Henry held her back.

"Yes?" he called over his shoulder.

His mother pushed the door open. "We're going out now, to the club and you need to leave. I can't trust you. You know that. He'll leave without locking up, or he'll leave the shower running, or he'll leave the stove on — who knows?" She said this last bit conversationally to Megan, despite not having acknowledged her to this point.

"She's right," Henry said, sitting up and brushing the hair

out of his eyes. "I have done all of those things and more. Come on, let us go."

"Do you need money?"

"No, mother, I don't. My monthly stipend suffices as always, but thank you."

"For the love of god, put a coat on over that getup," his mother said and she opened a closet, revealing a display that would rival the menswear section of Club Monaco. She pulled out a modern-day navy pea coat and tossed it at him. "Don't argue, Henry. I don't care if you throw it away when you get around the corner, but please do me the favour of wearing it."

Henry stood up and pulled the coat on. Megan thought he looked like a fashion model. "Happy, Mother? Now the neighbours will really think I have lost my mind because they know I would never wear anything like this."

"Thank you for indulging me, Henry." His mother flicked a finger at one of the model airplanes. "We're going to get rid of this junk one day," she said, waving her hand around.

"If you do," Henry said evenly, "then I will know that you never want to see me again. That will be our little signal, Mother. When I come home and this room has been cleared out, then I will know to leave, never to return."

"Oh, Henry," his mother sighed, and for a moment she looked slightly human. "Why must we do this? Why? Look at you. So handsome. So clever. Why can't you be halfway more normal than you are? Why? I really, truly do not understand. You could have the world at your feet."

"If you think about it, Mother, we all have the world at our feet, quite literally. And why am I like this, you ask? Why? Your and Dad's genes are to blame, I guess." Henry pulled Megan to her feet. "Although that is not fair," he added. "I do need to accept some responsibility. But this is what you and I do, Mother. We hurt each other. That is how we know we are still family. When we lose the power to hurt one another, well, then we will just be strangers."

He led Megan through the hallway and down the stairs.

Henry's father was still standing in the doorway where they had left him.

"Dad." Henry tipped a mock cap.

"Son. Do you need any money?"

"Nope, Mother already asked me. See you around, Dad."

"Take care, son."

"Always."

Henry closed the front door gently behind him and he and Megan walked down the path to the gate.

Megan thought it was better to remain silent and she did, all the way to the train station and even on the journey back to her apartment. Once they reached her stop, she leaned in towards him.

"Henry? Do you need to be alone for a bit?"

He nodded, unable to look at her. "Thank you," he said, looking at his hands. "I will try to come back tonight."

"That would be lovely," she said. She kissed him and got off when the doors opened.

She watched the train pull away and as it did, she caught sight of his downcast head and she thought her heart would break.

3. MEGAN

HENRY RETURNED LATER THAT NIGHT, much to Megan's relief. She was lying on the sofa, smoking and watching re-runs of *Bonanza* on TV. "Crazy people out there today," Henry said, settling down next to her and putting his arm around her shoulders. "How are you?"

Megan nodded. "I'm good." She rubbed his leg. "You feel like heading out to meet my folks tomorrow? We may as well get the family dynamics established—"

"And thenceforth ignored," Henry added. "Yeah, sure."

His head drooped.

"Tired?" Megan asked and he nodded.

"I think I will take a shower if that is okay," he said. "Wash away my sins."

He ambled off the bathroom and Megan turned her attention back to the television set, happy in the normalcy of their domesticity. She heard him turn on the shower and when he started singing loudly, she grinned. Until there was a knock at her door. The evil landlord, no doubt, she thought.

"This apartment's rented to ONE person and one person only," the landlord said self-righteously, his hands on his pregnant belly.

"And I'm the only one living here," Megan insisted. "A friend of mine got cold and I said she could take a shower."

"Pretty manly sounding she, if you ask me," the landlord said as Henry crescendoed to a particularly vocal piece of opera.

"That's hardly her fault," Megan was indignant and she moved to close the door.

"I'm watching you," the landlord said, and he gestured with a two-fingered eye-poke at himself and then at her. "That's me, watching you, girlie."

She shut the door, and decided not to tell Henry what had happened.

He strolled out of the washroom, naked and content. "Clean can feel like heaven sometimes," he said. "Have you not had enough TV? I am feeling largely positive that I can find another way to entertain you…"

"Largely, I agree you can," she said, looking pointedly at his enthused erection and she pulled off her T-shirt. "Let's head for the bed, Mister."

"I don't know," Henry said the following day as the train headed east. "I don't know if this is such a good idea."

"Are you high?"

"Yes."

"Then everything should be fine. I'm the one who should be nervous, not you. To put things in perspective about my family, you should know that our lives are furnished by The Brick, we dress at Sears, and we shop for groceries at the No Frills."

"Consider me in the know," Henry said. "And just so you know, that that kind of stuff matters naught to me."

"True." She snuggled up to him.

He was wearing a new hospital uniform. This one was pale yellow with white diamonds and squiggles, and he had a new pair of sandals she hadn't seen before. They were a neon green.

"It's like four degrees out there," she said. "Even though I know you don't feel the cold, I worry. It's like those people who hold their hands over flames — their skin must get burnt. You must suffer ill-effects."

"I suffer all right," Henry muttered, "but not from the cold.

It is my head, darling, you were right, my broken, broken head. Humpty Dumpty's got nothing on my head."

"I love your head," she said, and she stopped short. The L word.

"As I love yours," he returned simply, and she could breathe again.

They had to catch a bus after the train and Megan thought the ride would last forever. She hated Canada in November; everything was grey and dreary, dull and dark.

"At least it was Halloween a few days ago." she said out loud.

Henry turned to look at her. "I thought you didn't like Halloween."

"I don't, but at least the houses are brightly decorated. I hate this time of year because I don't like the fact that winter is coming."

"Everybody does. You'll be okay once we get snow. Snow makes people happy."

"Not everybody," she reminded him and he nodded.

"Where are we?" he asked. "I can't see out the windows, they're too dirty. No wonder you moved to Toronto. This is the far side of the eastern world."

"We're nearly there," she said as she pulled her scarf tight around her neck. "Don't say I didn't warn you."

They walked up a long tired street, the houses fronted by dead grass lawns and the smatterings of left-over dollar-store Halloween cheer. A few dogs barked noisily and someone was testing the revs on a car that needed a new muffler.

"Here we are," Megan said and she turned into the driveway of a low-slung bungalow with mock-stone aluminum siding.

"Here's the garden gnome collection," she pointed as they walked toward the porch steps, although the procession of gnomes that lined the pathway would have been hard to miss. A large one-toothed cardboard witch that had seen better days sailed across the front door on her broomstick and cobwebs hung in clumps around the door frame.

"Mom loves Halloween," Megan explained unnecessarily, putting her key into the front door lock.

"Mom? Dad?" she called out. "You home?"

"Meggie!" Her mother sounded delighted. "What a surprise, sweetie!" It sounded like she was in the kitchen. "Dad's in the basement, I'll go and call him. Megan heard her open the door to the basement. "Dad, Dad," she yelled. "You'll never guess who's here!"

Megan could hear her father clumping up the rickety basement stairs and he and her mother rounded the entrance to the living room at the same time, coming to an abrupt halt when they spotted Henry.

"This is Henry," Megan said.

"Of course it is," Megan's mother replied. "I'm Ethel and this is Ed."

"Pleased to meet you," Ed said and he shook Henry's hand. "Beer for you?"

"Ah, no, I'm good, thank you, Ed. I would love some water though."

"Sure thing, come on. Meggie, you want a beer?"

"Love one, Dad," Megan said, pulling off her coat and flinging it onto the sofa.

"Not home five minutes and already making a mess," her mother scolded and Megan laughed.

"You love it," she said.

"I love you, so that makes it okay."

As Henry inspected an oil painting of a wide-eyed kitten, Megan's mother gave her a quick thumbs up and Megan relaxed.

Ed returned with their drinks and they sat in the living room.

Megan cracked open her beer. "Henry's never been this far east before," she teased him and all eyes turned to Henry who had crossed his legs, balancing the glass of water on his knee.

"True," he agreed. "I have not. I am not a well-travelled man."

"But you are poet," Ethel said with a genuine smile. Megan was sure her mother was flirting with Henry, just slightly but still, there it was, and she exchanged a grin with her father.

"Guilty as charged," Henry said. "Here is a sample of my wares." He closed his eyes, paused for a moment, and then he let fly a stream of poetic consciousness that left his audience speechless.

"That sort of thing," he said, into the silence after he finished.

"Bravo," Ed said, raising his beer can. "I didn't understand a single word but it sounded very impressive."

Henry laughed.

"Megan said you're studying math or something," Ethel said.

"I am trying to untangle syllogistic logic," Henry said and a look of frustration crossed his face. "Mainly to explain my own … issues … I guess. I am fascinated by time, space, cause, effect, and consequence and how they logically interact. As humans, we like to find explanations for fundamental actions and behaviours, and we are not happy unless there's a reason for things. We like to know that this led to this, that led to that. But what if nothing led to this and that, but random chance? I think that is the underlying truth, but most people cannot handle it."

"I know I can't," Ed said. "Call me square, Henry, and I don't mind if you do, but you're right, I need my reasons for things. I need my *this causes that*. Otherwise, we're all just corks bobbing on the crazy seas of some unnamed ocean and if that is truth, son, then I don't want to know."

Ethel and Megan stared at Ed in surprise.

"I tell you what, Ed," Henry said. "If I ever prove my theory conclusively, I won't tell you, how's that?"

"Sounds good to me," Ed said and he sounded relieved. "You want to see some birdcages?"

"I'd love to!" Henry jumped to his feet and the two men wandered off, leaving Ethel and Megan behind, both of them speechless.

"Well, I never," Ethel finally said. "You ever heard your father talk like that?"

Megan shook her head. "Nope. But Mom, Henry's lovely, isn't he?"

"He is, sweetie, he really is. Are you hungry? I can make you something if you like."

"Oh, yeah, Mom, an omelet! With three kinds of cheese and onions and green pepper and olives."

"You're not pregnant?" her mother asked and Megan swatted her.

"No, Mom! Don't be silly! Let me ask Henry if he wants something but I'll bet he says no. He had mushroom soup for breakfast and that's usually all he has in a day."

"Tell him I've got fresh-baked caramel cookies if he likes. I made them for the bingo ladies for tomorrow's game, but I can make some more later."

"He says yes, please, that'd be wonderful," Megan said when she returned.

Her mother handed her a plate with a pile of cookies. "They're still talking birdhouses down there?" she asked.

"Yeah, non-stop. Wait, save one of those cookies for me, for after my omelet."

Megan carried the plate downstairs and handed it to Henry who was gesticulating angles with his long arms. He took a cookie without pausing, bit into it with relish, and carried on talking.

"They're in their own world," Megan reported with satisfaction as she sat down at the small Formica-covered table and watched her mother cook. "So, Mom, what's up with you? How are the bingo ladies? Spill the beans, give me the down and dirty."

"Now that you mention it, Frances's boy is in trouble again...." Her mother got right into it, with Megan nodding and saying the right things, but the only thing she was actually listening to was the happy murmur coming from the basement.

Later, she had to drag Henry away.

"We have to go, or we'll miss the bus and even now, it will

be ages before we get home," she said. Henry looked glum at having to leave.

"See you soon, son," Ed said. "We can even come and visit you lot in Toronto, take you out for a meal or something. Wait one second though."

He rushed back down to the basement and returned with a birdhouse that he thrust at Henry. "Here," he said and he turned a dark purple. "You liked this one best."

Megan was about to object and say that Henry didn't like possessions when she saw Henry's eyes light up and he reached for it like a kid at Christmas.

"Wow, thanks Ed! This is the best thing anyone's ever given me!" He cradled the birdcage to his chest.

"Can we leave now?" Megan asked, smiling. "Come on, Henry. Goodbye Mom, Dad. I'll phone you soon."

They walked down the driveway with Henry examining his birdhouse and chatting happily to Megan while Ethel and Ed watched from the window.

"Going to break her heart, isn't he?" Ethel said and Ed put his arm around her waist and sighed. "Yup. And ours, Eth. And ours."

Megan and Henry settled into a routine of sorts. "I had a word with the landlord," Henry said. "I'm going to pay him an extra seventy-five a week and he'll leave us alone."

"Seventy-five? We could live somewhere much bigger for that."

"Yeah, but we would have to find it, sign documents, move. It's much easier to just pay him. Besides, I like your apartment. You have a nice view of the park and there is good light."

Megan wondered what domestic life with Henry would entail. She didn't think it would resemble anything like the living arrangements that the rest of the world were used to. And she was right. Henry did surprise her by being more scheduled than she had thought he could or would be, although he still came and went at startlingly obtuse hours. She couldn't sleep when he was out; there was always a part of her that worried he wouldn't come back, so she found it hard to get the sleep she needed.

Henry began to write down his poems and he pinned large sheets of paper to the wall, tracking the flow of his thoughts. Megan loved coming home, opening the front door, and seeing Henry standing there, gnawing on a pencil, mumbling, shirtless, and most of the time, entirely naked.

The first few times she came home and he was engrossed, she tiptoed past him, not wanting to disturb him, but she soon realized that she could play the drums on the kitchen pots and pans and he wouldn't hear a thing.

When he was done writing for the day, he lay down on the floor, exhausted, and slept for a while. Then he would slip out to find his drugs and return at odd hours to crawl into bed with Megan, smelling of wood smoke, and holding her tight.

"How will you know when you're done?" she asked him, watching from the bedroom doorway as he scratched a new word across an old one on one of the sheets of paper. She had been fast asleep but a bad dream had woken her and she had wanted to see if Henry was still in the apartment or out for the night.

He turned to her and she could see him gathering his thoughts, moving away from the world inside his head and back to her. "I will never be done. I have an editor coming around tomorrow. He's going to read them and see what he thinks."

"He's going to read them on the wall?"

"Yes." He squinted at the writing. "Come and tell me if you think it is legible."

"It is," she said. "I read everything every day. I've got no idea what it all means, but I can read the words for what they are."

"Oh, good." He sounded relieved and he pulled her down onto the sofa with him and put her feet on his lap. "I never thought I could have this," he said. "You and me. I am so afraid of this happiness. Because that's what I feel, Meg, happy."

"Me too, Henry."

They grinned at each other.

"I am hungry," he said. "I think a stack of pancakes would go down a treat now, what say you?"

"It's two a.m.!"

"Exactly," Henry replied, getting up. "Time for supper."

Megan did wonder how much longer she would be able to function with the odd sleeping hours. She tried to be vigilant and maintain a regular schedule, but the days crept into the nights and the wrong hours stayed, like overdue library books gathering late fees. Megan felt as if her life was gathering late fees. She knew her concentration was slipping. She forgot to buy milk when it was the very thing she set out to get. She forgot to take her contraceptive pill for a few days, and then she took three to make up for it. She wore odd combinations of clothing to work, not realizing that she had done so until her boss looked at her strangely and remarked that it was a good thing they were a call centre, and not in full view of the public eye.

Megan apologized and decided to plan a week's outfits in advance but when she came home, either Henry distracted her or she fell asleep waiting for him, or she lost herself in some mindless TV.

The evening after the editor's visit, Megan arrived home to find the walls bare. The living room felt bereft and Henry was nowhere to be seen.

Megan was worried. Had the editor hated the poems? She couldn't bear to think of Henry's devastation. She looked at her watch. It was only early evening but it was already dark.

She had no idea where to start looking for Henry and she wished she'd taken a more careful note of where he went.

Too restless to sit and wait, she headed out to try and find him, thinking he might be in the park, but there was no one there apart from a few teenagers passing a bottle back and forth. The wind picked up and she thought she'd get Chinese take-out and wait it out for Henry back at the apartment.

She pulled her coat tight and slipped down a side road, heading for a Chinese restaurant that Henry loved. She thought she'd get him his favourites and have them ready for his supper, although, knowing him, he'd have them for breakfast.

And it was then that she saw him. She didn't recognize him at first. She only saw a tall figure in the darkness of a doorway, but something about the posture was familiar and she slowed down. Yes. It was Henry. His eyes were rolling back in his head and he was muttering and moaning and making unfamiliar noises, noises that brought a coldness to her stomach.

She wanted to call out to him, to try to help him, but she was worried that she would startle him and she sensed that could be dangerous. At one point he seemed to look at her and she waited for him to recognize her, but he looked right through her and his eyes rolled back in his head again.

"One of our regulars," a voice said and Megan jumped. She turned to see a police officer standing next to her, one hand on a bicycle.

"He's harmless," the cop said. "Hangs around doing his crazy eye-rolling thing and next thing you know, he's gone. Probably from the psych ward down the road."

Megan couldn't find words. She stood there, watching Henry writhing in the doorway.

"What's wrong with him?" She managed to get the words out, and they sounded as if they had come from someone else.

The cop shrugged. "Who knows? No shortage of loonies around here. You from around here?"

"No, just passing through," Megan lied.

The cop looked as though he would have liked to chat her up a bit. He was short and not bad-looking, youngish, dark-haired.

"I must go," she said.

"Officer Kaminski," he called after her. "In case you ever want to look me up. Fifty-Two Division. Kaminski!"

She tucked her head down and hurried home.

She had no idea what to think. She was ice cold and damp to her marrow but she couldn't move. She sat on the sofa in the living room with the newly-stripped walls and waited for Henry to return. When she finally heard the key turn in the door, it was close to dawn and she was still wide awake.

Henry was alarmed to see her sitting there under the light of a single lamp.

"Meggie? You okay?"

She started to cry. "I saw you, Henry. You were so out of it. You didn't know who I was or anything. You were in a doorway and some cop saw you too. What's going on? Is that what you do when you're not here?"

His face closed. "I do what I have to," Meg, he said. "You know that. I can't face an interrogation now. You know there are things I do that I don't have the answer to either. I wish I did. And I wish you hadn't seen me like that."

"I was so worried, that's all." Megan followed him into the bedroom. "I was frightened. A cop was there, and he said that you're there often, in that state."

"I don't want to hear it," Henry said. "I can't. Please Meg."

"What happened to the poems on the wall?"

He shrugged. "The editor loved them. He understood what I was doing, the progression and regression, and he said he could read it fine. He took them down and said he is going to typeset them and even though it is a crazy deadline, he wants to have a book out by spring."

"Henry! That's amazing! You must be so happy!"

He shrugged and slipped into bed, wearing his usual hospital uniform. "I don't care," he said. "One way or the other. It seemed like a thing to do, so I did it, but it doesn't mean anything to me. The voices I hear are not my voice. Who knows whose voices they are, anyway? I am just the conduit: the mad, empty vessel they have chosen to fill."

"But they're your poems, Henry. No one else could have

written them." She climbed into bed with him and set the alarm. "Oh god, I'm going to get about three hours sleep. I must stop doing this. I must get more sleep."

Henry stroked her head. "I am sorry you were worried," he said. "I love you, Megan."

It was the first time he'd said it like that.

"I love you too, Henry," she said sleepily, snuggling into him. "And even if you are not, I am very excited about your book."

She kissed his face and was startled to find it wet. "Henry. You're crying."

"Tough day," he said. "Some days just are."

The book was published in spring and it was memorable for two things: Henry's spectacular meltdown and Megan's realization that she was pregnant.

Shortly before the launch, Henry's behaviour became increasingly erratic.

"But how can you tell when he's never done things the normal way?" Megan's mother asked, reasonably.

"Because there's a normal, even for Henry and this isn't it. Are you and Dad coming to the launch?"

"Of course we are. Maybe we can take the two of you out for supper before or after?"

Megan sighed. "I've no idea, Mom. I'd love to. But, to tell you the truth, I've been feeling exhausted lately. I've been trying to get more sleep but it's not easy."

It was then that she recalled her two missed periods, but she pushed the thought out of her mind. "Maybe things will get back to what they were once the book launch is over," she said hopefully.

"I'm sure they will," her mother agreed. "Are Henry's parents coming?"

"I don't think they even know about it. He said you two are more like parents to him than his ever were. Oh Mom, I don't have a good feeling. I've been smoking so much that

I feel sick all the time. I must cut down and eat better. I feel like throwing up."

"Not pregnant are you?" her mother asked jokingly and Megan went cold.

"Of course not," she said heartily. "Just not taking good care of myself. I will, though, once the launch is over."

The launch night came arrived and Henry was nowhere to be seen.

"Is he coming?" the editor asked Megan an hour after the event had started.

Megan shrugged. "I can't tell you," she said. "You know Henry.

"I thought this meant something to him," the editor snapped. He was angry. "It's important that he's here. We need him."

"Well," Megan repeated, "you know Henry."

Henry chose that moment to arrive, and he wasn't in a good state. He was wet and filthy and wild-eyed, and his hair was matted.

"I found him," Bob said, the one who would be Zimmerman. "I know a few of his haunts and I tracked him down."

"Which might not have been the best idea," Megan commented and the editor agreed.

"Henry!" The editor called out to him. "Are you up for a reading?"

Henry rolled his eyes at the ceiling and swayed.

"Meg? Is he all right?" Megan's mother arrived at her side with her father in tow.

"I don't know, Mom," Megan said and she sat down.

The evening was going where it was going and all she could do was watch. She drank beer from someone else's glass, and shrugged when some snotty girl shouted at her.

"Come on, Henry," the editor urged and he led the writhing Henry up to the stage.

"Here he is," the editor announced. "Our genius poet, here at last! Come on, Henry! Honour us with a reading!"

Henry stood under the spotlight, swaying, and the whites of his eyes showing.

"He's always so dramatic," the snotty girl commented. "Such a drama queen. I can't understand what the fuss is about, his so-called brilliance, blah-di-blah."

Megan was sorry she'd finished the beer or she would have tossed it at her. She looked around but there wasn't anything else she could throw.

Meanwhile Henry hadn't progressed from eye rolling to spouting verse and Megan wondered what the editor would do next.

It didn't help that the crowd had picked up a chant: "Henry! Henry! Henry!"

Henry shrank back but then he opened his eyes and seemed to focus for a moment. The editor seized the opportunity to thrust a copy of the book into his hand. Henry turned the book over this way and that, examining it.

"Read! Read! Read!" The crowd chanted.

A small smile crossed Henry's face and he looked like a child finding that extra present under the tree, which Megan thought, was how he had been at Christmas, when they were all together, and Dad had hidden that last one especially for him.

Henry held the book wonderingly and then he tugged at the drawstring of his hospital trousers and he let the filthy garment fall to the floor. He flipped the book open at the centre and he took his penis in his hand and proceeded to piss on the pages, carefully drenching the book with yellow urine. A flood fell from the pages and onto the stage.

When he had finished, and the piss seemed to go on for a lifetime, he snapped the book shut, spraying those close to him. He laid it very carefully onto a small table. Then he pulled up his trousers and tied the drawstring with a neat bow. He slowly closed his eyes and leaned in towards the microphone.

The crowd, already silent, didn't move muscle. Not even a chair creaked.

"Empty." Henry said. "Empty." He opened his eyes and looked at Megan. Then he pushed through the crowd and made his way out into the night.

"Fucking genius my ass," the snotty girl said. "Although the rumours are true, he's hung like a donkey, I'll give him that."

Megan wanted to slap the girl but she got up and went up to the stage instead. She gingerly picked up the drenched book, and dropped it into a small plastic bag she had found in her purse.

"Come on," she said to her parents. "How about we go and get that supper?"

"Are you okay, dear?" her mother asked. "Goodness me, poetry readings have changed since my day."

"They're not usually like this," the editor remarked, over-hearing her. "But look, the book is selling like hot cakes. It's a good thing I printed double the usual run. Trust Henry to do something utterly original."

"And utterly disgusting," the pub owner said, his hands on his hips. "I've had a lot of acts up here but no one ever pissed on my stage before."

Megan left the editor to deal with the outraged owner and she and her parents threaded through the crowd and out the door.

They stood outside in the fresh spring evening, looking for Henry but he had disappeared.

"I'm worried about Henry," her father said. "That's the most out-of-it I've ever seen him."

"I've seen him like that once before, Dad," Megan admitted. "I just didn't want to worry about it. Let's not talk about it, okay? Please. I can't. I need to tell you both something."

"You're pregnant," her mother stated and Megan nodded.

"I am," she said.

Henry stayed away from home for a full week after the disaster of the launch. It was not an unmitigated disaster; his book was already on its way to a second print run.

Megan's parents had been supportive when they heard she was pregnant but they were also concerned.

They had gone to dinner as planned after the book launch but the mood was somber.

"But dear, how will you make a living?" Her mother asked. "A baby is full time and you can't rely on Henry. He'd be a danger to the child. How far along are you?"

"I think about six weeks," Megan said and she ordered a rare steak and wished she could have a cigarette. "I know, Mom, I know."

She could see her parents thinking, each engaged with their own scenarios and while they busied themselves with plans and concerns, she ate her steak and her baked potato and her bread roll. She finished her beer and ordered a second pint, her glance ordering her mother not to say a thing.

Her mother picked at a salad. "Have you told Henry?" she asked and Megan shook her head.

"I've been trying not to think about it. I missed a pill here and there, and a couple of periods, but there's been so much stress lately and I was hoping maybe I missed my period because of the stress. It happens. But then you mentioned it earlier this evening, and I think you're right, so we may as well face the facts."

"Well, you'd best have a doctor confirm," her mother said distantly. Megan bit her lip and nodded.

Her father was pale and she thought he looked old and tired. "You're so young," he said, shaking his head almost imperceptibly.

"How do you feel about it, dear?" her mother asked.

"I never thought about having a kid. And even now, I don't feel like it's real. Maybe it will sink in once it starts to grow. I don't know."

"I like Henry, you know I do, but this…" her father added.

"I know, Dad," Megan said. "Maybe I'll get lucky and miscarry or something. I don't know. Maybe it will never be real."

"It's real, Meggie," her mother said gently, "and the sooner you accept it, the better."

Megan pushed her plate away. "I'll have a double hot fudge sundae," she said to the waitress. "With extra whipped cream."

She eyed her mother, daring her to comment but her mother folded her arms and sat back.

"Times like this I wish I still smoked," Ethel said and Megan's father grinned in agreement.

"It's my worry anyway," Megan said, drumming her fingers on the table. "Mine and Henry's."

Her parents exchanged a glance. "We understand that, dear," her mother said, "but we're here if you need us."

Megan scowled and wished her dessert would hurry up.

"I want to show you something," her father said over the phone, two months later. "I'll come and get you, Meggie, and Henry, if he's there. Can you come out tomorrow?"

"Yeah, sure Dad," Megan said, rubbing what she was referring to as her baby bump. The truth was that she hadn't been able to stop eating since the poetry reading and the pounds had piled on faster than she had thought possible. She was like a furtive addict, cramming food into her mouth at every opportunity. She felt like the Titanic, already huge, and as hell-bent for catastrophe as that giant ship. "Sure. If Henry's here, I'll ask him to come with us."

Henry had not reacted well to the news of Megan's pregnancy and his solution was to stay away and take more drugs. His episodes of eye-rolling had increased even when he was home and Megan began to find him increasingly distasteful and ugly.

"Look at you," she said during one of his fits, although she couldn't be sure he could even hear her. "You look like a mad person, a crazy, homeless mad person."

Her solution was to eat and smoke and drink and she constantly felt sick, unsure if it was her toxic diet or her pregnancy or her new loathing for Henry.

"Crazy person," she'd say as she waved her spoon at him, her belly three times bigger than it should have been.

"Henry? Can you come with us? Please?" Her father asked him the next morning. Henry followed them down to the car like a suspicious stray dog. Ed opened the rear passenger door and Henry peered inside for a moment and then clambered in. Megan, sitting in the front seat, didn't say a word.

The drive to Scarborough took over an hour through the traffic and no one inside the car spoke the entire way, each staring out a different window, each in a different world.

When they got to her parent's home, Megan immediately sensed something was different. She baulked at going inside but her father put his hand on the small of her back.

"Come on Meg," he said. "It's going to be fine, you'll see. Come on, Henry, you too, come on in."

Downstairs first, her father said and he led them down into the basement, with Ethel following.

"What happened here?" Megan was startled. Her father's expansive former workshop was entirely gone and in its place was a furnished apartment, with a small washroom, a bedroom, and what was clearly intended to be a baby's area at the side.

"What is this?" Megan asked.

"Upstairs, Meggie. Now." Her mother's voice housed no room for discussion. "Kitchen table talk, now. You, too, Henry. Up you both go."

Kitchen table talk meant serious business, Megan knew that. She shut her mouth, followed her mother and sat down meekly.

When they were seated, her mother began. "You know Meggie, that's we've always loved and supported you and never questioned you. And we love Henry like a son. But it's not about the two of you any more. Do you understand that? You've gone beyond that and whether or not you meant it to happen, it did and now, someone needs to step up. And if you can't step up, we will. Because this is not about you. This is about a sacred life you are carrying. Megan, you need to come home and live with us. We'll help you through your pregnancy and the first thing you'll do is start eating better. I don't care about 'eating for two,' you've been eating for six! And you need to stop smoking, at least until the baby is born. And then, once the baby is born, you will carry on living here. A newborn is no joke, let me tell you. You'll be grateful for our help."

"A prison," Megan managed to say. "You've built me a prison."

You did that all by yourself, her mother wanted to reply but she didn't.

"No, Meggie, not a prison, a support system. Try to see it that way, okay? Now Henry, you can stay here too but you need to go to the hospital and stay there for a bit. I've spoken to some people about you and we can take you there now. You need help, Henry."

Henry, unlike Megan, looked relieved.

"Help," he repeated, rubbing his face, his hands and fingernails filthy. "I'll try. I'm so tired. I can't sleep, and I am so tired. Will they help me sleep?"

"Yes, they will. And then you can come back and stay here."

"I'll take you now," Ed said and he stood up. "And then I'll go and clean out your apartment," he said to Megan.

"I'll come with you, Dad," Megan insisted.

"We'll all go," her mother said and she stood up. "We need to get Megan registered at the hospital too."

"What about my job?" Megan asked. "And my apartment?" Although she didn't want to admit it, the thought of being told what to do, being guided through this horribly frightening time, even being told what to eat, was suddenly an enormous relief.

"You can phone your supervisor and say you need to resign from work because of the baby and that you are moving back home. Dad will go and take care of your apartment. If you like, you can go with him and help him pack things up. Come on, Henry. Let's go."

On the way to the hospital, sitting in the backseat of the

car, Megan turned to Henry. "Earth to Henry," she said, and he smiled.

"I'm sorry, Meg," he said. "I didn't mean to get this messed up. I thought I had everything balanced. I thought I had it under control."

"It's okay," she said. "I'll try to do better too."

"Are you still my girlfriend?" he asked her.

"Yes, Henry," she said, her hand on her belly. "I'm still your girlfriend. Will you be okay in hospital?"

He shrugged. "I don't know. Will you come and visit me?"

She nodded.

"We will too, Henry," Ed said loudly from the front seat. "You kids aren't alone in this."

Megan wanted to thank her parents but she couldn't find the words.

Henry seemed to know what she was thinking and he took her hand and they sat like that, all the way to the hospital, clinging to one another right up until the nurse led Henry away.

At the end of a long corridor, Henry turned and lifted a hand goodbye.

Megan waved back and then he vanished.

Megan's mother took her arm. "Come on, Meggie. Time to get you checked out."

What had looked like salvation soon became hell. Ethel took Megan for long walks, and monitored her diet, her smoking and her sleeping.

Henry was sent to detox and then began a long series of tests and experiments to see which diagnosis and medication suited him best.

"Everything hurts," he said to Megan when she visited. "My skin hurts. My tongue hurts. My eyeballs hurt. It hurts to breathe. They don't understand anything I tell them. They interview me in pairs — new people, the same people — asking new questions, the same questions. They have no idea about any of it. I swear they are crazier than me. I hate this place. I hate them. I can't sleep. I can't stand to be awake. The noises, oh. Meg, the noises these people make, they are not human. They're not human, but then I am in here too, so what am I?"

She wished she could touch him but contact was forbidden.

"My life's not much better," she said. "Mom gets me up first thing, and my whole day has a schedule. I have to eat my horrible breakfast, then go for a walk, then study things about the baby. Then I get an hour to myself, then lunch, then a walk. Then we go shopping for something for the baby, like that's my big reward, going to the mall, and if I've been really good, Mom lets me gets me a sorbet. Then we go back home and I can watch TV. Then Dad comes home and we have supper and then I watch TV till eleven and then it's lights out. And no smoking. It's ridiculous."

"I would trade with you in a heartbeat," Henry said and the shadows under his eyes looked like dark pits." Can you get me any drugs?" He had asked her for opiates, anything she could get her hands on, but she shook her head.

"I couldn't. Mom's like a pit bull, I swear she watches me when I go to the bathroom to pee. Henry?" she looked at him. "I've got something to tell you. The baby. It's a she. The baby is a she."

She wasn't prepared for Henry's reaction. His eyes lit up with the purest joy she had ever seen and she sat back in her chair, jealous of his happiness.

"A little girl!" He was delighted. "The whole thing just seemed so horrible. I will be honest, Meg, it felt to me like some kind of alien flesh had invaded you and taken you from me but now, it is not an alien. She is a little baby girl! What shall we call her? I must get healthy. I want to be a good father. I really do."

"And me, Henry? You never wanted to get healthy for me. What am I? Your precious daughter's human carrycot?" Megan had raised her voice and her tone was bitter.

Henry looked dismayed and bewildered by her outburst. "Meg, what is going on? Don't you love her?"

"Clearly I don't have the same passion for her as you do." Megan's eyes were cold and she got up.

"Wait, Meggie, please don't go. Please, let's talk about this. You know I love you."

"But you love her more." Megan was irrational and vicious and she walked away without looking back.

In the car, with her mother, she sobbed, inconsolably. "I hate this child," she said, tears streaming down her face. "I never thought he'd love it more than he loves me." She hit her belly with her fist and her mother swung the car off onto the side of the road and she grabbed Megan's hand.

"I understand your pain but don't you EVER, do anything like that again, do you understand me?"

Megan, cowed by her mother's anger and shamed, dropped her head and nodded. "I know it's not the baby's fault," she said. "But he's my true love, Mom, and you should have seen the way he looked when I told him. It's like the lights went on inside his heart and it should have been me who did that for him."

Life isn't fair, her mother wanted to say, but she didn't.

"I should go back," Megan said. "There's still half an hour of visiting time and I ran out. Can we go back, Mom?"

"Of course we can," Megan's mother said and she swung the car around.

"I'm sorry," Megan said to Henry when she got there. "I was jealous. Not admirable but there it is."

"Meggie, I love you, *you*. But this is something else. I can't describe how I feel. Tell me what does it feel, to have her inside you?

"Like a butterfly," Megan said. "Mainly I just feel fat even though I've lost some weight. Sometimes she moves and it's cool but she doesn't feel like a person to me."

"Let us think of a name," Henry said. "She needs a good

name. She needs to be named after a brave, bold, clever, adventurer who was not afraid of anything, someone who was fearless. I know! How about Amelia? After Amelia Earhart?"

"But she died young," Megan objected. "I don't want a flashy and tragic end to our daughter's life, thank you very much."

"Let's ask her what she thinks," Henry suggested. "I'll say some names and you tell me if you feel her move."

Henry listed a bunch of names and to Megan's annoyance, the baby was utterly still until he said "Amelia."

Megan shrugged. "Fine," she said. "Amelia it is."

"We should get married," Henry mused and Megan's heart leapt in happiness.

"You need to propose first," she said, grinning. "Ask me properly."

"Megan, my love, my only true love and mother of my daughter, the amazing Amelia, will you please, please, please marry me? Yes, me, Henry, crazy locked up poet who will one day, hopefully soon, be healed and well?

"Yes, Henry," she said," I'll marry you. I'll tell Mom and we'll start planning immediately! We can have it in the chapel here!"

"Time's up, Henry," the orderly arrived. "Hi Megan. How's the baby?"

"She's good. We've named her Amelia and we're getting married!"

"Good for you," the orderly said. "Come on, Henry, time for meds."

Megan rushed over to her mother who was waiting at the car.

"Mom, Henry proposed! We need to plan the wedding!"

Her mother sighed inwardly. "Sure, Meggie, sure," she said. She looked at the sky thinking now was as good a time as any to start smoking again, or take up drinking heavily.

"I don't know why you can't be happy for me," Megan scowled as she opened the car door. "No, wait," she said, slamming it shut. "We need to go back and book the chapel. Come on, Mom."

Her mother trailed behind her bouncing daughter, who turned to her. "We'll have to buy the rings too. Oh, Mom, isn't this exciting?"

Megan's father cried at the wedding. Megan wore a smile from ear to ear while Henry looked vacuous, close to drooling. He answered robotically and was unsteady on his feet.

The chaplain hurried the ceremony along and afterwards Henry's psychiatrist took a few photographs. "Now let's see," the psychiatrist mumbled, tripping over his own feet. "Um, wait, no, that's not it, hang on, okay smile, excellent. Come on Henry, give us a smile."

"He doesn't seem very organized," Megan whispered to her mother. "I don't like him being in charge of Henry's meds. No wonder he's so out of it. What happened to the other guy? I liked him better."

"I agree," her mother said. "We'll see what we can do. Just smile for now and don't let it ruin your special day."

"I can't work this thing. I'm going to find an orderly," the psychiatrist said. "Everybody wait here."

He returned with a nurse who handled the camera with ease.

"Henry," she called, "give us a smile, honey, come on!"

At the sound of her voice, Henry gave a lopsided smile and that was Megan's wedding picture: Henry smiling lopsidedly at the nurse, oblivious to what was going on around him.

But Megan didn't care. She fed pieces of wedding cake to Henry who seemed to have forgotten how to chew. Bits of cake fell out his mouth and onto his shirt. Ed had rented a suit for Henry that hung from him and he looked like he was drowning in the clothing.

Megan clung to Henry during the ceremony. Her belly jutted like a proud prow and raised the front of her cream satin Empire-waist wedding dress by nearly half a foot, and her feet were tiny in their sparkly shoes.

"Not what I had in mind, if you'd asked me some years back,"

Ed admitted quietly to Ethel and they smiled at each other.

"Me neither," Ethel said. "Oh, Ed, what a mess."

"Yeah, but we'll roll with it, Eth. It's what we do. So far, so good. Henry on the mend, Megan's happy and fitter. We've made progress."

"Don't know if I'd call Henry's state progress," Ethel said watching Henry drool more cake and Megan lovingly wipe it off. "This new guy's suspect, if you ask me. I'm going to come in and have a word with him as soon as I can get an appointment. He's not as accessible as Dr. Marks."

A couple of weeks later, it turned out there wasn't anything Ethel could do. Dr. Shiner was Henry's new state-appointed therapist and that was all there was to it.

"I understand you're worried," he stuttered, refusing to look her in the eye. "I'm trying a series of new medications. We need to find the right balance, which isn't easy. I admit we may have made the dosage a bit high, but we've cut back today and he's better."

"Can I see him?"

"It's not a good time. Come back tomorrow, you'll see an improvement." And with that, the therapist got up and held the door open and Ethel understood she had been dismissed.

She passed the nurses' station on the way out. "How's Henry, really?" she asked one of the nurses in an undertone.

"Dr. MultiMeds has gone crazy," the nurse muttered, "but you never heard me say that, right? Don't worry, though. He'll lower the dose. First he gives them enough to kill a horse and then he lowers it. Henry will be okay. How is Megan?"

"Fine," Ethel said, distracted. "She's fine, I guess." She laughed. "Actually, everything nuts, but like my husbands says, we're rolling with it. Rolling, rolling, rolling."

She went home to Megan who was putting her wedding pictures into frames and hanging them on the wall.

"Henry's hair's too long," she said, adjusting a picture.

"Mom, look, his hair's too long. You'd think they would have noticed, for such an important day as this."

"I'm going to lie down for a while, dear," her mother said. "I'm a bit tired out from everything. "

"Yeah, Mom. Listen, I've been really good with all the rules, haven't I? So can I have a grilled cheese sandwich with mayo and watch TV?"

"Yes, dear," her mother said, going up the stairs. She felt too weary to do battle with Megan over a sandwich, and she thought that one day's deviation wouldn't make any difference. "Today you can do anything you like. You can eat anything you like and watch as much TV as you like. We'll get back on track tomorrow."

"Awesome!" Megan rushed at the refrigerator and yanked open the door. "You're the best, Mom!"

4. MEGAN AND HENRY AND AMELIA

MONTHS PASSED AND HENRY SETTLED into a solid state of nothingness. Ed had wanted to let Henry's parents know what had happened, even though Megan protested, certain that they would not care. And she was right.

She guided Ed by memory to the large mansion in Rosedale and Ed gave a loud whistle when he saw the size of the house.

"No one's home," a neighbour said, after he saw them pressing the door bell at the front gate. "They're on a cruise. They asked me to keep an eye on things. Can I help you?"

"Do you know their son, Henry?" Ed asked and the neighbour gave a broad smile.

"Of course! What an original boy! Drove his parents mad but I thought he was a bit of genius. Is he all right?"

"Not so much," Ed admitted. "This is Megan, his wife. I'm Henry's father-in-law."

Ed took out a piece of paper and wrote down his phone number. "If you can get this to his parents and let them know I can chat anytime, that would be great," he said, handing it to the man who looked doubtful.

"They never seemed to care what Henry did," the neighbour said, "as long as he wasn't running around naked, which also happened a fair bit. I'll pass on the message but I wouldn't hold my breath that they'll be in touch. They're good neighbours but damned cold if you ask me."

"I told you, Dad," Megan said as they walked back to the car.

"Makes me very sad," Ed said. "Our poor Henry."

Megan snorted and Ed ignored her.

"If you keep him on his meds, you can take him home," Dr. Shiner said helpfully one day, and Ethel and Ed looked at one another.

"Sounds good," Ethel said, questioningly.

"Can do," Ed said, "but Doc, are you sure he's okay? Not going to burn the house down or anything?"

"No, no. Besides, he's never been violent. It's not in his repertoire of behaviours. And, given the cocktail of meds I've got him on, he's hardly going to develop any new psychoses." He studied the file in front of him. "No, no, you're safe as houses. Your house is safe as houses!"

"Well," Ed got to his feet, "let's go and get the fellow then."

"Bye Henry," the nurses called after him. "Have fun out there, be safe!"

Henry gave them a half smile as he shambled down the hallway to meet Ethel and Ed.

"Meggie was going to come," Ethel apologized to Henry, "but the baby's getting so big and she can hardly move."

Henry didn't appear to have heard her and Ethel was glad because it was a lie.

"He's like a frickin' retard," Megan had said on the way home from her last visit to Henry. "I'm not visiting him again if he's like that. He doesn't even know I'm there, for god's sake. There's no point. It's a waste of my time."

"He's your husband," her mother reminded her. "For better or for worse."

"Yeah, well, I kind of thought marriage would be different than this," Megan said. "Nothing's changed, if you ask me, except that Henry's disappeared into some no-man's land of weirdness."

Ethel and Ed loaded an uncomplaining Henry into the back of the car.

"What is Shiner giving him?" Ed asked. "I'm going to do some research."

"Oh Ed, don't mess with things you don't know about," Ethel said and Ed bit his tongue.

They got Henry home and led him inside. "This is your room," Ed said to Henry, guiding him up the stairs, past Megan who was watching TV in the living room and didn't even look up. Megan had refused to share the downstairs room with Henry.

"Put him in my old room," she had said. "There's only your sewing junk in there, Mom. There's no way I am having him near me."

"Henry? Can you talk to me?" Ed asked. "You'll be happy here. It's a nice room, don't you think?"

Henry sat down on the bed as if he wasn't sure if it was solid.

"Look, Henry," Ed pointed to the small desk in the corner. "I got you some model airplanes."

Ed couldn't be sure but he thought he saw a flicker of interest flare in Henry's eyes. "They're all yours, Henry," Ed said. "Are you hungry? Do you want a sandwich?"

There was no response.

"I'm going now," Ed said and he checked the windows, making sure they were locked shut. Ed stopped at the door and looked back at Henry who hadn't moved a muscle. "See you later, son," Ed said heavily and he went downstairs to find Megan arguing furiously with her mother.

"He's your husband!" Ethel said. "The father of your child."

"Words, Mom, just words. When the real Henry makes an appearance, I'll be behave like a wife. But this retard, he's nobody to me. He's like a zombie."

Ed decided not to engage in the quarrel and he went back upstairs to check on Henry who hadn't moved.

Ed went to his and Ethel's bedroom and emptied Henry's medications out onto the bed. He studied them for a while, and then he gathered them up in a plastic bag and left the house, with Megan and Ethel still shouting at each other.

Ed drove to the local pharmacy. "I need you to tell me exactly what this stuff is and what it does," Ed told the pharmacist. "Take your time. I want to know every single thing there is to know." He returned to the house two hours later, carrying a second bag filled with information that the pharmacist had given him, along with the notes that he had made.

"Frickin' flaming sugar," Ed said to Henry who was still sitting on the bed where he had left him. "I'd be in a coma too, if I took these meds. Listen, between you and me, we're going to start adjusting the dose. That all right with you, boyo? Now I'm going to get you a sandwich. You've got to eat."

Megan had vanished to cry in the basement and Ed found Ethel sitting at the kitchen table with her head in her hands. He sat down and put his arm around her.

"Eth," he said gently, "these are hard times but we'll get by. Why don't you go and have a nice bath and a big glass of wine? Take the treats when you can get them."

"You're a good man, Ed," she said. "You always have been."

"Glad you chose me over the poet?"

"You better believe it," she said fervently and he laughed.

As if by tacit agreement, Ed looked after Henry while Ethel managed Megan, who was growing grumpier by the day.

"Stupid baby's supposed to be born already," she commented a thousand times a day. "Why won't she come?"

"First ones are always late," her mother replied, also for the thousandth time. "Patience, Meggie, patience."

"I want her out of me!" Megan screamed and Ethel wanted to hit her.

"I understand, dear," she said, instead. "Why don't you watch some TV or have a nap?"

"I can't sleep! And I can't see over my stupid stomach. I am so tired of this, sick and tired!"

Meanwhile Henry, under Ed's careful ministrations, slowly improved. "You're messing with his meds, aren't you?" Ethel accused Ed and he blushed.

"Ah Eth, come on, you can't say he was okay like that?"

She nodded. "Be careful, Ed."

"I will, you know I will. But he's looking more human, wouldn't you say?"

"He does look better," Ethel agreed. "More awake."

"And I'm sure he said my name yesterday," Ed was excited. "Well, he said Dad, he called me Dad, I'm sure of it. But I'm going to have to get him to lie to Shiner," Ed mused. "He's got to look as drugged as he was, or Shiner will know I've been up to something."

"Now we're conniving psychiatrists," Ethel said and she gave a humourless chuckle. "Ed, how did it come to this?" she asked and Ed shook his head.

"Who knows, Eth? I wish Amelia would make an appearance, let Meg get on with her life."

"Her life won't be her own for the next dozen or so years," Ethel said. "She's got no idea what's coming."

"Who's got no idea?" Megan appeared, looking out of sorts as usual. "Mom, please can I have some ice cream? I need something nice in my life." She slumped down into her chair, her hands on her huge belly.

"Of course you can, dear," Ethel said, getting up. "Ed, you want some too?"

"Sure, hit me," Ed said, winking at Meg. "Let's go wild."

Henry appeared in the doorway. "Ice cream?" He said the words clearly, enunciating carefully. "I would like some too, please."

"Henry!" Ed jumped up. "Come on in. Sit down."

"Megan," Henry said. "Wow, you got so big. When did you get so big? Was I out of it?"

"You could say that," Megan said, bitterly and Henry looked confused.

"Don't be nasty, Meggie," Ed said. "Henry, you had to take a lot of meds and I've been lessening the dose but tomorrow, when we go back to the hospital, you have to act drugged. Can you do that? We're going to see Shiner and you can't let on that you're more in the know of things. Are you with me, son?"

"Act like a zombie," Meg said. "That's what you've been like, a zombie."

"A zombie. Okay, how's this?" Henry cocked his head to once side, let his jaw drop and gazed vacuously.

"Perfect," Megan said. "And don't talk. You don't talk. You never say anything."

"Got it," Henry said. "Thank you, Mom," he said to Ethel, tapping the bowl of ice cream with his spoon. "This is the most delicious thing I have ever eaten in my life."

"You do know we're married?" Megan asked. "Although I'm too fat to wear my ring and you're too crazy to be a husband."

"Married? Makes sense. Why are you so angry?"

"You'd be angry too if you were as big as a house," Megan grouched, and she pushed her bowl away from her. "Stupid baby, she should have been born already."

"Amelia!" Henry's face lit up. He leaned in towards Megan's stomach. "Amelia, come on baby, time to come on out, time to meet the world. Daddy is here, come on baby!"

"Yeah, like that's going to work," Megan said morosely but then she sat up and gasped.

"What honey? What's going on?"

"My water broke! Amelia heard him. She listened to Henry! She's coming!"

"I'll get your hospital bag," Ethel said. "Ed you get the car keys. Henry, are you coming?"

"Are you kidding? For sure!"

"But remember," Ed cautioned, "act like a zombie. You can't come unless you are a convincing zombie."

"Arggh!" Megan let out a cry. "I think I had a contraction. No one told me it would hurt this much."

"It's going to get a lot worse," her mother muttered, hustling her out the door.

"Hold my hand, Meg," Henry said. "Whoa, not that hard, you are hurting me."

"If I have to be in pain, you have to be in pain," Meg said through gritted teeth while Henry rubbed his hand.

"Meg, I hope it is because you are in labour, but you've become really mean. It is not like I wanted to be in hospital, dead to everything. I feel like you hate me now."

"I don't hate you," Megan said, breathing heavily. "Things just didn't turn out like I thought they would."

"And that's my fault?"

"Can you two maybe finish this some other time?" Ethel interrupted. She turned toward her daughter and grasped her by the shoulders. "Meg, breathe. Do the breathing like we've been practicing. Henry, hold her hand again."

"Not if she is going to hurt me," Henry said.

"Stop being such a pussy," Megan said.

"Megan!" Henry was shocked.

"She's a woman in labour," Ed said. "You need to ignore everything she says for the next twelve hours."

"Twelve hours!" Megan screamed. "I can't do twelve hours of this! I want pain meds! Where are my pain meds?"

"We're not at the hospital yet," Ed pointed out.

"I don't care!" Megan screamed.

Ed dropped Ethel, Megan, and Henry off at the main entrance. "I'll join you as soon as I find parking. Henry! Henry!"

Henry stopped and looked at Ed enquiringly.

"Zombie! There's a lot at stake. Please, son."

Henry nodded and his eyes went blank and he shuffled after Megan and Ethel, his head drooping sideways.

"Great," Megan said to her mother. "Fucking great. Arghhhh!" She screamed.

"Why don't you wait outside for Ed?" Ethel said to Henry but Megan grabbed his hand.

"No way, he's my husband, zombie or not, he's in this for the long run."

Under his zombie pose, Henry paled.

They reached the maternity ward and checked Megan in.

Megan gave a gut-wrenching howl. "I thought there were supposed to be gaps in between the pain," she said. "All I have is pain."

"Yeah, ain't life grand," the nurse said. "Well, come on y'all, let's get this party started."

The party, such as it was, dragged on for hours.

"Does it always take this long?" Henry whispered to Ethel who nodded. "I am exhausted," he said.

"How the fuck do you think I feel?" Megan said, but the fire had gone out of her voice and she sounded ragged.

"Meggie," Henry said, "you are doing so well. Come on, honey." He wiped her hair off her forehead.

"Talk to the baby again," Megan implored him. "Tell her to come out."

"Not yet, sweetie," the nurse said. "You're not dilated enough. You gotta wait this out more. Breathe into it."

"I hate fucking breathing!" Megan said. "Oh, this is hell. Why do people do this? Nothing in the world is worth this, nothing."

And later, when Amelia finally popped out, squawking and tiny, red-faced and crumpled, Megan still didn't think it had been worth it, while Henry fell in love without pause or hesitation. "Amelia," he said with reverence. "Oh."

He was the first to hold her and he couldn't bear to let her go. When the nurse insisted on taking her from him and giving her to Megan, Amelia cried, filling her little lungs with air and wailing like a banshee.

"Great," Megan said. "I can see how this is going to go. And why didn't I lose all the weight?" She asked her mother accusingly. "Look at me, I'm still like a whale."

"She just wants to feed," the nurse told Megan. "Here you

go, like this." The nurse helped the tiny screaming baby find the nipple and a blissful silence filled the room as Amelia sucked like pro.

Megan looked bored. "How long does she do this?" she asked the nurse.

"It depends, and she needs it every four hours too. We'll wake you up, don't worry."

"Great," Megan said.

"Oh, Meggie, she's so beautiful," Ethel said. She was as enraptured as Henry.

"Yup, she's an angel all right," Ed whispered, hardly able to talk as he held Amelia's tiny foot.

"You're all putting me in a bad mood," Megan said. "Give me some credit. I made her remember?"

"With some help from me," Henry smiled proudly.

"Henry!" Ed spun around and waved his hands urgently as Dr. Shiner tiptoed into the room and Henry adopted his zombie stance in the nick of time.

"I heard Megan was giving birth and I wanted to see how Henry was doing," he said, adjusting his glasses with fat little sausage fingers and looking around the room for Henry.

"He's fine," Ed said nervously. "We don't know if he knows what's going on, but he seems calm."

"Good, good," Dr. Shiner went up to Henry and stared into his eyes and Henry gazed vacuously over his shoulder. "Looking good, looking good," Shiner said. "I'll see you tomorrow for your check-up, Henry," he said loudly and Henry allowed a long strand of drool to hang like a jellied string from his mouth.

"Eughh, gross, enough," Megan said as soon as Shiner left the room. "Stop that, and wipe your mouth." She yawned. "I'm so tired."

"So are we, honey, we're going to go home," Ethel said. "We'll come back tomorrow."

"But will Amelia be okay?" Henry was worried. "Meg, are you paying attention to things? She is so little. Are you holding her neck the way you should? Mom, look, is Meg holding her right?"

"Oh god, of course I am, Henry. I'm her mother. You guys go home and sleep."

"I am staying here," Henry said and he sat down firmly in the chair. Ed grinned at him.

"You're the man, but remember, if you see Shiner, you do the thing. You want a sandwich or something?"

"I'd kill for a real coffee," Megan said. "An extra-large double double, with a Boston Cream doughnut and a blueberry muffin. Can you guys get that?"

"Sure," Ethel said, but she looked dead on her feet.

"You wait here," Ed said. "I'll get a bunch of stuff. Sit down for a moment, Eth."

"She is quite cute, isn't she?" Megan said, watching Amelia whose tiny fists were resting against her mother's breast. "Her face isn't so red anymore and I can see her features more clearly. Henry, I think she's got your forehead and cheekbones."

"And your nose," Henry said.

"No way. She's got your nose. It's perfect. Lots of hair though, and it's dark, like mine."

"Big eyes, Meggie, she definitely has your eyes."

"Yeah, that's true, she's got my eyes. And my ears, I've got pretty ears."

"If you say so yourself," Ethel said, amused.

"Yeah, even if I say so myself," Megan grinned. "Little sea-shell ears."

Ed returned with a tray of coffees and an array of baked goods.

"She's falling asleep," Megan said, and as if she had heard her, the nurse returned.

"I'll take her for a bit," she said. "You all get some rest now. Come on baby, time for you to sleep till your next feed."

"Look at us," Ed said, biting into a doughnut. "We're like a regular family. What say we keep it like this for a bit, eh? Those in favour say, aye."

"Aye," the other three chorused.

"A pretty good night," Megan said, sleepily. "Sorry I was such a bitch to everyone."

"It's fine," her mother said, kissing her. "You did very well, Meggie." But her daughter was already sound asleep.

Henry took to fatherhood as if he was born to it. Megan was not equally enamoured and soon it was Henry who was getting up at all hours to mix formula and change diapers. His energy was unflagging, his patience unfailing, and his delight in Amelia's every utterance was a joy to watch.

Megan did her part by expressing milk and moaning to her mother.

"You need to get a job," Ethel said, matter-of-factly.

"Yeah, like there are any jobs in the back-end-of-nowhere."

"Stop whining, Meggie. It's not attractive. Henry looks after Amelia, so there's nothing stopping you from looking for work. Knock on doors; make the effort. Come on. Let's go and find you something smart to wear and then you need to get out there and see what you can rustle up. You need to get back into your life."

"I'm busy being a mother!" Megan called after her, reaching for a bag of chips and her mother came back and snatched the bag out of her hands.

"Stop eating for god's sake. Come on, Meggie! Make an effort."

Megan sighed. "I am bored," she admitted. "Fine. Maybe I'll go and apply at McDonald's."

"If you work at McDonald's, you'll just eat everything. Why don't you try a gym instead? Or realtors' offices? Leave the fast food places as a last option."

"Fine," Megan grumbled. "Okay, come and help me find something to wear. Nothing fits any more." They found an outfit that stretched tight across Megan's chest and buttocks.

"Try not to sit for too long," Ethel advised.

"Great advice, Mom, thanks. Car keys?"

"Here," Ethel said. "Good luck."

Megan left despondent but she returned triumphant.

"You were right," she said to Ethel. "I tried a few realtors and they had nothing. But then I went into a gym and they liked me! I have to lose weight, they're going to use me as a before and after, and I'm going to be the receptionist. They're going to work out a fitness and nutrition plan for me and I have to read this book."

She held up a copy of *Calories In Versus Energy Out* and waved it at Henry who had come up from the basement. "Henry, I've got a job."

"I heard," he said, smiling and holding Amelia who was happily sucking on a pacifier.

"I swear she's got bigger since I left this morning," Megan said.

"Do you want to hold her?"

"No time, I've got to read my book." She grinned and left the room to go upstairs.

She and Henry had switched living arrangements shortly after Amelia was born. "It makes more sense," Megan had said, "for me to be upstairs. You're much better with her than I am and I need my sleep so I can express milk."

"Excellent!" Henry had been delighted and he had hugged Amelia close. "Dada wouldn't want to be anywhere else, would he, baby girl?"

Megan scowled at him and Ethel wondered if there was any way to rekindle their love. But what with Megan's fierce jealousy of Amelia, she didn't think so.

She had followed Megan upstairs that day. "Meggie, aren't you interested in trying to get things back to what they were, with you and Henry?"

Megan sat down heavily on the bed. "I don't care about sex right now," she said. "I'm a big fat whale. And all he's interested in is her. Once I get back on my feet, I'll have more confidence but what do I have to offer him now?"

"Love, Meggie. He loved that you loved him."

"I feel like we've been through too much, him going mad like that, me having the baby alone."

"Alone?" Ethel wanted to scream. "You really think you were alone? Meg," she said carefully. "You hardly had the baby alone. Me and Dad were with you every step of the way, and you lived here. You were hardly alone."

"I didn't have what most normal women have," Megan insisted. "A real husband, my own house, a proper family. And yeah, you and Dad were great, but it was like being fourteen again and me having done something wrong and both of you having to fix it. It wasn't the way it should have been."

Ethel couldn't argue with that. But she tried again.

"Try to bond with Amelia more," she added. "She's your daughter as much as his. She loves you too."

"She doesn't." Megan was firm. "She cries whenever I hold her. She's only happy when she's with him or you or Dad."

"It's up to you to try more," Ethel said but Megan shook her head. Ethel watched her daughter slump onto her bed clutching her book, with a look of determination on her face and she sighed. When she came back down the stairs, Henry was waiting for her.

"It will work out, Mom," he said. "I'm not worried. She just needs time. She and Amelia and me, we will be a real family. Meg just needs some space."

Ethel suddenly looked exhausted. "I hope you're right," she said. "I think I'll have a little lie down."

"You feeling all right, Mom?"

"A little tired, Henry, a little tired."

He watched her go slowly up back up the stairs again and he thought it was the first time that she had seemed old to him.

"Let us go for a walk, you and me," he said to Amelia and she smiled and gurgled as he strapped her into the stroller.

"Why is it so easy to take calories in and so hard to get the energy out?" Megan sighed, two weeks later. "I never realized how much I ate before and now I feel like I'm hungry all the time."

Emilio, the owner of the gym, and Megan's personal trainer and mentor laughed. "Most people don't ever realize what you just have. Don't worry. It gets easier. The stomach shrinks and other endorphins will start to make you feel happy and satiated, endorphins that will replace those that satisfy you by way of food."

Emilio had an accent that Megan couldn't quite place, soft curly hair, and large soulful eyes.

"You look more like a singer in a band than a personal trainer," she told him, trying to distract him from the pushups he was persuading her to do.

"I get that a lot," Emilio said. "Come on Megan, four more, come on, you can do it."

"I hate pushups," Megan grunted, doing a facsimile pushup of sorts.

"Now, the treadmill. Don't look so angry! Here, listen to my Walkman. When you are exercising, don't focus on the exercise. Take your mind off it by thinking about something you like or listening to music."

Megan allowed the thought to sneak in that what she really liked was when Emilio touched her, adjusting her in a position or helping her. She cast a sideways look at him but he had moved off to chat to another woman, a regular at the gym, a hard-body dressed in tiny gym gear. Megan stared at the woman's lean tight body and she was filled with a fierce determination to succeed as never before. She flicked on Emilio's music and started running.

Megan's determination paid off. She lost fifteen pounds in three months.

"Wow, Meg, you look great," Henry said.

"I'm so proud of you," Ethel and Ed said in unison.

"You have made a good start," Emilio commented and Megan threw an angry glance in his direction but he just laughed.

"Get as angry as you like," he shrugged, his accent melodic. "You will thank me one day. You can't see what I see," he said, and he moved closer to her. "You see here," he ran his hand down her leg, "I see the sinuous beauty hidden beneath the fat. You have lovely long legs, Megan, and we want to show them off to the world. And here," he put his hands on her waist, "you have a lovely little waist, we want the world to know that too. And these arms, we want definition here, shape and beauty. It's all here, Megan, we just need to keep working at it."

She nodded dreamily, loving the feel of his hands on her, and disappointed when he stopped. She was sure there was something going on between them. Sure, he was attentive to all the ladies at the gym, sure, he flirted with everyone, and he even batted his eyelashes at the boys, but she was sure there was something real between the two of them.

"Here is your midway picture," he said, putting a photo of Megan up next to her 'before'. "You think this should be your 'after' but once we have made more progress, you will be very happy that I didn't let you stop here."

"Okay, Emilio," she said. "But I'll tell you this for free. I'm starving."

"We will fix that." He leaned over the counter and looked at her. "We'll let Charles handle the front desk for half an hour and you and I will go and get a juice from that new takeout place. My treat."

She smiled at him. A date, she thought, and she shot to her feet. "Just don't get me one of those disgusting green ones," she said.

"Okay, but don't think you are getting anything with banana," he said, closing the gym door behind them. "You know the drill."

"Calories, calories," Megan grinned. "I know." She was

proud to be walking next to him. He was tall and muscular, dark-skinned and handsome. She hoped that people would think they were a couple and she leaned into him slightly and tried to match his stride.

"Megan!" She heard a voice call her name and she swung around, confused.

"That guy over there," Emilio said. "The one with the baby. Do you know him?"

"Hi Megan! We thought we'd come and see where you work!"

"He's my husband," Megan said, her heart falling with a thud to her feet. "And that's my daughter."

She stood where she was and let Henry and Amelia approach her. Amelia was waving her little hands in delight and cooing.

"I'm Emilio," Emilio said when it was clear that Megan wasn't going to introduce them. He held out his hand and Henry shook it. "I own the gym where Megan works."

"I'm Henry, her husband, and this is Amelia." Henry unstrapped Amelia and lifted her out of the stroller. "Say hi to Mama." But Amelia wrapped her arms around Henry's neck and buried her face in his neck.

"Daddy's girl," Megan said bitterly.

"We're going to get a juice," Emilio said. "You want to come along?"

"Yeah, sure," Henry said. "I'll give Amelia her bottle. "

"What do you do for a living?" Emilio asked once they had their juices and were sitting at a table.

"Nothing much," Henry apologized. "I was a poet and then I was sick for a while, and now I'm a house-husband and a father."

"Both are good things," Emilio said. "Being a father is a very good thing. I hope to have lots of children one day. You are very good with her," he observed.

"She's my angel," Henry said, and it was all Megan could do to stop from rolling her eyes.

"And how long have you been together?" Emilio asked.

Henry and Megan looked at one another. "Wow," Henry said. "I can't remember. I guess it is about two years now?"

Megan shrugged and shook her head and Emilio laughed. "You guys are funny," he said. "Most couples know to the hour how long they've been together. They remember what the moon was doing the night they met and what song was playing."

"We're not exactly like most couples," Megan said pointedly.

"That's what makes us special," Henry said, missing her sarcasm or choosing to ignore it. He picked up Amelia and burped her. "Megan is looking great," he said to Emilio. "And she's happier too."

"I'm right here, thank you very much," Megan said. "You can address me."

"I was trying to give you a compliment," Henry said mildly and he stood up. "Say bye-bye to Mama," he said to Amelia and he waved her little hand. "We will go home and see what Nana is up to. Nice to meet you, Emilio."

"You too," Emilio said, and he and Megan watched Henry amble off, chatting to Amelia, and pushing the stroller.

After they left, there was an awkward silence between Emilio and Megan.

"We'd better get back," he said and she shot to her feet.

"Yeah, I want to try the jazzercize class," she said and then she blushed. "Not that I can dance, mind you, but it sounds like fun."

"Everybody can dance," Emilio said distantly and she was certain that things had changed between them and whatever chance there might have been for romance had vanished.

But Megan, walking next to him, decided that the war wasn't lost. She would do what she had to do and in the end she'd get what she wanted. And she had decided that she wanted Emilio.

Amelia's first birthday party was a perfect. It was bleak January day and they held the party in a small community hall.

Even Megan had a good time and she basked in the glowing admiration of the other mothers that Henry had befriended in the parks and playgroups. For a disorganized, unscheduled fellow, Henry was a picture postcard father. He diligently took the meds that Ed handed him, and he stuck to the schedule Ethel made for him, and he consulted his wristwatch as if it was an oracle of wisdom that he didn't understand but feared and respected nonetheless.

"Family photo," Ed said, adjusting the self-timer on the camera. "Everybody say 'cheese.'"

The group shouted at the camera and grinned and the perfect moment was snapped and captured in space and time, and Ed allowed himself to relax just that little bit.

It wasn't four months later that the same group assembled, but this time it was minus one. They'd lost Ed. He'd been hit by a drunk driver and killed instantly.

Ethel was numb with pain, utterly still and quiet. Megan was confused and bewildered. Her father wasn't supposed to die. She kept expecting him to come home.

And Henry was panic-stricken. "Mom," he said. "I am sorry Mom, but I can't remember what medications Dad gave me. I just took them. I never paid attention to what they were."

"It's okay, Henry," Ethel said. "Ed would have written it down. We simply have to find out where."

While Ethel searched for the book, Henry fidgeted nervously. "I am worried," he said. "I'm afraid I won't be okay without Dad. I'm scared."

"So am I," Ethel wanted to say. She wanted to tell Henry to get a grip, that she was scared too. She wanted to tell him to be a man, for god's sake. But the rational Ethel knew that was neither possible nor fair.

"It'll be okay, Henry," she said gently, looking up from Ed's bedside table. "Look here, see? It's all written down. That's Ed for you." Two tears rolled down her cheeks and she didn't seem to notice. "I'll buy you those pill boxes that are broken down by the day and we'll add it to the schedule and you'll be fine."

She took Henry's hand. "Don't worry, Henry," she said. "Have you taken your meds this morning?"

He shook his head. "Not since Dad died."

"Three days," Ethel said, concerned. "I'm sorry Henry, I should have thought of this. How are you doing?"

"Not great," he said. "Not great. But I didn't want to say."

Ethel looked at him and she realized that he was shaking, that his whole body was shuddering.

She rushed to the washroom and shook out his pills and filled a glass with water. "Take these and lie down for a bit, I'll look after Amelia."

He swallowed the pills and closed his eyes in relief. "Yes, I think I will lie down for a bit," he said. "I'll wait for the noise to stop. I have been very dizzy too."

"I'm so sorry, Henry." Ethel stroked his forehead and he relaxed under her touch.

She tucked him into his bed. His breathing was shallow and he was pale and clammy to the touch. Poor fragile boy, she thought and she smoothed his blanket and left, quietly closing the door.

"Where's Henry?" Megan demanded when her mother got downstairs. "Amelia needs her bottle."

"Then I suggest you give it to her," Ethel said, her voice brokering no argument.

"But where's Henry?"

"Henry isn't well. I forgot about his meds and so did you." Ethel turned to face her daughter.

"Not my responsibility," Megan shrugged and her mother grabbed her by the shoulders and shook her.

Megan's eyes widened. "Get off me, Mom, what are you doing?"

"Trying to shake some sense into you," Ethel said. "Sit down, Megan. I've got something to say to you."

"But Amelia will wake up soon and she'll cry and you know how I hate that."

"Sit down."

Megan sat down at the kitchen table.

"I know you were young when it happened, but *you* got pregnant. *You* met Henry and decided he was the one and you wanted to marry him. Do you hear me, Megan? *YOU*. Not me, or Dad or even Henry. *YOU* made all this happen and now you shrug and say it's not my responsibility? It's time you stepped up, young lady, and took responsibility for the things you've done."

Megan eyed her mother and shook a cigarette out a pack. She'd taken up smoking again to help keep her weight down. She lit the cigarette and exhaled.

"I'm going the best I can," she said. "I am."

"And it's not good enough," Ethel said, and then she thought that was nothing that Ed would have said.

She sat down. "The point is, Meggie, we have to pull together, even harder now that your Dad's gone. Henry certainly can't help himself and neither can little Amelia. So we have to, do you see?"

Megan nodded but her mother could see that she wasn't listening at all.

"I'll make Amelia's bottle," Ethel said, getting up.

"Thanks, Mom," Megan said, inhaling deeply. "You are the best, you know."

Upstairs, Henry was terrified. He had fallen asleep under Ethel's soothing caress but then he woke in horror and fright. The room was contracting and expanding and growing dark and light with each expansion and contraction. The room was breathing and he was caught in its lungs and there was nothing he could do. Shadows fell in ominous shapes and drew back, claw-fingered and cackling, and then a strobe light began to whirl, blinding him and making him feel sick. He closed his eyes but the voices started shouting at him, choruses of accusing verses, overlapping and scratching.

Henry rolled over and stuffed his fingers into his ears.

"You are not real," he whispered. "None of you. You are not real. I am real. You are not real."

He was drenched in sweat and shaking. "I missed my medication. It's just that I missed my medications. I will be okay. Dad? Dad, where are you? Dad, talk to me, please Dad, talk to me".

But if Ed was there among the voices, there were too many others drowning him out.

"Oh god," Henry said despairingly, burying his face in the pillow. "Oh god."

Without Ed, Henry lost faith in his medication. The meds had seemed different when they were handed out by Ed. They came with the promise of wellness and good things, couriered by Ed's faith in both the pills and Henry. Without Ed, the pills were just tiny objects without efficacy or potency.

Henry continued to take them at the designated hour, in the Ed-designated dose, but his demons returned. The world wavered and became insubstantial. He heard things that weren't there and he couldn't hear the things that were.

He could hear the shouting words, but he couldn't hear Amelia crying. He could hear his heart beating like a bomb about to explode, but he couldn't hear Ethel, even though he could see her concern before his very eyes.

"Henry! Henry!"

But he was inaccessible and remote, locked in his prison of noise and shifting chaos and he covered his ears with his hands.

Ethel reached for the crying baby and jiggled her on her hip. She couldn't understand what was wrong with Henry. She had watched him take his meds and she had double-checked the dose but something had changed and she didn't know what it was. She fed Amelia her bottle and sought refuge by talking to Ed in her head. "Ed? What's going on with Henry?"

He's lost faith. He's lost his sense of all rightness.

"Can I help him?"

I don't think so, Eth. I don't think so. You'll have to take care of Amelia now.

"Great."

"I had the best day!" Megan exclaimed when she got home. "Mom, Emilio's going to send me for training to be a personal trainer! He says I can do it, he says I've got an innate understanding of physiology and that I've shown the necessary determination and fortitude. Isn't that wonderful? I'm so excited."

"It is wonderful, dear," Ethel said and she meant it. "I'm very happy for you." She burped Amelia, patting her warm little back.

"Are you okay, Mom? Why are you looking after Amelia again?"

"Henry's not well," Ethel said. "He's taking his meds but they're not working."

"We'll take him back to Dr. Shiner, then." Megan was firm but Ethel shook her head.

"Dr. Shiner was useless. It was your dad who helped Henry. Shiner deadened him to life."

"But there has to be something we can do?" Megan sat down at the table. "Here, give her to me."

Ethel handed the baby over and Amelia started crying and Megan sat her down on the kitchen table in front of her.

"Amelia?" Megan began. "I need you to listen to me. I am your mother. Granted, I haven't been such a good one but still, I am who I am. Now, stop crying. Your father's not well and you have to be nice to me so I can help Nana take care of you. Do you understand?"

Amazingly enough, Amelia stopped crying and Ethel gave a shaky laugh. "She really is something special," she said. "I'm going to make us some supper. You okay with grilled salmon and salad?"

"That'd be lovely. I'm going to check on Henry. Come on, baby, we're going to see what's up with Daddy."

The sight that greeted her was not hopeful. Henry was naked, and crouched on the floor, scribbling on sheets of paper.

"Henry? What are you doing?"

He looked up, wild-eyed. "They're back. The muse of many voices is back. I have to get them out of my head or I will go crazy. I must get them out now. There are too many voices."

"Henry, you're not well," Megan said. "Let me take you to the hospital. You don't have to go back to Shiner, I'll take you somewhere else."

"No! Leave me alone. I'm fine. Just leave me alone. Give me a couple of days, okay? I need some time, that's all."

"Don't you want to give Amelia her supper? You love giving her supper."

Henry's face was a blank. "What are you talking about?" He went back to his papers without a further glance at her or Amelia.

"Yeah, not good," Megan agreed with her mother when she went downstairs. "I said we should take him to hospital, not to Shiner, but he ignored me."

Her mother looked up from the salad she was chopping. "We can't make him go. Maybe it will work its way out of his system."

But they both knew better.

Henry soon regressed to the point where he wasn't eating and he wasn't sleeping. All he did was pace and scribble and tack pages onto the walls, pages that, when Megan tried to read them, made no sense.

"They're not even words," she said to her mother. "I never understood his poems before but they were real words and real sentences. Now it's just a bunch of nonsense. I worry about you being home alone with him all day."

"He's fine, dear. I don't think he'd hurt a fly." Ethel was convinced. "But this can't end well. I might have to call Shiner and get him to come here."

"Yeah, maybe that's a good idea," Megan said.

Amelia seemed to understand that something was going on and she was quietly obliging and well-behaved. However, Ethel had noticed things about Amelia that she had not yet mentioned to Megan, for fear of worrying her. Ethel was trying to pretend that there was nothing wrong with her granddaughter and she told herself that she was imagining things.

Luckily for Henry, Dr. Shiner was no longer with the hospital. He had been replaced by Dr. Margolin, who came to the house and consulted with Henry.

"I'm changing his prescription," Dr. Margolin told Ethel and Megan. "I don't believe in the chemical crapshoot that Dr. Shiner was loading into Henry's system. Let's try something different and see. I prefer to start with a small dose and then increase as needed, so it may be a bit of time before we see an improvement."

"Thank you for coming," Ethel said. "We couldn't get him to come to the hospital."

"Anytime," Dr. Margolin told her. "I've read his poetry. We need take care of this man."

It was June, the start of summer, and somehow they carried on, managing to muddle into the fall and trudge through a sad Christmas. Then it was time for Amelia's second birthday party and by then, Ethel knew for sure what she had suspected. All was not well with Amelia.

5. AMELIA

AMELIA NEARLY GOT THINGS RIGHT, but she also got them completely wrong. Ethel had seen the warning signs for a while and she had hoped that it was a passing phase and that Amelia would grow out of it. But instead, she got worse. Ethel's suspicions were confirmed when Amelia insisted on having her second birthday party outdoors in the freezing January rain. She insisted, despite the wails and protests of the other children, protests that were echoed by their horrified parents who quickly left the party when it became apparent that Amelia was not going to change her mind.

And that was just the tip of the iceberg.

"She needs to learn discipline," Megan shouted at her mother after the guests followed one another out the door.

"Oh, for heaven's sake, Meggie. You know better than that."

"I'm sorry I ever had her," Megan continued shouting. "She's ruined my life. And Henry's on his way out the door. I only had her for him, him and some stupid idea of us being a family and now I'm the one left holding the baby that I never wanted anyway."

Ethel slapped her hard across the face.

Megan stared at her mother, her eyes wide. Her mother, who had never even swatted her lightly, had belted her a heavyweight blow.

Megan raised her hand to the stinging welt and tears welled up in her eyes.

"You can think any range of selfish thoughts inside the privacy of your head," Ethel said. "But you are never to voice such disloyal nonsense about Amelia again. Not to me, not to anyone. You are not permitted to even mutter any such thing under your breath. Do you understand?"

Megan's face settled into an ambiguous scowl but she nodded and dug into her purse for a Kleenex and she blew her nose.

"I am serious, Megan," her mother said. "One more word like that, ever, and you are out the door, and I wouldn't care if I never saw you again. That's how strongly I feel about this. You have selective hearing so I need to know that you are getting this message loud and clear."

"I hear you, I hear you," Megan said. "She's like Henry, isn't she? She's not normal."

"Don't talk about her like that. What is wrong with you? You're the one with the problem, Megan. It's not normal to talk about your own daughter that way. It's true that Amelia appears to have inherited some of Henry's tendencies. She doesn't feel the cold, for one thing. I wouldn't have thought his problems had a genetic basis but it does seem to be the case. There must be more to Henry's condition than we realized with less of it within his control than we thought. Last night Amelia wanted to go for a walk in the middle of the night. 'Walk, Nana! Go walkies,' she kept saying and I tried to explain, 'No, sweetie, nighttime is when everybody is asleep, doggies, birdies, kitties—'"

"Yes, I get the idea," Megan interrupted her. "Oh god. Another Henry. She's doomed then, Mom. We may as well give up on her."

"You mustn't ever say that." Ethel was fierce. "She's also brighter and more intelligent than most kids and Henry's very loveable, you more than anyone, knows that."

"But his life is hell, and my life is hell because of it, and so will Amelia's be and anybody who wants to have any kind of relationship with her. I'm not going to think about it now. I've got too much going on. Work's crazy and it's just me supporting all of you. I'll have to take on more shifts at the gym, and god knows I hardly see you all as it is."

"What makes you think Henry's leaving?" Ethel asked. "I know he's been slipping out at night for months now and I'm always relieved when he comes back. But why do you think he's leaving? Has he told you that?"

Megan snorted. "That would mean acknowledging the truth of a thing and his whole life is about trying to prove the improbable logic of inconsistency and unreliability so he'd never say anything that definitive."

"He's so clever," Ethel mourned. "He was doing so well when Ed was here. It makes me so sad for him."

"You're sad for him? I'm sad for me. He ruined my life. Level-headed me and look what I ended up with. Stupid, stupid me."

"You fell in love," Ethel said.

"Yeah." Megan began to gather toys and clothes and crayons, her expression tired. "I think he's taking LSD again. I found him in the shower the other day washing his hair with dish detergent, marvelling at the beauty of the bubbles. And he told me he was due to give a talk at the university but he hasn't been there since before that terrible book launch."

Ethel was silent. She had no idea what to say.

"And now," Megan said, "Amelia's like him. Maybe it's better if he does leave us. Maybe he's taught her to do things like this, walking at midnight and sleeping in the day. Maybe it's better if he goes."

Ethel shook her head but Henry obliged Megan by doing exactly that. He left.

He came downstairs the following day and found Ethel and Megan in the kitchen, giving Amelia her breakfast. "You both know I have got to go," he said. "I will come back a better man, you will see. I need to consult with the spirit of the West. She is calling me. Hers is the loudest voice of all."

"It would be more helpful if you stayed here and became a better man," Megan said, sounding, she thought, perfectly reasonable but her voice broke.

"Oh, Meggie." He came and held her close and she buried her head in his chest.

"Don't go, Henry," she said. "Mom's right. You were doing okay with Dad. I'll help you. We'll speak to Dr. Margolin and see what else we can do, or we'll find you a new doctor. Don't go."

Henry stroked her hair. "I can't stay," he murmured into the top of her head. "I wish I could."

Megan jerked away from him and lit a cigarette. "Well, then, fuck off already," she said.

Henry crouched down next to Amelia. "I am sorry, baby girl," he said. "You know that, right?"

Amelia nodded and put her tiny hand on his face.

"I will come back, I just don't know when. But I will come back." He straightened up.

"I am sorry, Mom," he said to Ethel. "I let you down."

"You didn't, Henry. Look after yourself out there, okay?" Ethel was crying; big fat tears rolled down her cheeks.

Henry nodded and walked through the house to the front door. He was carrying a small plastic yellow and red grocery bag with a few of his possessions. Amelia pounded her fists, wanting to be taken out of her high chair and as soon as Ethel put her down, she toddled after Henry.

He hunkered down and gave her a hug. "*Noli timere*," he said to her. "Don't be afraid, okay, baby girl?"

Amelia nodded, a solemn expression on her little face, and Henry opened the door and left without looking back.

Ethel tided up the kitchen and Megan went to find Amelia. "I'm going to practice my routine again. Tomorrow's my big day," she said. "Mama's made up a whole new dance and exercise class and I don't want to screw it up. Do you want to come and watch Mama practice?"

The tiny figure at the window shook her head, her shoulders firm and unforgiving. "No," she said. "No."

When they woke the following morning, the house felt empty. Henry's inscrutable scribbles were still tacked to the walls and Megan took them down.

"I can't look at them," Megan said. "I know I was mean to him. I was trying to jolt him into some kind of normal. I know it was stupid. I miss him so much already."

"I do too," Ethel said. "There's something about Henry. Even when he's not doing well, it's nicer when he's here."

"Are you going to be okay?" Megan asked her mother. "I have to go to work today. I can't be unreliable."

"I'll be fine, off you go. It's not like Henry was helping me in any way. Good luck with your new class."

"I'll phone you later," Megan said and she gathered her gym gear and left. She made it through her class and it went fine but afterwards, the stress demanded release and she sat in a toilet stall in the washroom and cried. When she came out, the gym had emptied but Emilio was waiting.

"What's wrong?" he asked. "You did a great job. Don't misunderstand me but I could tell you were upset when you came in and now you've been crying."

Megan tried to laugh. "How much time have you got?"

"For you, all the time in the world. Come on, there's no one here. We've got a couple of hours before the next regulars arrive. Tell me what's going on."

Megan sat down in his small office and cupped a mug of green tea in her hands. "I fell in love," she said. "I fell in love with a crazy poet. And I thought I could handle the consequences that came with it, but I was wrong." She told Emilio the whole story.

"He left yesterday? Maybe he'll come back, just like he did before," Emilio said after she had finished her tale."

Megan shook her head. "No, not this time. He meant it. I could see that."

"But he was so great with Amelia," Emilio marvelled. "I was so impressed. I wished I could be like that with a child."

"Yeah, he was great. When he's doing okay, there's no one like Henry. He's magnetic, full of energy and life. Being with him was like watching an amazing movie come alive and being part of it for a moment. It felt incredible. But then there was the disaster area he left behind, time after time."

"It was probably your father's death that tipped him over the edge," Emilio said. "From the sounds of it, the first time he went crazy it was because you were pregnant and this time it's because of your father."

"I don't know. He went crazy before he knew I was pregnant, I hadn't told him. But you could be right about Dad. Henry loved him."

"Do you have any idea where he might have gone?"

"No. All he said was that he had to go west to follow the strongest voice. I can't see anyone letting him get on a bus in the state he's in, although, that said, he was remarkably lucid the day he left. It comes and goes with Henry."

"And all kinds of people get on buses," Emilio said. "Megan, you do know that I am here for you? I mean, really here for you?"

Her eyes filled with tears. "Oh, Emilio, thank you. I thought it was just me who felt what was going on between us. I'm so happy I wasn't wrong." She reached over and grabbed his hand and she immediately realized that it was the wrong thing to do.

Emilio froze, his soulful eyes wide and sad. "I am sorry," he said. "I am gay. Megan, you didn't know?"

"How would I ever have known?" she asked. "I thought you were flirting with me all this time, and not only me, but all the women at the gym."

He smiled ruefully. "I have the so-called Brazilian charm, my dear."

"Do you have a partner?"

He shook his head. "No, I haven't had one the whole time

we have known each other. I'm sorry, Megan."

Megan looked at him and grinned. "It's okay. In a way it makes things easier. Relationships are so screwy you know? Now we can be friends, at least I hope we can."

"Best friends! And you are a very good teacher too. We have a good thing here. Let's be happy about that, since life is such an up and down thing. We'll take the good stuff where we can, don't you think?"

"I do think," Megan said. She finished her tea. "I'd better phone home and see if Mom is okay."

"How was your class, dear?" Ethel asked.

"It went fine. It felt good, actually. It wasn't the best day for it. I was thinking about our stuff but still, it was good. You okay?"

"Yes, dear, I'm fine."

"And Amelia? Have you noticed any more Henry-isms?"

Her mother hesitated.

"Go on, Mom, tell me."

"Remember how Henry liked soup for breakfast and pancakes for supper? Amelia likes that too. And how Henry would wear odd socks? She does that, even with her shoes. And more than a few times, when I've gone to wake her, she's been sleeping on the floor. She said it's more comfortable than her bed. And often when I get up in the morning, she's awake. She sits quietly, playing with her toys, and from the mess, I can tell that she's been at it for hours. She doesn't understand seasonality or what the hours of a day mean. She can't grasp that morning is for breakfast, midday is for lunch, and things like that. And she's got Henry's wanderlust too. When we're out walking, she'll suddenly want to turn down a road for no reason and she just does things that seem, I don't know, so random. I think that's the best description for it really. She does such random things."

Megan sighed. "All we can do is keep an eye on things and do the best we can."

She hung up the phone and sat at the front desk, staring into space, not thinking about much of anything until the bell at the front door of the gym signalled that someone had come in for a workout.

Megan stood up. "Hi Mike," she said to one of the regulars. "Good to see you! Great day, eh?"

Megan stubbornly refused to give Amelia a party on her third birthday. "She'll just screw it up for everybody," she insisted.

"But it's not about everybody," Ethel said, wondering why her daughter was so unrelentingly selfish but she knew the answer: Megan was still trying to punish the vanished Henry by denying his daughter the things she wanted.

"It's about Amelia and celebrating her." But Ethel's efforts were in vain and Amelia's third birthday slipped by with the three of them wearing party hats and eating cake at the kitchen table.

"We're having a party," Ethel said, when Amelia's fourth birthday neared and Megan could tell by the set of her mother's jaw that this one wasn't up for discussion.

"Suggestions?" she asked, spooning a revolting mix of barley green and protein powder into a blender.

"We'll have it at Elves, Gnomes and Little People," Ethel said. "I'll book the *Sun, Moon and Stars* room and we'll have them cater cakes and things and the kids can come and go as they please and play on whatever they want to."

Elves, Gnomes and Little People was a party venue filled with jumping castles, slides, climbing apparatus, coloured balls, and all manner of soft surfaces for children to leap on and fall off.

"I think it's dangerous," Megan said. "Some of those slides are really high and I heard two kids broke their arms coming down off them. And some other little boy got tangled in the netting and nearly broke his leg. It's always such chaos. I don't see the appeal."

"They serve good enough food for everybody," Ethel said.

"And all the parents take their kids there. I'll send out invites and get it organized. All you have to do is show up, Megan, and be nice."

"Who will you invite?" Megan was honestly curious.

"Amelia's got more friends than you might think," Ethel was defensive. "She's a very popular little girl."

Megan snorted, poured her green drink into a bottle and left.

The party was scheduled for a Saturday and Amelia was beyond excited. She had her dress picked out: it was a ballerina tutu, with a peach frill and shiny stars on the bodice. She had purple fairy wings and purple leggings and she couldn't wait for the day to come.

The only trouble was, she truly couldn't wait for the day to come. Two Thursdays before the big event, Amelia arrived at the breakfast table in her ballerina costume, smiling and happy. "Birfday!" she announced, clapping her hands. "Yay, birfday!"

"No, honey, it's not for another ten days," Ethel explained. "Come on, Nana will help you get changed and we'll go to the park."

Amelia's face filled with darkness and confusion. "No," she said. "Birfday today!" She looked close to tears, crumpled and tiny, and Ethel made a quick decision.

"You know what, honey, you're right! Happy Birthday, my baby girl! Megan, wish Amelia a happy birthday and tell her how lovely she looks."

Megan gave her daughter a quick peck on the cheek. "I told you so," she said to her mother. "Good luck with your day. See you later."

Ethel grabbed her daughter and yanked her to a stop. "Amelia," she said, "can you play with your toys for a little bit? Mommy and Nana need to have a talk."

Megan's face filled with a darkness similar to Amelia's but she wasn't confused about anything. "You want me to play along and pretend her birthday is today?" she hissed at her mother.

Ethel nodded. "That's exactly what you'll do. You'll call

Emilio and tell him you'll be in by three, and then you go and get dressed into an outfit to celebrate your daughter's birthday."

"Great, it'll be you, me and Amelia, and the kids who work at the counters," Megan was scathing.

"I'm going to call a few mothers and see if they can come," Ethel said. "I thought this might happen, so I have a few contingency plans lined up."

"You're enabling her," Megan accused.

"She can't help it," Ethel said. "Go and get changed, okay? And then go to the bakery on the corner and get one of their birthday cakes."

"You're so bossy," Megan said but she dialed Emilio's number and explained the situation and then she went upstairs to get changed while Ethel worked the landline.

"Like I told you on the phone, nothing's set up upstairs," the kid at main counter said when Ethel, Megan and Amelia arrived, cake in hand.

"It's okay," Ethel said. "Amelia, do you want to stay and play down here, baby? There's nothing up there, they weren't ready."

"No, I want stars room."

"Please can we go up?" Ethel asked the kid. "It's fine if nothing's setup. It's her birthday, she really wants to be in the star room."

"Suit yourself," the kid shrugged and he went to unlock the room.

Just then a few of the other mothers arrived with their kids. "We didn't have time to get gifts," they apologized to Ethel, who reassured them it was fine.

"I've got a busload of presents," Ethel admitted. "I thought this might happen. The star room isn't set up either," she explained, "but Amelia wants to have her birthday in there. Can we all please go up and eat some cake in an empty room and let Amelia open her presents and play along as best we can?"

The mothers were used to Amelia's idiosyncrasies by now

and they agreed. They trooped up the stairs, with Megan lagging behind.

Ethel was happy to see that they'd dressed their children up as if it was a real party, and the two little girls and lone little boy didn't look unhappy to have the place to themselves.

"I prefer it like this," one of the mothers laughingly said to Ethel. "This is lovely. It can get dangerous in here on rainy days when it's packed. I wouldn't go in the big kids' jumping castle if you paid me, but Jackson dives right in. I spend the whole time white-knuckling it and hoping he'll gets out without hurting himself."

"I think it's strange to see it so empty," one of the other mothers said with a little shiver. "It's like a fairground with no one in it."

"We'll have fun," the third mother said. "Emma's play date cancelled today so if you ask me, this worked out perfectly."

"Since you already paid for a whole party," the kid at the counter said to Ethel, "I've sent out for mini burgers, French fries, cupcakes, soft drinks, and cookies. We'll do the best we can on short notice."

The food arrived quickly and the kid also whipped up a few decorations and within a short time, the vast empty party room was a hive of happy activity. Amelia was princess for a day, opening her presents and happily singing along with her three friends.

"Your daughter is amazing," one of the mothers said to Megan.

"Yeah?" Megan replied cautiously, wondering what was coming next.

"She's so generous," the woman said. "Most kids, mine included, are all about their stuff. The main thing on their mind is 'that's mine, mine, mine.' They're obsessed with what's theirs. Sharing is an alien a concept to them as monogamy is to adults.. Does she get that from you?"

"She's never cared about stuff," Megan admitted, careful to

stay away from the woman's last comment about monogamy, having no idea where that came from.. "She definitely gets her generosity from her father, not from me. I often have issues with it. She loses stuff or gives it away or she cuts the sleeves off her clothes for no reason. She drives me mad."

"I'm sure it would have its downsides, but I'd love to have a kid who isn't materialistic. It's crazy, they're four years old and everybody wants the latest toy and movie and it has to be new too. When I was a kid, I wore my older sister's clothes that she got from the one who came before her. Now everything has to be new and fabulous and matching, while Amelia comes in wearing odd socks and shoes and Ethel says that she hates new clothes and that they have to shop at Goodwill or Sally Ann or Amelia won't wear it. Now there's a kid after my own heart."

"Where you do know Ethel and Amelia from?" Megan asked, feeling stupid for asking but wanting to know.

"From Art and Move," the woman said. "Our kids have practically grown up together. Well, since they were about two."

"Art and Move?" Megan said, trying not to make it sound like a question but both women knew it was.

"Every Tuesday," the woman said. "We meet at the Scouts Hall in the Legion and two kindergarten teachers read stories and sing songs, and the kids dance and make artwork."

"And Amelia does all of it?"

"She has her own way of doing things, but yeah, she does most of it," the woman laughed. "Don't get me wrong, she's very gentle and super bright, she just has her own interpretation of things."

"Tell me about it," Megan said, and what she meant was that she agreed with the woman, but the woman misunderstood and thought that Megan had asked it as a question.

"For one thing, she always has to leave ten minutes before the end of class," the woman said. "No matter what we're doing, even if she loves it, it's like clockwork, ten minutes before we're set to end, up she hops and out she dashes. And it's not like there's a clock or anything for her to go by. I just noticed it."

"Her father used to leave at odd times too," Megan said. "He said he didn't know what made it so important for him to leave when he did."

Megan had no idea why she was talking to this woman with such frankness, while the kids' party blazed around her. "I also never have any idea how long he'll be gone for," she added.

"How long's the longest he's been away?"

"Right now he's been gone for two years, three months, and five days."

"No child support?" The woman looked sympathetic.

"No word from him at all."

"Sue the bastard," the woman said with feeling.

"You two are having a good chat, I see," Ethel joined them. "Thanks for coming, Monika."

"Hey," the woman said, "Amelia's a sweetie. Anytime."

Later they went back downstairs and the kids played on the slides and jungle gyms for a couple of hours and Ethel took the time to thank the mothers again for playing along. Amelia held Ethel's hand and waved goodbye to her guests when the party ended but she wasn't ready to leave.

"No go. Want more sun, moon star room," Amelia insisted.

"No, honey, it's over," Ethel said. "The party is finished. I'll take you up and show you."

She took Amelia upstairs and found Megan helping the kid clear things away. There was a curiously desolate feeling to the room, much like a summer beach stranded in the wintertime, lost and lonely. The kid had already stacked the benches and tables up against the wall.

"Play a game!" Amelia said, and she sat down on the floor of the empty room. "Duck, duck, geese!"

Ethel sat down. "Come on, Meg," she said. "This is the last thing you'll have to do today, I promise."

"I'll play too," the kid said and he sat down.

Amelia stood up. "Duck!" She shouted, touching Ethel's head.

"Duck!" Then she touched Megan. "GEESE!" she shouted and she touched the kid who jumped up and chased the giggling child around the room.

"Now your turn!" she yelled at him, and she sat down.

"Duck, duck, geese!" The boy chose Megan and she joined in the spirit of the moment and chased him around the room.

They played until Amelia was exhausted and Megan more so.

"I'd better get back downstairs," the kid said and Ethel thanked him.

"No problem, she's a cutie. I'm glad it worked out."

"Come on, Amelia," Ethel said. "Party's over, baby. Did you have fun?"

"Best birfday!" Amelia grinned. "Fank you, Nana and Mama."

"You're a nutcase, sweetie," Megan said. "But I love you."

"Don't say things like that to her," Ethel said tiredly.

"What? Don't tell her I love her?"

"You know what I mean," Ethel said and she gathered up Amelia's gifts.

"Sorry, Mom," Megan said. "I tell you one thing for darn sure. She's sure as heck lucky to have you."

"Tell me something I don't know," Ethel said wryly.

School, in regular terms, didn't work out either. Amelia simply could not understand the regulated hours or the uniforms or any of it, so Ethel dedicated herself to home schooling her. "Because of her condition, I can get a grant to home school her," Ethel explained to Megan. "I've got a doctor's letter saying it's for the best."

"Great, she's already a classified mental case," Megan said.

"I think you mean she's a genius in the making," Ethel corrected her. "I wonder what her specialty will be. Maybe she'll be a poet like Henry."

"Fuck poets and poetry," Megan said with venom and Ethel scolded her.

"What? Amelia's asleep. She can't hear me. Fuck poets, Mom, fuck them."

Much to Megan's fury, Henry, wandering around somewhere in the vast geography of the west, had managed to publish a second volume of poetry. Megan only knew this because advance copies had arrived from Zimmerman Bob. The would-be poet had turned publisher, having decided that his own offerings had run dry. That the volume of poems was dedicated to her and Amelia only fueled the flames of Megan's fury.

"Where is he?" she demanded of Zimmerman Bob when she visited him in his office. Zimmerman Bob had reverted to using his real name, Lionel Levinsky.

"Whoa, Megan, I know we only met a few times, but man, you look different. Like you could wrestle me to the ground if I don't give you the answers you want. The truth is, I don't know where he is. I just got a wad of scribblings in the post, with a note for me to do something with them, or get them to his previous publisher. Henry said he couldn't remember the name of the guy. He's very trusting, old Henry. I mean if I were a man of lesser ethics, I would have published them myself and taken the credit for writing them."

"They're too brilliant. No one would have believed you wrote them," Megan said shortly, despite the fact that she had tried to read them and hadn't understood a word.

Lionel laughed. "Yeah. Actually my ethics had nothing to do my not taking them. They had Henry written all over them. I wouldn't have had a chance of getting away with it."

"And you don't know where he is?"

"The postmark said Kamloops," Lionel said and he handed her the envelope that Henry had sent. "Funny," he said, "Henry's so out of it most of the time but every now and then he can pull it together to do something like find my address, go into a post office, fill out a form, and send a parcel. Amazing really."

"And he wrote you a note?"

"Yeah, here you go." Lionel handed a sheet of paper to Megan.

ZB, here's my latest. I hope they say what I think they say, and aren't the senseless ravings of a lunatic. If they are any good, will you do something with them? Find my publisher — what was his name? Or whatever you think.
Thanks, H

"That's it?" Megan was disappointed.

"That's it." Lionel leaned back in his chair and laced his fingers behind his head. "You two got married and had a kid, I heard?"

"Yeah, and we're busy living the happy-ever-after just like in the fairytales." Megan got up.

"Word is he's going to win a bunch of awards for this one, just like the first one. And students are already studying his first collection at university. You should be proud."

"Why? It's got nothing to do with me," Megan was bitter.

"He loved you as much as he could love anyone," Lionel said gently. "And remember, I knew him from when we were kids. None of this is his fault, Megan."

"I know what you're saying," Megan said and to her embarrassment, she began to cry. She sat down again and let the tears flow. "I miss him so much. When he and I met, and he came to live with me, I was so happy. I was so in love. It's like I'm waiting for him to come back and for our lives to rewind. I'm waiting for the love of my life to walk through the front door and say, 'Hey honey, I'm home. Where's the soup?'" She gave a shaky laugh.

Lionel handed her a box of Kleenex. "You want a scotch?"

"No. No, thank you, Bob. I mean Lionel. I don't usually lose it. I don't know what got into me. Hey, what happened to that girl I went to the reading with, what was her name again?"

"Alice. We've been married for three years now. We've got two kids. A two-year-old boy and a new little baby girl. She's only six months old. So much for my bohemian life," he said wryly. "Alice helps out here when she's not looking after the kids. She'll be in later if you want to see her."

"That's okay," Megan said, gathering her purse. She couldn't think of anything worse than making small talk with Alice. "Let me know if you ever hear anything more from Henry, will you?"

"Of course. Take care, Megan."

But, as Lionel put it, they heard ziltch from Henry until his next offering of poems that arrived in Lionel's office mail, five years later. Amelia had just turned nine.

"Another incredible work of staggering genius," Lionel said to Megan on the phone. He had called her as soon as the package arrived.

"Did he say anything about me?"

"He dedicated the book to you and Amelia again," Lionel said apologetically and Megan hung up the phone.

"Oh, honey," Ethel said, having overheard the conversation and she went to hug Megan but Megan jerked away from her, almost snarling.

"I hate him, Mom. I hate him."

"I wonder if we'll ever see him again," Ethel said. "And if we do, what will he be like?"

"I hope he stays away forever," Megan spat out the words. "I'm going for a run. I don't want to think about him."

Several months after the fourth volume of poems arrived from the west, a man showed up at Ethel's house: a tall skinny man with a wild shaggy head of hair and a craggy face like Nick Nolte after his run-in with heroin.

Amelia answered the door. She looked at the man who was wearing shorts in winter, a Hawaiian shirt that had seen better days, and bright pink flip flops.

"Mom's not happy with you," she said to the man she hadn't seen since before her second birthday. Amelia was fourteen.

"I can understand that," Henry said. "Listen, I am sorry

Amelia. I've been a pretty hopeless dad. Pretty much hopeless at anything except being a poet. Can you forgive me?"

She shrugged with perfect teenage nonchalance. "As far as I know," she said, "I'm too much like to you to be in any position to criticize. Are you back for good?"

Henry looked desperate. "How would I know?" he replied. "I would like to get to know you though. I did love you, Amelia, in my saner moments. I still love you. You were the sunshine of my life."

"I know, I remember you saying that. Would you like to come in?"

"Is your mother here?"

"No, she's at the gym, but Nana's here."

"Your mother's still going to that same gym?"

"She's a tangerine-coloured piece of beef jerky these days," Amelia said and Henry looked baffled.

"Amelia, who are you talking to?" Ethel called out.

"Dad's here," Amelia said.

"I hope he'll come in?" Ethel said. "One thing's for sure, you're both letting the heat out so one way or another, close the door."

Henry grinned and ventured in. "Hi Mom," he said, twisting his hands.

"Cream of broccoli, cream of tomato, or chicken noodle?" Ethel asked, getting up and giving him a hug.

Henry's face lit up. "It's a good day for chicken noodle," he said.

"Let's go and sit in the kitchen," Ethel said.

And that was where Megan found them.

She walked in, tired and strung out, hungry as a wolverine but unable to eat or drink because she was in the middle of competing and couldn't afford to retain a single drop of water. She hated winter, she was starving, and she was sure that she was going to lose the contest to her arch rival. All in all, it wasn't the best day for Henry to make his reappearance.

"Honey? We're in here," Ethel called out, and she got to her feet. "Meggie, guess who's here, honey?"

There was a grim silence.

"Unless it's Dad back from the dead, I'm guessing it's Henry," Megan said. "I don't want to see him. Not now, not ever. I'm going upstairs and if he comes near me, I'll kill him."

They heard her stomping up the stairs and they looked at one another.

"I always loved your mother for her passion," Henry said to Amelia who shrugged.

"She's in the middle of a competition," she said. "Never a good time."

"Never a good time," Ethel agreed.

"What competition?" Henry asked.

"Body building," Ethel said with a sigh. "She's fallen into some cult where the body is god. Never mind it being the temple of god, it just *is* god."

"Time for me to take my leave anyway," Henry said and he stood up.

"Will you be in Toronto for a while?" Ethel asked and Henry nodded.

"As far as I know, that's the game plan."

"Where are you staying?" Ethel asked.

"At my folks' place. They died recently," Henry explained. "They were holidaying on a cruise ship and they got some stomach bug and died of gangrene of the bowels. They left everything to me, mainly because there was no one else. I decided that I am going to live in the house but I plan to change it up a bit."

"I'll drive you home," Ethel said and she got her keys.

"That would be great," Henry said. "Thanks Mom. I am tired. I came right here after being on a bus for three days straight."

"I'll come too," Amelia said. "We may as well start this famous father-daughter bonding thing."

Amelia pulled on a pair of glittery flip flops and Henry laughed.

"I guess you do have my genes," he said.

"I don't understand one word of your poetry, so nix that idea," Amelia countered.

"Sometimes I don't understand it either," Henry admitted. "I'm merely the conduit for heavenly voices. The night I met your mother, I was wearing shoes like that only they didn't have any glitter on them. No, wait, I was barefoot. I wore the flip flops later."

"You were barefoot and she fell in love with you? Mom? I can't see that." Amelia was incredulous.

"Yes, we had something all right," Henry said. "Out of this world really."

"It was a marvel to behold," Ethel said and Amelia wondered if she was being sarcastic but Ethel took Henry's arm and there were tears in her eyes.

"She still loves you," Ethel said. "As much as she did then. And look what you two made: this wonderful girl."

"Eughh, Nana, let's not talk about the physicality of the whole thing," Amelia said. "I'd prefer to believe I simply sparked myself into being, rather than being the result of some gross bonding of sperm and ovum by two of the weirdest people alive."

"You are wearing purple feather fish hooks for earrings," Henry said, "and half of your hair is white and the other side is Kool-Aid blue. Every single fingernail is a different colour and you're covered in what I hope are henna tattoos, not because I have anything against tattoos, but because yours look like you drew them yourself with a brown sharpie."

"I did," Amelia said proudly. "Thank you for noticing."

"I could call you weird," Henry said mildly. "Or I could call you interestingly creative and I choose the latter, that is all I'm saying."

They went out to the car and Ethel noticed Megan staring down at them from the upstairs window but she didn't say anything.

"Give me directions," Ethel said. "I've never been to your home, remember."

"It wasn't my home until now," Henry said. He pointed the way until they pulled into the driveway of a huge mansion.

"Wow," Amelia said. "Cool."

"Will you be all right in there, Henry?" Ethel asked. "You can always come and live with us again if you want to. Meg will get used to it."

"Thank you, Mom, but I'm okay. Like I said, I have plans to redo the place, you'll see. And Amelia, now that you know where I live, please don't be a stranger. Come by any time."

"Your meds seem to be working," Ethel said hesitantly.

"Sometimes better than others," Henry replied. "And for now they are good. Don't worry, Mom. I've got a doctor here. I am going to do my best to keep it together."

He opened the car door. It had started snowing lightly.

"Goodnight, family of mine," he said and then he sauntered up the path and let himself into the house.

6. FAMILY

WHEN HENRY ARRIVED BACK IN TORONTO, he moved into his parents' house and then he gave every single possession away to Goodwill and the Salvation Army. Everything, except for a few items of his father's clothing, a paisley silk dressing gown being one of them. He also kept the mattress from his bed, and his collection of model airplanes that still hung as they had for all those years, but now fluttered dustily in an empty room.

Henry dragged his mattress into the living room and placed it neatly in front of the fireplace on the hardwood floor. He had no need for a blanket but he had kept one pillow and he had also kept the heavy drapes, so he could shut out the world when he chose.

"Minimalistic," Megan commented when she first saw the house, shortly after Henry's return.

Henry had arrived at the house in Scarborough early one morning.

It was three a.m. and only Amelia was awake.

"You want to go somewhere?" Amelia asked when she opened the door but Henry shook his head.

"I need to see your mother."

"She's sleeping and if you wake her up now, she'll kill you."

"I'll wait," Henry said. "You can tell me about you."

"Nothing to tell," Amelia said, leading him to the living room. But they chatted easily for hours until Megan stumbled up from the basement in search of her morning cigarette and coffee. "Henry? My god, you scared the shit out of me. What are you doing here?"

"Megan, is that you?" Henry was distracted by Megan's new look and he stared at her.

"Yeah." She lit a cigarette and blew the smoke at him. "What do you want, Henry?"

"I need your help," he said, twisting his hands. "Can you come to the house?"

"Now?"

"Yes, please."

"Sure."

Amelia was stupefied by her mother's acquiescence. She had expected Megan to bark a negative retort and slam back down upstairs. "I'll put some clothes on. Give me a moment. Amelia, will you make my morning shake?"

"Eughh, gross, but yes, I will," Amelia said, taking various protein powders and mixtures down off the shelf.

The three of them drove to Henry's house, with Megan smoking and sipping on her shake while she drove, and Amelia sitting in the centre of the back seat.

Henry led them inside the house. He took them to the kitchen that was also bare, save for a kettle, a can opener, a soup pot, and a spoon.

"There," he said, pointing to a mountain of mail on the polished marble island.

Megan began to sort things into piles, and then she opened the letters while Henry and Amelia watched her.

"Henry, do you know how to pay property taxes and keep the garden maintained and things like that?"

He looked at Megan blankly.

"I thought not," she said. "Fine, I'll take care of it. Some of these are overdue. Henry, if you want to live here, you're going to have to participate in some real-world activity. But it will just be for a morning. Can you do that?"

"What do you mean?"

"You need to come with me, to the bank. I can manage all of this for you so you can carry on living here but you need to try to seem normal for a morning when we meet people."

"No need to be nasty, Meggie," he said mildly. "Thank you for helping me. You have always helped me. I know I haven't been the ideal husband. Of that, I am perfectly aware."

"At least you dedicate your poetry books to me," Megan replied.

"And me, Mom," Amelia piped up. "He dedicates them to me too." But Megan ignored her.

"I will need to keep some cash on hand," Henry told Megan, "so I can take taxis to my appointments with my doctor. But Meggie, how will I remember to go?" He was panic-stricken.

"How often do you need to go?"

"Once a month. Not a lot but you know me. How will I remember?"

"I'll take you," Megan had said brusquely. "Come on, my family such as you are, let's be off."

"She's amazing," Henry said to Amelia. "I fell in love with her the moment I saw her."

Megan laughed. "Yes, he did." She started the car and Henry, sitting in the passenger seat, carefully snapped his seatbelt into place.

"But you looked different then," Henry mused.

"She's a body builder now," Amelia offered from the back seat and Henry studied Megan.

"But why are you so orange?"

"Oh for god's sake, it's just the tanning lamps, Henry. I go a bit orange is all."

"Tanning will kill you," Henry said, a worried frown creasing his forehead. "Even I know that. Those tanning lamps especially."

"They haven't proven anything," Megan argued. "Being tanned makes me look more cut."

"Cut?"

"Ripped, chiseled, sculpted."

"And your hair wasn't so red," Henry said. "It had red in it, yes it did, but it was beautiful, like chestnut with red, and it was shiny and long, and I loved how it smelled. I loved how you smelled."

"Too much information," Amelia said, from the back.

"You smell different now," Henry said, sniffing Megan. "You smell chemical. And your hair is very brittle."

He touched her hair and Amelia expected her mother to slap his hand away but instead she saw Megan lean into his touch and even close her eyes for a moment.

"Road, Mom, road," Amelia said, amazed that her mother seemed to love her father even now, despite her bitter fury at how things had turned out.

"We're here," Megan said as they pulled into the parking lot of the bank. "Let's do this thing."

They got out and Megan studied Henry who she had dressed in a pair of his father's dress suit trousers and a white shirt, items of clothing that he had thankfully also kept. "You look deceptively together."

"Meg, please, stop talking like that," Henry said and he took her hand and she grinned at him.

"You'll hold my hand even though I smell chemical?"

"You think I would let a few chemicals bother me?"

"You two are too weird," Amelia said.

Several hours later, Henry staggered out of the bank. "That was exhausting," he said, leaning against the car, looking haggard.

"But it's sorted out," Megan said. "Now you can go back to being a happy recluse."

"Can we get some breakfast?" Henry asked and Amelia brightened.

"Good idea, Dad!"

"It's nearly three in the afternoon but whatever," Megan said and she took them to an all-day breakfast diner.

"Pancakes and scrambled eggs," Amelia said. "With black coffee, please."

"You're too young to drink coffee," Megan said automatically. "I'll have a white egg omelet," she said to the waitress. "With one poached tomato. Easy on the grease, please."

"I'll also have pancakes and scrambled eggs," Henry said. "And can you bring lots of syrup?"

The waitress put a jug of syrup on their table and left without a word.

"Here we are," Henry said, beaming at Megan and Amelia. "Having a family breakfast."

"Yeah, like twelve years too late but it's the thought that count," Megan said. "Henry, where did you go, all this time?"

"Kamloops. It was nice there."

"You never wrote to us but you kept publishing books of poetry? Why didn't you write to me?" Amelia could hear the hurt in her mother's voice.

"I'm so sorry, Meg," Henry said and he took her hand. "I stepped out for longer than usual, I know. I wasn't in a good way after Ed died. I felt like I was going mad. Things seemed fine when he was around but then everything changed. So I left and then, when I was in Kamloops, the poems just kept coming to me, and I kept writing them down and then I posted them to Lionel and he did the rest. I didn't speak to him once the whole time. My job is to write the poems and send them. Lionel does the rest, and the rest doesn't matter to me."

"No more pissing on them?" Megan asked and Henry laughed.

"No. I don't even remember that night. There is so much I don't remember. I remember you being born though," he said to Amelia. "My whole world made sense then. It did. You were the sunshine of my life."

"But you left me too," Amelia pointed out.

"He couldn't help it," Megan defended Henry and Amelia turned to her, open-mouthed.

"What? How can *you* say *that*?"

"I never said he could help it. I always just said it wasn't fair how life had turned out, that he was this way."

"Life isn't fair," Henry said and their food arrived.

"I was so jealous of you," Megan said to Amelia as she blotted the excess oil off her food with a paper napkin. "He loved you more than anything. Much more than he loved me."

"I loved her differently, Meg," Henry said, drowning his eggs and pancakes in syrup. "You are the love of my life, and Amelia is the sunshine."

Two fat tears welled in Megan's eyes and rolled down her cheeks and she wiped them away with one hand.

"I don't understand any of it," Amelia said.

"You will, one day," Henry said.

"She does stuff like you," Megan said. "Gets on the wrong buses, doesn't feel the cold, does weird shit." Megan cut her omelet into tiny pieces and blotted them again."

"You do?" Henry looked at Amelia with interest but she focused her attention on her pancakes.

"Nana says the world sees things differently than me," she said.

"Yeah, so differently she has to be home-schooled," Megan said. "Mom's teaching her."

"Do you need money?" Henry asked.

"We're okay," Megan replied, "but if we ever do, you'll be the first to know."

"I am government-funded," Amelia said proudly.

"Who's this doctor you're seeing?" Megan asked Henry.

"Someone I got referred to by my doctor in Kamloops. I didn't go and see anyone by choice. I kind of lost it there and ended up in a hospital. But I was lucky, instead of some idiot like Shiner, I got a great doctor who understands me. He said I should see this guy. I hope he'll be okay."

"If not, we'll find you someone else," Megan said and Amelia was startled by her gentleness. Where was her brittle, angry mother?

"I'm done," Henry said abruptly. "Can we go?"

"Sure, you go and wait for me at the car," Megan said and Henry rushed out of the restaurant.

Amelia looked questioningly at her mother who shrugged. "That's Henry. He's always done that."

When they got outside, Henry had vanished.

"He's always done that too," Megan said, unlocking the door. "Don't worry about him. He'll be fine."

"But how can you be sure?" Amelia was panic-stricken.

Her mother looked at her curiously. "How can you not understand when you do the same thing?"

"But I know how to take care of myself," Amelia said.

"Believe it or not, so can your father."

"I still think we should look for him," Amelia said, refusing to open the car door.

Megan sighed and shrugged. "If you want to go hunting ghosts, that's fine but I've give a class in two hours and I need to catch up on my workout. I missed my morning session."

"I can't believe you!" Amelia stormed off and stood at the edge of the parking lot, watching her mother start the car.

Megan drove up to where Amelia was standing and rolled down the window. "Come on, Amelia," she said. "Last chance for a ride home or I'm leaving you here."

Amelia cast a desperate glance around but she knew that her father would be impossible to find and she had no yearning to be left wandering the neighbourhood of strip malls and dollar stores. "Are you sure he knows how to get home?" she asked, climbing into the car.

"He got himself all the way home from Kamloops, didn't he? And then he even managed to come and find me now, when he needed me. It's amazing what Henry can do, when he wants to." The old note of bitterness had crept back into her voice.

"He loves you, Mom," Amelia said, not wanting to lose the feeling of familial love and Megan nodded and put on a pair of sunglasses.

"Yeah, that's true, honey."

Amelia, happy to be called the rarely-used affectionate term, stayed silent until her mother dropped her off at home.

"See you later, Mom," she said and Megan gave a wave and drove off.

"We have the weirdest family ever," she said to Ethel after she had filled her in on the day's events.

"Ordinarily I would say something like all families are weird," Ethel said, getting out her notebooks. "But in this instance, I'll agree with you."

"Ah Nana! No school today!"

"And why not? It's not my fault you've been off jaunting. But you can choose, math or English."

"English. Why can't we study Dad's poems?"

"Because I don't have a clue what they mean. You'll have to wait until you get to university for that."

And when Amelia did, years later, she was amazed and baffled by the genius of the words and the magic of the imagery.

"Apparently he's mad as a hatter," one of her fellow students commented, a boy she had hitherto found cute.

"Real geniuses are," she had said coldly, and she gathered her books and left, and she never spoke to the boy again, much to his confusion.

Amelia had decided to study using her mother's maiden name. "I don't want any confusion or expectations by my teachers," she had said. "And if they know that Dad is my father, there won't be a way around it."

Megan understood. That Henry had achieved the level of national acclaim that he had, had come as no surprise to Megan but that he continued to be prolific, amazed her.

"He sees it as his necessary contribution to life," Amelia tried to explain to her, after Henry had told her how he felt.

"I get that, Megan had said, but still…"

PART II:
AMELIA AND MIKE (2011)

7. GROUP THERAPY: SESSION ONE

"GREETINGS ONE AND ALL! I am Doctor Frances Carroll and I am going to change your life forever!" The therapist's beady eyes glittered and his teeth clacked like tiny yellow castanets.

Amelia glanced at the cute young man across the room. He met her gaze and smiled. That caused an unexpected but pleasant flutter in her belly. She blushed slightly, hated herself for it, and turned her focus back to the manic Dr. Carroll.

"Yes, I am going to change your life. And in case any of you are wondering, I intend to change it for the better. Things could, and usually do, if left to their own inherently destructive devices, coupled with the humanistic natural condition and predilection for disaster and destruction, get much, much worse. But, in your cases, things will improve.

"There are no guarantees in life, this much is true. But if, and it's a big IF — because in the end it's up to you, people, I can lead to you to water but I can't make you drink — but if you follow my lead and take careful and accurate heed of my game plan, you WILL improve. You will no longer face the world as your phobic fear-ridden terrified selves. No! You will stride with confidence into every room, you will seize every bull by the horns, and you will shout your names from rooftops: I was here! You will tell the whole world: I AM here and I am here to STAY!" He paused and looked intently around the room. He was perched on the edge of his chair, with his small, red-sneakered feet planted firmly half a foot apart, his hands resting on his knees. He darted quick bird-like glances at each person in the circle.

"Now," he said gently, and his voice was a sweet caress after his abrasive high-energy sales pitch, "now, I know that Rome wasn't built in a day and the same can be said for your mental health but we have twelve beautiful weeks, twelve sturdy sessions and by the end of that sound dozen, if you follow my directions, D.T.O.T. will have changed your life."

He grinned, a flashy, self-satisfied grin and cocked his head to one side. "And what exactly is D.T.O.T. you might ask? We'll get to that in a moment. Before we do, I'd like you to introduce yourselves and tell us a bit about your problems. There's no need to feel ashamed. We know that each of you is here because you've got a problem. You've been diagnosed as such or you wouldn't be sitting here, sponsored by the government in a generous effort to cure you."

He brought his hands together in a prayer-like pose, leaned his chin on his fingertips, and reflected for a moment. "I believe in being frank," he announced abruptly and he sat up, ramrod straight, his expression kindly and suggestive of benevolent friendship. "Yes, I believe in being frank. There's no point in beating about the bush. Would a physician tell an ill man that he's healthy? He would not. Therefore, don't hold back. Let there be no shame in the things you tell each other. Just put it on the table. Throw it down."

He stroked his goatee with one hand and then he scratched his jaw, leaving visible red tracks on his skin. He leaned forward. "It is hard for me," he admitted in a confidential tone, "not to get impatient with you at the beginning. You creep into this first session, frightened and even more panic-stricken than usual, and most of you are hardly able to form the words to describe your particular malaise. Can we agree to compromise?"

He was imploring. "I will try not to be impatient and you'll try to tell us clearly what your name is, and why you're here.

It's very simple really. Just your name and your condition. Don't ramble or elaborate or start telling me about your sad little childhoods. Just give me the facts. For example: I am Frances Carroll and I have agoraphobia. Full stop, next person. This is a great way for us to start our work together, particularly if public speaking is your phobia. Dive in and swim with the sharks, but don't worry, we won't eat you."

Amelia wondered if the good doctor would ever shut up. She was, however, mildly entertained and she thought that the therapy might not be as tedious as she had been dreading. She wondered what the cute guy was in for. He looked too normal for anything too bizarre. He was lovely, with clear grey eyes, a clean strong jaw, high cheekbones, and a movie star mouth. She blushed again and studied her hands, noticing that the fellow next to her was pumping his knee up and down in a distracting and annoying way. She glared at him and saw a bead of sweat dribble down from his temple, past his ear, and make its way to his jaw. She shifted as far away from him as she could.

"Great!" Dr. Carroll announced. "You, go first." He pointed to a plump middle-aged woman who nearly fell off her chair in fright.

"Ah, I, um, I, well…"

"No! No! No!" Dr. Carroll said. "Listen up, it's easy. It goes like this; I am Amanda and I have claustrophobia. Try again."

"My name is Whitney and I have depression and anxiety and I am worried I am giving it to my daughter."

"Anxiety and depression are not like a prom corsage that you 'give' someone," Dr. Carroll corrected her. "But certainly your daughter can learn and mimic your anxieties and yes, you could be severely impacting her life in a potentially negative and destructive way. But you won't, once we're done here. Well done on your introduction! Tell me, was that so hard?"

Whitney looked down and shook her head, ripping a tissue to snowflake shreds and giving a quick sniff.

"Moving on! Next: you boy. Go on, spit it out." He pointed at the boy sitting next to Amelia. He was wearing a black baseball cap, mirrored aviator sunglasses, and a girly t-shirt cut to a low oval on his chest with a red sequined heart.

When the good doctor pointed in his direction, the boy's leg started pumping triple time. He suddenly jumped up. "I'm Kwon. I have social anxiety order," he barked out and he sat back in his chair, his relief palpable.

Amelia assumed she would be next but the doctor was stabbing his finger at people in a random fashion and she assumed it was part of the therapy to not follow order. Which was, she reasoned, predictable in itself, and she was inclined to point this out, but Doctor Carroll had signaled another hapless fellow.

Not that this fellow seemed hapless, at second glance. He was huge, with his long legs stretched out in front of him. The laces of his construction boots were untied and he was shaggy-haired, like a giant bear.

"I'm Alexei. I have anger management problems. Or so they tell me," he growled. Alexei had a strong Russian accent. "I don't think I get angry. I just don't put up with bullshit. You want the truth, Doctor? You like us to tell you the truth? Me, I don't have problems, other people have problems. I have no problems!"

He sat back, satisfied, and Dr. Carroll who was slightly subdued, consulted his notes. "Right, you're that person. Uh, okay then, whose next?" He stabbed his finger at the cute young man Amelia had been eyeing.

"I'm Mike. I'm a business entrepreneur but I have difficulty with public speaking."

Dr. Carroll peered at him. "You seem fine to me. You sure about this?"

Mike blushed scarlet. "Dr. Carroll, don't you remember our consultation?"

Dr. Carroll rifled through his notes. "Oh yeah, right, you belong in here. Sorry, it slipped my mind."

He sighed. "I've forgotten who has introduced themselves. Let's start with you," he pointed at a girl, "and we will go around from there. If you've already told us who you are, then wave to next person."

"I'm Ainsley and I have panic attacks," the skinny blonde girl offered. She clapped a bony hand to her mouth as soon as she finished talking, thereby flashing a gigantic engagement ring.

"I'm Persephone and I have social anxiety disorder and generalized anxiety disorder and borderline personality and agoraphobia."

Amelia eyed Persephone with interest. She was a hefty gothic girl in her twenties with long dark hair. Her upper arms were like giant albino bat wings. Amelia felt ashamed of her unkind thought but Persephone, wearing a sleeveless tank top, kept twisting her hair into a bun and showing off those strangely pale and middle-aged upper arms. Amelia forced her thoughts away.

"I'm Joanne and I'm a lawyer with generalized anxiety disorder and OCD. I also steal things when I get nervous."

Joanne was skinny with wiry grey hair and black sunken hollows under her eyes. Her mouth was twisted to one side as if her tongue had got stuck trying to dislodge an errant piece of food. She was tall, in pinstriped trousers with a no-nonsense grey shirt unbuttoned to reveal an equally no-nonsense chemise. Amelia watched her pick at the cuticle of her thumb until it bled.

"Oy, stop that! No self-harming in here," Dr. Carroll said and he flapped a binder at her.

Mortified, Joanne stuck her thumb into her mouth.

"Next!"

Next up was a pale porky fellow in his forties. He had a remarkable hairdo and Amelia could not help but stare. The man had an absolutely round head, the shape of which was accentuated by his greasy, grey, pudding-bowl-with-bangs haircut. His hair was combed forward over his head, starting at the nape of his neck and gelled and sprayed into an un-compromising position on his forehead. And he was wearing enough blush and lipstick to stop a patrol car.

The man touched his stiff bangs with his fingertips before speaking. "I'm Gino. I'm in sales and like Mike, I have difficulty with public speaking. I'm also an entrepreneur and I am hampering my own progress in my chosen field and—" The man waved uncooked-sausage fingers and was about to continue but Dr. Carroll interrupted him.

"Good! Good, enough! Good, moving on. You." He pointed at Amelia who shrugged.

"I don't think I have a problem," she said. "The rest of the world is out of time, not me. It's not my fault that everybody else has got things back to front. I'm here so I don't lose out on my welfare."

"Right, you're the young woman with the undiagnosed disorder. Interesting, interesting."

"Dr. Carroll," Amelia said. "You met me before, at my evaluation. Don't you remember?"

He ignored her. "Next!" He yelled at a sixty-something bottle-blonde woman who jiggled in fear. "I'm Angelina, I'm terrified of doctors. I keep making appointments because I'm sure I have a terminal illness but then I cancel and I can't go."

A girl with long dark curly hair put up her hand. "I'm Shannon and I have claustrophobia."

"And I'm David, businessman, afraid of talking to clients."

"Good, good, well done." Dr. Carroll said. "Has everyone gone? There were supposed to be twelve of you, like the disciples," he chuckled, pleased with himself. "But there were two cancellations, so ten will just have to do."

He looked at his watch and sighed. "Introductions eat up so much time. The first session is nearly a waste of time but I am sure you are keen and eager to learn about what comes next, to find out about that which will set you free! Hands up all of you who are interested in learning about D.T.O.T.? Come on!

Raise your hands! There you go, well done!

"D.T.O.T.," Dr. Carroll continued, "is revolutionary. D.T.O.T. is my invention, my contribution to the field of psychology. I started out fifteen years ago as a fan of the traditional Cognitive Behavioral Therapy programs and I could see there was some measure of success to be had. But? But not enough. I wracked my brains. I tell you, I've never worked so hard at anything as I did to try and find that thing, that elusive secret ingredient that would make this stuff really work. After all, we're here to heal, not stick a Band-Aid on a leprous wound, but to heal. We're here to heal!

"I started experimenting. Slowly of course, with what I call *Do The Opposite Thing*. That's what D.T.O.T. stands for: *Do The Opposite Thing*. It takes C.B.T. to a whole new level.

"Now, don't worry, this is perfectly above board. I had to prove myself endlessly, which was the hard part. I had to track statistics, medications, field studies and control groups, and the other bumpf that scientists demand. And I am delighted to tell you that D.T.O.T. passed every test and then some. It has been greeted as a revolutionary healing technique and you're extremely fortunate to be here, if I may be permitted to say that myself. This is a rare and fantastic opportunity for you.

"How does it work? The name should be fairly self-obvious but we'll work together, never fear, on the specifics. I wouldn't leave you with a bunch of ingredients and ask for a cake upon my return. No, we'll walk through this valley together. We'll traverse the cliffs, we'll take shelter when storms threaten, and we'll rejoice in the sunshine!"

Amelia looked over at Mike who gave her a quick grin and then studied his hands. Amelia snuck a surreptitious glance at her wristwatch. She felt as if she had been in the room for a lifetime but it had only been an hour. There was still half an hour to go.

"I want you to take out a piece of paper and a pen," Dr. Carroll said. "You were told to bring paper and a pen. None of you brought any? Of course you didn't, why am I not surprised? Luckily for you, I am prepared. I am at the ready."

He handed out sheets of paper and ballpoint pens.

"Now, write down something that you do, as a result of your disorder. Come on, let's be Speedy Gonzales. People, you all know what your disorder is! No news there, write down one example of something you do."

I take the wrong buses, Amelia wrote and she put her pen down.

"Now, let's go around the room," Dr. Carroll said. "Come on, oh, I've forgotten your names, next time I'll bring name tags, but for now, just say your name and read what you wrote."

"I'm Mike and I avoid talking on the phone."

"I'm Alexei, and I hit people."

"I'm Joanne and I cry in the washroom after meetings."

"I'm Amelia, and I catch the wrong buses."

"I'm Kwon, and I don't help out in my parent's store because I'm afraid someone will talk to me."

"I'm David, I avoid my clients."

"I'm Shannon, I don't take elevators."

"I'm Angelina, I cancel my medical appointments."

"I'm Gino, I don't talk at meetings."

"I'm Persephone, and I don't leave the house."

"Excellent!" Dr. Carroll grinned. "We're off to a fine start. Now, here are the rules: this is your homework and you must do it. This week, each of you, every single day, will do the opposite of what you have written down there. The exact opposite. Joanne, no crying in washroom. Kwon, you must work in the store and Angelina, you will go to an appointment. You get the picture."

"But, Dr. Carroll," Joanne spoke up. "If it was that easy, don't you think I would have done it before? *Don't cry in washroom.* Don't you think I haven't tried telling myself that before?"

"And me," David piped up. "Sorry, Doc, but this is too simplistic."

"Oh ye of little faith," Dr. Carroll sighed. "That's what it comes down to. Faith. Faith in me. Faith in yourself. Look the logic here: you all have different disorders, correct? Well, some of you have the same disorder but the specifics differ. Now why is that, you ask yourself, or you should ask yourself. Why do I have this one and not that one? The answer is that they all have the same irrational base. You could just as easily have one or the other, there's little rhyme or reason, despite exhaustive tests on nature versus nurture etcetera, blah blah blah. Therefore, I propose that if you simply do the thing you are most afraid of, and do it repeatedly, it will become a walk in the park, a piece of cake, or even, a walk in the park while you are eating cake!

"But," he added, and he eyed Joanne, "I get that you need tools to help you transition. In fairness, disorders weren't amassed overnight, they were built over a long period of time and you need the correct tools to help break them down. And I will help you by giving you the tools today. One of them, anyway."

He looked at his watch.

"Joanne," he said, "stand up."

She did so, hesitantly.

"I want to you pretend that you are driving your car," he said. "Do you like to drive?"

She nodded.

"Good. So, pretend you are in your Ford Mustang or your ten-ton truck or whatever gets your rocks off. Come on, hands on the steering wheel, there you go, ten and two. Now, you're going to drive your car and I'm going to follow you around and shout at you but you mustn't stop driving. No matter whatever happens, you must not stop. And, people, you've got to follow me and you must shout at Joanne too, and no matter what, she must carry on driving."

He opened the door of the room.

"We're going to do this in the hallway?" Joanne was horrified.

"Oh yes! Don't worry, no one will blink an eye. That's another thing, you people are all so *me, me, me*. No one's thinking about you, no one's watching you, no one cares! Off we go, so Joanne, get those hands on the wheel, ten and two, head out the door. You have to walk the whole way around the floor and back here to our room. You've got it?"

Joanne nodded. She looked close to tears and her twisted, pursed mouth was even more puckered than usual, and the hollows of her eyes were violent black smudges. And Amelia had noticed that an ugly red patch was creeping up her neck.

"Ready, steady, go!" Dr. Carroll shouted and Joanne started her slow walk down the hall with Dr. Carroll in tow and the rest of the group wandering haphazardly behind him.

"You're such a crybaby," Dr. Carroll shouted at her. "All you want to do is run away and cry! Stupid crybaby, you're no good at anything. You're a useless crybaby! How does it feel to be such a stupid crybaby?"

Amelia noticed that Joanne had picked up the pace, and so did Dr. Carroll, who trotted close to her, shouting up at her. "Crybaby! Useless, what a failure! I bet all you want to do is run away and cry, run away and hide and cry, don't you? Don't you?"

Joanne kept her hands steady on the imaginary steering wheel and she lengthened her stride. Her jaw tightened and by the time she rounded the final corner, she was close to power-walking and Dr. Carroll was practically running.

The group re-entered the room and Dr. Carroll closed the door, his chest heaving. "That was a good one! Well done, Joanne!" He nodded and grinned and looked more like a rabid chipmunk than ever.

"And that was supposed to show me what, exactly?" Joanne was icy.

"First off, you're not crying now, are you?"

"I'm furious," Joanne told him." I've never been subjected to that kind of thing before and frankly I won't stand for it.

Who do you think you are, with this cockamamie therapy?" She stood up and grabbed her purse.

"Joanne," Doctor Carroll said quietly. "Are you going to the washroom to cry?"

"Are you crazy? Cry over you, over this? Not on your life!"

"Then it worked," he said. "Please sit down."

Joanne thought for a moment, dropped her purse and sat down.

"Each of you is pursued by your own individual fears," Dr. Carroll said, and for a moment he sounded close to normal. "Each of your fears is a loud irrational voice shouting at you. So what you need to do, this week, is drive your cars — drive them straight to your goal and never mind the idiot in the backseat yelling at you to cry, or to leave, or to do whatever it is you do. You ignore that voice or those voices, and you carry on driving! Notice, you do NOT talk to the crazy thought, you do NOT engage with it. Why don't you talk to the thought? Ask yourself this: What would have happened if Joanne had stopped driving and started arguing with me? She never would have made it back to this room and she most likely would have ended up in the washroom crying. But she ignored me and she pushed though it and although it felt terribly uncomfortable and she got angry, she reached her goal without giving in to her fear."

Doctor Carroll sank back into his chair. "That's it for the day. I'll tell you, I'm exhausted. I give you guys my all, you will see that, every week. I am unstinting in my desire to help you. And now, we will finish off with a meditation. Much like Savasana in yoga, we always end our sessions with a meditation to allow the fruits of our work to take seed. Now, remember, if you don't show up for a session, you owe me $50 per, so that's $550 if you decide you're not coming back. You signed up for this; you made a commitment. You can back out but then you must pay the price, that's the way it goes in life. Any questions before we end?"

He looked around, but the group was stunned and mute.

"Excellent!" He grinned. "I'm going to ring this bell and we'll do a ten-minute meditation and I'll set my phone alarm because sometimes I fall asleep during this part. But try to think about what happened and try to contextualize it in terms of your own phobia. I can only do so much. You have to do the rest."

He set his phone alarm and rang a bell.

"I'll walk you through the start," he said and he yawned. "Your feet are planted firmly on the floor, your eyes are closed, and you're aware of your breathing, in and out. You feel your back against the chair and you can feel the blood tingling in your veins. You open your mind to receive the fruits of what we have learned today. You open your spirit to the acceptance of learning and you open your arms wide to receive the healing of the light."

With that, he promptly fell asleep and snored ever so gently.

Amelia opened her eyes and saw that the others had their eyes tightly shut and were following the rules. All except for Mike, who grinned at her. She gave a small wave. They sat there, desperately trying not to giggle, and the alarm eventually sounded and woke Dr. Carroll.

"Off you go, then," he shouted. "Have fun with it, D.T.O.T. wherever you can, and see you next week!"

The group scuttled out and much to her consternation, Amelia found that Mike was walking next to her. She couldn't think of a single thing to say.

"What did you think?" Mike asked Amelia, breaking the silence.

Mike was even more handsome up-close than Amelia had thought. His grey eyes were clear and wide-set and he had dimples when he smiled. And oh, that mouth. Never had a mouth had such an effect on her.

"It was interesting," she said. "But since I don't have a problem, I find therapy irrelevant."

"But you're here," he said. "There must be someone who thinks you have a problem?"

"Yeah, but that doesn't mean anything. We're forced to live according to social constructs and rules that we did not create. Those rules don't work for every individual. Some of us never agreed to them in the first place."

"But if we didn't have rules, there would be anarchy," Mike argued.

They were standing with the others from the group, waiting for the elevator to arrive. The others were trying to persuade Shannon to get on the elevator with them. "I don't know," Shannon said doubtfully. "It's taking an awfully long time to get here. It's a sign that it's going to get stuck and I shouldn't take it."

"All it means is that there are too few elevators for a hospital this size," Gino piped up eagerly.

"Exactly why I shouldn't take it," Shannon said.

"They may be slow but that doesn't mean they get stuck," Gino countered.

"Who made you come here?" Mike whispered and his mouth was close to Amelia's ear and she thought it felt delightful.

She sighed. "I'll lose my welfare benefits if I don't come," she told him. "And we can't afford that. I'm working toward my Masters in English literature and unless I get welfare, I can't afford to do it. Therefore, I don't have a choice but to be here. I am writing a thesis on Joan of Arc and the pervasive impact she has had on the image of female heroism in literature. I am quite obsessed with Joan and I can't lose my place at university."

"She was an epileptic and a schizophrenic," Mike commented and Amelia shrugged.

"Perhaps, but she was also so much more than that."

The elevator arrived with a noisy ping and the battered steel doors shuddered and shook themselves open.

"Come on," Gino said. "You can do it, you can!"

But Shannon took one look at the crowded steel box and turned and ran the other way.

"Not going to get better like that," Gino remarked.

"Very chatty for a person who's scared of public speaking," Mike whispered to Amelia who smiled and nodded.

They reached the ground floor.

"There's my gran," Amelia said, reluctantly. "She's waiting for me. No one trusted me to come. Frankly, they were right."

"Hello, I'm Mike," Mike said, going straight up to Ethel. "I'm in the group with your granddaughter."

"Nice to meet you, Mike," Ethel said, smiling.

"I thought you were shy?" Amelia countered. "You don't seem very shy to me."

Mike laughed. "I have trouble in boardroom situations, not person-to-person interactions. See you next week?"

Amelia was disappointed. She had been hoping he'd ask for her telephone number or email address.

"Yeah," she said. "See you next week. Come on, Nana, let's get the heck out of here."

They headed towards the revolving doors at the entrance, and Amelia spotted Shannon staring at the triangulated glass cage with distrust. Shannon finally gave up and pushed her way through the wheelchair-access door and left, looking despondent.

"That young man looked very nice, dear," Ethel said. "How was the whole thing? It took longer than I thought it would. I guess the doctor's not particular about keeping exact time."

"It was weird, Nana, it was very weird. I don't want to talk about it. Can we get Swiss Chalet for dinner?"

"I don't see why not. We'll see what your mother says."

Amelia gave a snort. "She'll say it's fine for us but then she'll have some stupid protein drink or something. Don't you think she looks more bizarre than ever, Nana?"

Megan's body building obsession had progressed to the point where she did, in fact, look bizarre. Ripped and taut, her skin glowed a strange orange from tanning lamps, and her face had the odd rictus of a botoxed smile.

"I hate it," Amelia said. "She looks like a freak."

"It makes her happy, dear," Ethel said. "It makes her happy."

"She'll get cancer from that all that stupid tanning," Amelia predicted. "And she smokes like a chimney to stay skinny. The whole thing is sick, if you ask me. She should be in here, doing this stupid group thing, not me."

Ethel privately agreed with her but couldn't admit it out loud. "We all have our issues, dear," she said.

"You don't," Nana, Amelia said.

"Tell me about Mike. He seems like a nice young man," Ethel said, trying to change the subject as Amelia was in a funk.

Amelia shrugged. "Nothing to tell. What's the bet he's got a girlfriend? I can't imagine him being single."

"He probably thinks the same thing about you, dear." They reached the car and Ethel beeped it open.

"You're very lovely, you know," Ethel said, putting the key in the ignition. "In fact, you've grown into a beautiful young woman. Your hairstyle is a bit unusual, but I do like it better all one colour and the black is very nice."

"I'm not bad looking, Nana, but I'm not right in the head, am I?" To Amelia's disgust and Ethel's surprise, Amelia started to cry. "Mike could never go out with me, even if he wanted to," she wailed, "because I don't do things right. I'll be alone the rest of my life."

"Aw, honey, that's not true," Ethel said and she unbuckled her seatbelt and hugged Amelia. "Come on, dear, don't cry. If you ask me, you're perfectly fine. It's just that society has a bunch of rules and we're expected to play by them. You can learn the rules, dear, you can. You may not like them or understand them, but you can learn them. I know you can. You can do anything you want to in this life."

"But what if I end up like Dad?" Amelia blew her nose loudly.

"He's different, dear, he always has been. Different from

you, I mean. Henry's troubles always ran much deeper. He's a wonderful, tragic, sad boy, and he always has been."

Amelia laughed. "Dad, a boy! He's practically middle-aged."

"And I'm a geriatric," Ethel started the car and smiled. "But seriously Amelia, you don't have what your Dad's got. You've got your own brand of unusual, but it's not like his, you don't have to worry about that."

She pulled out of the hospital parking lot. "He loved you so much when you were a baby," she said. "I never saw anybody love a child like Henry loved you. But then Grampa died and Henry just went away."

"I don't want to end up like him, Nana, or, even worse, like Mom. She's so bitter, so angry. I don't want to be like either of them."

"And you won't, dear," Ethel sounded certain.

"How can you be so sure?"

"Because, dear, you've got a large helping of your grandfather and me running through your veins and neither of us is anything like your parents, so there you go!"

Amelia gave a small laugh. "Yeah, okay. Swiss Chalet?"

"Swiss Chalet it is."

Take the right bus, take the right bus. Amelia consulted her notepaper.

Nana had helped her. *If I am going to the university, I need to take the 55 East. If I am coming home, I need to take the 55 West.*

She had a list of instructions for all the places and bus routes she could possibly take.

"Try to pause before you act, dear," Nana had said. "Don't give in to impulse. Even if you have to wait for the next bus, that's fifteen minutes, so what?"

"Fifteen minutes is forever, Nana!"

"Read a book, listen to music, but don't give in to impulse, dear."

THE NEARLY GIRL   133

Take the right bus, take the right bus.

Amelia stood at the bus station, waiting for the 55 East to come along.

Oh, the temptation. Bus after bus pulled up, each promising a new adventure and a brand new experience. It was true that she had taken many of them before, but who knew which stop would call out to her? Who knew which person she would follow home, just to see where they lived, and what their lives were about.

"That's creepy," Megan had said, piling lettuce onto her plate at dinner one evening when Amelia tried to describe why she felt the urge to explore the way she did.

"It's not creepy," Ethel had defended Amelia. "She's interested, curious. You should write books," she told Amelia. "Make up stories about people and their lives."

"I'm not interested in fiction," Amelia said. "I like to witness real people's lives. But most of them are so boring. I wish they could see how boring their lives are because then they would change them."

"No, they wouldn't," Megan commented, her lasered-white teeth glowing eerily in her tightly-stretched orange face. "Because they wouldn't think they were boring. Most people are happy as clams. Clams who don't know how bored and boring they really are."

But catching a random bus was a thing of the past. Today, there could be no whim-sponsored rides and no following of arbitrary people home. And why? Because of Mike, that's why.

Amelia clutched her piece of paper. Mike wouldn't take a random bus or follow people home. He just wouldn't and she wanted to be like him, so he would like her.

She wondered what he did for a living. She felt certain that it had to do with computers. He had that look about him, clean-cut, like he liked the world to be neat and tidy and defined by lines of ones and zeroes.

Amelia was twenty-two and she'd never had a boyfriend. She

hadn't wanted one either, until Mike. She wondered if perhaps it was the setting in which they had met that had sparked her interest. She had considered that him being there indicated that he himself must have issues, in which case he would hardly be in a position to judge hers.

But when his issues turned out to be less warped than hers, it was back to being an unequal affair, not that anyone matched Amelia on the warped scale of equalities, and she recognized that. And she knew that her attraction had very little to do with his being able to stand in judgment of her or not. It had to do with sheer physical attraction, which, for her, was a first.

If I can just take the 55 East and then come straight back home at the end of day on the 55 West, then maybe he'll like me, she thought. It will be a test, a test of our future.

She shook her head. What future? There was no future for Amelia Chameleon, not with anybody. The boy who had called her that had liked her, but he had admitted that her inability to control her erratic lifestyle was more than he could take. "I need to know that if you say you'll meet me somewhere, that you will," he had said. "Not that you fell asleep and turn up four hours later. Or, that you decided to go for a walk instead. You live inside your head and I can't go there with you."

But she hadn't liked him, not like that, so it hadn't mattered. But she liked Mike and so it mattered now.

The 55 East eventually arrived and Amelia found herself unable to get onboard.

I can't do what I should. I am allergic to shoulds. Shoulds are for losers. Losers do what they should. I do what I like. I am free, they aren't. Don't get on the bus, don't follow lists, don't follow rules, don't be boring like the rest of the world, be me, be free.

Amelia watched the 55 East bus pull away and then she turned and walked home.

"I couldn't do it," she said to Nana, despondent. "I couldn't do it."

"Did you take another bus?" Ethel asked.

"No. I waited and waited for the 55 and then when it came, I couldn't get on. It would have been like admitting to the biggest failure yet, that I am doomed to be boring, doomed to live a boring stupid life like everybody else."

"Back up a moment," Ethel said. "That you didn't get on another bus was a big step forward. You would have, you know. In the past, you would have."

"Yeah, maybe."

"No maybe's," Ethel insisted. "You'd be halfway to hell and gone, phoning me at midnight to come and get you from wherever you ended up."

Amelia grinned. "I usually find my own way back," she said.

"Yes, dear, for the most part you do. And for the record, I never mind coming to get you. Now off you go again. Go and try again."

What? Now?

"Yes, dear now. Off you go, go and catch the 55 East."

"But I'm tired!"

"Who said life was easy? I'm sure it wasn't me. Come on. I'll walk there with you."

"Ah, no, Nana, you don't have to, I'll go, I will." She kissed her grandmother on the cheek. "I'll try to come back with a positive report."

"Good luck!" Ethel called after her and she felt a wave of sadness as she watched Amelia's determined form disappear around the corner, setting off to try again.

This time, when the 55 East came to a stop, Amelia rushed at it, clambered on and sat down, her heart pounding. What had Dr. Carroll said? "You will experience unpleasant body sensations. You will feel as if your sanity is being threatened. You will feel sick. You will feel vulnerable. Identify these feelings in your body and notice them, but know they are not you, they are just feelings, just sensations. Imagine if you were in a room and the fire alarm kept going off by mistake and every time it did, you leapt up and ran out? That's what this panic is. It's an over-active fire alarm going off when it shouldn't."

Thinking about this made Amelia feel slightly better although her heart was still racing. Who on earth felt this level of panic simply because they took the bus they were supposed to? But it didn't matter about anybody else.

When she arrived at her destination, she got off the bus and waited for the return ride to take her home. She was exhausted and she spent the journey back leaning her head against the window with her eyes closed. It was easier to manage when she did not see all the places that beckoned her to get off.

"Well done, dear!" Nana exclaimed when she got home.

"I'm shattered." Amelia slumped down in her chair.

"It will get easier," Ethel told her. "Everything does, with time."

"Time and your macaroni and cheese," Amelia told her. "Hint, hint."

Ethel smiled. "With pleasure."

"I'm going to play some video games," Amelia said. "I need to lose my mind for a bit. Dr. Carroll says we mustn't engage with our problem areas, so I'm having nothing to do with my mind for the rest of the night."

"Sounds good, dear. Of course you can always watch *Murder She Wrote* reruns with me."

"Nana! Kill me first!"

When the day of the next therapy group arrived, Amelia got up early and washed her hair.

"You don't need to take me today," she told her grandmother. "I will get there by myself and don't worry, I *am* going."

Ethel hid a smile. "Fine, dear. Call me if you want a ride home. But wait, it's ten in the morning! Why are you leaving now? Your group only starts at one!"

"So I'll be a bit early," Amelia said. "I'll read a book or something. Don't worry Nana. I'm focused, I promise you I am."

"I'll say," Ethel muttered, putting the dishes away. Odds are, she thought, that if Mike's involved, this therapy may just work out. Of course if he rejects her, the opposite could occur too and send her spiraling the other way.

"Oh Ed," she said out loud. "What a thing, what a thing. Henry's locked away in his mansion like Howard Hughes, Megan thinks she's Arnold Schwarzenegger and Amelia's fallen for some boy she met in therapy. Although," she added, "Mike did seem nice. Oh I miss you, Ed, I miss you every single day. I know you're looking down on me but I wish you could actually talk to me, like say, 'hey, Eth, you batty old lady, why're you talking to yourself?' *Why would I need to say it if you just did, for me?* She could hear Ed plain as day and she laughed. I'll take myself to library, she thought, spend a pleasant time there and maybe find some ladies to rope into a game of rummy or something. She felt unusually tired but she dismissed the idea that there might be anything wrong with her and told herself that all she needed was a bit of fun in her life, a bit of levity.

8. GROUP THERAPY: SESSION TWO

M EANWHILE, AMELIA HAD EVER-SO-CAREFULLY taken the right bus and she also managed to get off at the hospital stop. It was a gusty gloomy November day, and she had hours to kill. She went for a long walk, happily thinking about seeing Mike later and she lost track of time. The next thing she knew, time was running out and she had no idea where she was.

She started crying and ran up to a stranger on the street. "Where's the hospital?" she shouted at him and grabbed his arm. He was elderly man and he looked startled and started pulled away. "Which way is it to the hospital?" she repeated, holding onto him.

The man jerked back and stared at her, his eyes wide.

"Are you deaf?" she yelled. "Which way is it to the hospital?"

A red car suddenly pulled up next to her. "Amelia?" It was Dr. Carroll. "What are you doing? The hospital's in the other direction. Come on, I'll give you a ride."

Amelia pulled the car door open and sank down into the passenger seat, sobbing. "I got lost. I came early. I was doing so well. I took the right bus and everything and then I nearly messed it up again." She hit herself on the forehead with her palm.

"Now, now, none of that," Dr. Carroll said disapprovingly. "You took the right bus, you did well. In any therapy, there are times of regression although they aren't necessarily regressions, they are further opportunities for learning new behaviours. Let's look at what happened. You planned to get on the correct bus, you got here early and then you took your eye off the ball? Right?"

"Yeah," Amelia said. "But I don't remember the moment when I took my eye off the ball. Next thing the ball had vanished and I was seven streets away from it."

"That's where meditation comes in." Dr. Carroll grinned his hamster-grin and swung into the hospital parking lot. "And if you don't mind, I'd like to use your very experience in group today. It will help you too, you'll see. It will solve a lot of issues."

"I'll look like an idiot," Amelia said, following him into the hospital.

"No more than any one else in the room," Dr. Carroll said cheerfully and he chuckled. "Don't be so serious, Amelia. It's not like you, or anyone else in the group has a life-threatening disease. There are people in here with cancer and all kinds of terminal illnesses. If anybody shouldn't be laughing, it's them, not you."

"I should be laughing?"

"You should lighten up. Look, there's Shannon, staring at the elevator. Let's see if we can help her."

"Shannon!" Dr. Carroll said and for a small man he had a loud if somewhat shrieky and high-pitched voice. "Going up? We'll join you! How have your elevator experiences been this week?"

"Bad," Shannon squeaked. "Bad. I haven't…"

"Oh look, here it is, in we go." Dr. Carroll bundled Shannon in and pulled Amelia in after him.

Amelia thought Shannon was going to die of respiratory failure. She was gasping and clutching at Dr. Carroll like a drowning guppy.

"It's all good, it's all good," Dr. Carroll said as the elevator gave a clanging sound and the doors opened, one floor higher. "No, we're not getting off here, one more to go. You're doing superbly, you know that, well done! Well done!"

Shannon closed her eyes and buried her face in his chest.

"No, no," he said, forcing her off him. "You must see it. You must experience it. Tell yourself, here I am, in an elevator, which could conceivably get stuck at any moment but even if it does, I won't die. No one has ever died of suffocation in an elevator, did you know that? They die of accidents, like being mauled between the floors after their scarves or ties get caught in the doors. And a number of elevator technicians suffer a fair amount of work-related injuries but the average Joe, like you and me, we're just fine! And look, we're here."

The doors opened and Shannon stumbled out, gasping.

"We should ride it down one more time, and then come up again," Dr. Carroll said but Shannon rushed into the therapy room before he could grab her again.

"We don't have time anyway," Dr. Carroll mused as he followed her into the room and set his briefcase and plastic bag down next to his chair. "Right, roll call, people, roll call!"

Amelia looked around and saw Mike. He was waving at her, pointing to a chair next to him.

"I saved it for you," he said, removing his sweater from the seat. "Hey, are you okay? Have you been crying?"

"I'm fine," Amelia said. "Just fine." She stared at the floor, thinking that Mike was even better looking than she remembered.

"Hmmm, we are missing Whitney, our neurotic housewife, and Alexei, our angry Russian," Dr. Carroll said.

"They're in the lavatory having sex," Joanne told him. "I wanted to use it and before I could, they ducked in there together like school kids. I mean, really. There aren't that many washrooms near this room. Couldn't they find a broom closet or something?"

"I'll go and get them," Dr. Carroll said and when he got up, the group stood and followed him.

"All for one," Joanne said with an evil smile on her twisted lips. "You followed me, now it's their turn."

Dr. Carroll shrugged and banged on the washroom door. "Alexei, Whitney, we know you're in there. You're late for therapy. Come out now. You can do this later."

"Is he for real?" Mike whispered to Amelia who was wishing that it was her and Mike in the washroom."

The door opened and Alexei came out, zipping up his jeans, followed by Whitney who was pulling down her skirt.

"You've been at it for over half an hour," Joanne said. "I timed you."

"You wish it was you, lady," Alexei said with fire in his eyes and he poked a finger in her direction. "But in only your dreams."

"No anger, no anger," Dr. Carroll said. "Okay everyone, back to group."

"This is hilarious," Gino said loudly to Shannon. "Want to have sex with me in a locked room? That would cure your claustrophobia big time!"

Shannon glared at him. "Don't be such a pervert," she snapped.

"People, people!" Dr. Carroll admonished, waving them to their seats. He ran a hand over his thinning hair. "Come now, a moment to regroup. There's been a lot of excitement today in a short space of time. First, I found Amelia wandering the streets dazed and confused, and then together she and I helped Shannon take an elevator…"

"Helped? You forced me in! I still can't breathe from the shock of it."

"But you're alive and well and you didn't die or go nuts," Dr. Carroll reminded her. "Therefore progress was made. And then we find two of our group engaging in coitus in the washroom. Tell me, Alexei, was it D.T.O.T. in action? You know, make love not war?"

Alexei looked confused. "Whitney is a sexy and beautiful woman," he said. "What do you mean, D.T.O.T.? What is D.T.O.T.? You mean detox?"

Dr. Carroll sighed. "How quickly they forget. *Do The Opposite Thing*," he said. "It was your homework for this week. It's the basis of this course. What about you, Whitney? Was your having sex with Alexei an example of D.T.O.T. in action?"

She laughed. "Sorry, Dr. Carroll, but no. He's hot as hell and you know what they say about therapy. Whatever goes on inside the cinder block walls of a madhouse, stays inside. It was just glorious fantastic sex."

"Hmmmm," Dr. Carroll said, and he jotted down some notes. "I posit that both of you were subliminally and subconsciously engaging in D.T.O.T. Sex, for Alexei, is the opposite of anger and for you, it's the opposite of anxiety. Good for you. Good for both you. Well done!"

"What?" Whitney and Alexei spoke at the same time, raising their objections, but Dr. Carroll dismissed their protests. "The beauty of D.T.O.T.," he explained, "is that it shows you the pathway to your truest desires, your most pure self. Alexei, you aren't an angry man. You're a virile young man who likes to have sex and Whitney, you aren't anxious. You are suppressed and crushed by the suburban stagnation of your life. Imagine if you could have sex with Alexei every day, wouldn't your life improve? Wouldn't you be happy? And, Alexei, imagine if you could have sex with Whitney every day? Of course I don't mean you two specifically, because neither of you is capable, or desirous, of that kind of commitment. You both want sex with randy strangers in washrooms, which, by the way is not exactly something either of you invented."

"You're saying that if I had sex every day with a stranger in a washroom that I'd be my happiest self?" Whitney asked.

"Well, tell me, wouldn't you?"

A smile crossed Whitney's face. "Sure, but it's amoral."

"Aha! Morality versus sanity! A whole different ball game to be explored and not one that concerns me in the least. What is morality anyway?"

"The fear of getting caught," David, the businessman, offered.

"No, that's consequence", Dr. Carroll said.

"Religion is morality," Ainsley piped up. She was the skinny blonde with the enormous engagement ring said. "It's against most religions to have sex with random people."

"I'm not convinced that religion is morality, per se," Dr. Carroll frowned. "What makes something truly wrong or evil? Think about it, people. But, most importantly, please pay attention to the fact that the events of this afternoon demonstrated beautifully how D.T.O.T. helps shine a light on the real truths of your hearts and psyches. I'll say more about this in a moment. Now I'd like to go around the room and check in with everybody and then we can look at Amelia's conundrum."

Amelia was hoping he had forgotten about their encounter.

"Don't worry," Mike whispered. "If he gets weird, I'll protect you."

Amelia broke into a broad grin and relaxed in her chair.

"Chatty Mike, let's start with you," Dr. Carroll said, with a rodent smile. "How was your week? Did you talk to anybody on the phone?"

"Actually, I did," Mike said. "I called a bunch of people and it got so easy that eventually people were trying to get me off the phone! I had fun with it. It was like because you had told me to do it, it took the fear away."

"That's because your secret desire is to talk to everyone. You're a very sociable, likeable fellow and you like to talk and you love to be heard. Alexei and Whitney, we're fully aware of how your week went."

"But—" Again, they spoke at the same time, and again, he ignored them.

"Joanne, what's the status on your weeping in the toilet?"

"I did not weep," Joanne said, through gritted teeth. "I am still angry with you."

"Joanne, you're angry with the world," Dr. Carroll said helpfully. "Depression, or sadness, is anger turned inward. If you started expressing your anger with the world to the world, you'd be a lot happier."

"And a lot less employed," Joanne commented and Dr. Carroll shrugged.

"The jobs of our choosing are not always the right ones for our personalities. You might be better off being a prison warden or, I don't know, a policewoman, who knows. But there you go, food for thought."

"Kwon, did you help out in your parents' store?"

Kwon jiggled his leg. He shook his head.

"Can't win 'em all," Dr. Carroll said cheerfully.

"David, did you engage with any of your clients?"

"I did," David said. "I felt like I said the wrong things, but one guy signed a new contract so I must have done something right." He grinned.

"Hmmm," Dr. Carroll said, "fear of accepting success. David, I want you to please stand up."

David did so, hesitantly, not sure what was coming.

"Now, shout, as loudly as you can: *I am David and I love the fact that I am a successful businessman!*"

"I…" David started. "I can't," he said.

"You can, you can. Come on, group, shout at David until he gets going. You are David and you love the fact that you are a successful businessman!"

Alexei, Mike, and Gino joined in with gusto while the women looked on bemused and Kwon clearly wanted to melt through the linoleum floor.

"Okay, okay," David yelled. "I am David and I LOVE THE FACT THAT I AM SUCCESSFUL BUSINESSMAN!" He shouted it three more times and Dr. Carroll had to pull him down into his seat.

"Good, good, well done. You should do that in the shower and in your car. But not in your office. Shannon, we all saw you take the elevator, so you're good."

Shannon glared at him.

"You want the world to hug you," Dr. Carroll said. "You

feel abandoned by life, lost and lonely. You think you suffer from claustrophobia when in reality, you feel forsaken in a desert of loneliness. Come on everyone, let's hug Shannon."

"No! No, no!" But Shannon's protests were drowned in a group hug led by Gino.

"Get OFF me, you pervert!" Shannon yelled. She shoved Gino hard in the solar plexus with her elbow and he grunted loudly.

"Easy now," Dr. Carroll said, assisting Gino back to his chair. "He was trying to help you, Shannon."

"Help? He groped my buttocks!"

"He did? Gino, did you grope Shannon's buttocks?"

Gino looked shamefaced. "I did," he admitted. "I am sorry," he said to her. "I think you are so beautiful."

"That's no reason to do it," Dr. Carroll said musingly. "You know what the Buddhists say. Do not take that which is not freely given. Apologize, without any conditions of why you did it."

"I apologize, Shannon," Gino said. "I am sorry."

"Gino, you feel as if the world doesn't hear you and that's why you're afraid of talking. You are certain that if you speak, your fears will be validated and you will be universally rejected. You believe that you don't have a voice worthy of hearing. Stand up and say: I have a voice and it has a message of importance."

Gino stood up, and he smoothed the creases of his trousers and clasped his hands nervously. "I am Gino, and I have a voice of importance," he whispered.

"It's *message* not *voice*," Dr. Carroll corrected him. "I have a voice and it has a message of importance. Louder, louder."

"I HAVE A VOICE AND A MESSAGE OF IMPORTANCE," Gino screamed and everybody in the room jumped.

"Very good," Dr. Carroll said. "Group, we are making great strides today! I am delighted, just delighted. Moving on. Angelina, did you make an appointment and keep it?"

"No," she whispered. "And don't make me stand up and shout anything because I won't."

"Fair enough," Dr. Carroll said. "Ainsley, did you leave the house and if you did, did you have a panic attack?"

"I left the house to go clubbing," Ainsley said. "I took a tranquillizer to go out and then, when I got to the club, I got drunk. When I drink, I don't panic and so I drank."

"Not optimal," Dr. Carroll said disapprovingly. "Next time, leave the house and suffer. Endure the panic attack. That would be worth much more than trying to numb yourself. Ask yourself, Ainsley, what are you trying to avoid? Your dead-end future with your fiancé?"

Ainsley gasped. "How dare you!" She stood up. "I'm leaving. Screw you Mr. High-and-Mighty. You think you know everything but you don't know shit! How dare you!"

She grabbed her purse and marched out.

"Guess I hit a nerve," Dr. Carroll said, making a note on his chart. "Always good to elicit a strong reaction. Next, Persephone, did you leave the house?"

"It was too cold," Persephone said. "I couldn't."

"I am noting resistance and passive aggression," Dr. Carroll said. "Be that as it may for the moment. I'd like to turn our attention to Amelia here. I believe that we can all benefit today by exploring her actions earlier. Tell us, in your own words, what happened to you today."

"I can hardly use anybody else's words, can I?" Amelia retaliated and Dr. Carroll chuckled.

"Diversionary conversation won't work," he said, tapping his knee with his plump fingers. "Use any words you like, but tell us what happened."

"I left the house early," Amelia said with a sigh. "I didn't want to be late."

"What time did you leave?"

"Around ten," Amelia admitted and the group gave an audible collective gasp and she turned on them. "What? I wanted to be here on time."

"Fair enough," Dr. Carroll said. "And you got here when?"

"Just before eleven."

And then what happened?"

"I don't know." Amelia sounded miserable. "I guess I thought I had time, so I'd go for a walk. It's a nice day outside."

"It's frickin' freezing," Persephone butted in. "I know you think I was making excuses for not leaving the house, Dr. Carroll but I wasn't. I work from home. I had no reason to leave the house. My boyfriend brings whatever groceries I need, so why should I leave the house?" She raised her giant albino batwinged arms above her head and adjusted her ponytail.

"We're not talking about you right now," Dr. Carroll said gently. "But we can return to you later. Amelia, I concur with Persephone. It's not a pleasant day for a walk. It's unseasonably windy and blustery."

Amelia shook her head. "I don't notice things like that. I've got a condition I inherited from my dad, although I don't have it as badly as he does. He doesn't feel the cold at all whereas I do a bit, but not much. I don't mind being in the rain either. I love walking in the rain or going to the beach on wet and windy winter days. It's much more beautiful than in the summer time."

"Hmmm," Dr. Carroll said. "Let's backtrack. The thought occurred to you to go for a walk and then you lost track of time and the next thing you remember, you were late for the group and I drove past you in the car and saw you shouting at some poor old fellow."

"I didn't mean to shout," Amelia said. "I just wanted to know which direction the hospital was in and he wouldn't tell me."

"Perhaps he was startled to have a young girl yelling and screaming in his face," Dr. Carroll commented. "But let's look into this more deeply. Do you often arrive that early for appointments?"

"Um, no," Amelia admitted. "But I wanted to make sure I was on time for this one. I wanted to factor in any deviations but then my calculations failed anyway."

"No," Dr. Carroll said. "I think that you wanted to be

here very much and you wanted to establish that here was still here. I believe there are levels of impermanence in your life that threaten the very firmaments of your trust. You're so deathly afraid of finding out that things have vanished, that you go out of your way to avoid looking at them. Does that make any sense?"

"I'm not sure I do understand," Amelia admitted. "I admit that I don't believe that this world is the way most people think it is. But more than that perplexing me, I am terrified that everything is so deathly boring. Most people are so bored and so boring. Their lives are prison cells and they don't even know it."

"Maybe they're happy," Dr. Carroll suggested.

"At what cost? They don't even know the cost. Their freedom, their choice, their sense of adventure is destroyed daily and they don't even know it."

"Ah, now we're getting somewhere," Dr. Carroll said. "Freedom, choice, and sense of adventure. Tell me, did you take the wrong buses this week?"

"No, I took the right ones," Amelia said in a small voice. "But it exhausted me." Her voice dropped to a whisper and Mike looked at her in concern.

"Your knight in shining armour," Dr. Carroll commented, catching the look, Amelia looked up in confusion.

"Him!" Dr. Carroll pointed. "He wants to protect you from yourself, from your fears. But he only wants to do it because it will make him feel good about himself. He wants to be the quarterback hero, saving the day on big screen TV, his hair blowing in the breeze, endorsements flooding in."

"Not true," Mike flushed.

"Is so," Dr. Carroll countered. "That's what you want in life: the cheerleaders and the accolades. And you're afraid that if you express yourself, voice what you really think, then none of the fame and glory will happen and you'll be crushed, so you'd rather sit on the sidelines in silence. But here, you have a perfect vessel for the validation of your fantasies of being Captain America. A tiny fragile girl, tremulous and vulnerable, waiting for you to rescue her. Only you aren't any of those things, Amelia, are you? Fragile and tremulous and vulnerable. You're a big adventurer, a warrior, and your biggest fear is that no adventures or battles await you. You fear that more than death."

Amelia looked at him wide-eyed. "Yes, but so what? I mean it's true but you say it like it's wrong or irrational. *Your* way of looking at the world is wrong, if you ask me."

"Wrong, right, right, wrong," Dr. Carroll shook his head. "Everybody's so hung up on right and wrong, good and bad. I say do what's true for you. If you want adventure, don't get on the wrong buses for god's sake. Take an ocean liner to Alaska, go and live large, girl. Go and volunteer in Africa, look for exotic snakes in the Amazon, sail hot air balloons over Egypt."

"None of that interests me." Amelia was scornful. "I am talking about freedom of the mind. Something entirely different."

"I see. So because you get on random buses, work strange hours of the day and night, have picnics in the snow and the rain, this makes you free? What's the difference? Think about it. But we're done for the moment, we need to move on. You've got lots of food for thought. Chew on it or spit it out, it's up to you." He looked carefully around the group.

"So, people!" He clapped his hands. "Mindfulness. We all need mindfulness in our lives! Why? Because then we become cognizant and fully present. As you know, I'm not a great fan of the meditation bit, but it's a necessary evil. Studies have shown that it works. Today we are going to focus on sound. Close your eyes and focus on the sounds that you can hear. Don't think 'oh, there's an announcement or a siren or a bird,' just acknowledge whatever the sound is, and then return to your mindfulness. Meditation is not about making lists. It's about finding the spaces between lists and thought. I will ring the bell and set the alarm."

"Fabulous," Joanne muttered and Gino grinned at her.

"One day you'll look back on this and think *that man saved my life*," Dr. Carroll commented. "And I accept your grateful thanks now. Okay, here we go." He rang a bell and the group closed their eyes.

Amelia shut her eyes, grateful to escape for a moment. She wondered if there was any truth to what Dr. Carroll had said and whether her assumptions about freedom were indeed valid. She tried to recall how it had started. Could she have inherited this anomaly of thought from her father just as she had inherited her lack of sensitivity to temperature?

So when Mike ran his fingers along her leg and gently took her hand in his, she was caught utterly unaware. Her eyes flew open and she turned to him, her face close to his. He took a quick glance around and seeing that everyone else still had their eyes shut, he leaned in and kissed her. His lips touched hers gently and then his tongue probed hers and next thing they were kissing full on, trying not to make any noise.

Considering that it was her first real kiss, Amelia thought that she did pretty well. She was first to pull back, worried the others would see them. When she opened her eyes, she saw Angelina watching them, grinning, her chins wobbling. Amelia let go of Mike and tried to scoot away, but Angelina shook her head and gave a thumbs ups. Mike grinned at Amelia and rubbed his foot on her leg and then the alarm bell rang and Dr. Carroll woke up and straightened his pullover.

"How was that for everyone?" He asked and the group muttered an assembly of replies.

"I know. It sort of kills the mood," Dr. Carroll said, yawning. "Meditation sucks the life right out of a person, if you ask me." He looked at his watch. "Hmm, time flies, time flies. So, homework for this week, continue doing D.T.O.T. with regards to whatever your specific case is and try to find new ways in which to express your voices. I want to hear a list of the things you did, not what you thought about doing. Any questions? Persephone," he said, "back to you for a moment. Next week, I want to hear that you left the house even if there was a snowstorm or a blizzard. Get out there and make a snowman or something, lemonade. You know, make lemonade. Are you with me?"

Persephone looked sulky and confused.

"Any questions?" There was silence. "We've done well today, group, well done! Off you go then, get out there and *Do The Opposite Thing*!"

Almost as one, the group rushed for the door.

"Stairs," Mike said to Amelia and they rushed down the seven flights of stairs and staggered out into the large lounge area adjoining the cafeteria.

They sank down into chairs, breathing hard, as if they had run a race.

Neither of them spoke for a while and Amelia wondered if Mike would say anything about their incredible kiss.

"What the fuck?" Mike eventually said, running his hand through his hair. "This shit is crazy. Excuse me, Amelia, I don't usually swear so much but is this guy for real?"

Amelia shook her head. "He's a genius or the devil," she said.

"Or both," Mike said.

They sat in silence for a bit. Amelia was trying to find a way to ask him something and he was trying to find a way to tell her.

"Amelia—" he began, and she knew the answer to her question.

"It's okay," she said, getting up, quickly. "I understand. I really do. See you next week?"

He nodded and she rushed out into the cold wind and she ran to the bus station, wishing she had asked Nana to fetch her instead.

"Concentrate," she told herself. "Today is not the day for adventures, just get home to Nana, okay? Concentrate. No wrong buses, no wrong stops." She talked herself onto the right bus and was surprised to find that her teeth were chattering. It couldn't be from the cold, she didn't feel the cold. No, it was shock of everything that had happened. "Concentrate, where's your stop? Look and listen. Don't lose concentration."

She got off at the right stop, ran home, and flung herself at Ethel in despair.

"Oh Nana, he's got a girlfriend!" She looked despairing at her grandmother and ran upstairs to her bedroom.

Ethel waited for half an hour and then she followed Amelia upstairs, a cup of tea in hand. "Tell me what happened, dear."

"Nothing happened," Amelia said, her face in the pillow. She sat up and took the cup of tea. "Okay, not exactly nothing. He kissed me during the meditation and then, afterwards, when the group ended, he just said 'Amelia' and then I knew."

Ethel knew better than to question Amelia's intuition. If Amelia said that one word had carried the weight of a hundred words, then Ethel believed her.

"Oh, sweetie, I'm very sorry."

"The whole group is so weird, Nana. There's this big Russian guy and he got caught having sex with this fat old woman — she's there for anxiety and he's there because he's got anger issues. And the doctor said it was good, what they were doing! And then he told a girl that her engagement was giving her panic attacks and she left. He's very argumentative."

"I've never heard of a therapist being so forthright," Ethel mused. "But maybe that's the secret to his success."

"He can't seem to figure me out," Amelia was glum. "Oh, I wish I was normal. Maybe Mike would like me if I was normal."

"Obviously he likes you, dear. He kissed you. Him having a girlfriend doesn't mean that he doesn't like you. And remember this, not that I should say this, but girlfriends can be broken up with. He just met you. Wait and see how things unfold."

"But I'm too weird," Amelia said. "And there are no benefits to my weirdness. Look at Dad. At least he's contributing to the world with his poems. I don't fit in and I don't contribute either."

"Sweetie, you're twenty-two. When your father was twenty-two, he wasn't contributing anything either. And there are different definitions to what contributing means. Look at your granddad. He didn't do anything literary or spectacular but he contributed by being a good, honest, loving man. He made the world a better place when he was in it, and that's not something you can say about most people. Besides, you've got Joan of Arc and your studies. You're doing so well."

"Yeah, but it's not like I'm saying anything other people haven't said before. I thought I was onto something unique but the research isn't supporting me and I feel like that's a dead end too. I want to matter, Nana. What's the point if you don't matter?"

Ethel was silent for a moment. "You have to do what matters in life to *you*, Amelia. And you'll figure that out, I know you will because you're too smart not to. In the meantime, don't give up on Mike yet, because you don't know. I'm going to lie down, I feel a bit tired, I don't know why."

Amelia was immediately concerned. "Oh Nana, I am sorry." She put her cup down. "Do you need me to do anything, get you anything?"

"I'm fine, sweetie. I'm seventy, not exactly a spring chicken!"

"But you never get tired."

"Everybody gets tired. I might have a bit of a flu. What are you going to do with yourself? I don't like you to be up here, miserable."

"I think I'll go for a walk," Amelia said. "Maybe walk to the gym and watch Mom do her weird body flexing stuff."

"Take your phone with you, in case you get sidetracked and you need me to come and get you," Ethel reminded her.

"I will, but I mustn't get sidetracked. I must work on being normal. I want to be a normal person."

"You're perfect as you are," Ethel said. "It's the world that's odd, but it's the only world we've got." She kissed Amelia on the head and went to her room.

Ethel wondered, as she lay down, if she should see a doctor but it seemed like too much effort. It was true that her stomach had been worrying her for a while and she didn't really think she had the flu but she was too tired to get checked out. I'm sure it will get better, she thought. It just needs to work its way out of my system. She was soon asleep.

Amelia slipped out of the house and locked the door. Despite what she had said to Ethel, she was craving escape, her kind of escape. It was late evening and it had begun to rain and Amelia smiled and headed towards the bus stop.

It was a perfect day to go the beach.

The lake was black and blustery when she arrived. The wind was strong, causing the breakers to crash onto the rocks with a flourish of exuberant wild white spray. The rain was a film of fine drizzle and the trees were black skeletons that glistened under the lights that lined the deserted boardwalk. The clouds were layered, like thick charcoal batting that played heave-ho with chalk and thick granite. The lights were on in the washrooms even although they were locked for the season and the pumpkin-lantern warmth of the yellow windows made Amelia feel happy and cheered. She turned her face up towards the falling rain, loving the lit cones of raindrops that fanned out from the lamps.

She strolled along and thought about Mike. What a kiss! She relived the moment when he leaned in, that fraction of a second when she thought she knew what was about to happen but she couldn't quite believe it. Then she thought he'd change his mind but there was the softness of his lips when he didn't, and that electrical magic of his tongue greeting hers. The perfect angles of their faces, that locked moment of togetherness and the reluctant pulling apart. He was so beautiful, so perfect! She hoped Nana was right, that girlfriends could be broken up with.

She passed a man with a dog, a huge golden retriever. The dog wagged its tail and tried to reach Amelia's outstretched hand but the man jerked the dog away, yanking the leash hard.

"Perfect night, wouldn't you say?" Amelia said politely to the man and he lowered his umbrella and hurried along.

Amelia stretched her arms out wide and imagined that hordes of summer-time beach revelers were lining the boardwalk. She imagined their picnic tables loaded with hot dogs, drinks, and salads. Their children were throwing Frisbees and playing with the family dogs. Bicycles, coolers, barbecues, baskets, umbrellas, towels, and shoes were strewn about, like a haphazard summer blanket on the beach sand and green grass.

The rain continued to fall and the darkness thickened and the clouds obscured the moon but Amelia felt happy, surrounded by the ghosts of happy people that she could see so clearly, with everyone enjoying themselves.

It's as if, she thought, those moments of joy are captured in time, and I'm the only one who can see them. And I get to play them over and over again, like a home movie except that I can step into the movie and become part of it. I don't ever want to lose this, no matter how 'normal' I need to pretend to be. This is my special magic, when time and place and people come to me, and I can see them and they're never lost.

She walked among hot dog vendors, and she watched sunbathers baking in bikinis while kids wheeled around on tricycles and old folk ate ice creams.

She walked through teams of little kids playing soccer in the central field, ringed by parents in camping chairs She walked past the tennis courts and heard the sound of balls being volleyed back and forth with that unmistakable and particular *thuk thuk thuk*.

She passed the lawn bowlers in their traditional whites, stooping to roll their balls. She entered the park and saw the immigrant families having their reunions, dressed in saris and clothes from home, firing up barbecues and chatting.

And finally, soaked to the bone, her thin T-shirt glued to her, her hair dripping, she caught the bus back home. She knew she was being stared at but she did not care. She was replete.

9. AMELIA AND HENRY

LATER THAT WEEK, AMELIA WENT to visit Henry in his mansion in Rosedale. She let herself into the house and found him in the living room, staring at the walls.

"Anything good happening, Dad?" she asked as he darted forward and corrected a line on a piece of paper tacked to the wall. He didn't seem to hear her and she waited while he made his annotation.

"Amelia!" He turned to her once he was done, delighted to see her. "Come and give your dad a hug! How are you?"

She hugged him, feeling the sharp jut of his bones through the thin silk dressing gown he was wearing over a pair of brightly-coloured boxer shorts. "Dad, have you been eating?"

"Of course," he said, jovially. "But I am on a roll here. I haven't been sleeping much. But who needs sleep? Everyone says you need this much sleep or that much, but what do they know? I think they sleep out of boredom. I've got too much exciting work to do to waste my time sleeping."

"I know what you mean," she said. "Dad, what if I am destined to live one of those boring lives like other people? I don't think I could stand that."

He stared at her. "I think you need a cup of tea," he said and he led her into the kitchen.

Amelia was no longer startled by the décor of the house but she didn't like the ghostly emptiness. Rather than minimalistic, she thought the house felt abandoned.

"How's the work going?" Amelia asked. "Dad, you really need a new dressing gown."

"Oh, there is no tea," Henry said, disappointed, rooting through bare cupboards. "Look, there is nothing here. I am sorry."

"I know Mom put in an order for your delivery this morning," Amelia said.

"There is soup," Henry said. "Would you like some soup?"

"There's always soup," Amelia laughed. "Yeah, Dad, I'll have some soup. Cream of broccoli."

"Excellent choice," Henry nodded his approval. "Tell me about you. What is happening in your life?"

"I'm afraid of being boring," Amelia told him.

"Ah right, you said that. And that led us to tea, which led us to soup. Let us explore this topic. What constitutes boring?"

"Doing things like everyone else," Amelia said promptly.

"But does one have a choice?" Henry asked. "If I had had a choice, I would have lived a normal life with you and your mother and been happy."

"Even if it meant giving up your poetry?"

"Yes, even then. My life is very hard work with not a lot of fun. The only time I ever had fun was when I was with your mother."

"So why didn't you stay with her?"

"I had no choice. You think my life is more interesting this way, than if I had stayed with her?"

"For sure! Of course."

"It is eccentric, and unusual, and it is who I am but it is no more or less boring than a fellow who has a family of four and a mortgage and a job at the bank that he hates."

"You hate your job?"

Henry paused for a moment. "Well, it is very tedious, some days. Trying to find that exact word. There are many words in my head but then sometimes I cannot find the right one and it drives me crazy, I tell you."

He laughed. He still had a beautiful deep laugh and a rich made-for-radio voice and Amelia loved to listen to him talk, but she loved it more when he laughed.

"Yeah, right, Dad," she said, smiling. "But your contribution to the world is worth more than some bank manager with a truckload of snotty kids. I mean, your contribution to the world is poetry! That's worth more than anything."

"But where would we be, if we didn't have bank managers? Or grocery stores, for example? I, for one, would be lost. Imagine me trying to farm and harvest my own food! I think, Amelia, that each of us in life has a job to do, and that job has moments of tedium and moments of joy. And that is just the way life is."

"Adult life isn't much fun," Amelia commented.

"That's a fact. Here's a spoon. Tell me if the soup is too hot."

Amelia tested the soup. "It's perfect."

Henry carried it over the marble island and they stood together, companionably sharing the soup from the pot.

"How is your thesis coming along?" Henry asked.

"It's better than it was. I thought I was getting road-blocked but I found a bunch of material to support my idea of Joan as a metaphor for freedom and imagination."

"Joan of Arc." Henry tapped his spoon on the pot and three tinny ringing sounds chimed. "Have you considered the possibility that you love her so much because you can relate to her?"

"Her solitary nature? Her ability to see the metaphoric and imagined dimensions of reality? Of course I have, Dad. And I do like her for that. People wanted to cage her and trap her, just like they want to trap me. That's my whole point. Joan wasn't afraid of death but she couldn't stand the idea of being cut off from the voice of her imagination and neither can I. I'd rather be dead too."

Henry looked at her thoughtfully. "Is there something going on that I am not aware of?"

"You know I'm in therapy?" Amelia asked and Henry was startled.

"No, I did not. You? Why?"

"Because of my so-called 'issues'. If I want to finish my thesis on Joan and one day be a teacher, which I don't even know if I do want to do, then I have to complete this course of therapy. If I don't go, I'll lose my welfare funding as well as my grant for university."

"I can give you money," Henry said. "I have always told you and your mother that."

"Yeah, well, Mom and Nana don't want you to, for some reason. I think they are worried that if you die, there'll be no money and then if I am no longer on the welfare system, I won't manage to make a living by myself."

"If I die, you and your Mom and Ethel get everything split three ways," Henry said. "However, I don't plan on dying for some time. Despite the tedium of trying to find the perfect word, I do actually like being alive."

"Why?"

"Why do I like being alive? Because it is fascinating! All of it is incredible! I marvel at life, Amelia, and I find it fascinating. Develop your powers of fascination, my child, and you will see that nothing is boring. Not really."

"Cream of broccoli soup is fascinating," Amelia said, teasing him, and he shook his spoon at her.

"It is! The nuances of taste, the saltiness, the very broccoli-ness of it! Magical, I tell you! But what is this therapy you have to go to?"

"It's called D.T.O.T., and it works in tandem with cognitive behavioural therapy. The doctor invented it himself, and D.T.O.T. stands for *Do The Opposite Thing*, and so whatever your phobia is, you have to do the opposite. One guy in our group is there for anger management and he got caught having sex with woman who has anxiety disorder and Dr. Carroll was very pleased. He said they were both finding ways to practice D.T.O.T., even if they weren't consciously aware of it."

Henry frowned. "Sounds over-simplistic to me," he said.

They finished the soup and Henry took the pot over to the sink and washed it carefully. "I mean," he added, rinsing the pot and putting it in the dish rack, "I could not do it. I could not just tell myself stop hearing voices—"

"You hear voices, Dad?" Amelia interrupted him. "I didn't know that."

Henry gave her a rueful smile. "Much like your beloved Joan. Although, by the way, some people thought she simply had tinnitus, epilepsy and schizophrenia."

"And anorexia and post-traumatic stress disorder and tuberculosis," Amelia said. "They can't bear the fact that she lived such a brave life. She heard her 'angel voices' on the church bell chimes. How do you hear yours?"

"They shout at me a lot. They are responsible for most of my poetry," Henry said. "I write down what they say. Which takes a lot of concentration, I will tell you that much. They all talk over each other and they yell at the same time, but thankfully they also repeat themselves a lot, too. So if I miss something the first time, I catch it on the next go round."

Amelia laughed. "You should hear how they dissect your words in a class, Dad! They can go on forever explaining how you reached certain logical conclusions. Apparently you find ways of expressing logic that no one has ever done before."

"Is that right?" Henry looked delighted.

"No one would believe they were just voices in your head," Amelia laughed.

"They are not *just* voices, my mocking child. They are the diverse and multiple facets of myself seeking expression. I simply have too many facets of thought for there to be only one channel of expression."

"That makes perfect sense," Amelia agreed. "Exactly like Joan. And me too, although I don't hear any voices, but I can see things other people can't."

"Do people at the university know that you are my daughter?"

"No, they don't, and not because I am ashamed of you, it's

the opposite. I can't live up to you, and that's my biggest fear. I'm not like you or Joan. I'm boring and ordinary, with no special gifts of madness, only annoying ones that inconvenience other people and won't ever let me live a happy life."

"That sounds like your mother talking," Henry said. "The annoying and inconvenient bit, I mean."

"Yes, she does worry. But she's right, Dad. What hope is there for me? I've never had a boyfriend and I doubt I ever will."

"Ah, so that's what this is about. I should have known. All of life boils down to two things: love and poetry. Although poetry may come first. Tell me about your love interest."

"There's nothing to tell. He's got a girlfriend."

"That is not cast in stone, sadly for her," he said.

"That's what Nana said."

"And how is Ethel?"

"I don't think she's well. She won't say but she's been taking a lot of naps and that's not like her."

"No, not like her at all. Has she seen a doctor?" Amelia could tell he was worried.

"She says she doesn't have to, that it will pass."

"Tell your mother about this." Henry was firm. "She might not notice what is going on, knowing her. But if you tell Megan, she'll do something about it."

"I will, Dad. Thanks for the soup and the chat. I'd better get going."

"Anytime."

He walked her through the empty hallway and Amelia noticed that everything sparkled and shone: the chandeliers, the parquet flooring, even the windows. "Do you get a cleaner in?" she asked.

"I do it myself," Henry said, proudly. "It is an excellent way to think. When your hands are busy doing menial tasks, your mind is freed up to run around and play. Some of my best ideas come to me when I am cleaning."

"I should try it," Amelia said, thinking about her room that looked like a disaster area. "If nothing else, it'd make Mom and Nana happy. Goodbye, Dad."

She hugged him and walked down the pathway, turning to wave when she got the end.

Henry waved back and then he closed the heavy wooden door. Amelia stared at the silent house, picturing him inside, going back to his papered walls to catch the messages from the voices with the butterfly net of his mind.

10. GROUP THERAPY: SESSION THREE

WHEN AMELIA RETURNED TO THE THIRD WEEK of Opposite Thinking therapy, as she had taken to calling it, she took care to sit down between Persephone and Ainsley and when Mike arrived, he looked disappointed. She avoided making eye contact with him and doodled on her notepad instead, ignoring the conversations going on around her. She did notice that he was particularly handsome in an open-collared steel-blue shirt and she was further saddened by the situation. In an effort to distract herself, she turned to chat to Ainsley and realized the girl was crying solemnly into a wad of tissue. Amelia wondered if she should say something but she couldn't think where to start and she returned her attention to her notepad.

"Hey, that's really good," Persephone said, looking at Amelia's drawing.

"You think so?" Amelia was surprised. "They're just weird scratching and caricatures that I do."

"You should do a graphic novel," Persephone said. "I love graphic novels. There's a whole world of them out there, right here in this city. I think you'd be great. What with your, I won't call it a disorder, your whatever-thingy, I bet you could imagine all sorts of things."

"That would be very true," Amelia said. "I did have an art teacher once and he said I showed a unique potential but I thought he was being kind because I was being home-schooled and couldn't even go to a normal school."

"Normal schools are very no great shakes—" Persephone started to say but just then Dr. Carroll flapped into the room, breathless and shaking.

"Late, I'm sorry, I am a bit late!" He sat down with a heavy thump and took out his notes and looked around. "I supposed Alexei and Whitney are at it again? Can someone go and get them?"

"I will," Joanne said, getting up.

"In the meantime," Dr. Carroll said. "Let's have a quick, and I do mean quick, no rambling streams of consciousness, thank you very muc, a quick check-in as to how your week was and specifically if you made any progress with D.T.O.T. Ainsley, I see you are back. You can start."

"I broke up with my fiancé like you said and I'm not happier. I'm very, very sad," she wailed. "I can't stop crying. I feel horrible."

"Firstly, I did not tell you to break up with your fiancé. I never tell you to do a thing or not to do a thing."

"That's not true," Shannon interjected. "You told me to take that elevator and I nearly died of fright."

"Don't interrupt please, Shannon. You'll get your turn. And secondly, Ainsley, you are simply working through a plethora of emotions right now, which, although it may not feel like it, is great. Carry on! You are resolving issues and making progress."

The door opened and Alexei and Whitney staggered in, followed by Joanne.

"Welcome, sex fiends!" Dr. Carroll said cheerfully. "Take a seat. Next we'll have Angelina. Any progress on making an actual medical appointment?"

Angelina shook her head mournfully and Dr. Carroll sighed audibly.

Amelia was reminded of her father's words to tell her mother about Ethel. She scratched a reminder on her notepad and missed the advice that Dr. Carroll doled out to Angelina.

"David?"

"Spoke to more clients. I even took one out for dinner."

"Excellent. Whitney, are you feeling less anxious?"

"I'm loving life! Things are much better at home too and my daughter is much more cheerful." Whitney cast a big smile at Alexei.

"And I have my anger issues under control," Alexei said, folding his hands across his belly, his long legs stretched out in front of him.

"Great! Shannon?"

"I've got nothing to say. I didn't take any elevators or go in any revolving doors and if anything, my fear is worse. I had trouble even taking the subway to come here."

"That's good," Dr. Carroll said encouragingly. "Before improvement, there is regression. Have faith. Persephone?"

She looked downcast. "Nothing. A nothing-much week really."

"Did you leave the house?"

"Ah, yeah, well…"

"Did you leave the house? Yes or no."

"No."

"Well then, moving on. Amelia?"

"I took a few buses that I was supposed to," Amelia admitted, and in so doing, she felt as if she had betrayed herself.

"And how did you feel?"

"Like a lemming, a suburban lemming, headed for a tedious, deathly-dull life."

"Humph," Dr. Carroll snorted. "A lemming, eh? You are overly attached to your idea of your uniqueness. You can still be singularly unique and yet, do the things that the rest of the world does. Think about that, please. Mike?"

Mike shrugged. "I was supposed to talk to a lot of people about a lot of things but I didn't."

"Classic avoidance. I would say that list of people was too long. I suggest you pick one person per week. You need to break it down to manageable parts. Joanne? Any toilet weeping?"

She shook her head, her twisted mouth grim, her cheeks sucked inward. "I haven't cried in the washroom, but now I sit in there for hours. I can't go back to my desk. I just sit there, on the toilet, trying to propel myself to get back to work. And I can't move and I get so behind, and then I have to work all night to get things finished, to do the things I was supposed to have done during the day."

"You hate your job," Dr. Carroll said, simply. "And you have no after-hours life, do you?"

Joanne shook her head.

"Work on finding something you like to do at night. For example, find a club of Scrabble players or something. I've got no idea what your interests are, but there will be something. You need to find a community and become part of it."

"Groups of people annoy me," Joanne said. "Everybody talks at the same time."

"Groups of people are merely gatherings of interesting individuals," Dr. Carroll retorted. "You need to approach life from the opposite direction. I can't make you do it, but it would help if you tried. Opposite, people, think opposite! You're being a little slow to catch on here. D.T.O.T., remember?" He consulted his notepad. "We're missing Gino today. Kwon chose to leave and pay the price. Goodbye, Kwon."

Just then Gino burst in and he looked frantic and sweaty.

"Gino, have a seat," Dr. Carroll waved at him. "How was your week?"

"Not good." Gino was breathing heavily and he hugged his jacket tightly to him.

"It happens," Dr. Carroll said. "You missed check-in, your bad. We'll hear from you later. People, this week we are going to concentrate on problem solving. I want each of you to write down a problem you have. Not your usual big phobia but a little problem, like say for instance, you don't visit a relative that you feel you should, or your neighbour drives you nuts by playing music at all hours, or some girl sits next to you and chews her lunch too loudly. Come on, all of you, write down one thing."

Amelia chewed on her pen. She didn't think she had any problems apart from her main one. She thought hard and wrote: *I can't make myself tidy up my room.*

She finished and looked up and saw Mike staring at her with desperation and she wanted to rush across the room and kiss him, regardless of the situation or timing. She dropped her gaze and gnawed on her pen instead.

"Joanne? What did you write down?"

"I can't choose clothes when I go shopping. I'll stare at a thing for hours and then I will leave without buying anything."

"Hmm." Dr. Carroll didn't seem to find that one particularly appealing. "David?"

"I procrastinate when it comes to doing chores around the house, like taking out the garbage or changing batteries in the fire alarm."

"I see." Dr. Carroll wasn't keen on that one either.

"I hoard things," Angelina piped up suddenly in a breathy voice and Dr. Carroll perked up. Amelia could almost see his nose twitching with excitement.

"You do? Really? Tell us more. Be specific and detailed."

"I have a lot of newspapers. A lot." Angelina paused to think for a moment. "The newspapers line the hallway, floor to ceiling. And I have boxes filled with things, boxes piled on top of each other."

"Filled with what kind of things?"

"Old telephones, alarm clocks, broken dolls, children's toys, and clothes from when the children were babies."

"How old are your children now?"

"Oh, in their forties. They've got kids of their own but they don't want my broken old stuff and they keep trying to get me to get rid of it but I can't."

"I thought you were married?" Dr. Carroll shuffled through some notes.

"I was, but my husband died a year ago. Stomach cancer."

"Was this when your phobia about medical appointments began?"

"No, I had that long before but him dying of cancer didn't help."

"Back to your hoarding, would you categorize yourself as being as bad as those people on TV?"

"Well. Bad? That sounds so judgmental. Would I say I have as much stuff as they do? Yes. I guess. My living room, spare bedroom, my bedroom, and even the bathroom are filled pretty much to the ceiling and it's hard to get inside. For a while, I had so much stuff that I had to put it into the bathtub and I showered at the YWCA. But then my daughter threatened to get rid of my stuff herself, and I couldn't bear to let her touch it, so I cleaned out the bathtub. I've got lots of books and magazines too, oh, and bottles. Empty bottles."

"You mean alcohol bottles?"

"No, I don't drink! I mean shampoo bottles and dish deter-gent bottles and I've got no idea why I keep them."

"Wow. Excellent. I mean not excellent per se, but an excellent problem for us to try to help you to solve."

"Oh, and I've got rabbits too."

"What?"

"Rabbits. They've got the run of the house and there's rab-bit poo everywhere although I do try to clean it up. And they chew things, so there's a lot of chewed up stuff. And there's their food, of course, and their water dishes."

"I see." Dr. Carroll was momentarily at a loss for words. "Why has this not come up before?" he asked. "Surely this would have been acknowledged as a problem before now? It sounds fairly large scale?"

"Yes, it is. But I'm here for anxiety and not being able to make appointments and keep them. I thought that if I could get rid of my anxiety, then I would be able to tackle my issues with hoarding."

"How many years has this been going on? It must have been while your husband was still alive?"

"Oh, yes, but he never minded. As long as I left an area clear around his lounge chair and the TV, it was fine."

"And your children? They grew up in among all this stuff?"

"Yes, and it always annoyed them. They were always trying to throw my stuff away and I wouldn't let them. When they were in their teens, we got them a trailer and we put it in the garden and they lived in that."

"Fascinating."

Dr. Carroll wasn't the only one mesmerized by Angelina's story. The entire group was leaning forward in their seats, eager to hear what she would say next but Angelina just shrugged. "That's it," she said.

"Well." Dr. Carroll leaned back in his chair and folded his hands behind his head. "I propose we take a short break for a meditation and we think about this. We're not supposed to actually think about specific things when we meditate but in this instance, we need to take a moment."

"I hope you can help me," Angelina said, looking around, her chins wobbling and her face earnest.

Amelia thought about her father's house and how empty it was. She imagined his horror at being confronted by Angelina's abode.

Dr. Carroll set his alarm clock and rang the bell. The room was eerily silent during the meditation. Amelia wanted to open her eyes and look at Mike but she didn't want him to see her doing it, so she kept her eyelids pressed firmly shut, and she clenched her hands in her lap. She felt sorry for Angelina but all she could think about was Mike and she relived the memory of his kiss instead.

Ding! The bell sounded and everyone opened their eyes and sat there, blinking in the silence.

"Well." Dr. Carroll rubbed his hands together and leaned forward. "Does anyone have any ideas to help Angelina? Don't be shy, people. This is how it works. We brainstorm together, so you say whatever you think and the ball gets rolling that way."

"She could start at one end of the house and fill a bag of junk every day," Shannon suggested.

"If I did that, it would take me the rest of my life to clear out one room," Angelina said.

"Then get one of those massive containers that you can get delivered to you," Dave suggested. "You can fill up to the top with crap and then, when you're ready, you phone them and they'll take it away."

"I tried that," Angelina said despondently. "But in the middle of the night, I climbed in to get some of my stuff back and I fell in and broke my arm. So they had to take the box away and I never dared get one again."

There was silence.

"More ideas, people, more ideas, come on!" Dr. Carroll said.

"You could have an open house," Amelia suggested. "Invite people to come in and take what they want?"

"I tried giving things away," Angelina said, "but then at the last minute, I took everything back. And most of the stuff is rubbish, I admit that."

"And the newspapers?" Mike asked. "I don't get the newspapers."

"There might be something I want to read in them," Angelina said, earnestly. "I might have missed something, and I like knowing they are there for me to refer to."

"There are archives and online resources for that," Joanne said but Angelina shook her head.

"They don't keep everything, like I do. I am much more organized than them, and I don't make arbitrary decisions like they do about what to keep and what to take out."

"Why don't you contact that TV show that helps hoarders?" Whitney asked. "I bet they'd love to have you on it."

"My daughter tried that and there was a long waiting list, so long, I'd probably never even get on the show. There are more of us in the world than you think."

"God help us," David said. "My wife collects dolls and those tiny spoons and even that drives me mad."

"At least those have value," Joanne commented.

"Some of my stuff has value," Angelina objected.

"Circles, we're going in circles, people," Dr. Carroll said. "Come on, we have to come up with something new. Ideas?"

The group sat studying their fingernails.

"What do you think, Dr. Carroll?" Persephone asked.

"I think that apart from Angelina burning down her entire house and starting from scratch, I don't have any suggestions," Dr. Carroll admitted.

"That's stupid!" Gino burst out and Dr. Carroll looked at him.

"Is it really? She seems to have tried everything else."

"But the rabbits!" Angelina said. "What about the rabbits? I can't burn them too!"

"How many are there?"

"I have no idea. They are rabbits and so there are a lot, and more keep coming."

"You'd have to get wildlife services in first, I guess," Dr. Carroll said and he sounded tired. "Anyway, we need to move on."

"But you haven't helped her," Gino said. "And look at Ainsley sitting there, still crying. What good are you, doctor? And look at that little Asian guy who didn't come back and you never listen to me either."

"Tell me, Gino," Dr. Carroll said patiently, "what are you trying to tell me that I'm not hearing?"

"That I need your help! Like Angelina needs your help! We came here so you would help us, but you don't do anything but cause more damage and pain."

"I'm not a magician," Dr. Carroll said in a mild tone. "And besides, this is only the third session. Why don't we continue and then see if you still feel the same about me at the end?"

"I can't wait that long, I can't." Gino started crying. "Yesterday I was humiliated in a meeting. Someone asked me a question, a very simple question, and I couldn't get my voice to say anything. I sat there, turning more and more red in the face and finally someone else answered for me. I got up and rushed from the room. I couldn't face anyone so I left the building and then today I phoned in sick. I waited the whole day to come here and you have to help me now, so I can go back to my job tomorrow."

"Oh my God!" Dr. Carroll shouted and the whole group looked at him. "Who and what exactly do you people think I am? You all come here with problems you've been carefully creating for decades and then you expect me to fix you in a day or two? It's always the same thing: you have the same ridiculous expectations, time in, and time out. Think about it, people, how long have you been this way? Let's go around the room. Each of you ask yourselves, how long have you had your problem and what have you done up until now to fix it? Angelina, how long would you say you've been hoarding and anxiety-ridden?"

"About fifty-five years," Angelina whispered.

"You see!" Dr. Carroll said. "And yet, I am expected to fix that in one day. I'm expected to go up to this white board and write down one sentence that will not only cure Angelina but all of you. Well, there is no magic secret. It doesn't work like that. It's a long hard road, and you need to commit to it and take responsibility for yourselves. I can show you the way but I can't make you walk the path. That's up to you."

"So," Gino said in a small voice. "What should I do about work?"

"Go back. Just go back," Dr. Carroll said and he sounded exhausted. "It's the opposite of staying at home, so it's good enough. Just go back."

"I can't go back," Gino said and he was still crying, dribbling sad tears, and he must have been wearing makeup because his tears left watery black trails down his face. "I can't. I feel so stupid. They laughed at me."

"Who cares about them? Gino, you need to care less. 'They' and that goes for all the 'theys' out there, they only matter as much as you let them. You can take control by thinking, 'I don't care what you think. I do a good job. So what if I'm not great at public speaking and so what if meetings make me nervous, that doesn't make me any less of a success in my job.' You can say that and mean it. Write it down and say it to yourself a hundred times a day and make it your truth. You can choose, Gino, whether to care of not."

"No," Gino whispered, "I can't. Because *I do care.* And I will always care. And they will always laugh at me. I'm a stupid failure and I always have been."

He reached into his jacket pocket and pulled out a gun. Angelina and Joanne, who were sitting next to him, sprang in opposite directions. The rest of the group pushed themselves back in their chairs as if trying to teleport into the next room through the walls.

Dr. Carroll seemed unperturbed. "I see," he said and his little eyes glittered. "And how long have you had the gun?"

"It was one my cousin's. I stole it from him years ago. He's so stupid. He thought he lost it."

"And what are you planning to do? Kill me or kill yourself?"

"Me, but maybe you first, and maybe Shannon too because she said I was a pervert and I'm not."

"I'm sorry," Shannon sputtered.

"No, you're not," Gino said and he waved the gun at her. "You're just saying that. Maybe I should take you into the elevator and have sex with you right now, that would serve you right."

"Yeah, as if you could get it up," Joanne said, sarcastically and he swung the gun towards her.

"Now, now," Dr. Carroll said. "Let's stay calm. Trading insults isn't going to help anyone."

Gino stood up and he sidled around the room, so that his back was against the door. "All of you, he shouted, get up and move to the corner. Stand there. Now Dave, move the chairs to that wall and stack them. Do it now, do it!"

"Sure, no problem, buddy," Dave said and he edged towards the chairs, lifting the one nearest to him.

"I'm not your buddy! You didn't even know who I was till now. All you do is whine about yourself and your stupid stuff, so don't think you can fool me, 'buddy'."

While Dave stacked the chairs, Gino waved the gun at the others. "Sit down, with your backs against the wall."

Amelia ended up sitting next to Mike and, despite the circumstances, she was thrilled. Their shoulders and the whole length of their arms were touching and Mike rested his hand on top of hers, which was palm down against the floor. She could feel the linen of his shirt sleeve brushing her bare skin, and he smelled wonderful: spicy, clean, soapy and masculine.

Amelia did not want to move, ever again. She would have been happy to stay like that for days, at least she was until Gino started shouting again.

"Doc! Are you listening to me?"

"Yes," Dr. Carroll said and Amelia could have sworn he sounded bored. "Yes, Gina, I mean Gino, what is it?"

"Gina! You called me Gina!" Gino was practically foaming at the mouth.

"A slip of the tongue," Dr. Carroll said. "What did you want to tell me?"

"How did you know?" Gino nearly shrieked.

"Know what?" Dr. Carroll looked perplexed. "I have no idea what you are talking about."

"Gina! How did you know about Gina?"

"There are some things a doctor just knows," Dr. Carroll said wisely, while the rest of the group knew as well as he did that he had no idea what was going on with Gino.

"So, then, can I?"

"Can you what? I am sorry, Gino. I am not following you here."

"Can I have a sex change?"

"Ah. Well, that's not a simple procedure to get state approval for, by any means. But let's not rule it out," he said, hastily when Gino frowned and was clearly unimpressed by Dr. Carroll's reply.

"Tell me more about Gina," Dr. Carroll said. "That would be very useful in helping us move the whole process forward, okay? Work with me here. Gina, if I may call you that. When did you first become aware that you were a female and not a male?"

"My mother knew," Gino said. He waved Dave down into a seated position and then he too slid down with his back against the frosted glass door.

"My mother knew," he continued. "But it was our secret, hers and mine. *La mia bellissima Gina*, she would call me. I had no father, you see. He left my mother when she got pregnant. The pig! But we didn't need him, my Mammi had me, her little *principessa*."

Mike squeezed Amelia's hand and a shiver ran through her belly. She nudged her body weight ever so slightly in his direction. Mike wrapped his fingers around hers and she cupped her palm towards his.

"How old were you when she started dressing you in girl's clothes?" Dr. Carroll asked conversationally.

"She did it ever since I can remember. She put makeup on me too. But only when we were alone. One time, *zia* Paola, my mother's sister, came to visit and I was in my little ballerina outfit and *zia* Paola, she shouted at my Mammi." Gino smoothed his bangs carefully, keeping the gun balanced on his upraised knees and steadying it with one hand.

"How old were you when your mother died?" Dr. Carroll asked.

"I was nine. And *zia* Paola and her husband took me to live with them and their four horrible sons. They laughed at me all the time, and *zia* Paola, she took me to one side and she said,

'Gino, that ballet dress nonsense, none of that here, you hear me?' And I nodded and we never spoke of it again."

"But you would dress up in her clothes whenever you knew you were home alone?" Dr. Carroll said and Gino nodded sadly.

"And then, when I earned my own money, I bought my own clothes and makeup and I moved to my own apartment where I could be me."

"There's something I don't understand," Dr. Carroll said. "Why do you keep hitting on Shannon if you really feel like you are a woman?"

Gino looked shamefaced. "My cousins did that to women. They would grab them and shout things, sexual things. I tried to copy them from when I was a teenager because I thought that if I could just be a normal man, then all my problems would go away. And now, when I get stressed, it's like a reaction that I can't stop. I am sorry," he said to Shannon. "I didn't mean it."

"It's okay," she said.

"I'm not a pervert," he insisted and Shannon nodded.

"It's okay, Gino," she said.

"Gina," he corrected her.

The others in the group sat silent as mice, unmoving and hardly breathing.

"I can see that you couldn't be you, the real you, in the real world, could you?" Dr. Carroll said and Gino nodded.

Dr. Carroll studied his fingernails. Then he frowned and nodded. "We've done wonderful work today, Gina. Not that I think the methodology was sound, meaning the gun, etcetera, etcetera, but nevertheless, progress is progress and I applaud your bravery in being so forthcoming. Now, if you'll let the others go, I will put the paperwork into action for getting you that sex change you want and we can go on our way until next week. What do you say to that?"

Gino shook his head. "No. Nobody leaves until the paperwork is signed, sealed, and delivered to me here. Nobody leaves."

"But Gina," Dr. Carroll objected and he sounded annoyed,

"you know that's not reasonable. These things take a long time."

"My point exactly. And I don't have any more time and neither do you, Doctor."

"Hmm. I understand your point." Dr. Carroll stared up at the ceiling. "Give me a moment, will you, Gina, to think about what to do. Can you do that? Can you give me a moment?"

"Five minutes," Gino said, looking at his watch.

"I can help you," Joanne said.

"What do you mean?" Gino asked. "What can you do?"

"I'm a lawyer, right? I can put your demands into legalese, and get the paperwork done for you. Trust me, I'm a much better legal negotiator then the doctor here."

"She's right," Dr. Carroll agreed. "If it's airtight and legal you want, then Joanne's the one for you. Not me. Joanne can make it happen pronto, meanwhile it could take years with me doing it, and I doubt we'd survive that, if we all have to stay in this room together for the duration."

Gino eyed Joanne. "How can I trust you?"

She shrugged. "You do or you don't, it's up to you. I am offering you my expertise."

"Gina, I know it's hard for you to accept the hand of friendship," Dr. Carroll said. "But try, please, try."

Gino looked at Joanne. He was breathing hard. "What would you do?"

Joanne raised her hands slowly. "I am going to reach for my briefcase and then I'm going to come over there, and we'll draw up a contract of your demands and we will find a way to get it to the director of the hospital and get him to sign off on it. But first steps first, are you okay with me reaching for my bag and getting a notepad and pen?"

Gino nodded. "But don't come too close with me. Sit there," he pointed with the gun.

"Fine." Joanne was reassuring and her movements were slow and steady.

By this time, Amelia and Mike were practically glued to one

another, from hip to ankle and he was rubbing her palm with his thumb and it was so astoundingly sensual that Amelia felt transported and dizzy. She was hardly aware of the drama going on around her. All she could feel was the silvery tingling of every nerve ending in her body and her eyelids drooped with pleasure.

She half-noticed Joanne scooting over to Gino, sliding over on her bum, and sitting where he had directed her.

"I need to pee,' she heard Persephone say and she looked up and tried to concentrate on what was happening.

"Gina?" Dr. Carroll asked. "Can we please let Persephone out? She needs to use the toilet."

"No!" Gino shouted. "I am not stupid. Wet your pants for all I care."

"Fine, then I will," Persephone yelled and Ainsley and Angelina, who were on either side of her, shifted as far away as they could.

"Try to hold it in," Dr. Carroll advised Persephone. "How's it going over there?" he asked, turning to face Joanne.

"Fine," Joanne said, scribbling something. "Okay, Gino, Gina, sign here."

She shifted her weight towards him and Gino turned his attention to the piece of paper she had handed him. In one fluid movement, from her crouched position, Joanne rushed at Gino, and karate-chopped the gun upwards. She punched Gino soundly in jaw with her other hand as she did so. When he fell over sideways, she punched him in the gut for good measure, knocking the wind out of him, and then she kicked the gun, which skittered across the room, finally coming to a stop under one of the chairs.

Joanne hastily got up, retrieved the gun and emptied the clip of bullets, then laid it carefully on the table.

Dr. Carroll had grabbed his bag and pulled out a walkie-talkie. An alarm sounded throughout the hospital.

Code White on Level Eight! Code White on Level Eight!

"That's for us," Dr. Carroll said. "Everybody stay calm. Security will be here now."

Gino was lying on the ground in a fetal position, trying to catch his breath.

"That was so impressive," Whitney said to Joanne, who shrugged.

"Black belt," she said. "I haven't been to a class in years but it came back to me when I needed it."

"And the way you handled the gun too," Whitney's eyes were shining.

"My dad was a cop." Joanne was nonchalant as she pulled out one of the stacked chairs, sat down and crossed her long legs.

Dave got up and started reorganizing the chairs and then he helped Angelina to her feet and got her seated.

Two security guards rushed into the room and Dr. Carroll pointed to Gino who was still writhing on the floor. "Him. Take him to psych and lock him up. And please take this ugly gun too and put it somewhere safe. Call the police, but I'll only be able to talk to them in an hour. I must debrief my group first."

The security guards hauled Gino to his feet and led him out of the room.

The rest of the group straggled back into their chairs and Amelia, feeling stoned and post-orgasmic, sank down into her seat, unable to look at Mike who was staring at her with unrestrained longing.

Persephone had rushed out to use the washroom and by the time she returned, things had somewhat normalized.

"So," Dr. Carroll asked, "how is everybody?"

"You are a terrible therapist," Mike said. "I don't know if I want to come back and I don't care if I owe you any money after today."

"Now, now," Dr. Carroll admonished. "You are, as always, seeing things quite back to front. Gino was close to the edge from the start. That was plain to see. And this was an enormous breakthrough. Now that I am aware of what his true issues are, I can give him some real help, one-on-one, and we can monitor him as an in-patient. Generally speaking, it's very good when a patient acts out like that because it signifies a turning point in their healing. How are you, Mike? How has your week been?"

"I told you already. You see, you never listen!"

"I do listen," Dr. Carroll said, tiredly. "Today's session hasn't exactly been without some surprising and distracting elements."

"I don't care about me," Mike said. "But what about Angelina? You have to do something to help her, other than tell her to burn down her house."

"And I will. Angelina, do you want help with your hoarding or not?"

"I don't know," she said, looking troubled. "I guess I'd just like other people to be okay with it."

"Sounds like a health hazard," Joanne said. "And a fire hazard."

"Let me think about it," Angelina said. "I'll tell you next week if I think I can cope with changing the situation. Right now, I don't know if I can. You're right, Dr. Carroll. I did want a magic sentence to make everything all right. I wanted the magic sentence to be a way to make everybody else all right with it, the way it is. I didn't want it to be a way for me to have to change. I don't think I do want to change and right now, after today, the only thing I want is to be safely back home, surrounded by the comfort of my things and my bunnies."

"That's very honest of you, Angelina, and I thank you," Dr. Carroll said, and Angelina beamed.

"We should try to be as honest as we can, with ourselves," Dr. Carroll said, and he seemed to be talking mostly to himself. "Let's have a quick go around and see how everybody is doing and then we can reconvene next week. David, let's start with you, how are you, right now? How are you feeling?"

"Fine. But I lied. Things aren't good. I didn't take anybody out for dinner. I said that things were better but they aren't.

I get into work and my staff begin to arrive and I feel the first grip of fear seize my gut. It's like a hand dips down my throat, reaches into my gut and holds my intestines in its fist. My thoughts go like this: I will not do a good job. I will lose my temper. I will cry. I will walk out. I will humiliate myself in front of everybody. I will ruin everything I've worked so hard to build. I will make costly mistakes. I will be revealed for being a fraud. And never mind my thoughts, my body hurts from head to toe. I have tension in my jaw. My shoulders are as stiff as boards and my gut is gripped by that giant fist. Then I think to myself that this will all end badly. I will lose concentration. I will lose control. Everything will end badly. I'd better not leave my desk or answer the phone because if I do, all hell will break lose."

"Ah. I see. No, actually, I meant about today. The gun incident, how are you feeling about that?"

"Oh, fine. Gino was a wingnut. Anybody could see that right off the bat." David sighed. "Don't worry, Doc. I'll be here next week. I know Rome wasn't built in a day even though it burned down pretty damn quick. Goes to show you how quickly things can fall apart. See what I mean? Look how long it took them to build Rome and then what, three days and it was gone? That's like my life. Took me all this time to build it and it can destroyed in a day."

"I hear you," Dr. Carroll said quietly. "I hear you, David. But your Rome will not burn down. Trust me. Believe in me. I know it's hard but keep doing your exercises. Keep trying to do D.T.O.T. and things will get better. Alexei, how are you?"

"I am all right. I feel stupid for not being the one to get the gun from him. He took me by surprise. I never thought such a worried little man would do such a thing." Alexei cast a glance at Whitney. "I should have knocked him to the ground."

"You feel emasculated," Dr. Carroll mused. "It happened so fast. Mike, David, do you feel like you should have been the ones to tackle Gino instead of a woman?"

Mike shook his head. "No way, I don't care. Joanne was great."

David also shook his head. "She's got skills I don't have. I don't care either way. I'm not a fighting man."

"But I am a fighting man," Alexei was upset. "And then, when it counted, I sat here and did nothing."

"It was an unusual situation," Dr. Carroll said. "You're being too hard on yourself, Alexei."

Alexei looked over at Whitney but she was looking at Joanne.

"So, then…" Dr. Carroll seemed unsure how to continue. "You're all good then? Good to go? Shannon, how are you?"

She smiled broadly. "It was quite exciting."

"Okay. Ainsley?"

"I don't give a shit. The only thing I want to do is go home and tell my fiancé that I'm sorry I broke up with him. I hope he'll take me back and if he doesn't, I will never forgive you."

"Okay. And Persephone?"

"I'm pretty freaked," Persephone said. She was shaking and quivering. "There was this guy, one time, he was homeless, and I was in charge of a homeless shelter and he waved a gun at me. Turned out to be a fake gun but I didn't know."

Her shaking increased until her whole body was shuddering and she fell forward, sobbing loudly.

"I'll have to attend to this," Dr. Carroll said with a sigh to the rest of the group. "If anyone else needs seeing to, please wait behind. Anyone who's okay, off you go, and toodle-loo. I'll see you next week."

Amelia took him at his word and she ran. She chose the opposite direction to the route she and Mike had taken the previous week, and she ran like the wind.

Once she was outside, Amelia walked the perimeter of the hospital and then she spotted Mike coming out the front door. She hugged herself close to the wall, and made sure she was hidden. She held her hand to her crotch and she was sure she could still feel the heat radiating.

She sank down on her haunches for a moment, her hand between her legs, holding tight, and she thought about the crazy group. Angelina with her hoarding, Gino-Gina and the gun, Persephone and her meltdown, but most of all she thought about Mike.

She rushed home.

The house was quiet and Nana was napping. Before she could forget again, she sent her mother a text message: *Nana is sleeping too much. Dad says you must take her to the doc.*

Then she lay back on her bed with her eyes closed, unzipped her jeans and slid her hand inside.

11. GROUP THERAPY: SESSION FOUR

Amelia was late for the next meeting. She had taken the right bus but she missed her stop and had to wait for the return bus, which took fifteen minutes.

When she arrived, she was happy to see Mike wedged in between Joanne and David so she sat down in between Ainsley and Angelina.

"How are you?" Ainsley asked happily as she turned toward Amelia and flashed her enormous engagement ring. "We got back together! Now I am living in fear of being mugged and having my ring stolen. I am convinced someone is going to try to steal it. I went into a McDonald's the other day and I swear, this group of kids was looking at me, figuring out how to jump me and steal it."

"Is it insured?" Amelia asked.

"Yes, but I don't want my finger cut off!"

"They won't cut your finger off," Angelina said, dismissively. "That's just stupid and unrealistic."

Amelia wondered why Angelina was being so aggressive and she also wondered where Dr. Carroll was.

"Like it's realistic that you'll die if you get rid of the crap that fills up your house? People in glass houses and all that," Ainsley snapped back.

"We're here because we have issues," Mike said, standing up. "We all know that. Attacking each other isn't helpful." He looked at Angelina and as if by a pre-arranged signal, she got up and they switched seats. "You can't avoid me," Mike whispered quietly to Amelia.

"You've got a girlfriend," she hissed at him. "But that didn't stop you from doing what you did, did it?"

"I can't seem to help myself when I'm around you," he said.

"Did you tell your girlfriend about me?"

Mike blushed. "No, I didn't. I need to know if you think there's anything between us before I do that. I love her. We've been together since high school and—"

"High school sweethearts, yeah, we know the story." Amelia said, bitterly. "I'm no competition for such a pure and true love."

"Amelia! What's got into you?"

"Nothing. You think you know me? You think I'm nice and sweet and compliant? You think I'm going to sigh with happiness that you want me and that I'll fall into your arms and be the perfect girlfriend? Is that what you want me to tell you, before you break up with your girlfriend? Well, I can't say it. I have never been, nor will I ever be, the perfect girlfriend. I couldn't be that way, even if I wanted to and believe me, there are times when I'd like nothing more."

"You're putting too much pressure on yourself," Mike said and he took her hand. His hand felt so huge and warm and strong, and she wanted to cry because it felt so good. His skin was rougher than hers and she gripped his fingers, never wanting to let go.

"You see what's between us!" Mike said, grinning, his fine facial hair scraggly and rough and she wanted to mash that soft mouth, and kiss the fine hair that would tickle her lips.

"I see what?"

"That we've got chemistry! We're dynamite!"

"A solid basis for a stable relationship," Amelia observed wryly.

"*You* want stable? Seriously? I thought you'd want something exciting, something new every day."

"No, you're wrong. I want passion, yes, and I want to be able to show you my world. I've got keys to the doors of worlds that no one else knows exists. I want to show you that and I want to know that I can trust you, and then the world will magically revolve around us like a carousel but I want you and me to be—"

"…The fixed centre of gravity." He finished her thought.

"Yes. But even as I say that, I don't know if I can do it. I want to do it but I don't know if I can. I can't promise you anything."

"Except the possibility of you being the best damn thing that ever happened to me," he replied.

They were whispering, lost in their own world, unaware of the dynamic in the room around them when David's loud voice jolted them back to reality.

"Where's the doc, eh? He's twenty minutes late. That's not kosher."

"Are you Jewish?" Shannon asked.

"What's that got to do with anything?" David was aggressive.

"Nothing. I'm Jewish so I just wondered."

"Ah. Well, yeah, I am."

"Fucking Jews ruined my country," Alexei growled, stretching his long legs out in front of him and cracking his knuckles.

"Don't blame the Jews because the shiksa goddess is doing the karate champion in the washroom this week instead of you," David countered.

Amelia and Mike sat up in shock. "What's going on?" Mike asked.

"Whitney is more turned on by lawyer-by-day, Angelina Jo-lie-by-night than she is by big bad Alexei," Ainsley explained.

Alexei flushed red and he flicked his hair back from his forehead. "She was a useless fuck," he said. "Who cares?"

"You do," Shannon said. "But she's not the only woman in this room, you know."

"You?" David piped up. "You'd like to get one thrown into you by the Russian mafia bad boy?"

"Since we're here in therapy, baring our deepest secrets, I'd say yeah, he could put his shoes under my bed any time," Shannon said.

"I can keep my shoes on, baby," Alexei said, grinning at her. "I just need to drop my trousers."

Shannon was so clearly aroused by this idea that there was practically steam rising from her head. She was writhing in her chair in such a way that Amelia wondered if she was going to get up and do a lap dance on the giant Russian's groin, but Dr. Carroll burst in, his hands held up in supplication.

"I apologize, I apologize," he said. "*Mea culpa*. Nobody's perfect. A fact which if you'd internalize, would make your own lives much more tolerable and less tormenting but then hey, I'd be out of a job and where's the fun in that? You all carry on being neurotic and I'll carry on trying to unscramble your tangled wiring."

He sat down. "We lost Gino," he said matter-of-factly. "He managed to hang himself in his private room. I wanted him in a dorm where it's not so easy to self harm…. I take that back. You can self-harm, but generally not to the point of self-extinction. So, *sayonara* Gino, and we will meditate on that for a while later. Now today—"

"Aren't you accountable?" David interrupted, incensed. "*Sayonara?* That's all you've got to say? How can you be so callous! You are our healer and because of you, Gino killed himself! What the fuck! Somebody has to take responsibility! Somebody has to take the *blame!*"

"Not so, David, not so. That's a very antiquated way of looking at cause and effect. There are myriad causes for every event. So many, in fact, that we can't account for them all. We can't even find them. We can't track down the root cause of anything because for each individual that is different. For one person it was good that his mommy tucked him in tightly at night while for his brother, it was hell. And what causes that? Genetics? Who knows anything about genetics really, except that we don't understand it. Gino was a crockpot stew of bubbling disturbed identities. He had the misfortune of having a mother who wanted a little girl, so he never stood a chance. Throw in peer group pressure and the devastating undertow tug of loneliness, add to it the onset of adulthood — adulthood! Man! Life's just too hard for some people."

Dr. Carroll paused for breath, cracked open a bottle of water and drank it in a series of loud glugging swallows. "The period of adolescence," he continued, "gets the primo attention. We have pity on the poor, suffering, hormonally-confused adolescent who is packed to the gills with the explosives of crazy rage and burning lust and incomprehensible desire. But it's okay, we understand what's going on, because they're adolescents. Everybody agrees they allowed their teenage dose of craziness. *But*, and here's the biggest *but* of all … why, and I truly do ask do ask *why* — and I ask you to consider it with the utmost seriousness that you can muster — *why* do people expect all that crap to suddenly vanish when we reach the age categorized as adulthood?"

He looked around with an imploring expression on his face. "What, like some magic switch is flicked and your neuroses, your unrequited love affairs, your pathetic crushes, your wars with your parents and siblings, they going to vanish, because you're wearing a spanking shiny new adult suit? Look at you, hot off the production line, Model Adult, virgin pure, no clicks on the mileage. But that's not true and you know it. Your gears are already stripped, your engine overheats and your accelerator cable snaps when you're on a deserted road. You enter the Nascar race of adulthood fundamentally flawed and ruined. Your engine is shaky, your body work is weak and yet, you're expected to be the best you've ever been — these are *your* days. Mr High School Quarterback is injured and out of play, he's yesterday's glory-boy but YOU, adult you, you are the hope of the future, you beautiful flawless specimen of adult imperfection."

He paused and looked around. "And how was it for you?" he asked, stabbing a finger at the group. "How was your foray into the world of being a bright and shiny adult? Were you the conqueror of offices? Were you a king of industry, a man with a shooting star? Were you the next big thing? Tell me, how many of you rode into adulthood upon your trusty steed and found this gleaming shining fairytale to be the reality of your life, your happy-ever-after? Instead, what you got feels more like an interminable life sentence, I am sure."

He looked around. "David, that you feel such angst and personal failure and crippling fear is not your fault. You were presented with a Disney myth of the prince you were going to be. You were going to carry your princess bride off into the sunset and then what? The curtains closed and the audience rose in a standing ovation at the happy prognosis of your rosy future. Meanwhile, you trudged up a hill, leading a horse in the fading light, and in reality, your trusty steed was a stubborn hungry mule carrying a wife who wanted nothing more than a hot meal, a softly-quilted bed, and a night of uninterrupted sleep. How on earth could you not feel anxious, given the un-speakable pressures you faced of having to eternally provide? It's hardly surprising that your behaviours became more fur-tive. You fears burrowed into your belly and into the arteries of your brain, and they flowed like liquid poison among the pulsating blood and they brought terror with every breath."

Amelia noticed that the group looked stricken. They were frozen, impaled on the vitriolic spear of Dr. Carroll's rant. She knew there had to be an upswing in the making and she was not wrong.

"But!" Dr. Carroll shouted, and he cracked open another bottle of water. "But you have the power to make the torture stop! You can be the instrument of change in your dismal pres-ent and your even more dreary future. Yeah, sure that may be your life now. It is a hundred thousand million people's lives, but none of them have stopped to say hey, I don't want this, who cares what my peers think? How happy are my buddies anyway? They're mostly cokeheads, neurotics, potheads, and drunks. Their marriages are failing and killing them and their wives. So what do you do in order to save your own life? You do the opposite thing! You say: I choose to NOT care about what people think or say about me. I will simply do my job. I chose this job or it chose me and I will do it, but it isn't *me*, it doesn't define me. People let their jobs define them, therefore I choose the opposite. I define my own being in accordance with my truest self."

An air of skepticism greeted his epiphany and most of the group looked disappointed and disinterested. This was not the solution they were hoping for.

"The trouble with you lot," Dr. Carroll said, "is that, regardless of what I tell you, you're still looking for that magic pill. And I'm not saying that this is easy but if you start slowly and you keep at it, eventually you can create utopia in your life. Mind you, I'm not going to tell you that you deserve utopia. I don't think anybody deserves anything. Life's not fair. There is no balance between hard work and success, input and reward. You can work twenty hours a day, work your heart out, do a great job and then, someone — he can even be your arch enemy — trumps you at the eleventh hour. Because that's life. It's unavoidable. So it's not about getting what you deserve because none of us deserves anything. We get what we get and we choose our reactions from there."

"But I want to be a big shot," Mike spoke up. "I want to be the next Steve Jobs. There, I've laid it on the line, that's what I want. Deserve it or not, that's my dream."

"At least you're taking the first step towards realizing your dream," Dr. Carroll said. "Bravo! You have realized your shortcomings and you are addressing them. You have more chance than the rest of them. But there's sacrifice involved. Like the gods of old, success wants its virgin blood, its crucifixes, its buckets of pain and sorrow, dashed like rainwater to hallow the ground and make fallow the seeds of your desire. And that sacrifice will hurt. You, for instance, young Mike, might be called upon to break up with your high school sweetheart, the slim-hipped, large-breasted, cornflake-pure golden beauty who guided the cheerleaders in ritualistic chant and war cry as you carried the football team to unparalleled heights of success. Together you were king and queen and you reigned in glory and you both thought it would go on forever. But now, she's a dental hygienist and you're a wanna-be hot shot I.T. boy and she wants a house in the suburbs and babies while you want money, power, success, and blow jobs from your secretaries."

"First," Mike replied. "You don't refer them secretaries any more. They're executive assistants. And Jane is a law clerk not a dental hygienist. And doesn't everybody want babies and a nice house?"

Jane. Miss Perfect is called Jane. Sweet Jane. How nice. And no, I don't want babies. Amelia looked at her hands and wished she was alone so she could cry.

"You're missing the point," Dr. Carroll said. "And I can't make you see it. I can't. It's up to you."

"Enough about Mike. What about me?" David asked plaintively. "I'm trying to realize my dream but I'm going to bring it down, I'm going to destroy it."

"And if you do, so what? You wife might hate you but that's her issue not yours. Your peers might think you failed but what's their definition of failure anyway, and who makes them the oracle of light and wisdom? Even if they've reached the pinnacle of exclusive golf clubs and private schools for their kids, you can choose to NOT let that matter. You can choose to believe the opposite thing. You can take responsibility for who you are and do what makes you happy and that might see you end up being an alfalfa farmer in the prairies.

"You have to ask yourself this: What is my dream? Am I achieving my dream? What is not achieving my dream costing me? What would I lose if I changed my dream? And, does losing those things truly matter to me?

"Anyway, enough of that," Dr. Carroll said, and he changed the subject abruptly. "There was a lot of violence in this room last week…. But wait, where's Whitney and Joanne?"

"Having sex in the toilet," Alexei said, morosely. "I was nothing to her. I was just a fuck that meant nothing. And look at her, a fat housewife, and me, I have such beauty." He growled to show his manhood and his displeasure.

"They're still in there?" Dr. Carroll looked at his watch. "Who's going to go and get them this time?"

"I will," Alexei jumped to his feet but Dr. Carroll leapt up and blocked his path.

"Not a good idea", he said. "Time for you to do the opposite thing. I am sure you want to hit them—"

"I want to *kill* them!"

"So you are going to do the opposite thing. You are going to sit down and forgive them and love them and wish them happiness. Look at it like this: you're a spectacular specimen of manhood. You could get any girl you want, why get hung up on a middle-aged neurotic woman?"

"Because I love her! And she loves me! I thought she would leave her husband and be with me and we would fuck each other six times a day and have babies and be happy."

"You can be as happy with somebody else," Dr. Carroll insisted.

"Six times a day," Shannon murmured, and she sat up straighter in her chair.

"The only trouble is," Alexei said pointedly to Shannon, "I like blondes. Be a blonde next week and maybe we can try."

Shannon looked like she was ready to leave right then and there to go to the nearest hairdresser's.

"Sit down, Shannon," Dr. Carroll said tiredly. "I'll go and get them. Please, everyone, sit still and wait, preferably in silence."

Mike took hold of Amelia's hand again and they sat there, contentedly silent.

Alexei gave a few low growls now while Ainsley told Persephone about how worried she was that someone would cut off her finger in a McDonald's in order to steal her ring.

"Any luck with the hoarding?" Shannon asked Angelina who sighed.

"I tried to gather a tiny bag — just one little plastic bag and fill it with junk and throw it out. It took me two days to get the bag filled. And then I couldn't throw it away. I put it in a corner of my bedroom and left it there."

"It's good that you tried."

"That's nice of you to say so, honey, but it's not the truth. I've done that before and in fact, even better. I can package the stuff up but I can't give it away."

"What do you think will happen if you do give it away?"

"I feel like I will go crazy unless I get it back."

"Angelina, we don't use the expression 'go crazy'," Dr. Carroll said, returning to the room with Whitney and Joanne in tow. "We say 'experience a psychotic break'."

"Yeah, that's got a much more sympathetic ring to it," Persephone said. "Certainly reassures me."

"Deconstruct the term 'go crazy.'" Dr. Carroll said. "What do you think it means? It means that your psyche loses touch with reality. In other words, your psyche experiences a breakdown. Going crazy is such a loose phrase. It can encompass so many of the mild and ordinary sins of daily life.

"Now," he said, "I do want to check in with all of you, but first I'd like us to meditate. We need to lower the anger level and lower the testosterone in the room. We need try to dispel the feelings of blame and self-hatred. To this end, we shall empty our minds and hearts and we shall focus upon a lowly piece of fruit. We will engage our energies in studying this mild-mannered unsung hero: the crone of the vineyards, the wrinkled doyen of the magisterial court; behold, the raisin!"

"I hate raisins," Mike spoke up, and was soon supported by David, Shannon, and Persephone.

"Come now," Dr. Carroll raised his eyebrows. "Are you not open to new experiences albeit it with old partners? Do not make the mistake in life that each encounter with an individual will be the same. Give your friendships with food and men and women more credence than that. Each time you meet a person, or a dish of food, or even a book you've read many times before, say: 'Hello new friend, what lessons can you teach me today?'"

Alexei gave a snort. "I sure was surprised last week," he said, glaring at Whitney. "She gutted me like a fish, no mercy, no care. That was a new surprise. You got that right."

"Let's move *on*," Dr. Carroll said. "One day, Alexei, you will thank Whitney for what she did. You embraced sex rather than anger and that was good. But then you got too attached to the specific host of the sexual experience as opposed to discovering that the sexual experience is a transcendent act that unites the yin and yang of our human selves. You need to let go of attachment and find the opposite of that, and the opposite of attachment is love and forgiveness. Both of which are the opposite of hate, anger, and violence. You see how everything is leading you away from anger and hate?"

"You talk so much!" Alexei moaned, his head in his hands. "I can't listen to so many words, you're killing me!"

"No more talking, at least for a while," Dr. Carroll assured him. "Time to meditate and find new meaning in old things. Everybody, hold out your hands." They did and they received, into the palms of their outstretched hands, three tiny raisins.

"I heard that a raisin is a worried grape," Ainsley laughed. "Are we going to cure these guys and turn them back into their former plump juicy unworried selves?"

"You are in much better spirits," Dr. Carroll commented. "Group, before we meditate with our raisins, let's check in with Ainsley. What's up, cheerful chickie?"

"What's up is that I totally ignored you and went back to my fiancé. I told him I was sorry I'd let some nutcase screw with my mind and I asked him if he would he take me back. He said yes, that he'd realized this was just some messed up part of your therapy, and that he had to be patient and let it pass."

"But you are happier now than you were before, yes?"

"I didn't know how much he meant to me before. If that's what you mean, then yes, so what? Every relationship has wake-up calls."

"But your panics are less, yes?"

"I wouldn't ascribe that to you."

"I would. I would state that you have realized a sense of autonomy within the relationship, an autonomy that you never had before. You now have confidence in knowing that you truly love this man and that you are with him because you love him, not because your parents or his parents or even he, expects you to be there. This time, you are there for you."

Ainsley shrugged. "Whatever rocks your boat, Doc," she said.

Dr. Carroll looked disappointed. "It does lessen my joy when there is resistance to the internalization of the self-realization," he said. "Oh well. Moving on to raisins."

"Which are getting pretty sticky," Mike said. "We've been holding them for a while now."

"Raisins," Dr. Carroll said, dreamily. "Now I will not be doing this exercise along with you because personally I hate the puckered up little prunes, but let that not detract from your experience. The key to this meditation is to totally let go of all that has come before in our sessions: the gun wielding, the weeping, the sex, the anger. And how do we let go? We meditate. I am going to guide you through a meditation and I want you to follow my lead. Okay, here we go.

"*Ding!* Bring the raisin close up to your face, and study the raisin. See the colours, the textures, the folds in the tiny dehydrated skin. Look at the areas of dustiness along the surface, look at the ridges, the valleys, the pillows and sheet-like folds of this tiny ball. Can you see a face in your raisin? What does it look like to you other than a raisin?

"Now, smell your raisin. What does the raisin remind you of? Summer days, raisin bran breakfast cereal, fights with your brothers? Could it be sex with a neighbour when you were little and experimenting and looking at one another's tiny genitals?"

Mike and Amelia looked at each other and shook with silent laughter.

"Focus people, do not lose concentration! Now, close your eyes. Take the raisin and rub it against your lips. Don't eat it but feel what it feels like. Is it rough, or soft or how does it feel?"

Amelia took her raisin and carefully ran it against Mike's beautiful, full soft lower lip. He half-closed his eyes and he started to lick the raisin with the tip of his tongue. Amelia took the raisin in her mouth, in between her teeth and he licked it, then licked her teeth, and they both sat there clutching the other raisins in the sticky palms of their hands, not letting themselves eat the raisin that they were sharing, just licking it and one another.

Ding!

Amelia pulled back and Mike swallowed the raisin.

"To review," Dr. Carroll said and he sounded aggrieved. "Alexei ground his raisins underfoot. David threw his away. Persephone ate hers. Amelia and Mike engaged in sex play. Joanne and Whitney also seemed to think this was some kind of sex game, and Angelina put hers in her pocket."

"I studied mine," Ainsley said and she sounded saintly and wronged. "If you ask me, Doctor, my life is like a raisin, puckered and dehydrated and prunish and dead. I need to find a way to make my life expand and bloom and be filled with nourishment and moisture again. But it's hard. I broke my back playing soccer four years ago and without warning, I dropped like a stone, and then I'm incapacitated by pain for weeks. I can't hold down a job. I can't have any kind of regular life because I could fall down at any second."

"Have you seen a physician?" Dr. Carroll asked.

"Yes. I can have an operation but there's a fifty-fifty chance I could end up paralyzed. And then I'd be even more like this stupid raisin. Puckered-up like an old lady before I'm thirty."

"Wow. Thank you for sharing, Ainsley." Dr. Carroll sounded deflated, as if his raisin exercise hadn't had quite the desired results.

"That's all you can say? Thank you for sharing? You're not very helpful," Ainsley was angry.

"I can't exactly say go and play soccer if it might paralyze you, can I? But you could take up art, or knitting, or crocheting, or pottery. You are thinking in very limited terms, Ainsley, and that's hardly my fault. The opposite of being a raisin is not being a soccer player and if you can't see that for yourself, you need to stretch the muscles of your imagination. Come on now! What else are you good at? What else do you enjoy?"

"I do enjoy baking. And making clothes for dogs. And teaching kids to paint."

"There you go then."

"I also love acting in amateur theatre and making costumes for them, and I like making hats and quilting and—"

"Yes, we get the idea," Dr. Carroll interrupted her. "So, can you see there's more to life than your being a tiny dried up raisin?"

"Yes. I can."

"Good. Now, Alexei, you crushed them under your boot."

"I was trying to make wine," Alexei said, with a lopsided smile.

"Others may believe you but I don't. You're angry, Alexei. Are you going to be okay this week, out there in the world?"

"Yeah. Sure."

"You don't sound too certain. I think we need to find some tools for you to put in your toolbox."

"I've already got every kind of tool there is," Alexei looked confused.

"Emotional tools, Alexei, not real tools. For example, let's say someone enrages you on the construction site. Let's say they call your mother a whoring pig."

"I will kill him," Alexei said instantly.

"Now that's the kind of thing I'm trying to help you avoid," Dr. Carroll said. Remember with D.T.O.T., you want to do the opposite thing, okay? What would be the opposite thing?"

"Buy him a coffee," David offered helpfully.

"I'm supposed to listen to advice from the guy who can't even leave his desk in case he cries or loses control?" Alexei was scathing.

"Alexei, be gentle now. David is only trying to help. We're all trying to help. What if you ignored the man who insulted you?"

"He would think I was a pussy."

"What if you said look, I could fight you and win but I'm not into that today, so pick on someone else."

"He would think I was a pussy."

"And so what if he does? What do you care what some moron thinks?"

"It's my reputation at stake, that's what."

"But Alexei, take the heavyweight boxing champion of the world. Do you think he feels he has to fight every punk who insults him or his mother? You need to pick the fights that matter."

"Like the one with Gino. That fight mattered and I didn't pick it and now look." Alexei scowled at Joanne and Whitney.

"You feel betrayed by Whitney," Dr. Carroll said. "But Alexei, what Whitney felt for you wasn't personal. She just liked the excitement. Her life has been so terrifyingly bland that she could hardly breathe and then you came along, offering danger and excitement but just about the time she was getting bored of being with you — not because she was bored of *you* but because the danger was lessening — then along came Joanne. Whitney is an addict of misery and of excitement. She thinks she's cured now, because she's with

Joanne, but pretty soon she'll need a new fix or all her anxiety symptoms will return."

"That's utter nonsense!" Whitney shouted and the group could tell she was searching for a stronger phrase but her adherence to social niceties kept her language scrubbed. "Doctor, you've got no idea what you're talking about."

"Actually I do. I was delighted when you and Alexei hooked up. I thought you were D.T.O.T.ing but now you're repeating yourself and D.T.O.T. means doing the opposite constantly, in order to keep things even and balanced, while you're just doing more of the same."

"So we're supposed to swing between behaviours as if we have some kind of psychosis?" Mike spoke up. "One week I should be king of public speaking and the next I should avoid people?"

"No. One week phone them, the next week email them, then meet them for coffee. Make a list of fear-inducing situations and rotate them. Whitney has come up with one solution for tranquillizing her anxiety, and that's sex. She needs to find other things. Whitney, have you had any kind of honest conversation with your daughter?"

"About what?"

"About her anxiety?"

"No, I've been too happy. I didn't want to get depressed."

"Nice," Dave commented. "She's the reason you came here and now the only thing you can think about is who you can roll in the hay with next."

"That's not true!" Whitney flushed. "I really like Joanne. I mean I liked Alexei too but it was just sex, sorry Alexei. But with Joanne, I don't know … I can be myself."

"Be myself," Doctor Carroll mused. "Such a bandied-about phrase and what does it mean? This would be a good time for us to look at values. I know it's been a longer session than usual, but we are making great strides here. So, our actions and behaviours are largely influenced by our values. What do each of you value? Take out a piece of paper and write down five values."

"I don't have any," Alexei said.

"Of course you do," Dr. Carroll said. "You value your masculinity and you value being respected for that. You value being liked for your body."

"I mean I don't have any paper," Alexei elaborated. "I do have values. I value my mother and my brothers and sisters. And loyalty to family is everything."

"I don't have real values," Angelina said. "I value my stuff over everything, at the expense of everyone and everything."

"I value helping people," Shannon said, looking at Alexei with a helpful expression.

"I value family," Persephone said.

"I value money and family and success and love," Mike said.

"I value harmony, peace and tranquility," David said.

"I value excitement," Joanne said.

"I value me," Whitney said, "and I'd like to increase my knowledge of the values that make me happy."

"Amelia?"

She was quiet. She wanted to say that she valued being part of society, that she valued being a contributor to the world, being a good daughter and granddaughter. She valued being a girlfriend, even though she'd never been one. But she couldn't say any of those things and so she simply lifted in shoulders in a hapless gesture. "I value the potential of having values," she said. "That's all I've got."

"Ainsley?"

"I value love, marriage, babies, and family. Being part of a community."

"Wait." Amelia piped up. "I want to contribute something to the world. I'd value that. I value the courage of people who do bold things in life, people who save other people's lives or stand up for a cause even if it means putting their own lives at risk."

"Very noble. Well, group. We did a lot and we achieved a lot. For your homework this week, I'd like you to meditate upon the foods you eat. Eat slowly, with deliberation. Taste the food, every bite. The saltiness, the sweetness, the texture, the temperature. And drink water, really taste the water."

"Angelina," Dr. Carroll asked abruptly, "can you stay back? I've found someone who might be able to help you with your hoarding."

A look of fear crossed Angelina's face. "But I've decided that I don't think I'm ready to change," she said, her chins quivering.

"Don't worry, it's okay, the therapist I've found for you is very nice, she won't rush you. Will you just sit and chat with me a bit about it? You can always say no, once I've told you about her."

Angelina sat down with the enthusiasm of someone going to the electric chair while the rest of the group left the room.

"See you next week," Dr. Carroll cried out as they left, "and don't forget: D.T.O.T.! D.T.O.T. till the cows come home!"

As Amelia prepared to make her great escape, Mike grabbed her by the arm. "No, you don't," he said. "Not this time. This time, you're coming with me."

12. AMELIA AND MIKE

"I HAD THE WORST WEEK BECAUSE OF YOU," Mike said. "We're going to have a chat. I'm taking you for coffee and not here at the hospital. We're going somewhere nice. Come on."

Amelia wasn't happy but she followed him to an old beat-up white car. "Nice ride," she said. "I thought you were the next Steve Jobs."

"It takes time," Mike said. "Here, let me clear the seat off for you." The passenger seat was covered in papers and books about marketing and computing.

Amelia gave the stack that Mike put on the back seat a cursory once over, and announced, "We've got nothing in common." She looked at him pointedly and then pulled on her seatbelt.

"I think we eat a raisin together pretty well," Mike said and Amelia smiled.

"Yeah, we do. Does your girlfriend know you're taking me out for coffee?"

"She does not and I'm not proud of that."

"Not being proud of your actions isn't good enough. I should leave," Amelia said but she made no move to unfasten her seatbelt.

Mike rested his head on the steering wheel. "Fine," he said. "Go, then. I'm tired of chasing you. These groups knock the shit out of me if you must know and I'm tired. I have to make up the hours I spend here and work is super pressured. So if you really want to go, then go and I won't bug you again."

"No, I'm sorry." Amelia spoke quickly. "I do want to talk to you too. I'm sorry. I'm afraid of getting to like you too much. And I most likely shouldn't have said that either but it's true."

He put his hand on hers and next thing they were necking across the gear stick, with Amelia still strapped into her seat belt.

"You make me so hot," Mike said and he cupped his hand behind her neck. "But let's go. I want to tell you about Jane because I want you to know who she is, so she's not just some arbitrary name. We started dating when we were both fourteen. Babies. We went through high school together and she was head of the cheerleading squad and I was the quarterback hero. It was like Dr. Carroll said, and it was great. But then school ended and I feel like we did too, but I don't know how to tell her. How do you tell someone you've spent eight years with, that you don't want to be with them any more? It's killing me, Amelia. And the truth is, maybe things won't work out between you and me, but the fact that I feel about you the way I do means that Jane's not right for me."

Amelia wanted to throw up. Her stomach lurched when he said that things might not work out between them. She gulped and didn't want to say anything in case she cried, so she sat very still.

Mike put the car into drive. "Let's go somewhere better than this to talk," he said.

He took her to a coffee shop with leather sofas and low-slung wooden coffee tables and original art on the walls. Amelia felt out of place. She knew nothing about the cool trendy side of the world. There were galleries and coffee shops and boutiques and all manner of things that she was completely in the dark about. Her idea of a good time was to walk down a street she had never been on, and looking for treasures. She loved nothing more than the glowing shimmer of light behind tightly closed curtains, where she imagined a family enjoying peace after a long day and sharing the adventures they had had with each other.

She sat down on a sofa and waited for Mike to return with their lattes. He settled in close to her, his thighs touching hers.

"I want to kiss you so much," he said, "but we must talk first."

"Mike, can I say this?" Amelia dipped the tip of her finger into the foam of her latte and stirred it. "I'm not part of this world." She gestured around her. "And it never mattered to me before I met you. But now I realize how out of touch I am. The only thing I know about is Joan of Arc and the English literature that I study. I don't know about art or politics or economics or the best music to listen to or places to eat, or anything like that. You'll think I am exaggerating, that I can't be that much in the dark, but I am. I don't watch TV. I never have. TV just seems so stupid. And I don't go to the movies either. And you might think that my way of living sounds unusual and interesting and it is to me, but it won't be to you or anybody else. And you'll get annoyed when I repeatedly have no idea what you are talking about."

He listened intently while she spoke, his eyes focused on hers. "Amelia," he said, "you can teach me things about your world that you find wonderful and I can share things with you that will enrich yours. I'm not some big party guy. I go snowboarding in winter. I ride bicycles in summer. I rollerblade a bit and that's me."

"I can't snowboard. Or ski. But I can ride a bicycle," she offered. "And if you wanted to go to a movie with me, I would like to try. I shouldn't dismiss movies. Maybe I'd like them with you." They smiled at each other.

"But first," he said. "I have to tell Jane." His face clouded over. "She's a good woman, she is."

Amelia ripped a piece of paper from her notebook. "Here's my email and my phone number. Contact me only if you break up with her."

He agreed and took the piece of paper from her. "Stay a little while, though. Let's trade stories," he said. "What's your earliest childhood memory?"

Amelia laughed. "You sound like Dr. Carroll. Well, Doctor, my earliest memory is of my second birthday party. It was a day of freezing rain and I still wanted to have my party outside. I couldn't understand why no one else wanted to be out there in the rain with me. I cried and cried and everybody left and my mother was mad at me for ruining everything."

"Where was your father?"

"He had left by then. He's back now. My dad's a whole other ball of wax. I'll tell you about him one day. He's a saga, no haiku there."

Mike looked confused.

"And you," Amelia said, changing the subject. "What's your first memory?"

He grinned. "It was the first time I rode my bike without training wheels. My dad was running next to me and my mom was watching us and she was smiling. It was a summer's day and I felt so proud of myself and happy."

"That's a lovely memory," she said. "Are you still close to your parents?"

"Very. And you?"

"Yeah, I am. But they're not what you'd call ordinary. The only ordinary one is my Nana and she raised me. She home-schooled me and she was more like a mother to me than my Mom. If you must know, my mom's an obsessed body-builder and a fake tanning freak, and I live with her and my Nana in Scarborough. My dad's a nationally-acclaimed poet who lives in an empty mansion in Rosedale."

"When did they get divorced?"

"They didn't. They're still married. And, I swear, they're still in love. Like I said, it's a very long story."

"Sounds like a very interesting story," Mike said and he looked at his watch. "Oh, man. Listen, I have to go. I'm so sorry. I don't want you to think I don't want to talk more because I do. There's nothing I'd like better but I have to get back to work. Can I drop you anywhere?"

"No, I'm good here for a bit."

"Are you sure? I hate to leave you. I've got a project I've got to get finished and—"

"You don't have to explain," Amelia said. "But promise to always tell the truth."

"I promise. Oh, Amelia." He pulled her to her feet and held her close, and she fitted perfectly into him. She laid her head on his chest, wrapped her arms around him, and both of them pressed tightly together.

"You smell so good," he said. "You smell like strawberries and wet grass and trees after a storm and electricity in the air and hot sunshine. You smell like all those things and more. And you're so tiny, Amelia. You're like a tiny little bird that landed near me by mistake and I'm so afraid you'll fly away."

"I won't," she said. "Not yet. Only if we can't be together. Then I'll have to."

"I know," he said. "See you soon?"

"See you soon?" She echoed his question and he left and she watched him through the window. She saw him drive away, his face intense with concentration and she saw a glimpse of the old man he would become. She thought it would be nice to watch him grow old and be by his side as he did.

She meandered home happily, trying to focus on the good things he had said and she avoided thinking about the ghost of Jane who hovered between them.

When she got home, she found her mother in a panic and her thoughts and dreams about her own day fled in a rush.

"Nana's in hospital!" Megan said, greeting Amelia at the door and leading her quickly inside. Megan, a wrinkled, chain-smoking, muscle-bound tangerine, paced the room in a neon pink bikini and a cropped sheer white gown. "I took Nana to see the doctor," she explained to Amelia. "And they immediately made her go to the hospital for tests. I had to take a class so I left her there. I should never had left her there by herself."

To Amelia's horror, Megan started crying and it sounded like she was having an asthma attack.

"Mom," Amelia said gently, and she knelt down next to her mother who had collapsed on the sofa. "Mom, take little breaths, okay? Breathe out more than you breath in. That's right. Little breaths. That's better. Now, go and get dressed into something less stripper-like and then we'll go and see Nana."

"You're right. I must get changed." Megan padded up the stairs and into her bedroom with Amelia following. Megan matched Amelia for disastrous messiness, and she picked up a pair of track pants off the floor.

"What's wrong with Nana?" Amelia was afraid to ask.

"They don't know. Something to do with her stomach. She's got a blockage, they said, and they have to try to remove it. They even said she may need surgery tomorrow."

"How do you know this? Did you speak to a doctor?"

"No. Nana phoned me. She sounded so calm. She even told me not to come back to the hospital today. As if."

"Why didn't you call me?"

Megan looked dazed. "I don't know. You were at therapy. And I wanted to try and be calm for when you got home, which obviously didn't happen."

"Does Nana need us to take her anything?"

"I don't know, I never thought to ask."

"If she went there thinking she'd be home soon, she probably didn't take anything. I'm going to get her toothbrush and pack her slippers and her gown and pajamas."

"We should take her some fruit."

"Not if she's being operated on tomorrow," Amelia said. "She won't be allowed to eat anything."

"You're right. You're so much better with these things than me."

"Nana trained me well," Amelia said and she tried to smile. The thought of Nana in hospital had banished the joy that Mike had brought her.

She packed the bag and returned to find Megan still sitting on her bed. "Come on, Mom, let's go."

"We should tell your father. He loves her too," Megan said and she started crying again.

"There's nothing to tell yet. Come on, Mom. Find some shoes. Let's go already."

She finally got Megan bundled into the car, the car that Megan seemed unable to start.

"Mom! What's going on with you?" Amelia looked her mother who was hugging the steering wheel and shaking.

"I hate hospitals," Megan said. "I'm afraid of them. They put the fear of god into me. The last time I was in one was when I had you. That's why I left Mom there earlier. I'm afraid to go back."

"Get a grip, Mom. Nana needs us. We don't have time for your drama."

"When did you become such a nasty little bitch?" Megan sniped but she started the car and put it into drive. "I'll be interested to see what you're like when you're my age and life's given you a few knocks of your own."

"I thought I was a gift, not a knock," Amelia pointed out and Megan looked slightly shamefaced.

"You are, sweetie, you are. I meant losing my dad and Henry going screwy on me."

"Dad was screwy when you met him," Amelia commented and her mother gave her such a dark look that Amelia decided to shut up.

"And then Emilio turned out to be gay. He's the only other man, apart from your father, that I have ever loved and he's gay. That's what I mean by knocks, Amelia. You'll see."

Amelia thought about Jane and she wanted to tell her mother that she already had an inkling, but she wasn't in the mood to talk about it, and certainly not with her mother.

They drove to the hospital in silence and Amelia thought about how familiar the place was becoming.

"Here we are. Mom, no hysterics, please. Promise me. This is about Nana, not you."

"I am an adult," Megan said, affronted, but as soon as she caught sight of her mother in a hospital gown, she dissolved into a fit of tears. Ethel was asleep, fragile-looking and vulnerable and Amelia found tears rising to the back her of throat too.

"Please take my mom outside," Amelia said to the nurse. "I don't want her upsetting Nana." The nurse nodded and led an unprotesting Megan away.

"Nana?" Amelia said softly. "I brought you your jammies."

Ethel opened her eyes and smiled. "Thank heavens. Come on, child. Let's get me out of this ridiculous nonsense that they call a gown."

Amelia helped Ethel get dressed and she was dismayed to see how thin her grandmother had become. "Nana, look at you. You are skin and bone. I feel terrible. I never noticed."

"I didn't want to worry anyone, so I wore more layers. I thought it was something that would go away and that I would put the weight the back on."

"What did the doctors say?"

"It's a blockage. They have to operate."

"I'll stay with you the whole time."

"You don't need to do that. I'm fine."

"You may be fine but I'm not. And Mom's a mess."

Ethel laughed. "I'm sure she is." She tied her dressing gown tightly. "I'm so glad you brought my things. I feel so much more human in my own clothes. Besides, I was freezing wearing that oversized dishcloth. You brought my toothbrush, that's just lovely. My teeth feel like a lawn that needs mowing."

Ethel gingerly made her way to the bathroom to brush her teeth while Amelia went to find the nurse to ask her if she had an update on Ethel's results.

Ethel still had a mouthful of foam when Megan, somewhat more composed, rushed into the tiny washroom and clung to her mother. "I couldn't bear it if anything happened to you," she wailed. "I am sorry I'm such a selfish horrible daughter. You can't die. I need you too much."

Ethel spat into the sink and rinsed her toothbrush. "I'm not going anywhere," she said. "Now get off me. You're heavy, Megan."

"Are you telling me I've put on weight? Jeez, thanks Mom, when I've a competition coming up too."

"Meggie, I've got the strength of a half-starved sparrow right now, that's all I'm saying. A Q-tip feels heavy."

Amelia came back and helped Ethel into the bed and Megan rubbed her temples.

"I'm sorry, Mom, There I go again: me, me, me. Listen, do you need me to stay? I'm supposed to take a class in an hour but I can get someone to sub for me."

"No, you go on. I've got Amelia here with me. I'm fine."

"Good! Amelia, you will phone me if there's anything?"

"Will do, Mom, but they've said that the operation is not tomorrow, but the day after, so we've got some waiting time ahead."

"I should tell Henry," Megan said and Amelia agreed.

"I'll see if he's in any state to come back to the hospital with me later," Megan said. "But he's close to finishing a collection and that's never a great time for him, as we know too well."

Megan left and Ethel and Amelia looked at each other with relief.

"So, dear," Ethel patted the blanket on the bed. "Come and sit next to your Nana and tell me the gossip about today's group. Was it crazier than the last one?"

"Oh Nana! You have no idea! It's like a soap opera, only worse, and this is real life!"

"Start at the beginning and don't leave anything out," Ethel ordered. "And I mean the bits about you and Mike too."

Amelia blushed and told her gran the whole story in detail. But she did leave out one bit — how she and Mike had meditated with the raisin.

The doctors removed the blockage and kept Ethel in hospital for a further week. Amelia, while relieved that Nana was on the mend, was distressed that she hadn't heard from Mike. "He's taken my heart and slain it upon a butcher block," she told Ethel.

Ethel, propped up and pale, tried to reassure her. "Breaking up is hard to do, dear. Particularly with them having been together that long. I think it speaks very well of him that he won't just ditch her, or that he can't. Imagine if it was you, in love with him and thinking that the two of you were going to be together forever and then hearing that it was over."

"Over because he met some nutcase during therapy at a hospital," Amelia added. "But Nana, how will I even face him at group today? "

"Be strong, dear. I know it's so easy for me to say, but you can't let him see how hurt you are. He hasn't earned that right. "

Amelia nodded. "I'll come and see you right away after group," she told Ethel.

"Unless Mike wants to take you somewhere," Ethel said but Amelia shook her head. She knew better.

And she was right.

13. GROUP THERAPY: SESSION FIVE

MIKE WAS WAITING FOR HER IN THE CORRIDOR outside the therapy room. "I am so sorry, Amelia," he said. "I couldn't tell her this week. But don't give up on me, please don't."

She shook his hand off hers. "Don't sit next to me," she said, and her eyes filled with tears despite her assurances to Ethel that she would not let her pain show. She pushed past Mike, strode into the room and found a seat in between Angelina and Persephone.

Amelia dug into her bag for her notepad, noticing as she did that there was a new woman in the group. She turned to Angelina, signaling her question with her eyebrows raised.

Angelina laughed. "It's Shannon," she said. "She went blonde like Alexei told her to!"

Amelia stared and Shannon laughed.

"You like it?" Shannon tossed her head from side to side. "I got bangs too. I love it! I feel amazing, so sexy. I wish I'd done this years ago."

"Very nice," Amelia muttered and she opened her notebook.

Dr. Carroll arrived and took roll call. "Where's Alexei?" he asked.

"He got arrested," Joanne said. "He kept following me to work and threatening to beat me up unless I promised to leave Whitney and the group. Eventually, I had to call the cops on that crazy Russian bastard."

"He's not coming back to group?" Shannon was aghast. "But I changed my hair like he said."

"Shannon, are you not hearing me?" Joanne asked. "Alexei is nuts. You don't want to have anything to do with him."

"That's not for you to decide," Shannon said and Dr. Carroll held up a hand.

"Shannon, wait for a moment, please. I need to hear what happened. Is he still in custody?"

Joanne shook her head. "He's been released but I am pressing charges."

"He only has himself to blame," Whitney piped up. "He challenged her to a bare knuckle fight in the parking lot, with her colleagues watching. It was just after work and everybody was leaving and I was waiting for Joanne."

"What happened then?" Dr. Carroll asked.

Joanne chuckled. "I hit him in the goonies. He dropped like a stone. Not a clean fight, but he's crazy, I had no choice."

"Everybody at work thinks she's such a hero," Whitney said, her eyes shining.

"He was released on bail?"

Joanne nodded.

Dr. Carroll sighed. "I'll try to get in touch with him later. Persephone, how are you feeling? Any more post-traumatic stress symptoms following Gino and the gun incident?"

She smiled. "No. I'm good. You were very kind and understanding, Dr. Carroll. I'm fine."

"I'm sick of this," Shannon said and she stood up. "I don't want to be here any more. I'll send you a cheque, Dr. Carroll. I'm out." She stormed out before anyone could say anything or try to stop her.

Dr. Carroll watched her leave. "Natural attrition," he said. "Moving on. David, I'd like to focus on you for a bit. Please tell us honestly, how have things been with you?"

"The same. Bad. Really bad."

"Let's take a moment to chat about what's going and see

if we can help you. David, I haven't asked you this but what does your company produce?"

"We provide a range of office furniture for the small business entrepreneur who wants to start up his or her own office."

"I've seen you on TV!" Angelina said, her chins jiggling with excitement. "I thought you looked familiar. Your furniture looks like it's from IKEA. It comes in those kinds of parts, but then you send people to assemble it in their offices. You don't leave them to figure it out by themselves."

"I design everything myself too," David said, proudly.

"But I thought, from the ads, that your business must be doing very well," Angelina said.

"It was, but it's going down the tubes, I can feel it. I'm not being neurotic, there are things I can't control and I'm losing my grip."

"David," Dr. Carroll said, standing up. "I think it's time for a field trip. We, all of us, need to go and see you in action. Let's go to your office!"

David paled. "Out of the question. I think that's the worst idea I've ever heard. You'll embarrass me and then my business will be kaput for sure."

"You're right, we need to make a plan first before we go rushing in," Dr. Carroll said, and he sat down, drumming his fingers on his knees. "Let's say Joanne wants to start a gym—"

"In which case, she'd need gym equipment, not office equipment," Dave pointed out.

"But she'd need office equipment too," Dr. Carroll said. "All businesses do. Whitney, you could be Joanne's girlfriend and you can pretend to be a decorator."

"I *am* a decorator." Whitney was insulted. "I told you that before."

"Persephone and Angelina, you're investing in the gym and want to see that the funds are being well spent. Ainsley, you're going to be the receptionist, so you need to make sure you like the colour and fit of the chairs and desks."

"What abut us?" Mike and Amelia asked.

"You're Whitney's kids, along for the ride, so no incestuous lovely-dovey stuff."

"I'm not *that* old," Whitney protested.

"And who will you be, Dr. Carroll?" Mike asked.

"I'm not sure yet but I will think of something. David, are your employees at work right now?"

"Yes." David looked pale and sweaty and he wiped his forehead. "Listen, Dr. Carroll, stop. This is the worst idea I have ever heard. I think you're mad. I don't want to do this."

"Trust me," Dr. Carroll said. "You want to get better, don't you? Give us the rundown on who's who in your workplace."

Dave sighed. "Cathy's the receptionist and the bookkeeper, and by the way, she's also my wife. Jeff and John are the sales guys. John is Cathy's brother. Then there's the carpenter, Nick, and he's Jeff's brother."

"Very tangled," Dr. Carroll observed. "Mixing business and family is a highway to hell. How long have you had this business?"

"Fourteen years. It used to just be me, Jeff and Nick. Jeff was my original sales guy, and Nick's in charge of production. There's another boy too, our social media specialist. He's in charge of our Twitter, Facebook and Instagram presence."

"I wouldn't have thought there would be much call for that in your sort of business?" Joanne asked.

"There isn't really. But he's John's son and Cathy's nephew and since he can't find a job, they said he should be our social media expert."

"I am reconsidering," Dr. Carroll said. "We're a team of specialists, brought in to ascertain the success and, or, failure of the current business model. You, David, the general manager, have brought us in to determine the efficiency of current business practices. Does anybody know you come to this group today?"

"Yeah, they know I have a regular appointment so it would be really weird if a group of us walked in together on the day

I have therapy." David sounded desperate in his efforts to stop Dr. Carroll.

Dr. Carroll held up his hand. "David," he said. "Calm down. We won't do anything without your full consent. We are just brainstorming, okay? Bantering, if you will. It's all hypothetical at this point. The central most important thing you have to first ask yourself is this: do you truly want to make a change? I asked Angelina the same thing and she replied very honestly that the answer was no. But how about for you? Are you ready to make changes, real fundamental changes to your life?"

"God, yes," David said. "The thing is, this is *my* business. At least it used to be until it was taken over two years by Cathy and her family, and sales have been plummeting ever since. I'd keep Jeff, my original sales guy, and Nick the carpenter. I can do the rest. Cathy's bookkeeping is creative to say the least. She keeps finding ways to lend her family money that never gets paid back."

"You looking to offload your wife, Cathy, her brother, John and his son, the social media guy, and then life will be good?"

"Yes." David seemed to be warming to the idea. "I need peace and quiet. I'm harassed by my family at home, then I'm harassed by my family at work, and no one listens to me in either instance. In all seriousness, Dr. Carroll, I would do anything to have things back to the way they were. This only happened because my receptionist got pregnant and Cathy said she'd fill in for her. Then she said she would do the bookkeeping, and then she insisted I needed more sales help, which I didn't. She brought in her brother and they both brought the kid in."

"How would you characterize your relationship with your wife?"

"She's very bossy. Won't take no for an answer."

"This may have an impact on your marriage," Dr. Carroll advised him. "You're looking to make a lot of changes here. Are you sure you're ready for the consequences?"

"I am ready for any and all consequences," David said, and he looked determined.

"Because however the dominoes fall, as a result of what we do, you can't come back to me and blame me for screwing up your life. This is your choice."

"I won't blame you for anything, you have my word," David said.

"What does each of us have to do?" Mike asked.

"We need to pare things down from my original idea," Dr. Carroll said. "That was a good example of free-rein brainstorming that needed to be refined into a realistic plan. How is everybody's availability for tomorrow? Can you all free yourselves up to do this thing and help David?"

The group nodded.

"We will be employees of a firm called Efficiency Workplace Solutions and we've been hired by David. Mike, you're in charge of looking at ways to streamline the company's computing systems. Next, who knows anything about social media?"

"I do," Persephone said. "I used to be in charge of the social media program for a big retail outlet before I had my breakdown."

"Joanne, you're the lawyer, so you need to check the books are in order."

"The books are fine!" David was indignant. "At least they are, apart from Cathy shaving off funds."

"Joanne, can you pretend to be an accountant?"

"Piece of cake," Joanne said, giving a twisted smile.

"Excellent. Here's the plan. David, you've called us in. After our visit, we will submit our findings in a report that will state that you need to change your business structure or you will go under. Will you be able to go through with it, because you'll be the one who needs to fire them, not me?"

"Totally fine. But this can't ever be traced back to you, can it? What if John or Cathy tries to look up the business or asks for ID's or anything?"

"I can help out there," Angelina said, eagerly. "I once found a box with business cards and clipboards and those plastic thingies for name tags and even pens with a company name!"

"But what is the company called?" Joanne was skeptical.

"It was Best Business something." Angelina was triumphant. "It will work. Trust me."

Dr. Carroll nodded. "Angelina, you are a gem! Best Business something is our name and our game. Come on, people, let's go."

"Go where?" Mike asked. "I thought we were doing this tomorrow."

"We are. But first, we're taking a road trip. We're going to check out Angelina's box of goodies. I will admit," Dr. Carroll said getting up. "I have cabin fever today. I need to get out of this hospital, which is why I initially had the idea for us to visit Dave's workplace. But now we need to get the business cards and, bonus, we can take a look at Angelina's home, which, as her therapist, I must do, if I am going to help her."

"Okay, sure, you can all come by," Angelina said. "But no one is allowed try to throw away anything. And no one is allowed to tell me how stinky it is. I don't even smell it anymore but I know other people do."

"We won't say a word," Dr. Carroll promised and the group nodded.

"I don't think I've got anything to offer," Ainsley said. "So I won't be joining you unless you need me for anything?"

"No, you're okay to go," Dr. Carroll said. "But wait, how are you? I realize this has turned into an odd session."

"I'm fine. Although I am sure someone is going to cut off my finger to take my engagement ring but other than that, I am fine."

Dr. Carroll looked tempted to dive into this problem but he shook his head. "No time today," he said. "Ainsley, we'll address that next week. I take it you must be leaving your house, if you're worried you will be in places where other people could attack you? Let's view that as a step forward. Well done!"

Ainsley looked confused as she left.

"I'm coming to Angelina's," Whitney said. "This is exciting. And I want to come tomorrow too."

"I want to come too," Amelia said to Angelina and David.

"You guys can do inventory tomorrow," David suggested. "Make lists of the supplies in the stationary closet. Also, my carpenter is convinced that wood and materials have been going missing so take stock of what there is and I can tally it up with orders placed. And printer paper. I swear I am going through printer paper at twice the speed I should."

"No wonder you've been stressed," Joanne said. "Sounds like they've been taking advantage of you left, right, and centre."

David nodded vigorously.

"As for me, I am the big boss," Dr. Carroll said. "I'll wander around and talk to each person. David, you have described me to any of them?"

David shook his head. "Cathy and John don't want to hear anything about you or my coming here. They think I'm a loser for seeing you. They'd prefer me to be Xanaxed and like a robot."

"It would suit their purposes," Dr. Carroll agreed. "Now, off we go, to Angelina's place."

"Someone is welcome to hitch a ride with me in my old station wagon," Angelina offered and Amelia and Persephone chose to ride with her. Dr. Carroll followed in his car, as did David and Mike. Whitney and Joanne left together.

They arrived at Angelina's house and gathered at the front door. "This doesn't look bad," Whitney commented. "Everything looks neat and tidy."

She was right. The garden was well-maintained and the house looked as if it had recently been given a fresh coat of paint.

"My children," Angelina explained. "They like the outside to be presentable."

Lulled into a false sense that the interior would match the serene outer facade, the group was stunned when Angelina opened the front door and a violent stench hit them with full force. They gagged at the wave of ammonia, rotting newspapers, mould, boiled eggs gone bad, vile kitty litter, and rancid cheese.

Angelina stepped inside and waved at the others to follow her. Paralyzed, none of them moved. They were hardly able to breathe and they had not yet entered the house.

"Come in. Close the door! Close the door!" Angelina shrieked. "You can't let the bunnies run outside."

They filed in, reluctantly, and Mike closed the door.

They were standing in what was once a hallway. Now it was a tunnel. A tunnel of newspapers that literally arched and joined, leaving a small crawl space below. The group eased their way carefully through the narrow space, emerging in what one presumed was formerly the living room. It was as if a landslide of broken rubbish had poured in through an open window and again, the contents were ceiling-high.

Amelia looked down. She was standing on a pile of old magazines, and when she tried to make sense of the sea of objects around her, she discerned clothes from bygone eras, clothes that were stained and torn. Jackets with enormous, brightly-coloured flowers, piles of yellow, blue, and tan trousers, and all manner of filthy T-shirts and stained blouses. Dolls, one eyed and broken. Cat toys, covered in filth and muck. And there were droppings, animal excrement everywhere.

"Oh, Angelina." Amelia was the first to speak. "I am so sorry but I can't be in here. You've got too many dead things here. All the good dreams are dead. I'll have to wait outside."

She crawled back through the newspaper tunnel, opened the front door and ran outside. She stood there, gulping in the sweet purity of the clean air, and she wondered if she'd ever be able to get the funk of death out of her nose.

Mike followed her out. "You okay?"

"Yeah, sorry about that." She scuffed the ground with her foot and refused to look at him.

"Don't worry about it. Man, it stinks in there. I think a few of the bunnies and a couple of other things died too. I'd better get back in and help the others find that box so we can get the heck out of here."

He went back into the house and Amelia sat down on the lawn to wait. She was trying to figure out how she had never smelled anything bad on Angelina. How had that stench not stuck to her? In fact, to the contrary, Angelina always smelled like fresh laundry, cotton clean and sunshiny.

The others wandered through the house, losing each other among the stacks of boxes and papers and magazines and rubbish.

"Angelina?" Dr. Carroll called out after a while. "Where you are?"

"In the study," she replied, which made no sense to him, but he followed the sound of her voice and he caught sight of the hem of her purple dress as she knelt on the floor.

"Can I help you?" he asked.

"I'm trying to get that box there," she pointed. "The one under those three small ones."

Dr. Carroll reached for the topmost box and it came tumbling down. As it did, it flew open and a torrent of tiny bones rained onto Angelina and Dr. Carroll before falling onto the floor. Dr. Carroll gave a high-pitched shriek and he jumped back, brushing at his clothes. "Mice! Oh my god! I am covered in dead mice."

"Oh, no," Angelina cried. "You've broken them!"

"You collect dead mice?" Dr. Carroll tried to recover his composure.

"Only once all the meat is gone and they're skeletons. They have the tiniest most beautiful skeletons and now look, you've broken them." She sounded ready to cry.

"I'm sorry Angelina," Dr. Carroll said and he put his hand on her arm. "I will be more careful."

He slid the next box carefully toward him and lowered it, wondering what was inside, and hoping to never have to find out. But it was only filled with rotted and stained tea cozies, stiff and crusted.

"It's the next box," Angelina said eagerly and Dr. Carroll lifted the box up and carried it out into the back yard where the others were waiting, having admitted defeat.

"Fantastic Corvette you've got in the garage," Joanne said. "1958?"

Angelina nodded. "It was my husband's."

"Looks in good shape. I love old cars. Would you consider selling it or are you hanging onto it too?"

Angelina shook her head. "I hate cars. You can have it for all I care. The keys are in the glove box. It's worthless to me."

"And yet," Dr. Carroll muttered, "the skeletons of dead mice are treasures."

"Done deal!" Joanne shot over to the car and dug inside the glove box. She soon had the hood raised and was examining the engine.

Dr. Carroll bent over the box he had carried out, hoping that Angelina hadn't sent them on a wild goose chase but there, amazingly enough, were clipboards with *Best Business M.B.A. Services Ltd.* on them, with printed letterhead, matching ballpoint pens, and plastic name tags holders with lanyards.

"Angelina, you are the best!" David was beside himself. "For the first time, I think this might work."

"The plan works as follows," Dr. Carroll said. "We meet at David's workplace at nine a.m. tomorrow."

"But the others won't be in by then," David said.

"Exactly. By the time they arrive, we'll be knee deep into it. Actually, let's make it eight-thirty a.m. Everybody needs to be in smart work clothes. Amelia and Whitney, you can't be there. I've been thinking about it and we can't have too many people. We'll have to join you later."

"There's a coffee shop on the corner of the main intersection," David said. "You can't miss it, Java Joe's. Wait for us there."

"I don't know if I can do it," Persephone said suddenly.

"I'm sorry." She was shaking and she reached into her large purse and dug out a prescription bottle. She dry-swallowed a pill and grimaced.

"Don't worry," Mike said reassuringly. "I can do your and my part. Piece of cake."

Persephone looked both humiliated and relieved and Mike patted her on the arm.

"Don't worry about it," Amelia told her. "You, me, and Angelina can wait together at Java Joe's. How long do you lot think you'll be?"

"At least three hours, maybe four," Dr. Carroll said. "We're going to do this properly."

"I'll get to the coffee shop around eleven, just in case," Amelia said and Angelina and Persephone agreed. Amelia wished them luck and strode off down the driveway.

"Wait, I'll give you a ride home," Mike shouted but Amelia had already disappeared around the corner.

"See you tomorrow," Dr. Carroll said. "Last chance, David, to pull out?"

"No pulling out. You're right, Dr. Carroll, it's time I took some responsibility for something in my life. And this way, I am actually doing D.T.O.T. Usually I'd wait for something to happen or for someone else to make the decision but I'm taking control, with your help. Thank you, everybody, for your help. I couldn't do this by myself."

"D.T.O.T.. till the cows come home!" Dr. Carroll shouted as he walked away, and he got into his car and drove off, waving and grinning like a manic hamster.

Angelina was left standing with Persephone, Joanne, and Whitney and she turned back to her house. "It really is bad, isn't it?" she asked and the three of them nodded.

"Maybe Dr. Carroll's right," Angelina muttered. "Maybe it should all burn down."

"But wouldn't you start doing it again?" Whitney asked gently. "I'm not judging you, I'm just asking."

"Yes," Angelina said sadly. "Yes, I probably would."

"What if we cleaned it out for you when you weren't there," Joanne suggested. "Has anybody ever tried that?"

"They did and I rushed home and stopped them. My daughter took me to Las Vegas and as soon as we landed, I knew what was going on. I made her bring me right back home on the next flight. When we arrived, there were packers and movers in the driveway and I made them put everything back where it was, exactly where it was."

"Angelina," Persephone asked, "did you ever make the doctor's appointment? The medical one? That was why you came to see Dr. Carroll in the first place."

Angelina's face went blank and expressionless. "I never did," she said carefully. "No, I never did. Now, I don't know about you but I am worn out. I'm going in to take a nap."

"Um," Joanne said, and she whipped out her yellow legal notepad. "I really want to buy the car from you. The battery's dead so I'll get it towed. Please let me pay for it."

"No, take it, take it," Angelina said. "Write a thingy saying you bought it for a dollar."

Joanne scribbled a note and Angelina signed it while Joanne dug in her purse for a dollar. "I'm calling a towing company now," Joanne said, scrolling through her phone to find a number. "And I'll get a ride back with them. Angelina, do you want us to come and collect you in the morning?"

"No, I'll be fine driving myself to the coffee shop. Let me move my car out the way, so you can get the Corvette out. Wait here."

They watched her walk toward the garage and get into her car.

"I can take the bus from here," Persephone said. "See you!" She waved and walked off.

Joanne and Whitney turned to one another. "I'll wait here with you for the tow truck," Whitney said.

Joanne gave her a wide smile. "I don't care if people think we are rushing into things," she said. "I've been so lonely, but that's not why I want to be with you. I want to be with you because you are you and you make me feel happy. And if it's a bad thing to have one's happiness dependent on another person, then so be it."

"I feel the same about you," Whitney said and she slipped her arm around Joanne's waist.

The next morning Amelia, Persephone, Angelina, and Whitney gathered at the coffee shop and waited. When it got to lunchtime and there had been no word, they were worried.

"I'm calling Joanne," Whitney said and she pulled out her cellphone.

"Hon? It's me, what's taking so long? What? Really? Wow... Wel, yeah, we'll be here, don't worry. Get here when you can."

She ended the call and turned to the others.

"Spit it out," Persephone said.

"A meth lab! Completely hidden below the carpentry area! Mike found it."

"Who was in on it?"

"Everyone except for David. Even his former partners, Jeff and Nick. Dr. Carroll phoned the cops as soon as Mike found the lab. Cathy and her brother and the nephew arrived at the same time as the cops and they tried to make a run for it but they were caught."

"How did David take it?"

"Joanne said he's in total shock. He feels very betrayed and who can blame him? No wonder he felt weird at work. His feelings of anxiety and paranoia were well-founded."

"Poor David," Persephone said. "Thank heavens for Dr. Carroll. His methods may be questionable at times but he certainly gets results."

"Except for Gino," Angelina said.

"Gino was long gone," Whitney was dismissive.

They chatted and waited for the others to arrive, who were jubilant when they finally got there. David was with them.

"I think we should have an impromptu session," Dr. Carroll said. "David is going to feel grief as well as triumph. There was a lot of betrayal."

"I'll get food and coffees for everyone," Whitney said and they gathered around a large table in the back of the coffee shop.

"I can't believe it," David said, shaking his head. "What an idiot I am."

"You couldn't have known," Mike said. "They hid the whole thing extremely well. I just thought it was strange how Nick kept looking over to that one area and that's why I asked you for the floor plan."

"Nick was the one who showed me the building in the first place," David said. "He must have known about the hidden basement all the time but he didn't show me. Of course, I should have studied the floor plan myself more carefully. Nick and Jeff were cooking meth this whole time and then when Cathy joined, she found out. She went back late one night to get some files and she found them. Of course she thought this was great, megabucks rolling in, and they had to cut her in as well as John and my nephew. And now they are all going to jail. I'm not bailing Cathy out, that's for sure. It explains why they were acting so strangely towards me. It would have suited them if I'd had a nervous breakdown and left the business. I'm so relieved I wasn't imagining things. They were trying to get rid of me by stripping the business financially. Jeff and Nick needed me in the beginning to lease the building but now I was in their way. Cathy would have stayed on as their landlord and they could have increased production."

"What are you going to do now?" Persephone said.

"The cops have seized the lab so my business has gone bust. I'll have to let my clients know. I've got a paid-off house and I am glad I was only renting that building because it's now damaged by the chemicals from the lab. The owner's none too happy, I'll tell you that much, but Cathy and the others are liable for damages. The cops have cleared me of everything.

I'm not destitute or anything, but I've got no idea what to do with the rest of my life."

"Let's do some brainstorming for David," Mike said, grinning. "Do you have any family in other parts of the country?"

"Yeah, mostly in Halifax. But I don't want to go back there."

"How about some interim travel? Is there anywhere you'd like to go?"

David shook his head. "I think what I'd like most is to start my business again. Find a new carpenter and new premises. I really like what I do, designing office furniture. I just wanted to stop worrying so much. I'm not going to leave the group just because we solved this, because even though it explains a lot, there are still a bunch of things I'd like to work on."

"Fantastic!" Doctor Carroll was beaming. "Well, then, I will be heading out. It's been a great day for D.T.O.T. and a great day for teamwork and friendship. See you next week and remember—" He paused and waited.

"D.T.O.T. *until the cows come home!*" the group called out after him and laughed.

"I'd better get back to work before they fire me," Joanne commented. "Whitney, I'll see you later?"

Whitney nodded.

"Amelia, do you want a ride?" Mike asked but she shook her head. She planned on going back to the hospital to check on Ethel. They were hoping that she would soon be released.

"And I'm going back to hole up in the safety of my home," Persephone said and she was seconded by Angelina.

"Angelina," Mike said, "this whole thing for David would never have worked without your Best Business supplies. You did a good thing. Doc had to tell the cops about the sting, because they wanted to know who we were and why we were there. The cops seemed a bit nervous of us, like we were all mental patients. It was funny."

"I'm glad my rubbish was of use for once," Angelina said and she looked old and tired. She got up and hooked her purse over her shoulder. "See you next week." She reached the doorway of the café and then suddenly whipped around and faced them. "KEEP ON ROCKING IN THE FREE WORLD!" she yelled with a giant smile. Then she hobbled to her car, and drove out of the parking lot with her face inches away from the steering wheel.

"She's such an awesome nutter," Mike said, following Amelia out of the coffee shop. "Amelia, c'mon let me give you a ride wherever you're going."

"No, I'm good, thanks."

"I'll call you as soon as I've broken up with Jane," Mike said. "Have a little faith, okay?"

"Faith needs to be earned, not begged, borrowed or stolen," Amelia said, and with that, she marched away.

14. DR. CARROLL

"IT WAS APPARENTLY CRAZY THERE, NANA," Amelia said, sitting on her gran's bed. "They arrested David's wife, her brother, her brother's son, the sales guy, and the carpenter."

"This Dr. Carroll certainly is unorthodox but he is effective," Ethel said, yawning.

"How are you feeling, Nana? Tell me the truth."

"A bit sore but fine, dear. Honestly. And now, be honest with me about you and Mike. What's going on there?"

"Nothing until he breaks up with Jane. I don't think he ever will. Would you like any orange juice or anything?"

"Just water would be lovely, dear. Thank you."

Amelia got a glass of water and then she added some water to Ethel's flowers as well. She kissed her gran and left.

After everything that had happened, she needed a brisk walk to clear her head. Before she knew it, she found herself on the road where she had shouted at the old man, asking him for directions to the hospital. She wondered if Dr. Carroll lived nearby since he had driven past her, but he could have been in the area for any number of reasons. She noticed a bus stop in the distance and she headed over. The sky was a greenish black and it was threatening hail. While Amelia had no qualms about walking in the rain, she was none too happy to be hailed on. She rushed inside the bus shelter just as the downpour of ice pellets started and she huddled into the furthermost corner, wondering how long the storm would last.

It soon began to ease off to a steady downpour, the hail spent. Amelia was about to leave when to her surprise, she saw Dr. Carroll's car pull into a driveway across the street. It was an unremarkable driveway adjoining an equally unremarkable bungalow with a lawn that needed mowing. Dr. Carroll parked under the garage awning and then he ran around to the front of the house, with a newspaper held overhead. He unlocked the front door and let himself in.

A light came on in the living room and Amelia saw Dr. Carroll draw the curtains closed. A lovely light emanated from the windows, and Amelia envied Dr. Carroll his warm glowy life and his house that was a sanctuary at the end of a long and, no doubt, typically chaotic day.

Amelia wanted to be home too, safe from the hope and worries of Mike. Although, she thought, hope was foolish and worries would follow her to her dreams. But she was tired and it would be lovely, nonetheless, to be home and be able to rest. She looked across the street at Dr. Carroll's house and she wondered if he had a family and if they had dinner together at a big shiny table. And did they watch TV together afterwards? Or did he help his children with their homework, if indeed he had children? Maybe he didn't even have a wife. If he did, did he tell her about his day, as much as he could, within the confines of patient confidentiality?

The rain eased to a mild drizzle and though a half an hour had passed, the bus had failed to come. Amelia couldn't help herself. She had to know more about Dr. Carroll's life after work. Going home to rest would have to wait.

She scuttled across the street and walked casually up the neighbour's driveway, hidden from Dr. Carroll's house by a tall hedge. When she came to the end of the driveway, she spied a convenient gap in the hedge. She crawled through it and made a quick dash to a large bush in the centre of Doctor Carroll's back lawn. Feeling utterly creepy but unable to stop herself, she rushed toward the house and crouched next to a window. She lifted her head carefully and peered into the window through a small, triangulated opening where the curtain had failed to close properly.

She had a full view of the dining room.

There, seated for dinner, was Doctor Carroll, with his family. And a perfect family it was, too. Mother, daughter, son.

There was mother, at the head of the table. She was young, with long dark curly hair and a pale oval face, the beauty of a pre-Raphaelite Madonna, with a slightly too-long nose and full lips.

The daughter was about twelve and although she felt guilty for the thought, Amelia sympathized with the girl for having inherited more of her father's looks than her mother's. The girl had short curly ginger hair that was more like a granny's permanent wave than the hair of a young girl. She had a little potato for a nose and a strong overbite that almost hid her thin lower lip. She was densely freckled and pale eyebrows were etched above her small, light brown eyes.

The son was around eight or so and he, like his mother, was a vision of loveliness. He had dark curly hair, enormous soulful eyes and he, in contrast to his sister, was petite, with fragile sloping shoulders and tiny delicate hands.

Dr. Carroll was sitting at the other end of the table and although Amelia couldn't see his face, she could tell by his hands movements that he was chatting vivaciously, waving his cutlery this way and that, and taking several large gulps from his water glass.

Amelia was curious to see if his family found him as amusing as he clearly found himself, and it was then that she felt the first frisson of shock. She realized what was horribly wrong. None of the family members showed any expression at all. None of them were eating. And neither were they looking at Dr. Carroll nor at one another. They were, the three of them, perfectly still and they gazed vacuously into space, without moving at all.

Amelia watched Dr. Carroll finish his meal. He wasn't in a hurry. Then he got up and moved clockwise to his daughter and he neatly cut her food up into bite-sized pieces. And then, without missing a beat of his clearly hilarious and engaging conversation, he fed small forkfuls to her until the food on her plate was gone.

Then he moved around to his wife, and he did the same with her, only this time, he draped his arm around her shoulder and he nuzzled her hair from time to time and he even planted a kiss on her cheek. When she was finished eating, he took her hand in his and rested his head on her shoulder for a long moment, and then he went around to his son and fed him in the same manner.

Neither mother, nor daughter, nor son moved the entire time except to chew slowly. After they had eaten, Dr. Carroll removed the dishes from the table and he returned with dessert, feeding it to them in the same painstaking, chatty and happy manner. After dessert, he disappeared for a few minutes and returned with a cup of coffee and a platter of cheese.

Amelia was pressed up against the glass, a witness to the entire tableau.

She watched Dr. Carroll finish his coffee and eat his cheese, and then he stood up and tenderly helped his wife to her feet. He lead her down a hallway, coming back a few minutes later, and then led the daughter away, returning to do the same with his son.

Thinking that she had seen enough for the moment, and worried that he would catch sight of her face through the tiny gap of the curtain, Amelia decided that it was time for her to leave. She took a deep breath and made a dash for the bush in the centre of the lawn. She ran back through the hedge and rushed down the neighbour's driveway. The night was still cloudy and dark and she was certain that no one had seen her but she was too unnerved to wait for the bus in such close proximity to Dr. Carroll's home so she ran back to the hospital.

Once she was there, she phoned her mother. "I'm going to stay with Nana for the night," she said. Her mother sounded more annoyed at having been disturbed than pleased by Amelia's rare effort to let her know of her plans. "That's fine," Megan said and she hung up the phone.

Amelia was shivering, not from the cold, which she did not feel, but from what she had seen. She climbed under the tangle of wires and got into bed with Ethel who mumbled something in her sleep. Amelia lay as still as she could, hoping that none of the nurses would catch her and make her leave.

Amelia would have told Ethel what she had seen but the following day, Ethel took a turn for the worse.

"Is it because I slept with her in her bed?" Amelia asked the doctor, sick with worry.

"Not in the least. Don't worry. Bowel surgeries do this regularly — have setbacks — but that's all it is, a setback. We're going to up her antibiotics and keep a careful eye on her."

Amelia sat next to Ethel, worrying about her, and worrying about what she had seen and wondering what to do. It wasn't as if she could go the police. She was, to all intents and purposes, a psychiatric patient and who'd believe some cockamamie story about her therapist holding his family as drugged hostages?

She couldn't tell her mother. Megan wouldn't believe her. She'd think that this was the latest Amelia-oddity and dismiss it. Amelia decided to go and visit Henry. She kissed Ethel and left the hospital.

It took her nearly an hour to get there but she finally had the mansion in sight and, with a feeling of relief, she opened the gate. But she knew, even as she walked up the pathway, that all was not well with Henry and her heart sank. She could feel it, even although the outward appearance of the house was unchanged. She knocked at the door repeatedly, knowing there would be no reply and she eventually let herself in.

The house was as silent as a tomb and the curtains were drawn. It was hard for Amelia to see anything until she switched on the hallway light. She headed for the living room, which was Henry's main work area, and she turned on the lights, and instantly saw the reason for the decline in Henry's mental health.

It was as Megan had predicted. Henry had finished his latest body of work.

The pages had been removed from the walls and, in his routine way, were neatly stacked in the middle of the polished floor. Amelia half-expected to see Henry asleep in front of the fireplace but the lumpy floral-patterned king size mattress was empty.

Amelia checked the kitchen and found no sign of her father there either.

She began to worry, even though this was not her first encounter with Henry when he was unwell. She ran up the stairs and found him lying on the floor of his boyhood bedroom, staring up at his model airplanes. His hands were behind his head and his eyes were half-closed.

"Dad?" She lay down next to him. "You finished your work I see. When?"

Henry opened his mouth but it was clear that it was hard for him to speak and he shook his head.

"I know, Dad," Amelia said gently. "But it's okay. The voices will come back. They don't have anything to say right now, but they'll be back."

Henry turned to look at her and his eyes welled with tears.

"No," he said, and his voice was hoarse and unused. "They're gone."

"Oh, Dad," she said. "We've been through this before. They always come back."

"This time is different," her father insisted.

"You've said that every time before too," Amelia reminded him, and Henry did not reply.

"Oh, Dad." She took his bony hand in hers and they lay there, looking up at the model planes.

"I think you need some soup," Amelia said but Henry shook his head.

"Fine," she said, "but I'm having some. I've come all this way to see you, so I'm going down to kitchen and I'll come back after I've eaten."

She got up and paused in the doorway. "Are you happy with your work?" she asked and Henry shook his head slowly.

"Don't know," he said. "No. Maybe. Can't remember any of it."

Amelia went downstairs and she opened the kitchen cupboard. She decided on cream of tomato. She emptied the can into the pot and added milk, thinking not about her father and his funk but about Dr. Carroll and his family. She had just turned off the stove when Henry appeared, looking unshaven and gloomy.

"Which one did you choose?"

"Tomato." She handed him a spoon and took the pot to the marble island and they stood there, eating in silence. Amelia was relieved to see Henry eating and as she watched, life seemed to flow back into his emaciated body.

"Dad," she said. "My therapist is holding his family drugged and hostage."

"We are all prisoners in familial relationships," Henry said, rapidly spooning soup into his mouth and spilling droplets on his t-shirt.

"I'm not being metaphorical, Dad. I'm being serious and literal."

Amelia told Henry what she had seen. "And I don't know what to do," she concluded. "Nana's sick and Mom won't believe me, or she won't care."

"Ethel's sick?" Henry dropped his spoon into the remainder of the soup and Amelia realized that Megan hadn't told him what was going on.

"She's in hospital. They operated on her colon. I'm sorry Dad. I thought Mom told you. She said she would."

"She could have tried to phone," Henry admitted. "I did

hear the phone ringing but I was busy. She should have come and fetched me."

Henry raced towards the front door, his dressing gown flying out behind him like a cape.

"Dad! Wait! Put some proper clothes on," Amelia shouted after him, and he stopped and looked down at his boxer shorts and his food-stained t-shirt.

"Right." He raced upstairs, threw on some clean clothes, and then he flew back down. He ushered Amelia out of the house, then he locked the front door and shot out to the street.

"I generally refuse to indulge in such monetary obscenities as a cab ride," he said, "but this is an emergency. Where are the cabs, for god's sake?" He peered up and down the quiet street.

"I'll phone for one, Dad, hang on."

It cost a small fortune and it took a while to get to the hospital. Henry gnawed on his knuckles the entire way. When they got there, he paid quickly and leapt out.

"Where's her room?" he asked urgently and Amelia guided him through the maze of corridors. He rushed inside Ethel's room and came to a shuddering halt next to her bed.

Ethel was fast asleep and Henry gently took her hand in his and pressed it to his face.

"Is she going to be alright?" He whispered to Amelia, voicing the thought he had wanted to ask the entire ride over.

Amelia nodded. "The doctor said she will be fine. He said a setback is normal and they've put her on more antibiotics."

Henry dug some money out of his shirt pocket. "Buy her some more flowers," he said. "Ethel likes flowers. Buy her two bunches, three. And cards and a basket or whatever you can find. She must wake and see that she is dearly loved. One vase of flowers is not enough."

Amelia nodded and went shopping. She returned with a stack of gossip magazines, several bouquets of flowers, and a great big teddy bear. "Nana loves these magazines," she told Henry. "Although she thinks I don't know that. I got her *The*

Sun newspaper too, She loves it, too." She sorted the display at the end of the bed and she and Henry settled down to wait.

"Dad?" Amelia whispered. "What about my therapist and his family?"

"Not now, Amelia. I can't think about anything until Mom wakes up."

Henry was still holding Ethel's hand gently and his chair was pressed up close to the bed.

Amelia rubbed her eyes with frustration. She had no idea what to do. She pinched the bridge of her nose hard, as if tiny attacks of pain would help her clear her own head and that a course of action would become clear to her. But nothing was forthcoming and she sighed. "I'm going to get some stuff from the vending machine," she said. "Do you want anything?"

Henry shook his head.

Amelia returned with a stash of junk food. She sat on the floor, flicked open *The Sun,* and bit into a granola bar. She paged through the paper idly, not paying much attention to any of it, when a story caught her eye and she gasped, pinning her hand to her mouth.

HOARDER AND RABBITS DIE IN FLAMING INFERNO.

Amelia stopped chewing in horror, her mouth half-full.

She had thought that the photo of the blazing house looked familiar. The garden was familiar, as was the shape of the burning house. And how could it not be, when she'd been there only days before?

Angelina had done what Dr. Carroll had suggested. She had burned down her house, with herself and her rabbits inside.

The fire chief said there was no doubt that it was suicide by arson. Amelia pictured Angelina's stoic resolve to end her emotional turmoil. She had, after all, been given a clear directive by Dr. Carroll that this course of action was her only solution.

"Amelia?" It was Henry. "Are you okay?" Even he had noticed her reaction.

Amelia shook her head and she spat her unchewed food into a napkin and got up. "I have to go," she said, throwing the napkin into the trash.

"What's wrong?"

But Amelia rushed out, unable to speak.

She sat under a tree in the hospital grounds, keening and hugging her knees to her chest. She wished there was someone, anyone that she could talk to but there was no one. She was utterly alone and this made her cry even harder. She'd always had Nana and sometimes she had Dad, but right now she had no one. She emptied the contents of her pockets out onto the grass, hoping to find a tissue. She discovered a dryer sheet, her cellphone, and a Werther's Butterscotch instead. She blew her nose on the dryer sheet and picked up her phone.

Five missed calls.

She stared at it in disbelief. It wouldn't be her mother. She didn't have that level of interest in Amelia's life and the only other person who ever called her was Nana.

She dialed her voice mail and listened to her messages and her heart skipped more than one beat when she realized the calls were all from Mike. He had read about Angelina and, from the sounds of it, he was as devastated as she was. Without pausing, she dialed his number and he picked up on the first ring. "What took you so long?" he asked without preamble.

"My gran's in hospital," Amelia said. "And I went to see my Dad. Never mind that, Mike—"

"I know. It's all his fault. He told her to do that. We all heard him. Just when I thought he was some kind of okay guy. We have to report him."

"I need to tell you something else about him," Amelia said. "Can you meet me at the hospital?"

"Yeah, sure. Are you there now?"

"Yes."

"Meet me in the lounge area near the coffee shop, where we went that time. I'll be there in half an hour."

He rang off and Amelia leaned against the tree, heartbroken about Angelina.

15. MIKE

MIKE ARRIVED AND WHEN HE WALKED towards her, Amelia thought that he looked more like a movie star than ever. She felt self conscious about her weepy appearance and swollen red face, not the mention the fact that she had neither showered nor changed since the last time she had seen him.

"So much has happened," she said, quickly. "Yes, I know I'm wearing the same clothes as the last time you saw me, and no, I haven't been home but I can explain."

"Amelia, you are so beautiful," he said in a rush. "I told Jane I've met someone, I did. I'm telling you the truth. After we helped David out, I thought about it. I thought about how he had been lied to by his wife and by everybody, and I thought that I couldn't lie to Jane any more. It's not fair to her."

"Oh. How did she take it?"

"She's furious. She said I've wasted the best years of her life and that she'll never forgive me. She said she hates me. She said I'll be sorry and she said a whole bunch of other stuff, but she'll be okay. Don't get me wrong, I nearly threw up before I told her, and I'm not exactly Mr. Popular in our crowd right now, but I don't care."

Amelia was alarmed. He had done what she had wanted him to do, she knew that, but now, instead of feeling happy, she was filled with dread. "I know I said you should do this," she told him, "but now that it's done, I'm kind of freaked out. I mean, you did all this for me and you don't even know me.

Now you'll see how strange and weird I am and you'll hate me because you lost all the good stuff that you had, because of a whim."

He took her hand and he touched her forehead with his. "It wasn't a whim. And just so you know, even if it doesn't work out between us, you helped me see that Jane wasn't for me."

"You agree that it's not going to work out between us?" Amelia sounded truculent.

"I didn't say that," he replied patiently. "I just said that if it doesn't, and I think it will, that you mustn't stress about anything."

He kissed her lightly and she folded into him, her hands clasped tightly around his neck and her body pressed close to his. When they finally pulled apart, Amelia ran her finger over his unshaven upper lip. "Feels nice when we kiss," she said.

"I shouldn't shave?" he grinned.

"I never said that," she burrowed her head into his neck. "You smell so good. So clean."

She pulled back suddenly. "Mike, Dr. Carroll is keeping his family drugged and hostage in their home."

He jerked away, his eyes wide. "What do you mean?"

"I saw him pull into a driveway and I wanted to see what the great doctor was like with his family and I watched them through the window."

Mike was silent.

"Don't you believe me?" she asked.

"Of course I believe you," he said. "He's responsible for Gino going crazy. He's responsible for Angelina setting herself and her house on fire. Of course I believe you, but I don't know what to do. Who will believe us?"

They were both silent.

"I don't know. But until we figure something out, come and meet my Dad and my gran," Amelia said. "I need to see how my Nana is doing."

Mike held onto Amelia's hand and despite the complex and

multiple disasters that swirled around them, Amelia thought that she had never felt so happy.

They found Ethel sitting up in bed, pale but chatting to Henry who was grinning with relief.

"This is Mike," Amelia said and Mike raised a hand in greeting. "This is Nana and my Dad."

"Good to meet you, Mike," Ethel said and Henry got up and shook Mike's hand. Henry seemed flummoxed, and didn't know what to say.

"I should be out in a week," Ethel told Amelia. "I'm feeling much better. I'm so sorry I gave you all a scare."

"Look," Henry said, "we got you some magazines." He stopped short, unable to say anything else and he stared at his hands and twisted them nervously.

The room filled with an awkward silence.

"Tell us about yourself, Mike, " Ethel said and he shuffled and looked as ill at ease as Henry.

"I work in computer programming. I graduated two years ago."

"Computer programming," Ethel said admiringly. "That's the way of the future."

"So they tell me," Mike said and Amelia wanted to get out of the room more than she'd ever wanted anything in her life.

"We've got stuff to do," she said. "Nana, I just wanted to check in again before we left. We'll see you later. Dad, will you still be here?"

Henry nodded furiously and hid behind the newspaper that he had flapped open.

"Good to meet you, Mike," he managed to say in a strangled voice.

"My Dad's a poet," Amelia told Mike, as if that explained everything. "Bye Nana, see you soon."

Amelia tugged Mike out of the room. "Nana's wonderfully normal," she said, "but Dad's like me, only he's three hundred and ninety-seven point five percent worse. Please tell me you've got some nutcases in your family." Mike shook his head. Amelia felt shut out by the normalcy of his life. He must have known what she was thinking because he pulled her to a stop.

"Hey, he said. "Don't do that, okay?" He kissed her. "Don't ever do that. And from what I've seen now, you guys are really close. Anyway, we've got bigger fish to fry than worrying about whether my family will be too normal for you to handle."

They fell silent.

"Let's go to Angelina's house," Mike said. "For no good reason except that I'd like to say goodbye to her."

He led her to his beat-up little white sedan and opened the door. "You may not believe me," he said. "But I'm going to make millions one day. I've got big dreams. I was a sports jock in school. I hit a pretty mean baseball too, but a career in sports is like playing the lottery. I prefer to rely on my brain."

To her dismay, Amelia found his earnest ambitions boring and she didn't know what to say. Was this the same Mike? It was as though the Mike she had previously connected with had disappeared and she felt as if she was on a blind date with a stranger. It suddenly occurred to her that she really knew very little about him. "Do you read books?" she asked, hoping to find a topic they could talk about.

"Yeah, business books mainly," Mike said, as he drove them to Angelina's house.

"Novels?"

"Nope, but I'm big into biographies and autobiographies. I study what the big-time winners did to climb the ladder of success, so I can do the same thing."

Amelia had no idea what to say in reply to that.

"What's your favourite movie?" she asked, scrambling to find a way to connect with him. She remembered him saying that he liked going to movies and it wasn't as if she hadn't ever seen a movie but generally they seemed like a waste of time.

"*Pirates of the Caribbean*. I love Johnny Depp."

Amelia felt despairing. "I liked him in *Edward Scissorhands*," she offered and Mike looked blank. This was not going well. Amelia decided to attribute the awkwardness between them to what had happened to Angelina and she focused on that instead of acknowledging that things between her and Mike were not quite the way she had hoped they would be.

"We're here," Amelia said with great relief and Mike parked and they got out of the car.

"Look," Amelia pointed. "There's Joanne and Whitney."

"And David, too," Mike said and they walked over to join the group.

"Such a terrible thing," Joanne said, and her eyes filled with tears. "I've been crying since I heard about it." Whitney put her arm around her.

David was pale and shaking. "It wasn't Dr. Carroll's fault," he said defensively. "He couldn't have known she'd take him literally."

"He's a maniac," Joanne said. "We trust him, and the things that he says, and look what happens."

"Hello group," Dr. Carroll piped up, appearing at Whitney's side and looking somber. "How is everyone doing? I thought I might find you here."

"This is all your fault," Joanne shouted at him. "You told her to burn down her house."

"Not with her in it," Dr. Carroll reminded her. "We were just brainstorming. The whole point is to come up with some of the most extreme ideas possible. She had tried everything else. I had no idea she was suicidal. There was nothing about that in her file, nor were there any signs."

"You're the expert," Joanne said, blowing her nose. "We rely on you. What good are you if you can't be relied on?"

"I do my best," Dr. Carroll said mildly.

"Your best isn't fucking good enough," Joanne shouted, and there were tiny flecks of white tissue stuck to her chin and Whitney brushed them off.

"I'm going to make sure they investigate you," Joanne said.

"I can do that. I can at least do that."

Dr. Carroll shook his head. "Good luck with that," he said, and his sharp little teeth flashed a grin. "I'm famous for my unorthodox methods and in this game, you win some, you lose some. Besides," he added, "She was on anti-depressants and everybody knows they can trigger all kinds of psychoses."

Amelia was staring at him in horror. She had not been able to utter a single word. She was hanging onto Mike's hand and he too, was silent.

"And may I remind you," Dr. Carroll said. "That we're only on the fifth of a twelve-week course and should you elect to not return, there will be a price to be paid." He grinned and turned to leave. "And," he added, "none of you read the fine print on the documents you signed, did you? You were all in such a hurry for me to fix you and clear the cobwebs of horror from the recesses of your addled brains that you happily signed on the dotted line without paying attention."

Even Joanne looked alarmed when he said this. "What did we miss?" she asked. "Bottom line, Doctor Loco, spill the beans."

"Tread lightly," Dr. Carroll admonished her. "The form says that should I feel the need, *vis-à-vis* that you might be a danger to yourself or anyone around you, that I can check you in for a four week period of inpatient treatment and trust me, you don't come out of that singing *Sunshine On My Shoulders*."

He cast a sad look at the smoldering remains of Angelina's house. "So unfortunate," he said, and he left.

The group stood looking at one another in the manner of car crash victims who were unsure what had just happened.

"Joanne?" Whitney asked in a tiny voice, "can he do that?"

"I guess he can," Joanne admitted. "Did anybody read the whole document? I know I didn't and I should have known better."

"We're utterly at his mercy," David said. "He's the crazy one and we're at his mercy."

"You've got no idea how crazy," Mike started to say, but David raised his hand to silence him.

"My game plan is this," he said. "Pay him, leave quietly, and make like this never happened. Besides, the guy really helped me. And he seemed to help you," he said to Whitney and Joanne, "and even both of you." He directed his last comment at Mike and Amelia. "Good luck with everything."

He turned and trotted off, his head down, his posture resolute.

"I'd better get home or my husband will be wondering where I am," Whitney said and she gave Joanne a deep tongue kiss. "See you tomorrow, honey. Try not to worry. We'll get through this." They watched her leave, her solid mom-hips clearly outlined in the white track pants she was wearing.

"She's still with her husband?" Mike asked and Joanne shrugged.

"Sure. She's got two kids and a twenty-year marriage. I wouldn't ask her to ditch all that and she wouldn't want to."

"But I thought you guys were having a thing?" Mike was perplexed.

"We are. We're having a great thing but life goes on. On a good note, she makes me happy just by being in my life and I'm not crying in the toilets anymore."

"Joanne," Amelia said. "Dr. Carroll is holding his family hostage. He's drugging them and feeding them and keeping them prisoner. His wife, his son, and his daughter."

To her and Mike's dismay, Joanne laughed. "Sweetie, we know you have a weird way of thinking and you see things that aren't there. I know the man's more than a few sandwiches short of a picnic but now that I've calmed down, I see what he's saying. I mean, who in their right mind would burn down their house, with themselves in it? Only a very unstable person and he can't be held responsible for that."

"But you said he was responsible!" Amelia was outraged.

"I did. I was, I am, really sad about Angelina. But if he was right and she was on meds, then who knows? That crap causes all kinds of suicidal tendencies. Trust me, I know. I took them for a year on the advice of my doctor and coming off them nearly killed me. Not to mention that I nearly killed myself being on them. I didn't know who I was."

"I can't believe you're saying this. I saw Dr. Carroll feeding his family. I saw what was going on. Mike, tell her."

"Did you see it?" Joanne turned to Mike who shook his head.

"But if Amelia says she saw it, then she did," he said.

Joanne laughed. "Sweetie, that's your dick thinking, not your head. Listen, I've got to go. This was very sad, very sad. But I agree with David. We got ourselves into this mess, let's do what we have to, to get ourselves out of it and then walk away. I'll see you at group. I'm going to carry on with it."

"I can't believe her," Amelia said, as they watched Joanne walk away. "I cannot believe her."

Mike sighed. "I don't know what we're going to do."

"I have to show you then," Amelia insisted. "We'll go to his house and I'll show you and if he sees us, we can pretend like we're there to talk about Angelina to him, like we need his help. Come on, let's go." Amelia had misgivings about her own suggestion but she figured they had little choice.

"I don't know," Mike said.

"We have to do something," Amelia insisted. "And we're the only ones who will."

Mike nodded and they got back into his car. "I feel like we're walking into a trap," Mike said and Amelia looked at him, narrowing her eyes with determination. "I know, we have to do it," he said and he started the car.

"Drive towards the hospital and I'll direct you from there," she said, her face worried and her arms folded tightly across her chest. Half an hour later, she pointed to a side street and Mike turned into it.

"Stop here, she said, we can walk to the house." She stopped and took her hand in his. "I know this may be stupid but else can we do?"

"Nothing. We have to do this." He stroked the back of her neck and she nodded.

"Joan of Arc wouldn't be afraid," she said.

"Joan of Arc never met Doctor Carroll," Mike replied and Amelia laughed and nodded.

"Let's go then," he said but she stopped him.

"I just realized something. It's only early afternoon. I was here around six thirty. We need to wait till then."

"Yeah, good thinking. While we wait, I'll ask you something I've been wondering. What would you like us to do for our first date, once we actually get to have it?"

She blushed. "I get to choose?"

"You get to choose. Anything."

She chewed on her lip and thought carefully. "I'd like to fill up a picnic basket with nice things and go to the beach with you."

"But it's November," he said. "It's like what, five degrees out, and rainy too."

"Perfect weather if you ask me," Amelia said.

"But we'll get wet and sick and then I'll miss work and lose my job and I won't be able to pay off my student loan and that will be the end of me."

He was joking, but not really. "What about going to a movie?" he asked but Amelia shook her head.

"That's a stupid date. You don't get to talk to the person you're with. You just sit there, staring at the screen like robots."

"But then you go out afterwards and you can talk about it and discuss what you thought."

"Okay. But what kind of movie? I'm not going to see *Pirates of the Caribbean*. It's stupid."

"Hey," Mike said. "I didn't call your idea stupid. I just said it could have bad consequences for me. How about we go and have dinner at a restaurant near the beach and then, if it's not raining, we can go for a walk afterwards?"

Amelia was silent for a moment, then she took his hand. "I'm sorry I said it was stupid. Dinner and a walk sound lovely. I guess I'm so freaked and I'm trying to show you that you and me won't work so you can back out now."

He stroked the back of her hand. "I'm not backing out. We'll figure everything out. You said your Dad's a poet. Has he had books published?"

"Oh yes."

Amelia told Mike the history of Henry's collection of works and Mike's eyes lit up. "I bet he'd be fascinating to talk to," he said. "If I could get him to actually talk to me."

"He can be amazing to talk to," Amelia admitted. "But when he's out to lunch, he's so out to lunch, and you think he'll never come back."

"Speaking of lunch, I'm so hungry," Mike said and he looked at his watch. "We've got time. I say we go to McDonald's and then come back, what do you think?"

"Great idea," Amelia agreed and Mike started the car.

"You know," he said, "as screwed up as all this is, I'm happy to finally be spending time with you. You've been driving me crazy, if you must know."

"Didn't you hear Dr. Carroll," she joked. "We're already officially crazy."

"Yeah, well then, *more* crazy."

"Are you sure we should go to McDonald's?" she asked. "Why not Wendy's? Or A+W? Or Burger King? Or Pizza Hut? Or wait, Baskin and Robbins!"

"I stand corrected," he said. "You're driving me more crazy now." But he grinned at her happily as he started the car.

16. INSIDE

"I KNOW I'M A GUY AND I SHOULDN'T admit to being scared," Mike said later as they crept up the neighbour's driveway, which was once again thankfully deserted. "But I am scared. Dr. Carroll freaks me out. I wonder if I should have told my dad what's going on."

"Would he have believed you?"

"I don't know. Anyway, it's too late now."

Amelia pointed to the kitchen window. "There, I looked in through there."

They crawled through the hedge, then ran across Dr. Carroll's garden and Mike peered through the window.

"There's no one there," he said.

"Let me see." Amelia couldn't believe it. There was no way she had imagined it, that surreal tableau of chatty manic Dr. Carroll and his zombie family.

She peered inside. Mike was right. The dining room table was there just as she remembered, all neat and tidy, but the place was eerily empty and quiet.

"Maybe he's running late or something," Amelia whispered and she turned to Mike and then she let out a piercing scream and Mike jumped.

"I see she's having a bad influence on you," Dr. Carroll said cheerfully to Mike. "If you want to come and see me, why not knock at the front door like everybody else?"

"We didn't think anybody was home," Mike said, lamely.

"Well, now that you're here, come on in," Dr. Carroll said jovially. "Good to see both of you. I understand you're both very upset about Angelina and I'm glad you came over. Come in, and I'll make some tea and we can have a good old chat."

"No thank you," Amelia heard herself say and her voice sounded a thousand miles away to her own ears. "We must be going."

But Dr. Carroll chuckled. "Oh, one cup of tea. You both came the whole way, you must have something on your alleged minds, so come on." He turned and walked around the side of the house. "Follow me," he called out.

"If we go in, we can see what's going on," Mike whispered to Amelia who shook her head.

"I don't like it," she said. "Let's leave."

"But how? How can we just leave? He caught us staring in his window. It would be strange and rude to leave."

"Strange and rude is what I do," Amelia said. "Let's go. Let's go right now."

But Mike was following Dr. Carroll and Amelia was following Mike and before she could say anything else, they were inside the living room. The room was immaculate.

"You like the seventies," Mike commented, looking around and Dr. Carroll nodded.

"Yes, I do. I go antique hunting on the weekends, if you can call the seventies part of the antiquities era. Let me get that tea and we can have a chat. Have a seat anywhere."

Mike sat down on a brown corduroy sofa while Amelia prowled the room.

"No pictures of them," she whispered. "No pictures of anyone."

They heard the kettle boil and snap off and then there was the sound of pouring water. Amelia felt as if sand was running through an hourglass and when the sand ran out, she and Mike would be trapped forever, bogged down, in the quicksand of Dr. Carroll's trap.

"Here we go," Dr. Carroll said. He was carrying a tray with three mugs. "I hope you like the tea. It's a blend I got while in a conference in Boston a while back. I made the cookies too. I love baking. It helps me to think."

He grinned his chipmunk grin and Amelia, following Mike's lead, picked up a cup of tea.

"It's delicious," she said, surprised and Dr. Carroll favoured her with another toothy little smile and a sideways glance.

"How are you both feeling?" he asked. "A lot has happened, this is true. Gino and the gun. Whitney swinging from one sexual partner to another. The episode with David. And now the death of poor Angelina. I want you both to know that my groups aren't generally this action-packed although I am gathering enough research with this one for an entire paper to be published. You certainly are an interesting group. But how are you both? Mike, you go first."

Mike had downed half his tea and was biting enthusiastically into a cookie. "These are great," he said. "Oh, crumbs, sorry Dr. Carroll."

Dr. Carroll waved a hand. "Doesn't matter. Carry on. What were you going to say?"

"Just that this therapy does seem to result in extreme behaviours," Mike said. "Far beyond the accepted norms. Would you say that D.T.O.T. would be a reasonable way for a person to live their day-to-day lives? The consequences are pretty intense."

"Hmmm." Dr. Carroll perched his chin on his fingertips. "Good point. You have to ask yourself what you really want in this life. I believe we're all entitled to live the lives we want, no matter how odd others may consider those lives to be. However, we are expected to mesh and meld with the fabric of so-called normalized society. If we all agreed to accept behavioural anarchy, that would be one thing, but we don't. Therefore, Mike, in answer to your question, I would say no. I would recommend that we employ the powers of D.T.O.T.

when we are attacking neuroses and phobias and the like, but not when we are holding down a job or having a relationship."

Mike didn't appear to know what to say to this so he ate another cookie.

"Do you have family, Dr. Carroll?" Amelia asked, taking a cookie to cloak her question in casual gesture.

"Sadly, no. But also, happily no," Dr. Carroll waved a hand around. "I like a neat and tidy ship and that's just not possible with family. Families are so messy, particularly kids. Stuff everywhere from the time they're babies. Worse when they're toddlers and an unimaginable nightmare when they're teenagers. It's impossible to control."

"Form and function trumps emotion," Amelia said and she gave a jaw-splitting yawn. "Sorry Dr. Carroll, that was rude of me. My gran's in the hospital and I haven't been getting much sleep."

"No problem," Dr. Carroll replied. "And how are you doing, Amelia?"

"I… Dr. Carroll, my, uh…"

Amelia was finding it difficult to speak. She looked over at Mike who was fast asleep, his head awkwardly bent to one side. She felt own eyes being pulled closed, as if gates were being lowered and locked tight. She tried to force her eyelids open but then she gave up and slid into the darkness of a deep black sleep.

Amelia swam through warm waters. Somehow able to breathe underwater, she glided among coral and floated into sea caves, emerging to be kissed by beams of sunlight that penetrated the depths. She and the large schools of fish eyed one another before swimming away. There were blue and yellow striped fish with disapproving little faces, slender red fish who blended in with the coral, and snake-like lizardfish that changed their colours, becoming white against the soft ocean sand. Angelfish, Butterflyfish and Amelia's personal favourite, the Squirrelfish with its huge eyes, reddish body and adorable yellow spiky fins, all kept her company.

Amelia found that she could bounce off the seabed with her toes buried in the soft sand, and this gave her purchase to springboard upwards, but no matter how much she shot up through that warm sunlit water, she could never reach the top. She ended up floating back down to the bottom to glide among the fish and then, for a while, she would forget about trying to reach the surface, and then she would remember and she would try that heavenward bounce again.

Jellyfish pulsated close by, the round curtains of their ball gowns opening and closing like bell jars, while wise-eyed turtles drifted past, and every manner of seashell lined the ocean floor and decorated the sea cave walls.

Amelia found that she could tumble and turn. She could do somersaults and torpedo forward with her arms tightly at her sides and her feet kicking wildly.

She studied her hands in the waxy green gloom of the lava lamp water and saw that her skin was pale and moonlike and her fingers were starfish. She saw her own reflection in the mirrored wall of dark water ahead of her and her eyes were staring. They were fixed wide-open and her mouth hung loose and her hair floated this way and that, like seaweed leached of life.

Then she was seated at a table, her limbs as heavy as lead, her arms pillars of concrete by her side, her legs numb, her appetite ravenous. Trapped inside her anesthetized body and her drugged mind, she wanted to look around but her head was a ballast in heavy waters, and she could not control it.

"Look family, we've got guests!" Dr. Carroll was ecstatic. "We're having a dinner party and I've made a feast. I've been cooking all day, slaving over a hot stove." He gave a high-pitched giggle.

"Mike, Amelia," he said, let me introduce you to my family.

"Yes, Amelia I know I told a porky pie, I do, in fact, have a family. I do! I do! I do! But, but, BUT, like I said, they were so messy! The chaos was incredible. I did what I could to run after them and tidy things up but it was beyond my control."

He dished out the food as he spoke, circling the table with a platter of meatloaf, carefully giving two slices to each person. "And," he continued, "as you know, I'm the master of D.T.O.T. and there I was, trying to live *with* the chaos, trying to be okay with the mess and it was getting harder and harder and I thought what should I do? Well, of course, I should *Do The Opposite Thing,* which was all well and good, but what would that be?"

He ladled servings of mashed potato onto the plates, and the aroma of salty butter, garlic, and heavenly potatoes made Amelia's mouth water and she drooled, feeling a trail of disgusting wet saliva slide down her face. She focused on trying to swallow and she discovered that she could. She found that she could even move her tongue around her mouth, explore her teeth and the roof of her palette, and just this modicum of control brought her joy. She could also think quite clearly and she wondered if the others could too. She looked over at Dr. Carroll's wife and, from the expression behind woman's clear unblinking gaze, Amelia believed that she too was aware of what was going on.

Oddly, though, the power of speech, like their limbs, had been stopped, sentenced to mute. Amelia tried to figure out how this was possible but she also wanted to hear what Dr. Carroll had to say and since she could not do both, she concentrated on Dr. Carroll instead.

"What," Dr. Carroll repeated, "would the opposite be, of me trying to live this normal, terrible, chaotic and uncontrolled life? Then answer pointed to one thing: control. But," he continued, spooning glazed carrots onto each plate, "how does one gain and maintain control? It's not easy when other people are involved. One can make a decision on behalf of the masses, for the good of the masses but will the masses understand, acquiesce and cheerfully agree? No, they will *not*!"

He sat down next to his wife and lovingly tucked a paper napkin into the neckline of her T-shirt.

"Take my sweet Charlotte here," he said tenderly and he carefully loaded a fork with mashed potato and meat loaf. "She had very definite opinions about things, one of which was letting the children have free reign. She was utterly convinced that they need their own space to grow and develop and I tried to explain that it wasn't working for me but she would not, or could not hear me. I tried reasoning with the kids too. Honestly," he said pausing for a moment, the food-laden fork suspended, "it wasn't as if they weren't party to this, they were. I involved them in the decision-making and choices every step of the way but they stubbornly resisted and persisted with their unacceptable levels of behaviour.

"It was difficult for me," he said, now holding a glass of water to his wife's mouth and gently cupping the back of her head with his other hand. "The idea of control came by degrees and at first I only dreamed of having one night, just one beautiful, perfect, quiet and peaceful night and when I achieved it, the results were remarkable and my life was irrevocably changed. I tidied the entire house and the quiet was sheer heaven!"

He grinned. "Nirvana! How did I do it? Chocolate milk-shakes! That's how I did it for the kids. And Charlotte had tea and cookies like you did," Dr. Carroll waved a hand at Amelia and Mike. "They gently fell asleep and I tucked them safely into bed and I cannot describe the sense of peace and order and tranquility that filled my heart and soul.

"The next morning after that pivotal night, I told Charlotte and the kids that they had food poisoning because they woke with headaches, feeling sick. I admit that it had been hard at the time to calculate the dose and I may have given them too much. I told them that they had gone to bed early and they believed me. Of course, I couldn't do it again as soon as I wanted to. I had to wait and that nearly killed me."

He had finished feeding his wife and had moved on to his daughter. "This is Bella," he said conversationally. "Bella is nearly ten and as you can see, she is the spitting image of me. Except for the fact that she's SO UNTIDY! Aren't you, princess?"

He struck the plate sharply with his fork and there was a resounding crack but none of the gathered party flinched or twitched a muscle.

"So, Bella's to blame too," he said accusingly but then he fell silent, with his head cocked to one side. "Well," he reconsidered, "if blame needs to be accorded which it does not. *Responsibility*, yes, we all share that, but not blame. There is no blame."

He mashed a forkful of potatoes into some meatloaf.

"They all have their own idiosyncrasies," he confided. "Charlotte likes to eat each thing individually and she doesn't even like her food to touch. Bella likes hers all smashed together and why I don't just put it into a blender and give her the resulting mush, I've got no idea. Actually I do know. It's because Daddy loves his honey pop *so* much!"

He paused again. "Where was I? Oh that's right, yes, I had that night of perfect peace and I found myself living for the next time it could happen again. I waited as long as I could and then, one Friday night I couldn't hold off any longer. I came home from a terrible day at work — you nutcases are so exhausting really," he waved a fork at Amelia. "And then there are all the politics about whose theories are proving more successful in the wards, who is getting RESULTS! I am constantly under tremendous pressure to achieve milestones and breakthroughs, you have no idea. And what did I come home to? Chaos. Utter chaos." He wiped Bella's chin.

"Now," he said, "you need to know that taking care of the kids and the house was Charlotte's ONLY JOB! How EASY is that? Huh? She didn't have jealous colleagues constantly trying to discredit her, She didn't have a career to maintain and sustain and fight and stress over. She didn't have any of it. The workplace jungle of psychotherapy is no easy arena let me tell you. It's not for pussies. It's a vicious war on a daily basis. Daily, I tell you.

"So, that Friday night, I arrived home and found a pigsty. The kids were running around like savages and there was Charlotte, reclining on the sofa, watching some ridiculous soap opera and drinking red wine, not a care in the world. It was," and he paused dramatically, "the moment when everything changed. I nearly lost it, but to my credit, I did not. No, I did not. I did not raise my voice or slam down my briefcase or do anything such unseemly thing. I just said, very calmly, 'Hi honey, how was your day' and she said, and I will never forget this, she said, 'Oh darling, I've never been so glad to see the back of a week. It was hell.'

"Hell? Her week was HELL? Pray tell, how was that even possible? I was gobsmacked, incredulous, but I didn't let it show. I said something like, 'Poor baby. I tell you what. I've got a great idea. How about I go and get takeout?' The three of them went crazy when I said that. It was like they had won the lottery. The only trouble was that they wanted pizza and it's impossible to crush sedatives into pizza, but all was not lost! Ice cream saved the day."

He finished feeding Bella and he put her knife and fork neatly onto her plate and moved to sit next to his son.

"This little guy's called Jason, which was Charlotte's naming choice. He should have been named Frank, which should have been my name too, but I was given the moniker Frances instead. Frances! It was my father's idea of a joke," he said in a confidential tone to Amelia. "To give me two girls' names; Frances, to go with Carroll. His name was Frank Bruce Carroll, nothing girly about that. But let's not get into my daddy issues or we will be here until pigs fly." He peered into his son's face. "Jason's no daddy's boy either, is he? Oh, you're a real mama's boy, aren't you, kitten? And Jason hates meatloaf," he added as an aside to Amelia who noticed that the only thing on Jason's plate was two slices of meatloaf. She also noticed that no napkin was tucked under Jason's little chin and that his father fed him so quickly that it was surprising the boy didn't choke.

"That Friday night I dosed them and I dosed them good and I cleaned and polished and scrubbed and vacuumed. I washed the walls and the light switches and the doors. I disinfected and sanitized and sorted and folded and I restored ORDER! I came to rest at about four in the morning and I realized then that I couldn't go back. Hadn't I tried that once before? And the crime of it was that when they woke after that first time, they never even noticed what I had done! All they did was complain about their sore heads and their aching tummies. That's gratitude for you. And they created disorder again in the blink of an eye. I couldn't let that happen again. I simply couldn't. I had to think fast. If I was going to maintain this, I needed to come up with a plan. The first thing I did was to race back to the hospital for syringes and more sedatives. I told the nursing staff that one of my patients was having a psychotic breakdown and that I'd fill out the paperwork later. Of course they believed me and I rushed back home to calculate the perfect dose to maintain the family peace. Operation Peaceful Family, that's the code name I have in my head for this!

"I carefully sedated them and then I sat down and created three fictitious files for three outpatients and I devised an experimental methodology and noted that I was doing a field study correlating a new type of sedative with psychoses that had a number of baseline characteristics. I was lucky. I had done something along those lines in my early years as a therapist and so I had a number of patients' files to draw on."

He stopped and looked from Mike to Amelia. "Hmm, who to feed next?"

Amelia's mouth was watering and she hoped it would be her. She couldn't understand how her whole body could feel numb and incarcerated and yet, she was starving, achingly hungry.

"I think I'll go with Mike," he said and he grinned at Amelia. "You wanted to be next, didn't you? You'll have to wait. You don't like to wait, do you? If you ask me, there's nothing psychologically wrong with you, you just need to structure your own life the way you want to, within the confines of this world and really, that's not very hard to do. And you," he said to Mike, "there's nothing wrong with your ability to speak in public, you just don't have anything to say yet. If you came up with some great idea that you wanted to share with the world, I bet we wouldn't be able to shut you up."

He loaded a fork with food and fed Mike who swallowed with evident enthusiasm, despite his deadpan expression.

"You are such a pretty, pretty boy," Dr. Carroll said, gazing at Mike. "Look at you. You're nearly girly you're so pretty. You're so big and manly, with your broad shoulders and your little waist but you're girly too. Maybe I should cut your pretty girly curly hair off and then we'll see how pretty you are." He peered at Mike. "No, you'd still be pretty then," he said, and he sounded sad and he gazed off into space.

"Now, me, I've never been pretty or handsome. And when Charlotte seemed to fall in love with me, I was baffled. It would be like Snow White falling in love with one of the Seven Dwarves. It was just wrong and yet, I couldn't dissuade her, not that I tried too hard."

He forked more food into Mike's eager mouth.

"Such pretty sensual lips," he said to Mike. "You've got such a beautiful mouth. Little dimples, cleft chin, high cheekbones, oh, I hate you, boy, and I'm not afraid to say it. That's enough food for you."

Amelia saw that he'd hardly fed any of the meal to Mike and her heart went out to him. She wondered what Dr. Carroll had in store for her.

"I couldn't believe my good luck when Charlotte married me," he said getting up. "I thought the sun, moon and stars had landed in my lap that very day. It was the best day of my life. I was her prince, we'd rule our kingdom together, and we would live happily ever after. She was MINE!

"But then she got pregnant and everything changed. It was all 'the baby this, the baby that.'"

Dr. Carroll left and went into the kitchen. Amelia heard drawers being opened and a blender sounded but Amelia couldn't turn her head. She heard his footsteps returning and he pulled her chair around to face him, and he sat down holding a bowl.

"Here, pretty girl," he said. "We know you like things to be different and so I got you a special treat."

He raised a spoon to her lips and she took it greedily, nearly weeping with disappointment when she realized what he was feeding her. It was vanilla pudding, the powdered kind you mix with milk, only from the taste of it, he had mixed it with water.

"Yucky pudding!" Dr. Carroll chortled." No succulent meatloaf or carrots or delicious mashed potatoes for you. I'll have yours."

He put the bowl of pudding on the table and he picked up her plate and proceeded to eat it with great gusto, and she, unable to move her head, had to watch him eat every mouthful.

"Oh yummy," he said. "I am such a good cook."

He finished eating and pushed the dirty plate away from him on the table. Then he leaned back and sighed with satisfaction.

"Charlotte is an orphan," he said. "No family whatsoever. She's a psychiatric nurse. That's how we met. I am quite the celebrity in the world of psychotherapists and no doubt that played a role in increasing my appeal. And I can be charming and empathetic. We learn a lot of empathy skills in medical school: how to control our body language to seem impassive, neutral and yet sympathetic. We are taught to smile but just a tiny bit, not so much that the patient will become confused and think we are friends; no, a reassuring smile, to let you know that we understand your pain. Which mostly we do not. Your pain is yours, but that said, we can and do have theories about what you are going through. Although the vast majority of you don't want to get better and so what we do is like banging our heads against a brick wall. But, I digress. I charmed Charlotte and she loved my intellect or psycho-prowess or whatever it was. And I found ways to keep her at home, keep her away from other people who might tell her that she had married far below her level, people who would no doubt help her to leave me.

"We are UNEVENLY YOKED," he yelled at Charlotte. "We always were. Why did you marry me? You made my life hell. And at first I was happy about the baby because I thought it would keep you at home with me more but then I thought NO! I will have to SHARE your love and I couldn't bear that. But it was too late. Too late, I loved you and then you had the baby and you wanted to go back to work and I thought no, no, and so I said we needed to have another child. And I love my Bella, my mini-me! I thought we would have another little me-clone, but no, out popped Jason, a mini-Charlotte and what could I do?"

Still leaning back in his chair, he rested his hands on his belly and closed his eyes. "Home schooling! I persuaded Charlotte to home-school the kiddies! And she agreed. By the time I suggested it, she had lost confidence in her nursing skills and I am ashamed to admit that's largely due to my repeated suggestions that she was a rather poor nurse, when in actual fact, she was excellent. Therefore," he said, sitting up, "no one missed her when she never returned because by that time, she had been gone for too long. She had vanished from their minds. There was no one to miss her, and no one to miss the kids, when I did what I did. It's almost like this was pre-ordained and meant to be. Sometimes I feel like the puzzle pieces fell into place so easily that I was a mere puppet in this as opposed to being the ringmaster.

"Time for the cheese platter," he said and he skipped off to the kitchen, returning with a large tray that he balanced underneath Amelia's nose.

"But you can't have any," he said, singsong, "You can't have any!" He popped a cube of smoked Gouda into his mouth and chewed noisily. "Now just so you know," he said, "we don't have supper together every night. The calories in this meal are enough to last you until the day after tomorrow. Maybe not you," he said and he looked at Amelia. "Or you," he said to Mike. "But you've both got meat on your bones. You might be hungry but you'll survive and it will be good for you.

"You," he said to Mike, "will realize that your fears were nothing when faced with the fear of death by starvation. And you," he turned to Amelia, "will long for routine and your granny and your lovely home life that you took for granted before.

"I bathe you every second day," he said. "And in case you're under the impression that your loved ones will be alarmed by your disappearance, I've got that worked out too. While you were both sleeping, I found your car parked down the street and I drove it to a parking lot in the Niagara, and I left it there. Niagara! So romantic! I took your journal from your backpack," he addressed Amelia, "and I copied your handwriting and you left a note that said that you and Mike were running away, that you didn't feel that you could be together here, and that you and he were leaving. I left your cellphones in the car too, and I bought two bus tickets to New York. Two little runaways," he smirked. "And the evidence to back up it too. I wore Mike's football jacket and his baseball cap and I used his credit card, so there he is, on camera at the Greyhound terminal, buying tickets to whisk his beloved away into the sunset. But it does mean I'm down two more in my group," he mused, "and really, that is not good. Despite the data I am collecting, this group hasn't been one of my better ones. Oh well.

"And now it's time to tidy up and put you to bed." He rolled a wheelchair into Amelia's view. "Come on my love, you first." He picked up Charlotte and put her in the wheelchair and he pushed her down the hallway. Then he returned and loaded Jason, putting heavy Bella onto the little boy's lap and then he rolled them out of sight.

Amelia recalled that the last time she had seen him having dinner with his family, that he had walked them back to their rooms. She wondered if Dr. Carroll had increased their dosage or if they were weakening. As if in answer to her unspoken question, Dr. Carroll pointed at the wheelchair. "I borrowed this from the hospital. Mike may be a pretty boy but he's much too heavy for me to carry. And," he continued, "I had to empty my study for you two. I had to move my things to the basement. And not only that, you've screwed up my stash of sedatives. I've had to increase the patient list and that's not good. I didn't want to do anything to draw attention to myself and now I have no choice. I just hope no one decides to investigate my outpatient study. And you'd better hope so too, because if they do, I'm leaving town and all of you will starve to death."

He wheeled Amelia to his former study and laid her down on a bare mattress. He returned with Mike and he turned them on their sides so that they were facing one another.

"Two little lovebirds," he said, tenderly. "Enjoy the view because you'll soon be asleep."

He returned what seemed like hours later with two syringes and by then Amelia couldn't help herself, she was aching for the escape. The hunger in her belly and the hopeless, nightmarishness of the situation made her long for oblivion.

As the sweet softness filled her blood and the soothing darkness filled her vision, she welcomed the respite.

17. MEGAN AND HENRY AND ETHEL

"SHE WOULD NEVER RUN AWAY," Ethel said firmly to Megan who drew hard on a cigarette and shrugged.

"Henry, what do you think?" Ethel asked and Megan barked a laugh.

"You use the word 'think' loosely, I gather," she said.

Ethel glared at her. "I didn't bring you up to be rude, Megan, and if you insist on it, then please leave the room."

"She's my daughter too," Megan said and Ethel and Henry exchanged a look.

"You two can think whatever you like," Megan said, exhaling two streams of smoke out of her nostrils. "I do care. And although I find it hard to believe she'd commit to a boy, I do think she ran away. You saw the note."

"It would be easy to fake her writing," Ethel said.

"But who would do that? And they left their cellphones. And they bought two tickets to New York."

"Amelia has never expressed an interest in New York," Ethel said and Henry agreed.

"Maybe her boyfriend did."

"I don't know," Henry volunteered. "He looked quite strait-laced to me."

"You met him?" Megan was astounded.

"Yes. At the hospital. He seemed like a nice boy. Too ordinary for Amelia, but nice. I can't see him running off. He didn't strike me as the type."

"And Amelia told me he was very career-orientated," Ethel said. "She said he was in the group because he struggled with public speaking, which interfered with his entrepreneurship, which made me smile because it sounded so earnest. He wants to be the next Steve Jobs apparently."

"From what I saw, he's heading for disappointment," Henry said.

"Did they see them on the security cameras?" Megan interrupted. "Buying the tickets for New York?

"The cameras weren't working that night," Ethel said. "The police said they are broken more often than not."

"Here's what I don't get," Megan mused. "Why leave the car? Why not sell the car? They don't have any money and they haven't made any ATM withdrawals even though their bank cards are missing. How have they bought food or got a hotel or anything?" She sat down. "I'm really staring to worry," she said.

"About time," Ethel remarked.

"So what can we do?"

"Nothing," Henry said. "That's what makes it worse. The police don't seem to care at all and they've bought the story that they ran away, hook, line, and sinker"

"What about Mike's family?" Megan asked.

"They're extremely worried," Ethel said. "We've spoken a few times."

Again Megan was surprised. "When? Where was I?"

"At the gym or not taking it seriously yet," Ethel said.

"Take me through it again," Megan said. "Start right at the beginning."

"I was in hospital and Henry was there," Ethel said patiently. "That was the Friday. Amelia and Mike came to visit and then they left. I didn't hear anything from her on Saturday and I didn't worry, but then the following day, I got worried. I phoned her five or six times and her phone went to voice mail, which it never does. Henry was with me the whole time and we didn't know what to do. I phoned the police from the hospital on Sunday afternoon and they told me I had to wait before I could file a report and was I sure she was missing? I told them she has never been out of touch for this long and that she was with a young man named Mike but I didn't know his last name. Because it was the weekend, they said I should wait, because plenty of young people get up to shenanigans on the weekend, and they would come home on Sunday night.

"And Henry and I didn't know it then but Mike's parents had already reported him missing and the police also told them they had to wait longer before a search alert could be issued. However, the police did take the registration number of the car and the license number, and they spotted the car at the bus station in Niagara on the Monday, along with Amelia's note saying she and Mike had run away. The police also found their cellphones and they phoned me. And then they came to the hospital and told us what they had found, and that Amelia and Mike had run away to New York.

"I asked them for Mike's family's telephone number and they wouldn't give it to me but they said they'd give mine to them, and thank heavens his parents phoned me. But they didn't have much to add.

"By Tuesday, the doctors figured I could come home and so Henry brought me here and he stayed with me and here we are, now."

Megan was silent, in deep thought. "You haven't seen or heard from her in five days. It doesn't add up. Amelia running off to New York. I mean it kind of does but it also doesn't." She lit another cigarette.

"Mom," she said, "tell me everything you know about this group. That's where she met this boy? When do they meet?"

"Yes, she met him there. Thursdays, from one to three, at the hospital."

"And the doctor's name?"

"Dr. Carroll Frances, or Frances Carroll, I can't remember which way around."

"I say we crash the group tomorrow," Megan said.

Henry paled. "I can't go there," he said.

"Fine," Megan replied, "I will."

"I'm coming with you," Ethel said.

Megan shook her head. "You're not well enough, Mom."

"But you won't know what to say," Ethel said and Henry nodded his head vigorously in agreement.

"Thanks for the vote of confidence but I'll be fine."

"Oh my god!" Henry gave a strange gasp and they both turned to look at him.

"Spit it out, husband," Megan said.

"She said something. Oh, what was it…?" Henry said. "Amelia came to see me at the house and I wasn't feeling good and she made me soup and she told me something about her therapist. Oh, what was it?" He slapped his forehead. "Think, think, think."

"I know it was a pretty weird group," Ethel said. "Some of the members started having sex with each other in the washroom, and the therapist said that was great. The therapy itself is about doing the opposite to what you'd normally do, given that your normal is not being productive or helpful in the real world."

"They had sex? All of them?" Megan was horrified.

"No, just some of them. And then some guy went crazy and waved a gun around."

"A gun! Mom, how could you let her keep on going?"

"It made sense in the context that Amelia explained it. It was a reaction to the therapy," Ethel said, miserably. "Although, hearing it now, it doesn't sound above board."

"What else?"

"I think there was a hoarder woman and – oh my god!" This time it was Ethel who exclaimed in horror and the other two looked at her.

"What, Mom? What?"

"I read it in *The Sun*, about a hoarder woman who killed herself and her rabbits. Amelia told me about this woman who was a terrible hoarder and that she had rabbits. I can't see there being two people like that, can you?"

"What did you read in *The Sun*?"

"A woman, a hoarder, killed herself and her rabbits! She burned down her house with them in it."

"That is the opposite of hoarding and being alive," Henry commented. "It must be the same woman."

"And there was some fellow whose wife was running a meth lab and the group pulled a sting and got the police involved," Ethel said.

Megan stared at her. "Mom? How on earth could you let Amelia continue with this?"

"Lots of reasons," Ethel said defensively. "She wanted to go because of Mike and like I say, when Amelia explained it in context, it made much more sense than it does now. I can hear how it sounds now."

"Recriminations are counter-productive," Henry said, patting Ethel's hand and giving Megan a look.

"Yeah, yeah," Megan grumbled. "My god, what a mess. No question in my mind. I have to go to the group. What do we know about this therapist? I'm going to Google him."

They followed her to her bedroom and waited while she booted up her computer. "Here we go. He looks like Paul Giamatti. Got a list of credentials longer than my arm, and he's won awards and citations for his work. I'm quoting here: his 'unorthodox but highly successful psychiatric therapeutic strategies.' He's a leader in his field. He was brilliant at university, and he's being hailed as the new Jung mixed with Freud, with a dose of existential, non-conformist philosophical idealism mixed in. In other words," she said, turning to Henry and Ethel, "he's a full-on mega wingnut."

"Where does he stand on medications?" Henry asked.

Megan studied the screen and scrolled down. "It doesn't say."

"I'm going to find his home address and pay him a visit," Megan said and she tapped at her keyboard. "Frick. He must have paid to be unlisted."

"Wherever he is, at home, at the hospital, wherever, I can't go near him," Henry said. "The sound of him scares the beje-sus out of me."

"It's okay," Megan told him. "I'll meet him. Let's Google this hoarder who died in the fire. Here we go: Angelina Sante Croce. She was sixty-six. She had two kids and four grand-kids, and her husband died a year ago. It says here that she had been undergoing psychiatric treatment for some time and that anti-depressants led to her suicide. That last by the way, was an observation from our good Doctor Carroll. Which lets him off the hook, wouldn't you say? 'Look, Ma, the drugs did it, it wasn't me.'"

She switched off the computer. "I'm going to have a shower. Henry, do you want to stay here with us until this is sorted out?"

He nodded and then he started crying. "I love her, Megan. You've got to get her back."

"I will, Henry, I will. I'll get out girl back. Don't you worry either, Mom. I'll get to the bottom of this."

18. GROUP THERAPY: SESSION SIX

MEGAN LOOKED AROUND THE ROOM. There was a giant blonde man, a large pale-skinned gothic girl, a plump blonde housewife-mom type, a balding middle-aged business-man, a tall girl with freshly-dyed platinum hair and thick bangs, and a skinny Paris Hilton look-alike who kept admiring her gigantic engagement ring. No one seemed to be talking so she kept quiet too.

Five minutes after the appointed hour, a short stocky man rushed into the room and sat down, hefting his plastic bag of papers to one side. "Hello Shannon," he said to the blonde girl with bangs. "Good to see you back. Now, group, a lot has happened since last we met," he said. "We have lost a few members of our group. One to suicide and two of the others have found love and run away."

It was tough for Megan to remain silent but she clenched her jaw and waited for him to continue. He seemed utterly self-absorbed.

"But Alexei has returned to us, and that is good news. I intervened with Joanne and I negotiated with the police and Joanne has kindly agreed to drop the charges and Alexei will complete his therapy. I know you are sad about Angelina and we will talk about that—"

"What happened to Angelina?" the Paris Hilton girl piped up, interrupting Doctor Carroll and a few of the others looked enquiring too.

"She died by her own hand," Dr. Carroll said solemnly. "The official verdict is that her medication led to psychosis, and there was nothing anyone could do."

There were a few gasps in the room.

"And who ran away?" the gothic girl asked.

"Amelia and Mike," Dr. Carroll sighed. "They abandoned everything and left for New York to follow the path of true love."

Megan wondered how he could knew so much about what had happened to Amelia and Mike but before she could follow that train of thought, the blonde housewife spoke up. "Shouldn't we abandon this group? Can't we? Please. I don't want to come any more, and neither do I want to pay you to be able to leave."

The middle-aged businessman agreed. "I want out too," he said.

"But David," Dr. Carroll looked confused. "We helped you reclaim your life. We helped you achieve liberation from those who were stealing from you and deceiving you. And Whitney, you have found happiness and peace in sexual liberation, so why would you want to leave? We can't abandon this group. Where is Joanne by the way, does anybody know?"

"She had to go on a business trip this week," Whitney said. "She said for you to send her the bill for a missed session.

"She should have told me," Doctor Carroll sounded aggrieved. "I will bill her. And who, exactly, are *you*?"

He addressed the last to Megan, having finally noticed that she was there.

Megan cleared her throat. "I'm Megan, the mother of the girl who supposedly ran away for love," she said, her voice dripping with sarcasm. "I'm here to find some answers."

"You can't just join in," Dr. Carroll was indignant. "There are protocols to be followed. We discuss sensitive issues in our groups!"

"I can't think of anything more sensitive than my daughter's disappearance," Megan commented. "And since you are being funded by the government to treat her and she's not here, I am stepping, in, in lieu of her." She looked at Dr. Carroll calmly. "You can try to throw me out, if you like," she said, flexing a bicep twice the size of his leg as she leaned forward to rest her chin on her hand.

"As far as I am concerned, she can stay," Whitney said. "She's Amelia's mother for god's sake and it's not like we've got anything to hide."

David agreed. "Let her stay," he said tiredly to Dr. Carroll. "Come on, Doc. I decided to come back instead of paying you out, so let's get on with it."

"Frankly, I've had enough of this shit," Ainsley said and she opened her purse and scribbled on a cheque. "Here. This is rubbish."

"Is it?" Dr. Carroll looked at her squarely. "How many panic attacks have you had since the group started?"

"None," she admitted.

"And how often have you left your home in the past two months?"

"A lot," she said. "I can pretty much come and go whenever I want to."

"Therefore I would call the treatment a success," Dr. Carroll said. "Wouldn't you?"

"Call it whatever you like," Ainsley said, "I'm done with it." She thrust the cheque at Dr. Carroll and rushed out the room as if she was worried he would try to stop her.

"I consider her a success," Dr. Carroll said, and he took some papers out of his plastic bag and made a note. "Excellent. No panic attacks, and she can leave the house whenever she wants to." He ticked off a list and grinned. "I do love a happy ending!"

He looked at the small remaining group. "Fine. We will continue, albeit with a stranger in our midst. Today we are going to examine our core beliefs. These are the underlying assumptions and life rules that we have developed along the way. These rules are supposed to help us but, in reality, they hurt and hinder us. We think to ourselves, if we do this thing perfectly, or that thing, according to the rules, then we will be safe but our rules don't work!"

He grinned. "Alexei, may I use you as an example?"

The big blonde giant shrugged.

"Thank you. I would say that despite your size and your muscle power, that you essentially feel invisible and unloved in this world. You react with expressions of anger and violence in order to make yourself feel alive and acknowledged. You only feel visible when you seduce women. Your core belief is one of 'if I don't assert myself daily in an aggressive or sexual way, I don't exist.'"

Megan expected the giant to roar with outrage but he sat up straighter and looked interested.

"But these core values that you rely on, only do you harm. Violence and sex bring you hurt and anxiety. You are always looking for the next fight, or the next woman, to affirm your place in the world. I want you to stand up."

"Now?" Alexei was bewildered.

"Yes, now. Please stand up."

Alexei stood up awkwardly and shoved his hands in the pockets of his jacket.

"Relax," Dr. Carroll said. "It's all right to feel nervous but everything is fine. Now, I want you to say: 'I am Alexei and I am a valuable human being.'"

Alexei mumbled something and Dr. Carroll shook his head. "But wait," he said. "Group, I'm going to bring you into this too. After Alexei says his mantra, we must all shout, and I do mean shout, '*We love you, Alexei.*' Let's try again. Come on, Alexei."

"What must I say again?"

"I am a valuable human being," Dr. Carroll reminded him.

"I am a valuable human being," Alexei repeated and Dr.

Carroll, Shannon, Persephone, Whitney, and David shouted
"*We love you, Alexei!*" and Megan jumped.

"I am a valuable human being," Alexei shouted and the
group yelled back at him.

This went on for about ten minutes and Megan watched
the giant man's body language change from that of a defiant
fighter to a happy schoolboy.

"Fantastic!" Dr. Carroll wiped his brow. "Okay, Alexei, you
can sit down now. I want you to say that to yourself every
day, a hundred times a day, and imagine us telling you that
we love you.

"Now group, it's time for meditation. As you know, this isn't
my favourite part but we must do what we must do. Today
I have brought some sounds and we will meditate on them.
Please get comfortable and close your eyes. Place your feet
firmly on the floor. Here we go."

He took a small, antiquated tape recorder out of his satchel. He rang a bell and switched on the recorder that made a
crackling sound, followed by crashing waves.

Megan opened one eye and looked around. Everybody's eyes
were closed except for Dr. Carroll who was staring at her with
an openly hostile expression. So venomous was his gaze that
Megan was alarmed and she could feel her heart racing. The
two of them stared at one another until Megan dropped her
gaze and closed her eyes, preferring the privacy of not having
to be the focal point of that laser stare. The bell finally rang
and the group opened their eyes and Dr. Carroll surveyed the
room. "I would like to ask our visitor a question," he said,
and Megan felt her stomach clench.

"Go ahead," she said, pleasantly.

"It's clear that you take enormous pride and care in your
body," Dr. Carroll said. "My question is this, what is it a
substitute for? What hole in your life are you trying to fill?"

"I lost my husband to psychosis many years ago," Megan
said evenly. "He was, and still is, the love of my life and we

are still married although we cannot be together. I work out because it gives me a sense of community and belonging. Also, I used to be quite fat and I like being this way better. Being fat," she said pointedly, her gaze on Dr. Carroll's little paunch, "is not an optimal way of thriving in this world. Did I answer your question adequately, Doctor? "

"Hmmm, yes, but I sense a lot of anger," Dr. Carroll said and Megan laughed.

"Doctor, this isn't even close to anger. But anger is what I do feel toward you, oh yes."

"Can you explain that further?" Dr. Carroll sat up, his beady eyes glittering. He was spoiling for a fight.

"I sent my daughter here to you, in good faith and now she's missing. Gone."

"Ah." He rubbed his hands together. "In a nutshell, I practice what is known as D.T.O.T. therapy, which is *Do The Opposite Thing*. Your daughter's interpretation of this was to run away. Running away is her way of expressing the opposite action to the life she was living."

"That doesn't make sense to me," Megan argued. "Amelia was always running off. Staying would have been the opposite thing. Having a relationship with this man, that would have been the opposite thing. So what you're saying doesn't make sense."

"Psychotherapy can never be fully understood," Dr. Carroll said, "particularly by those who are untrained in the field. In such matters you have to trust the experts to guide you. We have your mental health issues at heart, we take your healing very seriously and you are in good hands."

Whitney gave a loud snort and the group turned to her.

"Whitney, do you have something you'd like to add?" Dr. Carroll asked but she shook her head.

"Fine, then that's it for the day, we are going to end early. Group, for your homework, I want each of you to identify a core belief that you grew up with, and then I want you to dismantle it, in the same way we did with Alexei. I look forward to hearing your results next week. Go forth and D.T.O.T. *till the cows come home!*"

He gathered his plastic bag and his satchel and rushed out of the room.

Megan looked up to see Whitney standing next to her.

"Let's go and get a coffee," Whitney said.

"As you can see, I am blonde now," Megan overheard the tall girl say to the giant Russian, but she gathered her things and followed Whitney, and she missed hearing his reply.

"Frickin' nutcase, isn't he?" Whitney said, after they had grabbed a coffee and were seated in the cafeteria. "Although, he does get some things right, I'll give him that much. I am happier now and much less anxious. Having sex with people other than my husband is definitely the key to happiness in my life."

"Yeah, well. The only thing I'm interested in is if you know anything about Amelia's disappearance? Oh shit!" Megan smacked her hand on the table, causing Whitney to jump.

"What?"

"I forgot to ask Dr. Carroll how he knew so much about Mike and Amelia's disappearance."

"Did the police know they met at this group?"

Megan thought for a moment. "My mother and Mike's parents would have told them, yes."

"Then the police probably would have told Doctor Carroll," Whitney said.

"Maybe. But I just can't see Amelia running away," Megan said. "She loves her gran and her father. She might leave me but she wouldn't leave them. Did anyone say anything that could help? Did they ever mention New York?"

Whitney shook her head. "I've got to get going. I'll phone you if I think of anything and I'll ask Joanne, she's back tonight. I would say don't worry but I'd be sick with worry too. And you call me, if you hear anything."

Megan said she would and she sat there for a while after Whitney left, staring into space, and wondering what she could do next.

19. DR. CARROLL AND AMELIA

"THERE IS A PROBLEM WITH YOUR BEING HERE," Dr. Carroll said to Amelia. He had brought a chair in with him from the dining room, and he had his legs crossed and his hands were folded behind his head. "The problem is that I didn't invite you. You have brought with you a range of complications from small to large. On the small side of the problematic scale, there is hygiene. The thought of touching either of your bodies repulses me. As does, god help me, the idea of taking care of your bowel activities. And I don't want to have to cook for you either. After all, I am your therapist. You are both supremely inferior to me. You came to me for help, for guidance, by way of my intellect. The intention was not — although some do see therapy in this light — the intention was NOT for me to be your NANNY!"

Amelia was lying on her back as he had positioned her and the only thing she could see was the ceiling. She swallowed and tried to form a sound but her voice was still mute.

Dr. Carroll sighed. "I don't know what to do really. I'll have to think about this one." He got up and left the room. She heard the front door open and close, and Dr. Carroll was gone.

Amelia lay still. Mike was next to her, snoring slightly.

Amelia wondered how much time had passed since she and Mike had vanished. She wondered how Dr. Carroll had covered up their disappearance but she was sure his story was airtight. She wondered if anybody was worried about them and looking for them. She hoped Ethel was out of hospital and she tried to send her mind messages, telling her to look for them.

Amelia's eyes were wide open and she was forcing herself to make little growling noises in her throat and eventually she was able to make a sound. She graduated to trying to form words. "Ma….. Ma….. Mak….. Mak!"

"Mak?" The word was hardly decipherable but she was grateful for the utterance.

"Mike?" She said his name as quietly as she could but there was no reply.

She lay on her back and closed her eyes and concentrated hard on trying to roll over. It was impossible to do in one motion but she broke it down, first by just trying to move her right arm across her chest. By the time she achieved this gigantic feat, she was drenched in sweat and she felt exhausted.

She wasn't sure why but the sedative was metabolizing in her system in a different way to Mike and Doctor Carroll's family; it seemed to be leaving her bloodstream much faster. She was worried that Dr. Carroll would notice this and administer the next dose before the current one had worn off.

She was about to roll over onto her stomach when she heard a noise. Alarmed that Dr. Carroll had returned, she flopped over onto her back, and adjusted herself into the same position as he had left her. No sooner had she done this, than the doctor pushed his way into the room.

He sat down on the floor and heaved a great sigh. "You two have caused me an inordinate problem," he said. "Really and truly you have. Why did you have to come here? Why?"

He sat cross-legged and put his head into his hands. "I don't know what to do with you," he said, his voice muffled. "I have to get rid of you but I don't know how to do it. I'm not a violent man. I'm not. I never thought it would come to this."

He rubbed his face. "I could kill you easily enough, that part is not the problem. It's the disposing of the bodies. Hmmm…."

He fell into deep silence. "If your bodies were ever found,

the drugs in your system would lead you right back to me. And it's not easy to dispose of bodies, it's much harder than you would think. They make it look so easy in the movies but I wouldn't even know where to start. Although, that said, I could drive north for a few hours, find a couple of side roads and dump you in the swamps. But I'd have to wade into the swamps, carrying you, and you are both so heavy and there are snakes in those waters and frogs and god knows what, so no… that won't work.

"Oh, this is such a problem. I wonder if I should disappear instead. But why should I have to give up everything I have worked so hard to achieve? Why should I be the one to lose everything just because two nosy parkers poked their nosy noses where they shouldn't have?

"What about fire? I could try to burn you both, but bodies don't burn entirely in a fire and how and why and where would you have set yourselves alight? I don't think I would be able to create a scenario in such a way that it would be believable to anyone.

"There's dismemberment of course. I could dismember you in the bathtub but the blood, ugh, blood. And I would have to buy saws and knives and plastic sheets and containers and, from what I've read, evidence of blood is extremely hard to rid of. And what would I do with the body parts? I am back to square one. Problems with disposal.

"A lover's pact? Perhaps suicide? Yes… but I'd need to get you both into a motel which would be a logistical nightmare. Slitting your wrists would be easy but I'd also have to make sure that enough time passed for the drugs to clear out of your system. And how am I supposed to get you two lugs into a motel without being seen?"

He gave a great sigh. "I have to prepare dinner for my family. You two can starve to death for all I care. He got up. "I'm one of the top two percentile of brilliant geniuses," he said. "I will think of something."

20. RESCUE

APART FROM THE DOCTOR BEING a thoroughly unlikeable man, Megan reported to Henry and Ethel that she hadn't discovered anything. It was Thursday evening and Megan was close to tears. "I feel at a loss," she said. "I thought I could solve this but I can't. Did Mike's family have any updates?"

Ethel shook her head. "They've hired a private detective but there's nothing new. They said Mike has never been out of contact for this length of time. He phones or texts them twice a day."

The three of them fell silent and when the telephone rang, they leapt in fright. Megan nearly fell over the table rushing to answer it. "Yes?" She was breathless.

"Megan? It's Whitney. I've got Joanne with me. She remembered something that might or might not have any relevancy. She said that Amelia said something about Dr. Carroll holding his family hostage and Joanne feels terrible because she dismissed it and told Amelia she imagining things."

"Can I talk to Joanne?"

"Yeah, here you go."

"Wait, I'm putting you on speaker," Megan said. "Amelia's gran and dad are with me too."

"Hi," Joanne said and she spoke in a rush. "To cut a long story short, we all, from the group I mean, we bumped into each other at Angelina's burnt house and Amelia announced that Doctor Carroll is keeping his family hostage. I didn't know what to say or do. I mean we were standing outside the house where Angelina had just killed herself and I couldn't deal with it. I thought that Amelia was imagining things, but now I don't know. Mike was with her, and he said he believed her, but I think maybe they went back to the house so Mike could see for himself. He hadn't seen it with his own eyes and maybe she wanted to show him."

"Yes! That's what she told me too," Henry spoke up loudly, horrified. "That's what she said, about the hostage thing but I was in a funk and then Ethel was sick and then…"

"It doesn't matter, Henry," Megan said and she patted him on the shoulder. "We have to find out where the doctor's house is, and go there. I tried looking him up online but he's not listed."

"I know," Whitney said. "We'll go the hospital and I'll pretend I have to see him and I'll ask for his home address."

"They'll never give it to you," Ethel said. "But you could fake a breakdown and have him summoned and then Megan could follow him home when he leaves."

"I could do that," Whitney said. "I do hysterical exceptionally well."

"We must hurry," Henry urged. "We don't know what's going on. Amelia is in terrible danger. I can feel it."

"But if you have a breakdown, they will sedate you and keep you there," Joanne said to Whitney and the three gathered around Ethel's table could feel Whitney's shrug.

"I don't care," she said. "As long as you find a way to follow him and get those kids back."

"Let's meet at the hospital," Megan said. "Mom, you and Henry stay here."

"No way," they both said.

"Forget it," Ethel added. "We're all going."

"We'll leave now," Joanne said. "We'll meet you in the main reception area. We don't want to be wandering around the hospital trying to find each other."

They hung up and Megan helped Ethel to the car, and Henry

climbed into the back. "I really don't think you're well enough to do this," Megan told her mother.

"I'm not going to waste time and energy talking about it," Ethel was firm. "Let's go."

They arrived at the hospital and Megan rushed into the main area and she soon spotted Joanne and Whitney and Ethel and Henry caught up with them.

"Are you ready for the performance of your life?" Joanne asked Whitney who nodded.

"I've got a lot of stored-up rage," she said. "Watch me. But don't leave me in there, honey? You'll come for me as soon as you can?"

"Count on it," Joanne said and she gave Whitney a kiss.

They took the elevator to the eighth floor of the psych wing and Whitney started shuddering and shaking, and by the time they reached the reception desk, she was weeping rivers of tears, not bothering to wipe them away. Joanne led her to the nurses station.

"Dr. Carroll has totally screwed up," Joanne shouted. "He's driven Whitney over the edge, and now she can hardly speak. Call him and get him to come here NOW!"

"Calm down," the nurse said, looking nervous.

"I will NOT CALM DOWN," Joanne yelled. "This is all Dr. Carroll's fault. I want you to get him here NOW!"

The nurse was already dialing a number and Ethel, Megan and Henry, who were waiting around the corner, could hear as she urged Doctor Carroll to come to the hospital.

"What's her name?" the nurse asked Joanne.

"Whitney Abrien. She's part of his D.T.O.T. group," Joanne said.

The nurse repeated the name into the phone and listened. "He's on his way," she said reassuringly, but Whitney didn't let up. She carried on sobbing and Joanne kept a firm arm around her shoulder while Ethel, Henry and Megan kept a careful eye on the goings-on. All they could do was wait.

Back at the house, shortly after Dr. Carroll left the room, Amelia tried to sit up. She managed to raise herself upright and was startled to hear the ringing of a phone and, in the silence of the house, she could hear Dr. Carroll clearly.

"What? Whitney? Yes, she is. What? Now? No, I can't come now. What? Joanne? Oh for heaven's sake. All right, fine, I'll be there in ten minutes. Try to keep her calm. Try to calm them both down."

She heard him muttering and putting on his shoes and gathering his car keys and then she heard the slamming of a door and a resounding silence echoed through the empty hall.

Amelia rolled over onto her stomach and leopard-crawled across the room. Her progress was painstakingly slow and she soon had carpet burns from her elbows to her hands.

"Cheap, shitty carpet," she muttered, as she reached the doorway. "Why couldn't you be thick shag rug or a nice rich pile? Or a nice shiny parquet, like Dad's flooring. That would be super easy to slide along. But no, it has to be wiry brown office crap, the kind that's made out of plastic fibers if you look at them closely enough, which I am now, not out of choice. It looks like a scrubbing brush or something you'd see in the conference room of a cheap hotel."

Chatting quietly to herself, she made it to the doorway of her and Mike's room. She dragged herself around the doorframe and her heart sank. She only had about two kilometers to go before she reached the kitchen. She frowned and bit her lip and her brow furrowed in concentration. *Do or die.*

She inched forward in the unnatural silence of the house, the house that was inhabited by four sleeping bodies, four ghostly bodies, specters in limbo, unaware of what was going on, unaware that their lives depended on her actions and the success of her achieving her goal.

"You ruined my life!" Whitney wailed. "My husband found out about Alexei and Joanne and he's leaving me and the kids!

It's all your fault! And Angelina died because of you and Gino's dead because of you and…"

"Three milligrams of Clonazepam, now," Dr. Carroll said to the nurse.

"Three?" The nurse looked at him, one eyebrow raised.

"Don't question me," Dr. Carroll snapped. "She's experiencing a psychotic break. We need to sedate her immediately."

"You're to blame!" Whitney wailed again. "It's all your fault. I want to kill myself, and you. I want to kill you first and then me."

She gulped down the pills the nurse gave her.

"And I want you to tell my husband that it wasn't my fault it was all yours. I was just doing what you—"

She wailed for another few minutes, slowly winding down until she sank into the arms of an orderly who hauled her up onto a waiting stretcher.

"I'll come and check on her first thing tomorrow morning," Dr. Carroll said tiredly.

"What's going to happen to her?" Joanne demanded to know.

"None of your business," he replied. "Unless you're next of kin, which I happen to know you're not."

"I care about her and I know that was she said was true," Joanne said, trotting alongside him, hoping it wasn't apparent that all she really wanted to do was follow him to his car so that she could make a note of the model and license number and see which direction he went.

Ethel, Megan, and Henry had already left the hospital and were waiting for her call. They were ready to take off in whichever direction she told them to.

"True, truth, what is truth?" Dr. Carroll said. "You people, my god, you make me sick. You don't have the courage to face truth if it looks you in the eye. You'd rather hide behind the suburban safety of endless self-deception than face your real selves. Know thyself. You all think you want that but you don't."

"And you think *you* could handle the truth?" Joanne challenged him, happy that they were already in the elevator heading towards the ground floor and main reception area.

"I know I could," Dr. Carroll laughed. "I have done so, many times. I can always rely on myself for that."

"Will we still have group next week, if Whitney's not here?" Joanne was still gamely trying to make conversation and they finally crossed the polished acres of the reception area and pushed their way through the revolving doors.

Dr. Carroll looked surprised. "Of course, why not? Look, we are at my car. I cannot talk to you anymore. I must go home. I'll see you at group." He waved her away dismissively.

"I'll come by tomorrow to check on Whitney, whether I am family or not," Joanne said, and she fingered her phone in her pocket, getting ready to whip it out.

"Whatever rocks your boat," Dr. Carroll said shortly and he started his car and sped out the parking lot.

"Silver grey, Chrysler sedan, license plate, DTOTRULE, leaving via Midland exit," Joanne said breathlessly, thinking the phone had taken forever to ring through to Megan.

"Yeah, I can see him," Megan said. "Follow in your car and stay on the line. I'll let you know where we're headed."

Joanne ran to her car and wrenched the door open. "Oh Whitney," she said, accelerating out into the street. "I'll be back to get you tomorrow, I promise."

Amelia's raw and bloody arms were stinging by the time she was halfway down the hallway. When she reached the end of it, her flesh felt as it was on fire. She thought fleetingly of Joan of Arc, burning at the stake and what an excruciating way that was to die, and she felt renewed sympathy for Joan. She was also reminded of her bravery and she took courage from Joan's battlefield heroics.

"Be with me, Joan," she whispered. "I must prevail."

She could either drag herself forward through the living room to the front door but that meant she would have to face another vast field of painful iron-bristle carpeting, or she could turn right and drag herself across the comparative coolness of the white linoleum kitchen floor.

If she could only reach the kitchen door that opened out to the garage. Then, to her horror, she heard the sound of a car returning, an engine being switched off, and a car door slamming.

She kept her head down, trying not to acknowledge that the front door was being opened and she strained in concentration in the subsequent silence as Dr. Carroll padded into the house.

She hoped that he would stop in the living room and sit down for a moment, and her prayers were answered when she heard the squeak of his favourite leather armchair.

She turned right and dragged herself into the kitchen, believing that she could make it to the garage: she could, she could. She crawled around the kitchen table and realized in a fatal moment that two things awaited her: a door handle she could not reach and the unmistakable shoes of Dr. Carroll. She raised herself up on her bleeding raw elbows and looked at him.

"You've made a mess of my kitchen floor," he said. "Blood everywhere." He pulled out a chair and sat down. He studied her and rested his hands on his belly. "You really are an anomaly," he said. "The sedatives should have knocked you sideways into next Sunday."

"They nearly did," she said and she smiled at him.

"You're awfully cheerful for a person about to meet their death," Dr. Carroll remarked and Amelia managed a laugh.

"You won't kill us," she said confidently.

"Oh no? And why not, pray tell?"

"Because that would be the obvious solution. You're going to do the opposite thing."

He gaped at her. "Oh come now, that's a cliché attacking a cliché."

"You have no faith in your life's work? I think you do have faith. I think that of all the things that have gone wrong in your life, the one thing that you do believe in is D.T.O.T. And what's more, you know it works. It may be extreme, as seen in the cases of Gino and Angelina, but it does work. Honesty replaces self-delusion."

"And I'm going to stand up in front of the world and announce that I'm a kidnapper, a would-be murderer, and a liar?"

"Yes."

"That's utterly ridiculous," he said, but he thought about Joanne's challenge to him only moments before. Would he have the honesty to stand up and be his true self, when it counted?

And Amelia, unknowingly, pushed the point home further.

"Many of the things you proposed sounded insane. *Doing the opposite thing.* But we did them and they worked. Why not say that? Wouldn't that be honest? Wouldn't that be the truth? You've lived your life honestly all along, according to your own set of opposite rules, and I can't see you not doing it now."

"Interesting," Dr. Carroll said, and he tapped his fingertips together. "It would be a relief to come clean. I admit that. And you are not wrong when you say that that action would be more true to myself than if I murdered you and the boy and left your bodies to rot in the woods. That wouldn't really be me being myself. But me saying: look, I wanted control, I wanted order and I wanted peace and I took control and achieved it. Well, yes, that would be me!" His eyes glittered with happiness but then they clouded over."

"But I would be incarcerated," he added. "That wouldn't be pleasant."

"You live within the freedom of your own mind," Amelia reminded him. "You told us that. You told us that being true to ourselves in this worldly cage was preferable to us being our socially-conditioned castrated selves caged in the world created by others." Amelia was not sure if he had in fact said that but he nodded and she continued.

"Besides," she said, "you could write books on D.T.O.T. and

imagine the publicity. You would be lauded for having taken it to the nth degree, for having had the courage to explore its range and unlimited possibilities. You'd be regarded as a man of great courage for having faith in your own work to the extent that you'd give up what others regarded as a great career."

"I'd be kicked out of the profession," Dr. Carroll argued. "I'd be branded a lunatic."

"You'd be called a genius. An *avant garde* hero. A legend. A man of courage and foresight. But it's up to you. I, however, know what you will choose."

"You just don't want to die."

"Of course I don't. Neither would you. But if you are going to kill me, I have little choice in the matter and so be it."

"Hmmm. You do utter some words of wisdom, young lady. Perhaps you should go into the profession of psychiatry."

He got up and picked up the phone and dialed 911. "Hello?" he said. "Is this call being recorded? I want this to be recorded."

"It is being recorded, sir. What is your emergency?"

"I kidnapped my wife and my son and my daughter and I have held them hostage for the past six months. I also kidnapped and held two of my patients hostage and I was planning to murder them. I hereby give myself up and I admit to everything I have done. My address is 187 Milson Road and I will wait here, to be arrested. You should bring ambulances for five people. They will live but they have been heavily sedated."

"Please stay on the line, sir. Police cars and ambulances have been dispatched to your address and should be there shortly."

Dr. Carroll turned to Amelia and winked at her. "You're so right," he said, exultantly. "D.T.O.T. wins! Excellent thinking, young woman. Clearly, you were a student who heard what I was saying."

"Are you still on the line, sir?"

"I'm here, I'm here…" Dr. Carroll replied, his foot tapping the ground impatiently.

Amelia's chafed skin was burning but despite the pain, she

was fighting to stay awake. The adrenalin that had flooded her system when she confronted Dr. Carroll was fading and she was growing increasingly sleepy as the drugs regained their hold. She was struggling to keep her eyes open when she heard the sound of the front door being broken down and someone crashed into the living room.

And then, to her amazement, Amelia heard her mother's voice.

"Amelia, honey, are you here? Where are you? Amelia, answer me!"

"Mom?" Amelia couldn't believe her ears "Mom, is that you? What are you doing here? How did you find me? I'm in the kitchen."

Her mother burst through the kitchen door, took one look at Amelia and gathered her in her arms as if she was weightless. "Oh honey. Are you okay?"

"I will be. How did you find me?"

"It wasn't easy. Is your boyfriend okay?"

"I'm not sure if he's my boyfriend, but he's very drugged. He's alive but he's heavily sedated."

"Amelia!" Ethel and Henry both rushed into the kitchen, both of them in tears.

"Nana! Dad! You guys are so cool! Like superheroes!"

The sound of sirens filled the air and within minutes, police officers flooded the house and handcuffed the grinning Dr. Carroll.

But Amelia, on a stretcher at this point, asked to have one word with him before he was taken away. "Dr. Carroll," she said. "You know all that stuff I said to you in there?"

"Yes?"

"It was the opposite of what I really believe. What you did had nothing to do with any therapy that you believed in. It was just the psychopathic antics of a little man. And that you bought into my speech shows that you don't know anything about people at all. Have fun in prison."

Amelia watched his jaw drop and then she lay back on her

stretcher, worn out. "Mom," Amelia said. "If you don't mind, I need to sleep. You can fill me in later, how you guys all found me and everything." And with that she passed out.

"She's fine, " the medic reassured Ethel and Megan and Henry. "How she managed to stay alert like she did, with that level of drugs she's got in her system is incredible. She saved her life and the young man's life for sure. And most likely the mother and kids. They couldn't have taken much more in their systems. It will be hard to detox them. It's going to take a while. But your daughter, she's pretty amazing."

"She's our nearly girl," Megan said, stroking Amelia's hair. "Nearly miraculous, utterly loved."

EPILOGUE

I FINALLY CAME TO THE END OF MY STORY and I looked at Spencer and Ana. "What happened next?" Spencer asked and Ana nodded.

"Dr. Carroll fulfilled Amelia's prophecy and became a revered hero in prison. D.T.O.T. became a cult movement with thousands of fans all over the world. He got a life sentence, but he still managed to have a weekly reality TV show and he published another three books about D.T.O.T. in action; case studies which he conducted in the prison to support his hypothesis. Prison inmates became compliant, helpful, and charitable, and Dr. Carroll was soon appointed as a representative on the board of directors."

"You know, I do remember reading about him, the loony tune," Spencer said. "As far as I know, he's still going strong."

I nodded. "He is. His wife and children recovered and left the country to go and live in New Mexico. Mrs. Carroll never remarried and became a recluse, supported financially by the Foundation of Psychiatrists of North America. Jason's a wildlife conservationist, while Bella is a chartered accountant for a legal firm in New York."

"And what about Henry?" Spencer asked.

"He's still publishing poetry. He left his mansion in Rosedale and moved in with Ethel and Megan," I said. "That was where I saw him when I went to visit Amelia. Ethel got her good health back and she carried on playing bingo and took up lawn bowling. Megan cut down on her bodybuilding and became a yoga instructor instead, and when I saw her, she had stopped smoking and she wasn't orange anymore."

"What about Mike and Amelia?" Ana asked. "Did they stay together?"

I shook my head. "Mike realized that he and Amelia didn't have much in common and he went back to Jane who was very forgiving after everything he had gone through with Dr. Carroll. Mike and Amelia stayed in touch and she told me that Mike was so relieved to have his normal, safe life returned to him that he never had a problem speaking in public again. She said that Mike joked that more than a few people had remarked that it was hard to shut him up, so Dr. Carroll had been right about that. Amelia wasn't broken-hearted that he went back to Jane. I think she was quite relieved actually."

"And the other members of the group?" Spencer asked.

"Amelia told me that Whitney came clean to her husband about her affairs with Alexei and Joanne and not only did he forgive her, he suggested they tried swinging and it worked so well that Whitney never had another day of depression. David went to Vancouver and started a new life and married a woman with two small boys and he is very happy. But not everybody had a happy ending. Persephone's anxiety got worse until she was admitted as an inpatient and she's still in hospital. And, oh the horror, Ainsley's worse fears came true and her finger was cut off and her wedding and engagement rings were stolen. She was on honeymoon in Africa and she came out of it kind of okay but she has refused to wear jewellery ever again, and she won't ever leave Canada again for a holiday either."

"What a bunch!" Spencer commented, grinning. "And the big Russian with anger-management issues? I liked him."

"Shannon and Alexei hit it off and they got married. Shannon never came to grips with her claustrophobia, but Alexei did stop fighting the world and having sex with random women. Joanne met a human-rights lawyer who liked world travel and Siamese cats, and they were still together the last time I saw Amelia."

"And what about Amelia?" Ana asked. "What happened to her?"

"She finished her thesis and got her doctorate in literary metaphorical comparisons between historical figures and classical playwrights."

"She couldn't have been too dim-witted," Ana commented and I nodded.

"She was a clever girl, she just wasn't as up-there as Henry. I left university before she did and we lost touch but I heard she went to France after she graduated, to visit the village where Joan of Arc was born. I should try to get in touch with her again, see what she's up to. My bet is that she will have done everything she ever wanted to, in exactly the way she wanted to. Well, nearly, anyway."

"Speaking of nearly," Spencer said, getting up and smoothing his trousers. "It's nearly time for our meeting. Let's go and knock this one out the ballpark, no nearly's about it."

We followed him out into the freezing rain of the dark November day, and I suddenly had a vision of Amelia. She was wearing a thin yellow cotton summer dress and she was soaked to the bone, running along the stormy beachfront with the waves crashing wild and high against the rocks. Coal-black clouds swirled up above like swallow murmurations, and in her hand she held a bunch of jostling red helium balloons, while a giant golden retriever bounded along beside her. Amelia was smiling from ear to ear.

ACKNOWLEDGEMENTS

Many thanks to be my beloved Inanna Publications, particularly to my ever-wonderful Editor-in-Chief, Luciana Ricciutelli, and our wonderful Publicist, Renée Knapp.

Thanks and love to Tully and Grayson, little angels who taught me all about Art and Move, and Duck, Duck, Geese.

To my family for all their love and support and thanks especially to Bradford Dunlop for reading all the versions of every story and encouraging me every step of the way.

To the real Ethel and Ed: I borrowed your names and your kindness to strangers who were in need of a helping hand. My Ethel and Ed were also inspired by your generosity in sharing your home, as well as your unjudgmental love. Thanks also to Mike Shoss for helpful insights that went into the creation of my Mike.

Grateful thanks to early supporters of the book: Jill Buchner, Gina Buonaguro, Carolyn Shannon, Andrea Thompson, Michael Fraser, Heather Babcock, Elaine Ash, Lynne Murphy and Mandy Eve Barnett.

Thanks to the Mesdames of Mayhem, and thanks to the Toronto writing community.

Bibliography:

The Anxiety and Phobia Workbook, Fifth Edition, Edmund J. Bourke, New Harbinger Publications, Inc, 2010.

Mind Over Mood, Second Edition, Dennis Greenberger and Christine A. Padesky, The Guilford Press, 2016.

Credit:
Raisin meditation: various sites via Google.

Photo: Bradford Dunlop

Originally from South Africa, Lisa de Nikolits has lived in Canada since 2000. *The Nearly Girl* is her sixth novel. Previous novels include: *The Hungry Mirror* (2011 IPPY Awards Gold Medal Winner); *West of Wawa* (2012 IPPY Silver Medal Winner and a *Chatelaine* Editor's Pick); *A Glittering Chaos* (2014 IPPY Silver Medal Winner); *The Witchdoctor's Bones*; and most recently, *Between The Cracks She Fell* (2016 IPPY Bronze Medal Winner and a *Canadian Living* magazine "must-read book of 2015"). Her short fiction and poetry has also been published in various anthologies and journals. She lives and writes in Toronto.